LADY BYRON VINDICATED

A HISTORY

OF

The Byron Controversy,

FROM ITS BEGINNING IN 1816 TO THE PRESENT TIME.

BY

HARRIET BEECHER STOWE.

———————

BOSTON:

FIELDS, OSGOOD, & CO.

1870.

CONTENTS.

———————

PART I.

CHAPTER I.

CHAPTER II.

CHAPTER III.

CHAPTER IV.

CHAPTER V.

PART II.

CHAPTER I.

CHAPTER II.

5

PART I

CHAPTER I.

INTRODUCTION.

HE interval since my publication of "The True Story of Lady Byron's Life" has been one of stormy discussion and of much invective.

I have not thought it necessary to disturb my spirit and confuse my sense of right by even an attempt at reading the many abusive articles that both here and in England have followed that disclosure. Friends have under taken the task for me, giving me from time to time the substance of anything really worthy of attention which came to view in the tumult.

It appeared to me essential that this first excitement should in a measure spend itself before there would be a possibility of speaking to any purpose. Now, when all would- seem to have spoken who can speak, and, it is to be hoped, have said the utmost they can say, there seems a propriety in listening calmly, if that be possible, to what I have to say in reply.

And, first, why have I made this disclosure at all?To this I answer briefly, because I considered it my duty to make it.I made it in defence of a beloved, revered friend, whose memory stood forth in the eyes of the civilized world charged with most re pulsive crimes, of which I certainly knew her innocent.

I claim, and shall prove, that Lady Byron's reputation has been the victim of a concerted attack, begun by her husband during her life time, and coming to its climax over her grave. I claim, and shall prove, that it was not I who stirred up this controversy in this year 1869. I shall show who did do it, and who is responsi ble for bringing on me that hard duty of making these disclosures, which it appears to me ought to have been made by others.

I claim that these facts were given to me unguarded by any p'romise or seal of secrecy, expressed or implied; that they were lodged with- me as one sister rests her story with another for sympathy, for counsel, for defence. Never did I suppose the day would come that I should be subjected to so cruel an anguish as this use of them has been to me. Never did I suppose that, when those kind hands, that had shed nothing but blessings, were lying in the helplessness of death, when that gentle heart, so sorely tried and to the last so full of love, was lying cold in the tomb, a country man in England could be found to cast the foulest slanders on her grave, and not one in all England to raise an effective voice in her defence.

I admit the feebleness of my plea, in point of execution. It was written in a state of exhausted health, when no labor of the kind was safe for me, when my hand had not strength to hold the pen, and I was forced to dictate to another.

I have been told that I have no reason to congratulate myself on it as a literary effort.

0 my brothers and sisters ! is there then nothing in the world to think of but literary efforts ?

1 ask any man with a heart in his bosom, if he had been obliged to tell a story so cruel, because his mother's grave gave no rest from slander, I ask any woman who had been forced to such a disclosure to free a dead sister's name from grossest insults, whether she would have thought of making this work of bitterness a literary success ?Are the cries of the oppressed, the gasps of the dying, the last prayers of mothers, are any words wrung like drops of blood from the human heart to be judged as literary efforts ?My fellow-countrymen of America, men of the press, I have done you one act of justice, of all your bitter articles, I have read not one.

I shall never be troubled in the future time by the remembrance of any unkind word you have said of me, for at this moment I recol lect not one. I had such faith in you, such pride in my countrymen, as men with whom, above all others, the cause of woman was safe and sacred, that I was at first astonished and incredulous at what I heard of the course of the American press, and was silent, not merely from the impossibility of being heard, but from grief and shame. But reflection convinces me that you were, in many cases, acting from a mis understanding of facts and through misguided honorable feeling; and I still feel courage, there fore, to ask from you a fair hearing. Now, as I have done you this justice, will you also do me the justice to hear me seriously and candidly ?

What interest have you or I, my brother and my sister, in this short life of ours, to utter any thing but the truth ? Is not truth between man and man and between man and woman the foundation on which all things rest ? Have

you not, every individual of you, who must hereafter give an account yourself alone to God, an interest to know the exact truth in this matter, and a duty to perform as respects that truth ? Hear me, then, while I tell you the position in which I stood, and what was my course in relation to it.

A shameless attack on my friend's memory had appeared in the Blackwood of July, 1869, branding Lady Byron as the vilest of criminals, and recommending the Guiccioli book to a Christian public as interesting from the very fact that it was the avowed production of Lord Byron's mistress. No efficient protest was made against this outrage in England, and Littell's Living Age reprinted the Blackwood article, and the Harpers, the largest publishing house in America, perhaps in the world, re-published the. book.

Its statements with those of the Black-wood, Pall Mall Gazette, and other English peri odicals — were being propagated through all the
INTRODUCTION.

young reading and writing world of America. I was meeting them advertised in dailies, and made up into articles in magazines, and thus the gener ation of to-day, who had no means of judging Lady Byron but by these fables of her slander ers, were being foully deceived. The friends who knew her personally were a small select circle in England, whom death is every day reducing. They were few in number compared with the great world, and were silent. I saw these foul slanders crystallizing into history uncontra-dicted by friends who knew her personally, who, firm in their own knowledge of her vir tues and limited in view as aristocratic circles generally are, had no idea of the width of the world they were living in, and the exigency of the crisis. When time passed on and no voice I was raised, I spoke. I gave at first a simple story, for I knew instinctively that whoever put the first steel point of truth into this dark cloud of slander must wait for the storm to spend itself. I must say the storm exceeded my expectations,

and has raged loud and long. But now that there is a comparative stillness I shall proceed, first, to prove what I have just been asserting, and, second, to add to my true story such facts and incidents as I did not think proper at first to state.

CHAPTER II.

THE ATTACK ON LADY BYRON.

T N proving what I asserted in the first chap-ter, I make four points : 1st. A concerted attack upon Lady Byron's reputation, begun by Lord Byron in self-defence. 2d. That he trans mitted his story to friends to be continued after his death. 3d. That they did so continue it. 4th. That the accusations reached their climax over Lady Byron's grave in Blackwood of 1869, and the Guiccioli book, and that this reopening of the controversy was my reason for speaking.

And first I shall adduce my proofs that Lady Bryon's reputation was, during the whole course of her husband's life, the subject of a concen trated, artfully planned attack, commencing at the time of the separation and continuing dur ing his life. By various documents carefully

prepared, and used publicly or secretly as suited the case, he made converts of many honest men, some of whom were writers and men of letters, who put their talents at his service during his lifetime in exciting sympathy for him, and who, by his own request, felt bound to continue their defence of him after he was dead.

In order to consider the force and significance of the documents I shall cite, we are to bring to our view just the issues Lord Byron had to meet, both at the time of the separation and for a long time after.

In Byron's Memoirs, Vol. IV. Letter 350, under date December 10, 1819, nearly four years after the separation, he writes to Murray in a state of great excitement on account of an article in Blackwood, in which his conduct towards his wife had been sternly and justly com mented on, and which he supposed to have been written by Wilson, of the Noc.tes Ambrosianse.

He says in this letter: " I like and admire and he should not have indulged himself in such

outrageous license When he talks of

Lady Byron's business he talks of what he knows nothing about; and you may tell him 110 man can desire a public investigation of that affair more tJ\'7ban I do!' *

He shortly after wrote and sent to Murray a pamphlet for publication, which was printed, but not generally circulated till some time afterwards. Though more than three years had elapsed since the separation, the current against him at this time was so strong in England that his friends thought it best, at first, to use this article of Lord -Byron's discreetly with influential per sons rather than to give it to the public.

The writer in Blackwood and the indigna tion of the English public, of which that writer was the voice, were now particularly stirred up by the appearance of the first two cantos of "Don Juan," in which the indecent caricature of Lady Byron was placed in vicinity with other indecencies, the publication of which The italics are mine.

was justly considered an insult to a Christian community.

It must here be mentioned, for the honor of Old England, that at first she did her duty quite respectably in regard to " Don Juan." One can still read, in Murray's standard edition of the poems, how every respectable press thundered reprobations, which it would be well enough to print and circulate as tracts for our days.

Byron, it seems, had thought of returning to England, but he says, in the letter we have quoted, that he has changed his mind, and shall not go back, adding : " I have finished the Third Canto of 'Don Juan,' but the things I have heard and read % discourage all future publication. You may try the copy question, but you '11 lose it ; the cry is up, and the cant is up. I should have no objection to return the price of the copy right, and have written to Mr. Kinnaird on this subject."

One sentence quoted by Lord Byron from the Blackwood article will show the modern readers

what the respectable world of that day were thinking and saying of him : —

" It appears, in short, as if this miserable man, hav ing exhausted every species of sensual gratification, having drained the cup of sin even to its bitterest dregs, were resolved to show us that he is no longer a human being even in his frailties, but a cool, unconcerned fiend, laughing with detestable glee over the whole of the better and worse elements of which human life is composed."

The defence which Lord Byron makes, in his reply to that paper, is of a man cornered and fighting for his life. He speaks thus of the state of feeling at the time of his separation from his wife: —

" I was accused of every monstrous vice by public rumor and private rancor ; my name, which had been a knightly or a noble one since my fathers helped to conquer the kingdom for William the Norman, was tainted. I felt that, if what was whispered and mut tered and murmured was true, I was unfit for Eng land ; if false, England was unfit for me. I withdrew; but this was not enough. In other countries in

Switzerland, in the shadow of the Alps, and by the blue depth of the lakes, I was pursued and breathed upon by the same blight I crossed the mountains, but it was the same ; so I went a little farther, and settled myself by the waves of the Adriatic, like the stag at bay, who betakes him to the waters.

" If I may judge by the statements of the few friends who gathered round me, the outcry of the period to which I allude was beyond all precedent, all parallel, even in those cases where political motives have sharp ened slander and doubled enmity. I was advised not to go to the theatres lest I should be hissed, nor to my duty in Parliament, lest I should be insulted by the way ; even on the day of my departure my most intimate friend told me afterwards that he was under the apprehension of violence from the people who might be assembled at the door of the carriage."Now Lord Byron's charge against his wife was that SHE was directly responsible for get ting up and keeping up this persecution, which drove him from England, that she did it in a deceitful, treacherous manner, which left him no chance of defending himself.He charged against her that, taking advantage of a time when his affairs were in confusion, and an execution in the house, she left him sud denly, with treacherous professions of kindness, which were repeated by letters on the road, and that soon after her arrival at her home her par ents sent him word that she would never return to him, and she confirmed the message ; that when he asked the reason why, she refused to state any ; and that when this step gave rise to a host of slanders against him she silently encouraged and confirmed the slanders. His claim was that he was denied from that time forth even the justice of any tangible accusation against himself which he might meet and re fute.

He observes, in the same article from which we have quoted :

" When one tells me that I cannot ' in any way jus tify my own behavior -in that affair,' I acquiesce, be cause no man can justify ' himself until he knows of what he is accused ; and I have never had and, God knows, my whole desire has ever been to obtain

it any specific charge, in a tangible shape, submitted to me by the adversary, nor by others, unless the atrocities of public rumor and the mysterious silence of the lady's legal advisers may be deemed such."

Lord Byron, his publishers, friends, and biog raphers, thus agree in representing his wife as the secret author and abettor of that persecu tion, which it is claimed broke up his life, and was the source of all his subsequent crimes and excesses.

Lord Byron wrote a poem in September, 1816, in Switzerland, just after the separation, in which he stated, in so many words, these accusations against his wife. Shortly after the poet's death Murray published this poem, to gether with the " Fare thee well," and the lines to his sister, under the title of " Domestic Pieces," in his standard edition of Byron's poetry. It is to be remarked, then, that this was for some time a private document, shown to confidential friends, and made use of judi ciously, as readers or listeners to his story

were able to bear it. Lady Byron then had a strong party in England. Sir Samuel Rom-illy and Dr. Lushington were her counsel. Lady Byron's parents were living, and the appearance in the public prints of such a piece as this would have brought down an ag gravated storm of public indignation.

For the general public such documents as the " Fare thee well" were circulating in Eng land, and he frankly confessed his wife's virtues and his own sins to Madame cle Stae'l and others in Switzerland, declaring himself in the wrong, sensible of his errors, and long ing to cast himself at the feet of that serene perfection,

" Which wanted one sweet weakness, to forgive." But a little later he drew for his private par tisans this bitter poetical indictment against her, which, as we have said, was used dis creetly during his life, and published after his death.

Before we proceed to lay that poem before

the reader we will refresh his memory with some particulars of the tragedy of Eschylus, which Lord Byron selected as the exact par allel and proper illustration of his wife's treat ment of himself. In his letters and journals he often alludes to her as Clytemnestra, and the allusion has run the round of a thousand American papers lately, and been read by a thousand good honest people, who had no very clear idea who Clytemnestra was, and what she did which was like the proceedings of Lady Byron. According to the tragedy, Clytemnestra secretly hates her husband Agamemnon, whom she professes to love, and wishes to put him out of the way that she may marry her lover, Egistheus. When her husband returns from the Trojan war she receives him with pretended kindness, and officiously offers to serve him at the bath. Inducing him to put on a garment, of which she had adroitly sewed up the sleeves and neck so as to hamper the use of his arms,

THE ATTACK ON LADY BYRON. 19

she gives the signal to a concealed band of assassins, who rush upon him and stab him. Clytemnestra is represented by ^Eschylus as grimly triumphing in her success, which leaves her free to marry an adulterous para mour.

" I did it, too, in such a cunning wise, That he could neither scape nor ward off doom. I staked around his steps an endless net, As for the fishes."

In the piece entitled " Lines on hearing Lady Byron is ill," Lord Byron charges on his wife a similar treachery and cruelty. The whole poem is in Murray's English edi tion, Vol. IV. p. 207. Of it we quote the following. The reader will bear in mind that it is addressed to Lady Byron on a sick-bed.

" I am too well avenged, but 'twas my right ; Whate'er my sins might be, thou wert not sent To be the Nemesis that should requite, Nor did Heaven choose so near an instrument. Mercy is for the merciful ! If thou Hast been of such, 't will be accorded now.Thy nights are banished from the realms of sleep,For thou art pillowed on a curse too deep ;Yes ! they may flatter thee, but thou shalt feel A hollow agony that will not heal.Thou hast sown in my sorrow, and must reap The bitter harvest in a woe as real. I have had many foes, but none like thee For 'gainst the rest myself I could defend,And be avenged, or turn them into friend ;But thou, in safe implacability,Hast naught to dread, in thy own weakness shielded,And in my love, which hath but too much yielded,And spared, for thy sake, some I should not spare.And thus upon the world, trust in thy truth,And the wild fame of my ungoverned youth, On things that were not and on things that are, Even upon such a basis thou hast built A monument whose cement hath been guilt!The moral Clytemnestra of thy lord,And hewed down with an unsuspected sword Fame, peace, and hope, and all that better lifeWhich, but for this cold treason of thy heart,Might yet have risen from the grave of strife And found a nobler duty than to part.

THE ATTACK ON LADY BYRON. 21

But of thy virtues thou didst make a vice, Trafficking in them with a purpose cold, And buying others' woes at any price, For present anger and for future gold ; And thus, once entered into crooked ways, The early truth, that was thy proper praise, Did not still walk beside thee, but at times, And with a breast unknowing its own crimes, Deceits, averments incompatible, Equivocations, and the thoughts that dwell In Janus spirits, the significant eye That learns to He with silence* the pretext Of prudence with advantages annexed, The acquiescence in all things that tend, No matter how, to the desired end, All found a place in thy philosophy. The means were worthy and the end is won. I would not do to thee as thou hast done."Now, if this language means anything, it means, in plain terms, that, whereas, in her early days, Lady Byron was peculiarly char acterized by truthfulness, she has in her recent dealings with him acted the part of a liar,

The italics are mine.

22 THE ATTACK ON LADY BYRON.

that she is not only a liar, but that she lies for cruel, mean, and malignant purposes, — that she is a moral assassin, and her treatment of her hus band has been like that of the most detestable murderess and adulteress of ancient history,— that she has learned to lie skilfully and artfully, that she equivocates, says incompatible things, and crosses her own tracks, that she is double-faced, and has the art to lie even by silence, and that she has become wholly unscrupulous, and acquiesces in anyihmg, no matter what, that tends to the desired end, and that end the destruction of her husband. This is a brief summary of the story that Byron made it his life's business to spread through society, to propagate and make converts to during his life, and which has been in substance reasserted by Blackwood in a recent article this year.

Now, the reader will please to notice that this poem is dated in September, 1816, and that on the 29th of March, of that same year, he had thought proper to tell quite another story. At

that time the deed of separation was not signed, and negotiations between Lady Byron, acting by legal counsel, and himself were still pending. At that time, therefore, he was standing in a community who knew all he had said in former days of his wife's character, who were in an aroused and excited state by the fact that so lovely and good and patient a woman had ac tually been forced for some unexplained cause to leave him. His policy at that "'time was to make large general confessions of sin, and to praise and compliment her, with a view of en listing sympathy. Everybody feels for a hand some sinner, weeping on his knees, asking par don for his offences against his wife in the public newspapers.

The celebrated " Fare thee well," as we are told, was written on the i/th of March, and accidentally found its way into the newspapers at this time "through the imprudence of a friend whom he allowed to take a copy." These " imprudent friends" have all along been such a marvellous convenience to Lord Byron.

But the question met him on all sides, What is the matter ? This wife you have declared the brightest, sweetest, most amiable of beings, and against whose behavior as a wife you actually never had nor can have a complaint to make, why is she now all of a sudden so inflexibly set against you ?

This question required an answer, and he answered by writing another poem, which also accidentally fbund its way into the public prints. It is in his "Domestic Pieces," which the reader may refer to at the end of this volume, and is called "A Sketch."

There was a most excellent, respectable, well-behaved Englishwoman, a Mrs. Clermont,* who had been Lady Byron's governess in her youth, and was still, in mature life, revered as her confidential friend. It appears that this person had been with Lady Byron during a part of

* In Lady Blessington's Memoirs this name is given Charle-mont; in the late Temple Bar article on the character of Lady Byron it is given Clermont. I have followed the latter.

her married life, especially the bitter hours of her lonely child-bed, when a young wife so much needs a sympathetic friend. This Mrs. Clermont was the person selected by Lord Byron at this time to be the scapegoat to bear away the difficulties of the case into the wilderness.

We are informed in Moore's Life what a noble pride of rank Lord Byron possessed, and how when the head-master of a school, against whom he had a pique, invited him to dinner, he de clined, saying, " To tell you the truth, Doctor, if you should come to Newstead, I should n't think of inviting you to dine with me, and so I don't care to dine with you here." Different countries, it appears, have different standards as to good taste; Moore gives this as an amusing instance of a young lord's spirit.

Accordingly, his first attack against" this "lady," as we Americans should call her, con sists in gross statements concerning her having been born poor and in an inferior rank. He begins by stating that she was

" Born in the garret, in the kitchen bred, Promoted thence to deck her mistress' head ; Next — for some gracious service unexpressed And from its wages only to be guessed — Raised from the toilet to the table, where Her wondering betters wait behind her chair. With eye unmoved and forehead unabashed, She dines from off the plate she lately washed; Quick with the tale, and ready with the lie, The genial confidante and general spy, — Who could, ye gods ! her next employment guess, — An only infant's earliest governess ! What had she made the pupil of her art None knows ; but that high soul secured the heart, And panted for the truth it could not hear With longing soul and itndeluded ear ! "

The poet here recognizes as a singular trait in Lady Byron her peculiar love of truth, — a trait which must have struck every one that had any knowledge of her through life. He goes on now to give what he certainly knew to be the real character of Lady Byron :

* The italics are mine.

THE ATTACK ON LADY BYRON.

" Foiled was perversion by that youthful mind, Which flattery fooled not, baseness could not blind, Deceit infect not, nor contagion soil, Indulgence weaken, or example spoil, Nor mastered science tempt her to look down On humbler talent with a pitying frown, Nor genius swell, nor beauty render vain, Nor envy ruffle to retaliate pain."

We are now informed that Mrs. Clermont, whom he afterwards says in his letters was a spy of Lady Byron's mother, set herself to make mischief between them. He says: " If early habits, those strong links that bind At times the loftiest to the meanest mind, Have given her power too deeply to instil The angry essence of her deadly will ; If like a snake she steal within your walls, Till the black slime betray her as she crawls ; If like a viper to the heart she wind, And leaves the venom there she did not find,— What marvel that this hag of hatred works Eternal evil latent-as she lurks."

The noble lord then proceeds to abuse this woman of inferior rank in the language of the

28 THE ATTACK ON LADY BYRON.

upper circles. He thus describes her person and manner:

" Skilled by a touch to deepen scandal's tints With all the kind mendacity of hints, While mingling truth with falsehood, sneers with smiles, A thread of candor with a web of wiles ; A plain blunt show of briefly spoken scheming ; A lip of lies ; a face formed to conceal, And without feeling mock at all who feel ; With a vile mask the Gorgon would disown, A dieek of parchment and an eye of stone. Mark how the channels of her yellow blood Ooze to her skin and stagnate there to mud, Cased like the centipede in saffron mail, Or darker greenness of the scorpion's scale, — (For drawn from reptiles only may we trace Congenial colors in that soul or face,) Look on her features ! and behold her mind As in a mirror of itself defined : Look on the picture ! deem it not o'ercharged ; There is no trait which might not be enlarged."

The poem thus ends:

" May the strong curse of crushed affections light Back on thy bosom with reflected blight,

THE ATTACK ON LADY BYRON. 29

And make thee in thy leprosy of mind As loathsome to thyself as to mankind Till all thy self-thoughts curdle into hate,Black as thy will for others would create ;Till thy hard heart be calcined into dust,And thy soul welter in its hideous crust.O, may thy grave be sleepless as the bed,The widowed couch of fire, that thou hast spread !Then when thou fain wouldst weary Heaven with prayer,Look on thy earthly victims—and despair !Down to the dust! and as thou rott'st away,Even worms shall perish on thy poisonous clay.But for the love I bore and still must bear To her thy malice from all ties would tear,Thy name, thy human name, to every eye The climax of all scorn, should hang on high,Exalted o'er thy less abhorred compeers,And festering in the infamy of years."

March 29, 1816.

Now, on the 2Qth of March, 1816, this was Lord Byron's story. He states that his wife had a truthfulness even from early girlhood that the most artful and unscrupulous governess could

not pollute, that she always panted for truth, that flattery could not fool nor baseness blind her, — that though she was a genius and master of science, she was yet gentle and tolerant, and one whom no envy could ruffle to retaliate pain.

In September of the same year she is a mon ster of unscrupulous deceit and vindictive cruelty. Now, what had happened in the five months between the dates of these poems to produce such a change of opinion? Simply this:

1st. The negotiation between him and his wife's lawyers had ended in his signing a deed of separation in preference to standing a suit for divorce.

2d. Madame de Stael, moved by his tears of anguish and professions of repentance, had offered to negotiate with Lady Byron on his behalf, and had failed.

The failure of this application is the only apology given by Moore and Murray for this poem, which gentle Thomas Moore admits was not in quite as generous a strain as the "Fare thee well."

But Lord Byron knew perfectly well, when he suffered that application to be made, that Lady Byron had been entirely convinced that her marriage relations with him could never be renewed, and that duty both to man and God required her to separate from him. The allow ing the negotiation was, therefore, an artifice to place his wife before the public in the attitude of a hard-hearted, inflexible woman ; her refusal was what he knew beforehand must inevitably be the result, and merely gave him capital in the sympathy of his friends, by which they should be brought to tolerate and accept the bitter accusations of this poem.

We have recently heard it asserted that this last-named piece of poetry was the sudden off spring of a fit of ill-temper, and was never in tended to be published at all. There were cer tainly excellent reasons why his friends should have advised him not to publish it at that time. But that it was read with sympathy by the circle of his intimate friends, and believed by them, is

evident from the frequency with which allusions to it occur in his confidential letters to them.*

About three months after, under date March 10, 1817, he writes to Moore : " I suppose now I shall never be able to shake off my sables in pub lic imagination, more particularly since my moral

clove down my fame." Again to Murray

in 1819, three years after, he says: "I never hear anything of Ada, the little Electra of Mycenae,"

Electra was the daughter of Clytemnestra, in the Greek poem, who lived to condemn hei wicked mother, and to call on her brother to avenge the father. There was in this men tion of Electra more than meets the ear. Many passages in Lord Byron's poetry show that he intended to make this daughter a future parti san against her mother, and explain the awful words he is stated in Lady Anne Barnard's diary, to have used when first he looked on his

* In Lady Blessington's conversations with Lord Byron, just before he went to Greece, she records that he gave her this poem in manuscript. It was published in her Journal.

little girl, — " What an instrument of torture I have gained in you ! "

In a letter to Lord Blessington, April 6. 1823, he says, speaking of Dr. Parr :

u He did me the honor once to be a patron of mine, though a great friend of the other branch of the house of Atreus, and the Greek teacher, I believe, of my moral Clytemnestra. I say moral because it is true, and is so useful to the virtuous, that it enables them to do any thing without the aid of an Egistheus."

If Lord Byron wrote this poem merely in a momentary fit of spleen, why were there so many persons evidently quite familiar with his allusions to it ? and why was it preserved in Murray's hands ? and why published after his death ? That Byron was in the habit of reposing documents in the hands of Murray, to be used as occasion offered, is evident from a part of a note written by him to Murray respecting some verses so intrusted : " Pray let

not these versiculi go forth with my name except to the initiated"

Murray, in publishing this attack on his wife after Lord Byron's death, showed that he be lieved in it, and, so believing, deemed Lady Byron a woman whose widowed state deserved neither sympathy nor delicacy of treatment. At a time when every sentiment in the heart of the most deeply wronged woman would forbid her appearing to justify herself from such cruel slander of a dead husband, an honest, kind-hearted, worthy Englishman actually thought it right and proper to give these lines to her eyes and the eyes of all the reading world. Noth ing can show more plainly what this poem was written for, and how thoroughly it did its work ! Considering Byron as a wronged man, Murray thought he was contributing his mite towards doing him justice. His editor prefaced the whole set of " Domestic Pieces" with the fol lowing statements:

* Byron's Miscellany, Vol. II. p. 358. London, 1853.

" They all refer to the unhappy separation, of which the precise causes are still a mystery, and which he declared to the last were never disclosed to himself. He admitted that pecuniary embarrassments, disordered health, and dislike to family restraints had aggravated his naturally violent temper and driven him to excesses. He suspect ed that his mother-in-law had fomented'the discord,— which Lady Byron denies, — and that more was due to the malignant offices of a female dependant, who is the subject of the bitterly satirical sketch.

" To these general statements can only be added the still vaguer allegations of Lady Byron, that she conceived his conduct to be the result of insanity, —that, the phy sician pronouncing him responsible for his actions, she could submit to them no longer, and that Dr. Lush-ington, her legal adviser, agreed that a reconciliation was neither proper nor possible. No weight can be attached to the opinions of an opposing counsel upon accusations made by one party behind the back of the other, who urgently demanded and was pertinaciously refused the least opportunity of denial or defence. He rejected the proposal for an amicable separation, but con sented when threatened with a suit in Doctors* Com mons"

The italics are mine.

Neither honest Murray nor any of Byron's partisans seem to have pondered the admis sion in these last words.

Here, as appears, was a woman, driven to the last despair, standing with her child in her arms, asking from English laws protec tion for herself and child against her hus band

She had appealed to the first counsel in England, and was acting under their direc tion.

Two of the greatest lawyers in England have pronounced that there has been such a cause of offence on his part that a return to him is neither proper nor possible, and that no alter native remains to her but separation or divorce.

He asks her to state- her charges against him. She, making answer under advice of her coun sel, says, " That if he insists on the specifica tions, he must receive them in open court in a suit for divorce."

What, now, ought to have been the conduct

of any brave, honest man, who believed that his wife was taking advantage of her reputation for virtue to turn every one against him, who saw that she had turned on her side even the lawyer he sought to retain on his ; * that she was an unscrupulous woman, who acquiesced in every and any thing to gain her ends, while he stood before the public, as he says, " accused of every monstrous vice, by public rumor or private rancor " ? When she, under advice of her lawyers, made the alternative legal separa tion or open investigation in court for divorce, what did he do ?

* Lord Byron says, in his observations on an article in Blackwood : " I recollect being much hurt by Romilly's con duct : he (having a general retainer for me) went over to the adversary, alleging, on being reminded of his retainer, that he had forgotten it, as his clerk had so many. I observed that some of those who were now so eagerly laying the axe to my roof-tree might see their own shaken. His fell and crushed him."

In the first edition of Moore's Life of Lord Byron there was printed a letter on Sir Samuel Romilly, so brutal that it was suppressed in the subsequent editions. (See Appendix.)

HE SIGNED THE ACT OF SEPARATION AND LEFT ENGLAND.

Now, let any man who knows the legal mind of England, — let any lawyer who knows the character of Sir Samuel Romilly and Dr. Lushington, ask whether they were the men to take a case into court for a woman that had no evidence but her own statements and im pressions ? Were they men to go to trial without proofs ? Did they not know that there were artful, hysterical women in the world, and would they, of all people, be the men to take a woman's story on her own side, and advise her in the last issue to bring it into open court, without legal proof of the strongest kind ? Now, as long as Sir Samuel Romilly lived, this statement of Byron's that he was condemned unheard, and had no chance of knowing whereof he was accused never ap peared in public.

It, however, was most actively circulated in private. That Byron was in the habit of intrust-

ing to different confidants articles of various kinds to be shown to different circles as they could bear them, we have already shown. We have recently come upon another instance of this kind. In the late eagerness to exculpate Byron, a new document has turned up, of which honest John Murray, it appears, had never heard when, after Byron's death, he published in the preface to his "Domestic Pieces" the sentence: "He rejected the proposal for an amicable separation, but consented when threatened with a suit in Doc tors Commons? It appears that, up to 1853, neither John Murray senior, nor the son who now fills his place, had taken any notice of this newly found document, which we are now in formed " was drawn up by Lord Byron in August, 1817, while Mr. Hobhouse was staying with him at La Mira, near Venice, given to Mr. Matthew Gregory Lewis, for circulation among friends in England, found in Mr. Lewis's papers after his death, and now in the possession of Mr, Mur ray." Here it is : —

" It has been intimated to me that the persons under stood to be the legal advisers of Lady Byron have de clared 'their lips to be sealed up' on the cause of the separation between her and myself. If their lips are sealed up, they are not sealed up by me, and the greatest favor they can confer upon me will be to open them. From the first hour in which I was apprised of the inten tions of the Noel family to the last communication be tween Lady Byron and myself in the character of wife and husband (a period of some months), I called repeat edly and in vain for a statement of their or her charges, and it was chiefly in consequence of Lady Byron's claim ing (in a letter still existing) a promise on my part to consent to a separation, if such was really her wish, that I consented at all; this claim, and the exasperating and inexpiable manner in which their object was pur sued, which rendered it next to an impossibility that two persons so divided could ever be reunited, induced me reluctantly then, and repentantly still, to sign the deed, which I shall be happy most happy to cancel, and go before any tribunal which may discuss the busi ness in the most public manner.

" Mr. Hobhouse made this proposition on my part, viz. to abrogate all prior intentions — and go into court the very day before the separation was signed, and

THE ATTACK ON LADY BYRON. 4!

it was declined by the other party, as also the publication of the correspondence during the previous discussion. Those propositions I beg here to repeat, and to call upon her and hers to say their worst, pledging myself to meet their allegations, whatever they may be, and only too happy to be informed at last of their real nature.

" BYRON."

"August 9, 1817.

" P. S. — I have been, and am now, utterly ignorant of what description her allegations, charges, or what ever name they may have assumed, are; and am as little aware for what purpose they have been kept back, unless it was to sanction the most infamous calumnies

by silence.

" BYRON. " LA MIRA, near VENICE."

It appears the circulation of this document must have been very private, since Moore, not 0wr-delicate towards Lady Byron, did not think fit to print it ; since John Murray neglected it, and since it has come out at this late hour for the first time.

If Lord Byron really desired Lady Byron and

42 THE ATTACK ON LADY BYRON.

her legal counsel to understand the facts herein stated, and was willing at all hazards to bring on an open examination, why was this privately circulated ? Why not issued as a card in the London papers ? Is it likely that Mr. Mat thew Gregory Lewis, and a chosen band of friends acting as a committee, requested an audience with Lady Byron, Sir Samuel Romilly, and Dr. Lushington, and formally presented this cartel of defiance ?

We incline to think not. We incline to think that this small serpent, in company with many others of like kind, crawled secret ly and privately around, and when it found a good chance, bit an honest Briton, whose blood was thenceforth poisoned by an undetected false hood.

The reader now may turn to the letters that Mr. Moore has thought fit to give us of this stay at La Mira, beginning with Letter 286, dated July I, 1817,* where he says: "I have been

THE ATTACK ON LADY BYRON. 43

working up my impressions into a Fourth Canto of Childe Harold," and also " Mr. Lewis is in-Venice. I am going up to stay a week with him there."

Next, under date La Mira, Venice, July 10,* he says : " Monk Lewis is here ; how pleasant!"

Next, under date July 20, 1817, to Mr. Mur ray : " I write to give you notice that I have completed tJie fourth and ultimate canto of Childe Harold. .... It is yet to be copied and polished, and the notes are to come."

Under date of La Mira, August 7, 1817, he records that the new canto is one hundred and thirty stanzas in length, and talks about the price for it. He is now ready to launch it on the world ;

and, as now appears, on August 9, 1817, two days after, he wrote the document above cited, and put it into the hands of Mr. Lewis, as we are informed, "for circulation among friends in England."

The reason of this may now be evident. Hav ing prepared a suitable number of those whom

he calls in his notes to Murray " the initiated,'* by private documents and statements, he is now prepared to publish his accusations against his wife, and the story of his wrongs, in a great im mortal poem, which shall have a band of initiated interpreters, shall be read through the civilized world, and stand to accuse her after his death.

In the Fourth Canto of "Childe Harold," with all his own overwhelming power of language, he sets forth his cause as against the silent woman who all this time had been making no party, and telling no story, and whom the world would there fore conclude to be silent because she had no answer to make. I remember well the time when this poetry, so resounding in its music, so mourn ful, so apparently generous, filled my heart with a vague anguish of sorrow for the sufferer, and of indignation at the cold insensibility that had maddened him. Thousands have felt the power of this great poem, which stands, and must stand to all time, a monument of what sacred and solemn powers God gave to this wicked man,

and how vilely he abused this power as a weapon to slay the innocent.

It is among the ruins of ancient Rome that his voice breaks forth in solemn impre cation :

—

" O Time, thou beautifier of the dead, Adorner of the ruin, comforter, And only healer when the heart hath bled ! Time, the corrector when our judgments err, The test of truth, love, — sole philosopher, For all besides are sophists, — from thy shrift That never loses, though it doth defer ! Time, the avenger! unto thee I lift

My hands and heart and eyes, and claim of thee a gift.

" If thou hast ever seen me too elate, Hear me not; but if calmly I have borne Good, and reserved my pride against the hate Which shall not whelm me, let me not have worn This iron in my soul in vain, — shall THEY not

mourn ?

And thou who never yet of human wrong Left the unbalanced scale, great Nemesis, Here where the ancients paid their worship long,

Thou who didst call the Furies from the abyss,And round Orestes bid them howl and hiss For that unnatural retribution, just Had it but come from hands less near, in this Thy former realm I call thee from the dust.Dost thou not hear my heart ? awake thou shalt and must!

Jt is not that I may not have incurred For my ancestral faults, and mine the wound Wherewith I bleed withal, and had it been conferred With a just weapon it had flowed unbound, But now my blood shall not sink in the ground.

" But in this page a record will I seek ; Not in the air shall these my words disperse, Though I be ashes, a far hour shall wreak The deep prophetic fulness of this verse, And pile on human heads the mountain of my curse. That curse shall be forgiveness. Have I not, Hear me, my Mother Earth ! behold it, Heaven, Have I not had to wrestle with my lot ? Have I not suffered things to be forgiven ? Have I not had my brain seared, my heart riven, Hopes sapped, name blighted, life's life lied away, And only not to desperation driven,

Because not altogether of such clay

As rots into the soul of those whom I survey ?

" From mighty wrongs to petty perfidy, Have I not seen what human things could do, —
From the loud roar of foaming calumny, To the small whispers of the paltry few, And subtler
venom of the reptile crew, The Janus glance of whose significant eye. Learning to lie with
silence, would seem true, And without utterance, save the shrug or sigh, Deal round to happy
fools its speechless obloquy ? " *

The reader will please notice that the lines in italics are almost, word for word, a
repetition of the lines in italics in the former poem on his wife, where he speaks of a significant
eye that has learned to lie in silence, and were evidently meant to apply to Lady Byron and her
small circle of confidential friends.

Before this, in the Third Canto of "Childe Harold," he had claimed the sympathy of the

The italics are mine.

48 THE ATTACK ON LADY BYRON.

world, as a loving father, deprived by a severe fate of the solace and society of his only
child:

" My daughter, with this name my song began, My daughter, with this name my song
shall end, I see thee not and hear thee not, but none Can be so wrapped in thee ; thou art the
friend To whom the shadows of far years extend.

"To aid thy mind's developments, to-watch The dawn of little joys, to sit and see Almost
thy very growth, to view thee catch Knowledge of objects, wonders yet to thee, And print on thy
soft cheek a parent's kiss, This it should seem was not reserved for me. Yet this was in my nature,
as it is, I know not what there is, yet something like to this.

" Yet though dull hate as duty should be taught, I know that thou wilt love me ; though
my name Should be shut out from thee as spell still fraught With desolation and a broken claim,
Though the grave close between us, were the same. I know that thou wilt love me, though to
drain My blood from out thy being were an aim And an attainment, all will be in vain."

THE ATTACK ON LADY BYRON. 49

To all these charges against her, sent all over the world in verses as eloquent as the
English language is capable of, the wife replied noth ing. 'As a lamb before her shearers is dumb,
so she opened not her mouth.'

" Assailed by slander and the tongue of strife, Her only answer was, — a blameless life."

She had a few friends, a very few, with whom she sought solace and sympathy. One letter
from her, written at this time, preserved by acci dent, is the only authentic record of how the
matter stood with her.We regret to say that the publication of this document was not brought forth
to clear Lady Byron's name from her husband's slanders, but to shield him from the worst
accusation against him, by showing that this crime was not in cluded in the few private
confidential revela-•tions that friendship wrung from the young wife at this period.

Lady Anne Barnard, authoress of "Auld Robin Grey," a friend, whose age and experience

3

5O THE ATTACK ON LADY BYRON.

made her a proper confidant, sent for the broken-hearted, perplexed wife, and offered her
a woman's sympathy.

To her Lady Byron wrote many letters, under seal of confidence, and Lady Anne says : " I
will give you a few paragraphs transcribed from one of Lady Byron's own letters to me. It is sor
rowful to think that in a very little time this young and amiable creature, wise, patient, and
feeling, will have her character mistaken by every one who reads Byron's works. To rescue her

from this I preserved her letters, and when she afterwards expressed a fear that anything of her writing should ever fall into hands to in jure him (I suppose she meant by publication), I safely assured her that it never should. But here this letter shall be placed, a sacred rec ord in her favor, unknown to herself."

" I am a very incompetent judge of the impression which the last Canto of ' Childe Harold' may produce on the minds of indifferent readers.

" It contains the usual trace of a conscience restlessly

awake, though his object has been too long to aggra vate its burden, as if it could thus be oppressed into eternal stupor. I will hope, as you do, that it survives for his ultimate good.

" It was the acuteness of his remorse, impenitent in its character, which so long seemed to demand from my compassion to spare every semblance of reproach, every look of grief, which might have said to his con science, You have made me wretched.'

" I am decidedly of opinion that he is responsible. He has wished to be thought partially deranged, or on the brink of it, to perplex observers and prevent them from tracing effects to their real causes through all the intrica cies of his conduct. I was, as I told you, at one time the dupe of his acted insanity, and clung to the former delusions in regard to the motives that concerned me personally, till the whole system was laid bare.

" He is the absolute monarch of words, and uses them, as Bonaparte did lives, for conquest, without more regard to their intrinsic value, considering them only as ciphers, which must derive all their import from the situation in which he places them, and the ends to which he adapts them, with such consummate skill. Why, then, you will say, does he not employ them to give a better color to his own character ? Because

he is too good an actor to over-act, or to assume a moral garb, which it would be easy to strip off.

" In regard to his poetry, egotism is the vital princi ple of his imagination, which it is difficult for him to kindle on any subject with which his own character and interests are not identified; but by the introduction of fictitious incidents, by change of scene or time, he has enveloped his poetical disclosures in a system impen etrable except to a very few, and his constant desire of creating a sensation makes him not averse to be the object of wonder and curiosity, even though accompanied by some dark and vague suspicions.

" Nothing has contributed more to the misunderstand ing of his real character than the lonely grandeur in which he shrouds it, and his affectation of being above mankind, when he exists almost in their voice. The romance of his sentiments is another feature of this mask of state. I know no one more habitually destitute of that enthusiasm he so beautifully expresses, and to which he can work up his fancy chiefly by contagion.

" had heard he was the best of brothers, the most generous of friends, and I thought such feelings only required to be warmed and cherished into more diffusive benevolence. Though these opinions are eradicated, and could never return but with the decay of my memory.

you will not wonder if there are still moments when the association of feelings which arose from them soften and sadden my thoughts.

" But I have not thanked you, dearest Lady Anne, for your kindness in regard to a principal object, — that of rectifying false impressions. I trust you understand my wishes, which never were to injure Lord Byron in any way ; for, though he would not suffer me to re7nain his wife, he cannot prevent me from continuing his friend; and it was from considering myself as such that I silenced the accusations by which my own conduct might have been more fully justified.

" It is not necessary to speak ill of his heart in gen eral ; it is sufficient that to me it was hard and impen etrable, — that my own must have been broken before his could have been touched. I would rather represent this as my misfortune than as his guilt; but, surely, that misfortune is not to be made my crime ! Such are my feelings ; you will ju&ge how to act.

" His allusions to me in « Childe Harold' are cruel and cold, but with such a semblance as to make me appear so, and to attract all sympathy to himself. It is said in this poem that hatred of him will be taught as a lesson to his child. I might appeal to all who have ever heard me speak of him, and still more to my own heart,

to witness that there has been no moment when I have remembered injury otherwise than affectionately and sorrowfully.

"It is not my duty to give way to hopeless and wholly unrequited affection ; but, so long as I live, my chief struggle will probably be not to remember him too kindly. I do not seek the sympathy of the world, but I wish to be known by those whose opinion is valuable and whose kindness is dear to me. Among such, my dear Lady Anne, you will ever be remembered by your truly affectionate

"A. BYRON."

On this letter I observe Lord Lindsay remarks that it shows a noble but rather severe charac ter, and a recent author has remarked that it seemed to be written rather in a " cold spirit of criticism." It seems to strike these gentlemen as singular that Lady Byron did not enjoy the poem ! But there are two remarkable sentences in this letter which have escaped the critics hitherto. Lord Byron, in this, the Third Canto of " Childe Harold," expresses in most affecting words an enthusiasm of love for his sister. So long as he

lived he was her faithful correspondent ; he sent her his journals ; and, dying, he left her and her children everything he had in the world. This certainly seems like an affectionate brother; but in what words does Lady Byron speak of this affection ?

" I had heard he was the best of brothers, the most generous of friends. I thought these feelings only required to be warmed and cherished into more diffusive benevolence. THESE OPINIONS

ARE ERADICATED, AND COULD NEVER RETURN BUT

WITH THE DECAY OF MEMORY." Let me ask those who give this letter as a proof that at this time no idea such as I have stated was in Lady Byron's mind, to account for these words. Let them please answer these questions : Why had Lady Byron ceased to think him a good brother ? Why does she use so strong a word as that the opinion was eradicated, torn up by the roots, and could never grow again in her except by decay of memory ?

And yet this is a document Lord Lindsay

vouches for as authentic, and which he brings forward in defence of Lord Byron.

Again she says, " Though he wotild not suffer me to remain his wife, he cannot prevent me from continuing his friend." Do these words not say that in some past time, in some decided manner, Lord Byron had declared to her his rejection of her as a wife ? I shall yet have occasion to explain these words.

Again she says, " I silenced accusations by which my conduct might have been more fully justified."

The people in England who are so very busy in searching out evidence against my true story have searched out and given to the world an important confirmation of this assertion of Lady Byron's.

It seems that the confidential waiting-maid who went with Lady Byron on her wedding journey has been sought out and interrogated, and, as appears by description, is a venerable, respectable old person, quite in possession of all

her senses in general, and of that sixth sense of propriety in particular, which appears not to be a common virtue in our days.

As her testimony is important, we insert it just here, with a description of her person in full. The ardent investigators thus speak: —

" Having gained admission, we were shown into a small but neatly furnished and scrupulously clean apart ment, where sat the object of our visit. Mrs. Minns is a venerable-looking old lady, of short stature, slight and active appearance, with a singularly bright and intelli gent countenance. Although midway between eighty and ninety years of age, she is in full possession of her fac ulties, discourses freely and cheerfully, hears apparently as well as ever she did, and her sight is so good that, aided by a pair of spectacles, she reads the Chronicle every day with ease. Some idea of her competency to contribute valuable evidence to the subject which now so much engages public attention on three continents may be found from her own narrative of her personal relations with Lady Byron. Mrs. Minns was born in the neighborhood of Seaham, and knew Lady Byron from childhood. During the long period of ten years she was Miss Milbanke's lady's-maid, and in that 3*

capacity became the close confidante of her mistress. There were circumstances which rendered their relation ship peculiarly intimate. Miss Milbanke had no sister or female friend to whom she was bound by the ties of more than a common affection ; and her mother, whatever other excellent qualities she may have possessed, was too high-spirited and too hasty in temper to attract the sympathies of the young. Some months before Miss Milbanke was married to Lord Byron Mrs. Minns had quitted her service on the occasion of her own marriage with Mr. Minns, but she continued to reside in the neighborhood of Seaham, and remained on the most friendly terms with her former mistress. As the court ship proceeded, Miss Milbanke concealed nothing from her faithful attendant, and when the wedding-day was fixed she begged Mrs. Minns to return and fulfil the duties of lady's-maid, at least during the honeymoon. Mrs. Minns at the time was nursing her first child, and it was no small sacrifice to quit her own home at such a moment, but she could not refuse her old mistress's request. Accordingly, she returned to Seaham Hall some days before the wedding, was present at the ceremony, and then preceded Lord and Lady Byron to Halnaby Hall, near Croft, in the North Riding of Yorkshire, one of Sir Ralph Milbanke's seats, where

the newly married couple were to spend the honeymoon. Mrs. Minns remained with Lord and Lady Byron during the three weeks they spent at Halnaby Hall, and then accompanied them to Seaham, where they spent the next six weeks. It was during the latter period that she finally quitted Lady Byron's service, but she re mained in the most friendly communication with her Ladyship till the death of the latter, and for some time was living in the neighborhood of Lady Byron's resi dence in Leicestershire, where she had frequent oppor tunities of seeing her former mistress. It may be added that Lady Byron was not unmindful of the faithful services of her friend and attendant in the instruc tions to her executors contained in her will. Such was the position of Mrs. Minns towards Lady Byron, and we think no one will question that it was of a nature to entitle all that Mrs. Minns may say on the subject of the relations of Lord and Lady Byron to the most respectful consideration and credit."

Such is the chronicler's account of the faithful creature, whom nothing but intense indignation and disgust at Mrs. Beecher Stowe would lead to speak on her mistress's affairs ; but Mrs. Beecher

Stowe feels none the less sincere respect for her, and is none the less obliged to her for having spoken. Much of Mrs. Minns's testimony will be referred to in another place ; we only extract one passage, to show that while Lord Byron spent his time in setting afloat slanders against his wife, she spent hers in sealing the mouths of witnesses against him.

Of the period of the honeymoon Mrs. Minns says : —

"The happiness of Lady Byron, however, was of brief duration ; even during the short three weeks they spent at Halnaby the irregularities of Lord Byron occasioned her the greatest distress, and she even contemplated re turning to her father. Mrs. Minns was her constant companion and confidante through this painful period, and she does not believe that her ladyship concealed a thought from her. With laudable reticence, the old lady absolutely refuses to disclose the particulars of Lord Byron's misconduct at this time j she gave Lady Byron a solemn promise not to do so.

" So serious did Mrs. Minns consider the conduct of

Lord Byron, that she recommended her mistress to confide all the circumstances to her father, Sir Ralph Milbanke, a calm, kind, and most excellent parent, and take his advice as to her future course. At one time Mrs. Minns thinks Lady Byron had resolved to follow her counsel and im part her wrongs to Sir Ralph ; but on arriving at Seaham Hall her ladyship strictly enjoined Mrs. Minns to pre serve absolute silence on the subject, — a course which she followed herself, — so that when, six weeks later, she and Lord Byron left Seaham for London, not a word had escaped her to disturb her parents' tranquillity as to their daughter's domestic happiness. As might be expected, Mrs. Minns bears the warmest testimony to the noble and lovable qualities of her departed mistress. She also declares that Lady Byron was by no means of a cold temperament, but that the affectionate impulses of her nature were checked by the unkind treatment she ex perienced from her husband."

We have already shown that Lord Byron had been, ever since his separation, engaged in a systematic attempt to reverse the judgment of the world against himself, by making converts of all his friends to a most odious view of his

wife's character, and inspiring them with the zeal of propagandists to spread these views through society. We have seen how he prepared par tisans to interpret the Fourth Canto of " Childe Harold."

This plan of solemn and heroic accusation was the first public attack on his wife. Next we see him commencing a scurrilous attempt to turn her to ridicule in the First Canto of " Don Juan."

It is to our point now to show how carefully and cautiously this Don Juan campaign was planned.

Murray :

"VENICE, January 25, 1819.

" You will do me the favor to print privately, for Private distribution, fifty copies of ' Don Juan? The list of the men to whom 1 wish it presented I will send hereafter."

The poem, as will be remembered, begins with the meanest and foulest attack on his wife that ever ribald wrote, and put it in close

neighborhood with scenes which every pure man or woman must feel to be the beastly utter ances of a man who had lost all sense of decency. Such a potion was too strong to be administered even in a time when great license was allowed, and men were not over-nice. But Byron chooses fifty armor-bearers of that class of men who would find indecent ribaldry about a wife a good joke, and talk about the " artistic merits " of things which we hope would make an honest boy blush.

At this time he acknowledges that his vices had brought him to a state of great exhaustion, attended by such debility of the stomach that nothing remained on it; and adds, " I was obliged to reform my way of life, which was conducting me from the yellow leaf to the ground with all deliberate speed." * But as his health is a little better he employs it in making the way to death and hell elegantly easy for other young men, by breaking down the remaining scruples of a society not over-scrupulous. * Vol. IV. p. 143.

Society revolted, however, and fought stout ly against the nauseous dose. Even his sister wrote to him that she heard such things said of it that she never would read it ; and the outcry against it on the part of all women of his acquaintance was such that for a time he was quite overborne; and the Countess Guic-cioli finally extorted a promise from him to cease writing it. Nevertheless, there came a time when England accepted " Don Juan," — when Wilson, in the Noctes Ambrosianse, praised it as a classic, and took every opportunity to reprobate Lady Byron's conduct. When first it appeared the Blackwood came out with that indignant denunciation of which we have spoken, and to which Byron replied in the extracts we have already quoted. He did something more than reply. He marked out Wilson as one of the strongest literary men of the day, and set his " initiated " with their documents to work upon him.

One of these documents to which he re-

quested Wilson's attention was the private au tobiography, written expressly to give his own story of all the facts of the marriage and sep aration.

In the indignant letter he writes Murray on the Blackwood article, Vol. IV. Letter 350, — under date December 10, 1819, — he says : —

" I sent home for Moore, and for Moore only (who has my journal also), my memoir written up to 1816, and I gave him leave to show it to whom he pleased, but not to publish on any account You may read it, and you may let Wilson read it if he likes, — not for his public opinion, but his private, for I like the man, and care very little about the magazine.. And I could wish Lady Byron herself to read it, that she may have it in her power to mark anything mistaken or mis stated. As it will never appear till after my extinction, it would be but fair she should see it; that is to say, her self willing. Your Blackwood accuses me of treating women harshly; but I have been their martyr; my whole life has been sacrificed to them and by them."

It was a part of Byron's policy to place

Lady Byron in positions before the world where she could not speak, and where her silence would be set down to her as haughty, stony indifference and obstinacy. Such was the pretended negotiation through Madame de Stael, and such now this apparently fair and generous offer to let Lady Byron see and mark this manuscript.

The little Ada is now in her fifth year,— a child of singular sensibility and remarkable mental powers, — one of those exceptional chil dren who are so perilous a charge for a mother.

Her husband proposes this artful snare to her, — that she shall mark what is false in a statement which is all built on a damning lie, that she cannot refute over that daughter's head, — and which would perhaps be her ruin to discuss.

Hence came an addition of two more docu ments, to be used "privately among friends,"

11

* Lord Byron took especial pains to point out to Murray the importance of these two letters. Vol. V. Letter 443, he

THE ATTACK ON LADY BYRON.

and which Blackwood uses after Lady Byron is safely out of the world to cast ignominy on her grave,—the wife's letter, that of a mother standing at bay for her daughter, knowing that she is dealing with a desperate, powerful, un scrupulous enemy.

" KIRKBY MALLORY, March 10, 1820.

" I received your letter of January i, offering to my perusal a Memoir of part of your life. I decline to in spect it. I consider the publication or circulation of such a composition at any time as prejudicial to Ada's future happiness. For my own sake, I have no reason to shrink from publication; but, notwithstanding the injuries which I have suffered, I should lament some of the consequences.

"A. BYRON. "To LORD BYRON."

Lord Byron, writing for the public, as is his custom, makes reply :

says: "You must also have Trom Mr. Moore the correspond ence between me and Lacly B., to whom I offered a sight of all that concerns herself in these papers. This is important. He has her letter and my answer."

68 THE ATTACK ON LADY BYRON.

" RAVENNA, April 3, 1820.

" I received yesterday your answer, dated March 10. My offer was an honest one, and surely could only be construed as such, even by the most malignant casuistry. I could answer you, but it is too late, and it is not worth while. To the mysterious menace of the last sentence, whatever its import maybe,—and I cannot pretend to unriddle it, I could hardly be very sensible even if I understood it, as, before it can take place, I shall be where 'nothing can touch him further.' ... .1 advise you, however, to anticipate the period of your intention, for, be assured, no power of figures can avail beyond the present; and if it could, I would answer with the Floren tine :

" ' Ed io, che posto son con loro in croce certo
La fiera moglie, piii ch' altro, mi nuoce.
" BYRON. " To LADY BYRON."

Two things are very evident in this corre spondence. Lady Byron intimates that, if he

" And I, who with them on the cross am placed,. . truly
My savage wife, more than aught else, doth harm me." InfernOy Canto XVI., Longfellow's translation.

THE ATTACK ON LADY BYRON. 69

publishes his story, some consequences must fol low which she shall regret.

Lord Byron receives this as a threat, and says he does n't understand it. But directly after he says, " Before IT can take place, I shall be," &c.

The intimation is quite clear. He does un derstand what the consequences alluded to are. They are evidently that Lady Byron will speak out and tell her story. He says she cannot do this till after he is dead, and then he shall not care. In allusion to her accuracy as to dates and figures, he says: " Be assured no power of figures can avail beyond this pres ent " (life) ; and then' ironically advises her to anticipate the period, i. e. to speak out while he is alive.

In Vol. VI. Letter 518, which Lord Byron wrote to Lady Byron, but did not send, he says : " I burned your last note for two rea sons, firstly, because it was written in a style not very agreeable ; and, secondly, because I

wished to take your word without documents, which are the resources of worldly and • sus picious people."

It would appear from this that there was a last letter of Lady Byron to her husband, which he did not think proper to keep on hand, or show to the " initiated " with his usual unreserve ; that this letter contained some kind of pledge for which he preferred to take her word, without documents.

Each reader can imagine for himself what that pledge might have been ; but from the tenor of the three letters we should infer that it was a promise of silence for his lifetime, on certain conditions, and that the publication of the autobiography would violate those condi tions, and make it her duty to speak out.This celebrated autobiography forms so con spicuous a figure in the whole history, that the reader must have a full idea of it, as given by Byron himself, in Vol. IV. Letter 344, to Murray:

" I gave to Moore, who is gone to Rome, my life in MS., in seventy-eight folio sheets, brought down to 1816 Also a journal kept in 1814. Neither are for publication during my life, but when I am cold you may do what you please. In the mean time, if you like to read them you may, and show them to anybody you like. I care not "

He tells him also: —

"You will find in it a detailed account of my marriage and its consequences, as true as a party concerned can make such an account."

Of the extent to which this autobiography was circulated we have the following testimony of Shelton Mackenzie, in notes to the " Noctes " of June, 1824.

In the Noctes Odoherty says :

" The fact is, the work had been copied for the private reading of a great lady in Florence."

The note says :

" The great lady in Florence, for whose private read ing Byron's autobiography was copied, was the Countess

of Westmoreland Lady Blessington had the auto biography in her possession for weeks, and confessed to having copied every line of it. Moore remonstrated, and she committed her copy to the flames, but did not tell him that her sister, Mrs. Home Purvis, now Vis countess of Canterbury, had also made a copy ! . . . . From the quantity of copy I have seen, and others were- more in the way of falling in with it than myself, I surmise that at least half a dozen copies were made, and of these Jive are now in existence. Some particu lar parts, such as the marriage and separation, were copied separately; but I think there cannot be less than five full copies yet to be found."

This was written after the original autobi ography was btirned.

We may see the zeal and enthusiasm of the Byron party, — copying seventy-eight folio sheets, as of old Christians copied the Gos pels. How widely, fully, and thoroughly, thus, by this secret process, was society saturated with Byron's own versions of the story that related to himself and wife ! Against her there was only the complaint of an absolute silence. She put forth no statements, no docu ments ; had no party, sealed the lips of her counsel, and even of her servants; yet she could not but have known, from time to time, how thoroughly and strongly this web of min gled truth and lies was being meshed around her steps.

From the time that Byron first saw the im portance of securing Wilson on his side, and wrote to have his partisans attend to him, we may date an entire revolution in the Black-wood. It became Byron's warmest supporter, is to this day the bitterest accuser of his wife.

Why was this wonderful silence ? It appears by Dr. Lushington's statements, that, when Lady Byron did speak, she had a story to tell that powerfully affected both him and Romilly, a story supported by evidence on which they were willing to have gone to public trial. Supposing, now, she had imitated Lord Byron's example, and, avoiding public trial, had put her story into

private circulation ; as he sent " Don Juan " to fifty confidential friends, suppose she had sent a written statement of her story to fifty judges as intelligent as the two that had heard it; or sup pose she had confronted his autobiography with her own, — what would have been the result ?

The first result would have been Mrs. Leigh's utter ruin. The world may finally forgive the man of genius anything ; but for a woman there is no mercy and no redemption.

This ruin Lady Byron prevented by her utter silence and great self-command. Mrs. Leigh never lost position. Lady Byron never so varied in her manner toward her as to excite the sus picions even of her confidential old servant.

To protect Mrs. Leigh effectually, it must have been necessary to continue to exclude even her own mother from the secret, as we are assured she did at first ; for, had she told Lady Milbanke, it is not possible that so high-spirited a woman could have restrained herself from such outward expressions as would at least have awakened sus-

picion. There was no resource but this absolute silence.

Lady Blessington, in her last conversation with Lord Byron, thus describes the life Lady Byron was leading. She speaks of her as "wearing away her youth in almost monastic seclusion, questioned by some, appreciated by few, seeking consolation alone in the discharge of her duties, and avoiding all external demon strations of a grief that her pale cheek and solitary existence alone were vouchers for."

The main object of all this silence may be imagined, if we remember that if Lord Byron had not died, had he truly and deeply re pented, and become a thoroughly good man, and returned to England to pursue a course worthy of his powers, there was on record neither word nor deed from his wife to stand in his way.

His PLACE WAS KEPT IN SOCIETY, ready for him to return to whenever he came clothed

and in his right mind. He might have had the heart and confidence of his daughter un shadowed by a suspicion. He might have won the reverence of the great and good in his own lands and all lands. That hope, which was the strong support, the prayer of the silent wife, it did not please God to fulfil.

Lord Byron died a worn-out man at thirty-six. But the bitter seeds he had sown came up, after his death, in a harvest of thorns over his grave ; and there were not wanting hands to use them as instruments of torture on the heart of his widow.

CHAPTER III.

RESUME OF THE CONSPIRACY.

A/I 7E have traced the conspiracy of Lord Byron against his wife up to its latest device. That the reader's mind may be clear, on the points of the process, we shall now briefly recapitulate the documents in the orderlof time.

I. March 17, 1816.—While negotiations for separation were pending, — " Fare thce well, and if foreverr

While writing these pages, we have received from England the testimony of one who has seen the original draught of that " Fare thee well." This original copy had evidently been subjected to the most careful and acute revision. Scarcely two lines that were not interlined, scarcely an adjective that was not exchanged for a better;

showing that the noble lord was not so far over come by grief as to have forgotten his reputa tion. (Found its way to the public prints through the imprudence of a friend?\'7d

II. March 29, 1816. — An attack on Lady Byron's old governess for having been born poor, for being homely, and for having unduly influenced his wife against him ; promising that her grave should be a fiery bed, &c. ; also prais ing his wife's perfect and remarkable truthful ness and discernment, that made it impossible for flattery to fool, or baseness blind her; but ascribing all his woes to her being fooled and blinded by this same governess. (Found its way to the prints by the imprudence of a friend?)

III. September, 1816. Lines on hearing that Lady Byron is ill. Calls her a Clytemnestra, who has secretly set assassins on her lord ; says she is a mean, treacherous, deceitful liar, and has entirely departed from her early truth, and be come the most unscrupulous and unprincipled of women. Never printed till after Lord By ron's death, but circulated privately among the " initiated"

IV. Aug. 9, 1817. Gives to M. G. Lewis a paper for circulation among friends in England, stating that what he most wants is public investigation, which has always been denied him; and daring Lady Byron and her counsel to come out publicly. Found in M. G. Lewis's portfolio after his death ; never heard of before, except among the " initiated."

Having given M. G. Lewis's document time to work, —

January, 1818. — Gives the fourth canto of " Childe Harold " * to the public.

Jan. 25, 1819. — Sends to Murray to print for private circulation among the "initiated" the first canto of " Don Juan."

Is nobly and severely rebuked for this insult to his wife by the " Blackwood," August, 1819.

* Murray's edition of Byron's works, vol. ii. p. 189; date of dedication to Hobhouse, Jan. 2, 1818.

October, 1819.—Gives Moore the manu script Autobiography, with leave to show it to whom he pleases, and print it after his death.

Oct. 29, 1819, vol. iv. letter 344. — Writes to Murray, that he may read all this Autobiogra phy, and show it to anybody he likes.

Dec. 10, 1819. — Writes to Murray on this article in "Blackwood" against " Don Juan " and himself, which, he supposes written by Wilson ; sends a complimentary message to Wilson, and asks him to read his Autobiography sent by Moore. (Letter 350.)

March 15, 1820. — Writes, and dedicates to I. Disraeli, Esq., a vindication of himself in reply to the " Blackwood " on " Don Juan," containing an indignant defence of his own conduct in rela tion to his wife, and maintaining that he never yet has had an opportunity of knowing whereof he has been accused ; accusing Sir S. Romilly of taking his retainer, and then going over to the adverse part ', &c. Printed for private circula tion; to be found in the standard English edition of Murray, vol. ix. p. 57.

To this condensed account of Byron's strategy we must add the crowning stroke of policy which transmitted this warfare to his friends, to be continued after his death.

During the last visit Moore made him in Italy, and just before Byron presented to him his Autobiography, the following scene occurred, as narrated by Moore (vol. iv. p. 221) : —

" The chief subject of conversation, when alone, was his marriage, and the load of obloquy which it had brought upon him. He was most anxious to know the worst that had been alleged of his conduct; and, as this was our first opportunity of speaking together on the subject, I did not hesitate to put his candor most searchingly to the proof, not only by enumerating the various charges I had heard brought against him by others, but by specifying such portions of these chai-ges as I had been inclined to think not incredible myself.

" To all this he listened with patience, and answered with the most unhesitating frankness ; laughing to scorn the tales of unmanly outrage related of him, but at the same time acknowl edging that there had been in his conduct but too much to blame and regret, and stating one or two occasions during his domestic life when he had been irritated into letting the ' breath of bitter words' escape him, . . . which he now evidently

remembered with a degree of remorse and pain which might well have entitled them to be forgotten by others.

" It was, at the same time, manifest, that, whatever admis sions he might be inclined to make respecting his own delin quencies, the inordinate measure of the punishment dealt o^lt to him had sunk deeply into his mind, and, with the usual effect of such injustice, drove him also to be unjust himself; so nmch so, indeed, as to impute to the quarter to which he now traced all his ill fate a feeling of fixed hostility to himself, which would not rest, he thought, even at his grave, lut contimte to persecute his memory as it was now imbittering his life. So strong was this impression upon him, that, during one of our few intervals of seriousness, he conjured me by our friendship, if, as he both felt and hoped, I should survive him, not to let unmerited censure settle upon his name."

In this same account, page 218, Moore testi fies that

" Lord Byron disliked his countrymen, but only because he knew that his morals were held in contempt by them. The English, themselves rigid observers of family duties, could not pardon him the neglect of his, nor his trampling on principles : therefore neither did he like being presented to them, nor did they, especially when they had wives with them, like to cultivate his acquaintance. Still there was a strong desire in all of them to see him; and the women in particular, who did not dare to

look at him but by stealth, said in an under-voice, ' What a pity it is ! ' If, however, any of his compatriots of exalted rank and high reputation came forward to treat him with courtesy, he showed himself obviously flattered by it. It seemed, that, to the wound which remained open in his ulcerated heart, such soothing attentions were as drops of healing balm, which com forted him."

When in society, we are further informed by a lady quoted by Mr. Moore, he was in the habit of speaking of his wife with much respect and affection, as an illustrious lady, distinguished for her qualities of heart and understanding; saying that all the fault of their cruel separation, lay with himself. Mr. Moore seems at times to, be somewhat puzzled by these contradictory statements of his idol, and speculates not a little on what could be Lord Byron's object in using such language in public; mentally com paring it, we suppose, with the free handling which he gave to the same subject in his private correspondence.

The innocence with which Moore gives him self up to be manipulated by Lord Byron, the naivete with which he shows all the process, let us a little into the secret of the marvellous powers of charming and blinding which this great actor possessed.

Lord Byron had the beauty, the wit, the genius, the dramatic talent, which have consti tuted the strength of some wonderfully fascinat ing women.

There have been women able to lead their leashes of blinded adorers ; to make them swear that black was white, or white black, at their word ; to smile away their senses, or weep away their reason. No matter what these sirens may say, no matter what they may do, though caught in a thousand transparent lies, and doing a thousand deeds which would have ruined others, still men madly rave after them in life, and tear their hair over their graves. Such an enchanter in man's shape was Lord Byron.

He led captive Moore and Murray by be ing beautiful, a genius, and a lord ; calling them " Dear Tom," and " Dear Murray," while

they were only commoners. Pie first insulted Sir Walter Scott, and then witched his heart out of him by ingenuous confessions and poeti cal compliments ; he took Wilson's heart by flattering messages and a beautifully-written letter; he corresponded familiarly with Hogg; and, before his death, had made fast friends, in one way or another, of the whole Noctes Ambrosianas Club.

We thus have given the historical resum£ of Lord Byron's attacks on his wife's reputation : we shall add, that they were based on philo sophic principles, showing a deep knowledge of mankind. An analysis will show that they can be philosophically classified : —

ist, Those which addressed the sympathetic nature of man, representing her as cold, method ical, severe, strict, unforgiving.

2d, Those addressed to the faculty of associa tion, connecting her with ludicrous and licen tious images ; taking from her the usual protec tion of womanly delicacy and sacredness.

3d, Those addressed to the moral faculties, accusing her as artful, treacherous, untruthful, malignant.

All these various devices he held in his hand, shuffling and dealing them as a careful gamester his pack of cards according to the exigencies of the game. He played adroitly, skilfully, with blinding flatteries and seductive wiles, that made his victims willing dupes.

Nothing can more clearly show the power and perfectness of his enchantments than the masterly way in which he turned back the moral force of the whole English nation, which had risen at first in its strength against him. The victory was complete.

CHAPTER IV.

RESULTS AFTER LORD BYRON'S DEATH.

A T the time of Lord Byron's death, the Eng lish public had been so skilfully manipu lated by the Byron propaganda, that the sympa thy of the whole world was with him. A tide of emotion was now aroused in England by his early death, — dying in the cause of Greece and liberty. There arose a general wail for him, as for a lost pleiad, not only in England, but over the whole world ; a great rush of enthu siasm for his memory, to which the greatest literary men of England freely gave voice. By general consent, Lady Byron seems to have been looked upon as the only cold-hearted, un sympathetic person in this general mourning.

From that time, the literary world of England

apparently regarded Lady Byron as a woman to whom none of the decorums, nor courtesies of ordinary womanhood, nor even the consideration belonging to common humanity, were due.

" She that is a widow indeed, and desolate," has been regarded in all Christian countries as an object made sacred by the touch of God's afflicting hand, sacred in her very helplessness ;

and the old Hebrew Scriptures give to the Supreme Father no dearer title than " the widow's God." But, on Lord Byron's death, men not devoid of tenderness, men otherwise generous and of fine feeling, acquiesced in in sults to his widow with an obtuseness that seems, on review, quite incredible.

Lady Byron was not only a widow, but an orphan. She had no sister for confidante ; no father and mother to whom to go in her sor rows, — sorrows so much deeper and darker to her than they could be to any other human being.. She had neither son nor brother to uphold and protect her. On all hands it was

acknowledged, that, so far, there was no fault to be found in her but her utter silence. Her life was confessed to be pure, useful, charitable ; and yet, in this time of her sorrow, the writers of England issued article upon article not only devoid of delicacy, but apparently injurious and insulting towards her, with a blind unconscious ness which seems astonishing.

One of the greatest literary powers of that time was the " Blackwood :" the reigning monarch on that literary throne was Wilson, the lion-hearted, the brave, generous, tender poet, and, with some sad exceptions, the noble man. But Wilson had believed the story of Byron, and, by his very generosity and tenderness and pity, was betrayed into injustice.

In "The Noctes " of November, 1824, there is a conversation of the Noctes club, in which North says, " Byron and I knew each other pretty well ; and I suppose there's no harm in adding, that we appreciated each other pretty tolerably. Did you ever see his letter to me ? "

The footnote to this says, " This letter, which was PRINTED in Byroiis lifetime, was not published till 1830, when it appeared in Moore's Life of Byron. It is one of the most vigor ous prose compositions in the language. Byron had the highest opinion of Wilson's genius and noble spirit."

In the first place, with our present ideas of propriety and good taste, we should reckon it an indecorum to make the private affairs of a pure and good woman, whose circumstances from any point of view were trying, and who evidently shunned publicity, the subject of pub lic discussion in magazines which were read all over the world.

Lady Byron, as they all knew, had on her hands a most delicate and onerous task, in bring ing up an only daughter, necessarily inheriting peculiarities of genius and great sensitiveness ; and the many mortifications and embarrassments which such intermeddling with her private matters must have given, certainly should have

been considered by men with any pretensions to refinement or good feeling.

But the literati of England allowed her no consideration, no rest, no privacy.

In "The Noctes " of November, 1825, there is the record of a free conversation upon Lord and Lady Byron's affairs, interlarded with exhor tations to push the bottle, and remarks on whiskey-toddy. Medwin's " Conversations with Lord Byron " is discussed, which, we are told in a note, appeared a few months after the noble poet's death.

There is a rather bold and free discus sion of Lord Byron's character, — his fond ness for gin and water, on which stimulus he wrote " Don Juan ; " and James Hogg says pleasantly to Mullion, " O Mullion ! it's a pity you and Byron could na ha' been acquaint. There would ha' been brave sparring to see who could say the wildest and the dreadfullest things ; for he had neither fear of man or wo man, and would ha' his joke or jeer, cost what it

might." And then follows a specimen of one of his jokes with an actress, that, in indecency, cer tainly justifies the assertion. From the other stories which follow, and the parenthesis that occurs frequently, (" Mind your glass, James, a little more ! ") it seems evident that the party are progressing in their peculiar kind of civiliza tion.

It is in this same circle and paper that Lady Byron's private affairs come up for discussion. The discussion is thus elegantly introduced : —

Hogg. — " Reach me the black bottle. I say, Christopher, what, after all, is your opinion o' Lord and Leddy Byron's quarrel ? Do you yoursel' take part with him, or with her ? I wad like to hear your real opinion."

North. — " Oh, dear ! Well, Hogg, since you will have it, I think Douglas Kinnaird and Hobhouse are bound to tell us whether there be any truth, and how much, in this story about the declaration, signed by Sir Ralph " [Milbanke].

The note here tells us that this refers to a statement that appeared in " Blackwood " imme diately after Byron's death, to the effect, that,

previous to the formal separation from his wife, Byron required and obtained from Sir Ralph Milbanke, Lady Byron's father, a statement to the effect that Lady Byron had no charge of moral delinquency to bring against him."* North continues : —

" And I think Lady Byron's letter, the ' Dearest Duck' one I mean, should really be forthcoming, if her ladyship's friends wish to stand fair before the public. At present, we have noth ing but loose talk of society to go upon; and certainly, if the things that are said be true, there must be thorough explanation from some quarter, or the tide will continue, as it Jias assuredly begun, toflmu in a direction very opposite to what we were for years accustomed. Sir, they must explain (his business of the letter. You have, of course, heard about the invitation it contained, the warm, affectionate invitation, to Kirkby Mallory " —

Hogg interposes, —

" I clinna like to be intei-ruptin' ye, Mr. North; but I must inquire, Is the jug to stand still while ye're going on at that rate ? "

* Recently, Lord Lindsay has published another version of this story, which makes it appear that he has conversed with a lady who conversed with Hobhouse during his lifetime, in which this story is differently reported. In the last version, it is made to appear that Hobhouse got this declaration from Lady Byron her?elf.

North. — " There, Porker ! These things are part and par cel of the chatter of every bookseller's shop ; "a fortiori, of every drawing-room in May Fair. Can the matter stop here ? Can a great man's memory be permitted to incur damnation while these saving clauses are afloat anywhere uncontradicted ? "

And from this the conversation branches off into strong, emphatic praise of Byron's conduct in Greece- during the last part of his life.

The silent widow is thus delicately and con siderately reminded in the " Blackwood" that she is the talk, not only over the whiskey-jug of the Noctes, but in every drawing-room in Lon don ; and that she must speak out and explain matters, or the whole world will set against her.

But she does not speak yet. The public per secution, therefore, proceeds. Medwin's book being insufficient, another biographer is to be selected. Now, the person in the Noctes club who was" held to have the most complete informa tion of the Byron affairs, and was, on that ac count, first thought of by Murray to execute this very delicate task of writing a Memoir which

should include the most sacred domestic affairs of a noble lady and her orphan daughter, was Maginn. Maginn, the author of the pleasant joke, that " man never reaches the apex of civi lization till he is too drunk to pronounce the word," was the first person in whose hands the Autobiography, Memoirs, and Journals of Lord Byron were placed with this view.

The following note from Shelton Mackenzie, in the June number of "The Noctes," 1824, says, —

" At that time, had he been so minded, Maginn (Odoherty) could have got up a popular Life of Byron as well as most men in England. Immediately on the account of Byron's death being received in London, John Murray proposed that Maginn should bring out Memoirs, Journals, and Letters of Lord Byron, and, with this intent, placed in his hand every line that he (Murray) possessed in Byron's handwriting. . . . The strong desire of Byron V family and executors that the Autobiography should be burned, to which desire Murray foolishly yielded, made such an hiatus in the materials, that Murray and Maginn agreed it would not answer to bring out the work then. Event ually Moore executed it."

The character of the times in which this work was to be undertaken will appear from the fol lowing note of Mackenzie's to " The Noctes " of August, 1824, which we copy, with the author's own Italics: —

"In the ' Blackwood ' of July, 1824, was a poetical epistle by the renowned Timothy Tickler, to the editor of the 'John Bull' magazine, on an article in his first number. This article . . . professed to be a portion of the veritable Autobiography of Byron which was burned, and was called ' My Wedding Night.' It appeared to relate in detail eicry thing that oc curred in the twenty-four hours immediately succeeding that in which Byron was married. It had plenty of coarseness, and some to spare. It went into particulars such as hitherto had been given only by Faublas ; and it had, notwithstanding, many phrases and some facts which evidently did not belong to a mere fabricator. Some years after, I compared this ' Wed ding Night' with what I had all assurance of having been transcribed from the actual manuscripts of Byron, and was per suaded that the magazine-writer must have had the actual state ment before him, or have had a perusal of it. The writer in ' Blackwood ' declared his conviction that it really was Byron's own writing."

The reader must remember that Lord Byron

RESULTS AFTER LORD BYRON S DEATH. Q/

died April, 1824: so that, according to this, his Autobiography was made the means of this gross insult to his widow three months after his death.

If some powerful cause had not paralyzed all feelings of gentlemanly honor, and of womanly delicacy, and of common humanity, towards Lady Byron, throughout the whole British nation, no editor would have dared to open a periodical with such an article ; or, if he had, he would have been overwhelmed with a storm of popular indignation, which, like the fire upon Sodom, would have left him a pillar of salt for a warning to all future genera tions.

" Blackweod " reproves " The John Bull " in a poetical epistle, recognizing the article as coming from Byron, and says to the author, —

" But that_y<?«, sir, a wit and a scholar like you, Should not blush to produce what he blushed not to do, — Take your compliment, youngster : this doubles, almost, The sorrow tfaat rose when his honor was lost." 7

98 RESULTS AFTER LORD BYRON'S DEATH.

We may not wonder that the Autobiography was burned, as Murray says in a recent account, by a committee of Byron's friends, including Hobhouse, his sister, and Murray himself.

Now, the " Blackwood " of July, 1824, thus de clares its conviction that this outrage on every sentiment of human decency came from Lord Byron, and that his honor was lost. Maginn does not undertake the Memoir. No Memoir at all is undertaken ; till finally Moore is selected, as, like Demetrius of old, a well-skilled gilder and " maker of silver shrines," though not for Diana. To Moore is committed the task of doing his best for this battered image, in which even the worshippers recognize foul sulphurous cracks, but which they none the less stand ready to worship as a genuine article that " fell down from Jupiter."

Moore was a man of no particular nicety as to moralities, but in that matter seems not very much below what this record shows his average associates to be. He is so far superior to

Maginn, that his vice is rose-colored and refined. He does not burst out with such heroic stanzas as Maginn's frank invitation to Jeremy Ben-tham : —

" Jeremy, throw your pen aside,

And come get. drunk with me ; And we'll go where Bacchus sits astride, Perched high on barrels three."

Moore's vice is cautious, soft, seductive, slippery, and covered at times with a thin, tremulous veil of religious sentimentalism.

In regard to Byron, he was an unscrupulous, committed partisan : he was as much bewitched by him as ever man has been by woman ; and therefore to him, at last, the task of editing Byron's Memoirs was given.

This Byron, whom they all knew to be obscene beyond what even their most drunken tolerance could at first endure ; this man, whose foul license spoke out what most men conceal from mere respect to the decent instincts of humanity ; whose " honor was lost,"

— was submitted to this careful manipulator, to be turned out a perfected idol for a world longing for one, as the Israelites longed for the calf in Horeb.

The image was to be invested with deceitful glories and shifting haloes, — admitted faults spoken of as peculiarities of sacred origin,— and the world given to understand that no common rule or measure could apply to such an undoubtedly divine production ; and so the hearts of men were to be wrung with pity for his sorrows as the yearning pain of a god, and with anger at his injuries as sacrilege on the sacredness of genius, till they were ready to cast themselves at his feet, and adore.

Then he was to be set up on a pedestal, like Nebuchadnezzar's image on the plains of Dura; and what time the world heard the sound of cornet, sackbut, and dulcimer, in his enchanting verse, they were to fall down and worship.

For Lady Byron, Moore had simply the respect that a commoner has for a lady of rank, and a

good deal of the feeling that seems to underlie all English literature, — that it is no matter what becomes of the woman when the man's story is to be told. But, with all his faults, Moore was not a cruel man; and we cannot conceive such outrageous cruelty and ungentlemanly indelicacy towards an unoffending woman, as he shows in these Memoirs, without referring them to Lord Byron's own influence in making him an un scrupulous, committed partisan on his side.

So little pity, so little sympathy, did he sup pose Lady Byron to be worthy of, that he laid before her, in the sight of all the world, selections from her husband's letters and jour nals, in which the privacies of her courtship and married life were jested upon with a vulgar levity ; letters filled, from the time of the act of separation, with a constant succession of sarcasms, stabs, stings, epigrams, and vindictive allusions to herself, bringing her into direct and insulting comparison with his various mis tresses, and implying their superiority over

her. There, too, were gross attacks on her father and mother, as having been the instiga tors of the separation ; and poor Lady Mil-banke, in particular, is sometimes mentioned with epithets so offensive, that the editor pru dently covers the terms with stars, as intending language too gross to be printed.

The last mistress of Lord Byron is uniformly brought forward in terms of such respect and consideration, that one would suppose that the usual moral laws that regulate English family life had been specially repealed in his favor. Moore quotes with approval letters from Shel ley, stating that Lord Byron's connection with La Guiccioli has been of inestimable benefit to him; and that he'is now becoming what he should be, " a virtuous man." Moore goes on to speak of the connection as one, though somewhat reprehensible, yet as having all those advantages of marriage and settled domestic ties that Byron's affectionate spirit had long sighed for, but never before found ; and in his last resume of the

poet's character, at the end of the volume, he brings the mistress into direct comparison with the wife in a single sentence : " The woman to whom he gave the love of his maturer years idolizes his name ; and, with a single tmhappy exception, scarce an instance is to be found of one brought . . . into relations of amity with him who did not retain a kind regard for him in life, and a fondness for his memory."

Literature has never yet seen the instance of a person, of Lady Byron's rank in life, placed before the world in a position more humiliating to womanly dignity, or wounding to womanly delicacy.

The direct implication is, that she has no feel ings to be hurt, no heart to be broken, and is not worthy even of the consideration which in ordinary life is to be accorded to a widow who has received those awful tidings which generally must awaken many emotions, and call for some consideration, even in the most callous hearts.

The woman who we are told walked the

room, vainly striving to control the sobs that shook her frame, while she sought to draw from the servant that last message of her husband which she was never to hear, was not thought worthy even of the rights of common hu manity.

The first volume of the Memoir came out in 1830. Then for the first time came one flash of lightning from the silent cloud ; and she who had never spoken before spoke out. The libels on the memory of her dead parents drew from her what her own wrongs never did. During all this time, while her husband had been keep ing her effigy dangling before the public as a mark for solemn curses, and filthy lampoons, and secretly-circulated disclosures, that spared no sacredness and violated every decorum, she had not uttered a word. She had been subjected to nameless insults, discussed in the assemblies of drunkards, and challenged to speak for herself. Like the chaste lady in " Comus," whom the vile wizard had bound in the enchanted seat to be

" grinned at and chattered at " by all the filthy rabble of his dehumanized rout, she had re mained pure, lofty, and undefiled ; and the stains of mud and mire thrown upon her had fallen from her spotless garments.

Now that she is.dead, a recent writer in "The London Quarterly " dares give voice to an insin uation which even Byron gave only a suggestion of when he called his wife Clytemnestra; and hints that she tried the power of youth and beauty to win to her the young solicitor Lushing-ton, and a handsome young officer of high rank.

At this time, such insinuations had not been thought of; and the only and chief allegation against Lady Byron had been a cruel severity of virtue.

At all events, when Lady Byron spoke, the world listened with respect, and believed what she said.

Here let us, too, read her statement, and give it the careful attention she solicits (Moore's Life of Byron, vol. vi. p. 275): —

" I have disregarded various publications in which facts within my own knowledge have been grossly misrepresented; but I am called upon to notice some of the erroneous statements proceeding from one who claims to be considered as Lord Byron's confidential and authorized friend. Domestic details ought not to be intruded on the public attention : if, however, they are so intruded, the persons affected by them have a right to refute injurious charges. Mr. Moore has promulgated his own impressions of private events in which I was most nearly concerned, as if he possessed a competent knowledge of the subject. Having survived Lord Byron, I feel increased reluc tance to advert to any circumstances connected with the period of my marriage ; nor is it now my intention to disclose them further than may be indispensably requisite for the end I have in view. Self-vindication is not the motive which actuates me to make this appeal, and the spirit of accusation is unmingled with it; but when the conduct of my parents is brought for ward in a disgraceful light by the passages selected from Lord Byron's letters, and by the remarks of his biographer, I feel bound to justify their characters from imputations which I know to be false. The passages from Lord Byron's letters, to which I refer, are, — the aspersion on my mother's character (p. 648, 1. 4) : * ' My child is very well and flourishing, I hear ;

* The references are to the first volume of the first edition of Moore's Life, originally published by itself.

RESULTS AFTER LORD BYRON S DEATH. IO/

but I must see also. I feel no disposition to resign it to the contagion of its grandmother" 1 s society." 1 The assertion of her dis honorable conduct in employing a spy (p. 645, 1. 7, &c.) : 'A Mrs. C. (now a kind of housekeeper and spy. of Lady Ws), who, in her better days, was a washerwoman, is supposed to be — by the learned — very much the occult cause of our domestic discrepancies.' The seeming exculpation of myself in the extract (p. 646), with the words immediately following it, ' Her nearest relations are a ———;' where the blank clearly implies something too offensive for publication. These passages tend to throw suspicion on my parents, and give reason to ascribe the separation either to their direct agency, or to that of ' offi cious spies ' employed by them.* From the following part of the narrative (p. 642), it must also be inferred that an undue influence was exercised by them for the accomplishment of this purpose : ' It was in a few weeks after the latter communication between us (Lord Byron and Mr. Moore) that Lady Byron adopted the determination of parting from him. She had left London at the latter end of January, on a visit to her father's house in Leicestershire ; and Lord Byron was in a short time to follow her. They had parted in the utmost kindness, — she wrote him a letter, full of playfulness and affection, on the road; and, immediately on her arrival at Kirkby Mallory, her father wrote to acquaint Lord Byron that she would return to him no more.'

* " The officious spies «f his privacy," p. 650.

IO8 RESULTS AFTER LORD BYRON'S DEATH.

" In my observations upon this statement, I shall, as far as possible, avoid touching on any matters relating personally to Lord Byron and myself. The facts are, — I left London for Kirkby Mallory, the residence of my father and mother, on the 15th of January, 1816. Lord Byron had signified to me in writing (Jan. 6) his absolute desire that I should leave London on the earliest day that I could conveniently fix. It was not safe for me to undertake the fatigue of a journey sooner than the I5th. Previously to my departure, it had been strongly impressed on my mind that Lord Byron was under the influence of insanity. This opinion was derived in a great measure from the communications made to me by his nearest relatives and personal attendant, who had more opportunities than myself of observing him during the latter part of my stay in town. It was even represented to me that he was in danger of destroying himself. With the concurrence of his family, I had consulted Dr. Baillie, as a friend (Jan. 8), respecting this supposed mal ady. On acquainting him with the state of the case, and with Lord Byron's desire that I should leave London, Dr. Baillie thought that my absence might be advisable as an experiment, assuming the fact of mental derangement; for Dr. Baillie, not having had access to Lord Byron, could not pronounce a posi tive opinion on that point. He enjoined, that, in correspond ence with Lord Byron, I should avoid all but light and soothing topics. Under these impressions, I left London, determined to follow the advice given by Dr. Baillie. Whatever might have been the nature of Lord Byron's conduct towards me from the

time of my marriage, yet, supposing him to be in a state of mental alienation, it was not for me, nor for any person of com mon humanity, to manifest at that moment a sense of injury. On the day of my departure, and again on my arrival at Kirkby (Jan. 16), I wrote to Lord Byron in a kind and cheerful tone, according to those medical directions.

" The last letter was circulated, and employed as a pretext for the charge of my having been subsequently infliienced to ' desert' * my husband. It has been argued that I parted from Lord Byron in perfect harmony; that feelings incompatible with any deep sense of injury had dictated the letter which I ad dressed to him; and that my sentiments must have been changed by persuasion and interference when I was under the roof of my parents. These assertions and inferences are wholly destitute of foundation. When I arrived at Kirkby Mallory, my parents were unacquainted with the existence of any causes likely to destroy my prospects of happiness ; and, when I com municated to them the opinion which had been formed concern ing Lord Byron's state of mind, they were most anxious to promote his restoration by every means in their power. They assured those relations who were with him in London, that ' they would devote their whole care and attention to the alle viation of his malady;' and hoped to make the best arrange ments for his comfort, if he could be induced to visit them.

" With these intentions, my mother wrote on the I7th to

* " The deserted husband," p. 651.

Lord Byron, inviting him to Kirkby Mallory. She had always treated him with an affectionate consideration and indulgence, which extended to every little peculiarity of his feelings. Never did an irritating word escape her lips in her whole intercourse with him. The accounts given me after I left Lord Byron, by the persons in constant intercourse with him, added to those doubts which had before transiently occurred to my mind as to the reality of the alleged disease; and the reports of his medical attendant were far from establishing the existence of any thing like lunacy. Under this uncertainty, I deemed it right to com municate to my parents, that, if I were to consider Lord Byron's past conduct as that of a person of sound mind, nothing could induce me to return to him. It therefore appeared expedient, both to them and myself, to consult the ablest advisers. For that object, and also to obtain still further information respecting the appearances which seemed to indicate mental derangement, my mother determined to go to London. She was empowered by me to take legal opinions on a written statement of mine, though I had then reasons for reserving a part of the case from the knowledge even of my father and mother. Being convinced by the result of these inquiries, and by the tenor of Lord By ron's proceedings, that the notion.of insanity was an illusion, I no longer hesitated to authorize such measures as were necessary in order to secure me from being ever again placed in his power. Conformably with this resolution, my father wrote to him on the 2d of February to propose an amicable separation. Lord Byron at first rejected this proposal; but when it was distinctly notified to him, that, if he persisted in his refusal, recourse must be had to legal measures, he agreed to sign a deed of separation. Upon applying to Dr. Lushington, who was intimately ac quainted with all the circumstances, to state in writing what he recollected upon this subject, I received from him the follow ing letter, by which it will be manifest that my mother cannot have been actuated by any hostile or ungenerous motives towards Lord Byron : —

" ' MY DEAR LADY BYRON, — I can rely upon the accuracy of my memory for the following statement. I was originally consulted by Lady Noel, on your behalf, whilst you were in the country. The circumstances detailed by her were such as justi fied a separation ; but they were not of that aggravated descrip tion as to render such a measure indispensable. On Lady Noel's representation, I deemed a reconciliation with Lord Byron prac ticable, and felt most sincerely a wish to aid in effecting it. There was not on Lady Noel's part any exaggeration of the facts ; nor, so far as I could perceive, any determination to pre vent a return to Lord Byron : certainly none was expressed when I spoke of a reconciliation. When you came to town, in about a fortnight, or perhaps more, after my first interview with Lady Noel, I was for the first time informed by you of facts utterly unknown, as I have no doubt, to Sir Ralph and Lady Noel. On receiving this additional information, my opinion was entirely changed : I considered a reconciliation impossible. I declared my opinion, and added, that, if such an idea should be entertained, I could not, either professionally or otherwise, take any part towards effecting it.

"' Believe me, very faithfully yours,

"'STEPH. LUSHINGTON.

"'GREAT GEORGE STREET, Jan. 31, 1830.'

112 RESULTS AFTER LORD BYRON S DEATH.

" I have only to observe, that, if the statements on which my legal advisers (the late Sir Samuel Romilly and Dr. Lushing-ton) formed their opinions were false, the responsibility and the odium should rest with me only. I trust that the facts which I have here briefly recapitulated will absolve my father and mother from all accusations with regard to the part they took in the separation between Lord Byron and myself.

" They neither originated, instigated, nor advised that sepa ration ; and they cannot be condemned for having afforded to their daughter the assistance and protection which she claimed. There is no other near relative to vindicate their memory from insult. I am therefore compelled to break the silence which I had hoped always to observe, and to solicit from the readers of Lord Byron's Life an impartial consideration of the testimony extorted from me. " A. I. NOEL BYRON.

"HANGER HILL, Feb. 19, 1830."

The effect of this statement on the literary world may be best judged by the discussion of it by Christopher North (Wilson) in the suc ceeding May number of " The Noctes," where the bravest and most generous of literary men that then were — himself the husband of a gen tle wife — thus gives sentence : the conversa tion is between North and the Shepherd : —

RESULTS AFTER LORD BYRON'S DEATH. 113

North. — " God forbid I should wound the feelings of Lady Byron, of whose character, known to me but by the high esti mation in which it is held by all who have enjoyed her friend ship, I have always spoken with respect! . . . But may I, without harshness or indelicacy, say, here among ourselves, James, that, by marrying Byron, she took upon herself, with eyes wide open and conscience clearly convinced, duties very different from those of which, even in common cases, the pre saging foresight shadows . . . the light of the first nuptial moon ?"

Shepherd. — " She did that, sir ; by my troth, she did that."

North. —" Miss Milbanke knew that he was reckoned a rake and a roue ; and although his genius wiped off, by impas sioned eloquence in love-letters that were felt to be irresistible, or hid the worst stain of, that reproach, still Miss Milbanke must have believed it a perilous thing to be the wife of Lord Byron. . . . But still, by joining her life to his in marriage, she pledged her troth and her faith and her love, under probabilities of se vere, disturbing, perhaps fearful trials, in the future. . . .

" But I think Lady Byron ought not to have printed that Narrative. Death abrogates not the rights of a husband to his wife's silence when speech is fatal ... to his character as a man. Has she not flung suspicion over his bones interred, that they are the bones of a — monster ? ... If Byron's sins or crimes — for we are driven to use terrible terms — were unen durable and unforgivable as if against the Holy Ghost, ought

the wheel, the rack, or the stake to have extorted that confession from his widow's breast ? . . . But there was no such pain here, James : the declaration was voluntary, and it was calm. Self-collected, and gathering up all her faculties and feelings into unshrinking strength, she denounced before all the world — and throughout all space and all time — her husband, as excom municated by his vices from woman's bosom.

" 'Twas to vindicate the character of her parents that Lady Byron wrote, — a holy purpose and devout, nor do I doubt sin cere. But filial affection and reverence, sacred as they are, may be blamelessly, nay, righteously, subordinate to conjugal duties, which die not with the dead, are extinguished not even by the sins of the dead, were they as foul as the grave's corruption."

Here is what John Stuart Mill calls the lite rature of slavery for woman, in length and breadth ; and, that all women may understand the doctrine, the Shepherd now takes up his par able, and expounds the true position of the wife. We render his Scotch into English : —

" Not a few such widows do I know, whom brutal, profligate, and savage husbands have brought to the brink of the grave, — as good, as bright, as innocent as, and far more forgiving than, Lady Byron. There they sit in their obscure, rarely-visited dwell-

RESULTS AFTER LORD BYRON S DEATH. 115

ings; for sympathy instructed by suffering knows well that the deepest and most hopeless misery is least given to complaint."

Then follows a pathetic picture of one such widow, trembling and fainting for hunger, obliged, on her way to the well for a can of water, her only drink, to sit down on a "knowe" and say a prayer.

" Yet she's decently, yea, tidily dressed, poor creature ! in sair worn widow's clothes, a single suit for Saturday and Sun day ; her hair, untimely gray, is neatly braided under her crape cap ; and sometimes, when all is still and solitary in the fields, and all labor has disappeared into the house, you may see her stealing by herself, or leading one wee orphan by the hand, with another at her breast, to the kirkyard, where the love of her youth and the husband of her prime is buried."

"Yet," says the Shepherd, "he was a brute, a ruffian, a mon ster. When drunk, how he raged and cursed and swore! Often did she dread, that, in his fits of inhuman passion, he would have murdered the baby at her breast; for she had seen him dash their only little boy, a child of eight years old, on the floor, till the blood gushed from his ears ; and then the madman threw himself down on the body, and howled for the" gallows. Limmers haunted his door, and he theirs; and it was hers to lie, not sleep, in a cold, forsaken bed, once the bed of peace,

affection, and perfect happiness. Often he struck her; and once, when she was pregnant with that very orphan now smil ing on her breast, reaching out his wee fingers to touch the flow ers on his father's grave. . . .

" But she tries to smile among the neighbors, and speaks of her boy's likeness to its father; nor, when the conversation turns on bygone times, does she fear to let his name escape her white lips, ' My Robert; the bairn's not ill-favored, but he will never look like his father,' — and such sayings, uttered in a calm, sweet voice. Nay, I remember once how her pale coun tenance reddened with a sudden flush of pride, when a gossip ing crone alluded to their wedding; and the widow's eye brightened through her tears to hear how the bridegroom, sit ting that sabbath in his front seat beside his bonny bride, had not his equal for strength, stature, and all that is beauty in man, in all the congregation. That, I say, sir, whether right or wrong, was — forgiveness"

Here is a specimen of how even generous men had been so perverted by the enchantment of Lord Byron's genius, as to turn all the pathos and power of the strongest literature of that day against the persecuted, pure woman, and for the strong, wicked man. These " Blackwood " writers knew, by Byron's own filthy, ghastly

writings, which had gone sorely against their own moral stomachs, that he was foul to the bone. They could 'see, in Moore's Memoirs right before them, how he had caught an inno cent girl's heart by sending a love-letter, and offer of marriage, at the end of a long friendly correspondence, — a letter that had been written to show to his libertine set, and sent on the toss-up of a copper, because he cared nothing for it one way or the other.

They admit, that, having won this poor girl, he had been savage, brutal, drunken, cruel. They had read the filthy taunts in " Don Juan," and the nameless abominations in the Auto biography. They had admitted among them selves that his honor was lost; but still this abused, desecrated woman must reverence her brutal master's memory, and not speak, even to defend the grave of her own kind father and mother.

That there was no lover of her youth, that the marriage-vow had been a hideous, shameless cheat, is on the face of Moore's account; yet the " Blackwood " does not see it nor feel it, and brings up against Lady Byron this touching story of a poor widow, who really had had a true lover once, — a lover maddened, imbruted, lost, through that very drunkenness in which the Noctes Club were always glorying.

It is because of such transgressors as Byron, such supporters as Moore and the Noctes Club, that there are so many helpless, cowering, broken-hearted, abject women, given over to the animal love which they share alike with the poor dog, — the dog, who, beaten, kicked, starved, and cuffed, still lies by his drunken master with great anxious eyes of love and sorrow, and with sweet, brute forgiveness nestles upon his bosom, as he lies in his filth in the snowy ditch, to keep the warmth of life in him. Great is the mystery of this fidelity in the poor, loving brute, — most mournful and most sacred !

But oh, that a noble man should have no higher ideal of the love of a high-souled, heroic woman !

Oh, that men should teach women that they have no higher duties, and are capable of no higher tenderness, than this loving, unquestion ing animal fidelity ! The dog is ever-loving, ever-forgiving, because God has given him no high range of moral faculties, no sense of justice, no consequent horror at impurity and vileness.

Much of the beautiful patience and for giveness of women is made possible to them by that utter deadness to the sense of justice which the laws, literature, and misunderstood religion of England have sought to induce in woman as a special grace and virtue.

The lesson to woman in this pathetic piece of special pleading is, that man may sink himself below the brute, may wallow in filth like the swine, may turn his home into a hell, beat

and torture his children, forsake the marriage-bed for foul rivals ; yet all this does not dissolve
r~

the marriage-vow on her part, nor free his bounden serf from her obligation to honor his
memory, — nay, to sacrifice to it the honor due to a kind father and mother, slandered in
their silent graves.

Such was the sympathy, and such the advice, that the best literature of England could give
to a young widow, a peeress of England, whose husband, as they verily believed and admitted,
might have done worse than all this ; whose crimes might have been "foul, monstrous,
unforgivable as the sin against the Holy Ghost." If these things be done in the green tree, what
shall be done in the dry ? If the peeress as a wife has no rights, what is the state of the cotter's
wife ?

But, in the same paper, North again blames Lady Byron for not having come out with the
whole story before the world at the time she separated from her husband. He says of the time
when she first consulted counsel through her mother, keeping back one item, —

" How weak, and worse than weak, at such a juncture, on which hung her whole fate, to
ask legal advice on an imperfect

document! Give the delicacy of a virtuous woman its due; but at such a crisis, when the
question was whether her con science was to be free from the oath of oaths, delicacy should have
died, and nature was privileged to show unashamed — if such there were — the records of
uttermost pollution."

Shepherd. — " And what think ye, sir, that a' this pollution could hae been, that sae
electrified Dr. Lushington ?"

North. — " Bad — bad — bad, James. Nameless, it is horri ble : named, it might leave
Byron's memory yet within the range of pity and forgiveness ; and, where they are, their sister
affections will not be far; though, like weeping seraphs, stand ing aloof, and veiling their wings."

Shepherd. — " She should, indeed hae been silent — till the grave had closed on her
sorrows as on his sins."

North. — "Even now she should speak, — or some one else for her, — ... and a few
words will suffice. Worse the condition of the dead man's name cannot be — far, far better it
might — I believe it would be — were all the truth somehow or other declared; and declared it
must be, not for Byron's sake only, but for the sake of humanity itself; and then a mitigated sen
tence, or eternal silence."

We have another discussion of Lady Byron's duties in a further number of " Blackwood."
The Memoir being out, it was proposed that there should be a complete annotation of

Byron's works gotten up, and adorned, for the further glorification of his memory, with
portraits of the various women whom he had delighted to honor.

Murray applied to Lady Byron for her por trait, and was met with a cold, decided
negative. After reading all the particulars of Byron's harem of mistresses, and Moore's
comparisons between herself and La Guiccioli, one might imagine reasons why a lady, with
proper self-respect, should object to appearing in this manner. One would suppose there might
have been gentlemen who could well appreciate the motive of that refusal ; but it was only con
sidered a new evidence that she was indifferent to her conjugal duties, and wanting in that respect
which Christopher North had told her she owed a husband's memory, though his crimes were foul
as the rottenness of the grave.

Never, since Queen Vashti refused to come at the command of a drunken husband to show herself to his drunken lords, was there

a clearer case of disrespect to the marital dig nity on the part of a wife. It was a plain act of insubordination, rebellion against law and order ; and how shocking in Lady Byron, who ought to feel herself but too much flattered to be exhibited to the public as the head wife of a man of genius !

Means were at once adopted to subdue her contumacy, of which one may read in a note to the "Blackwood" (Noctes), September, 1832. An artist was sent down to Ealing to take her picture by stealth as she sat in church. Two sittings were thus obtained without her knowl edge. In the third one, the artist placed himself boldly before her, and sketched, so that she could not but observe him. We shall give the rest in Mackenzie's own words, as a remarkable speci men of the obtuseness, not to say indelicacy of feeling, which seemed to pervade the literary circles of England at the time : —

" After prayers, Wright and his friend (the artist) were visited by an ambassador from her ladyship to inquire the

meaning of what she had seen. The reply was, that Mr. Murray irncst have her portrait, and was compelled to take what she re fused to give. The result was, Wright was requested to visit her, which he did; taking with him, not the sketch, which was very good, but another, in which there was a strong touch of caricature. Rather than allow that to appear as her likeness (a very natural and womanly feeling by the way), she consented to sit for the portrait to W. J. Newton, which was engraved, and is here alluded to."

The artless barbarism of this note is too good to be lost; but it is quite borne out by the con versation in the Noctes Club, which it illus trates.

It would appear from this conversation that these Byron beauties appeared successively in pamphlet form ; and the picture of Lady Byron is thus discussed : —

Mullion. "I don't know if you have seen the last brochure. It has a charming head of Lady Byron, who, it seems, sat on purpose : and that's very agreeable to hear of; for it shows her ladyship has got over any little soreness that Moore's Life occasioned, and is now willing to contribute any thing in her power to the real monument of Byron's genius."

North. "I am delighted to hear of this : 'tis really very noble in the unfortunate lady. I never saw her. Is the face a striking one ?"

Mullion. " Eminently so, a most calm, pensive, melan choly style of native beauty, — and a most touching contrast to the maids of Athens, Annesley, and all the rest of them. I'm sure you'll have the proof Finden has sent you framed for the Boudoir at the Lodge."

North. " By all means. I mean to do that for all the Byron Beauties."

But it may be asked, Was there not a man in all England with delicacy enough to feel for Lady Byron, and chivalry enough to speak a bold word for her ? Yes: there was one. Thomas Campbell the poet, when he read Lady Byron's statement, believed it, as did Christo pher North; but it affected him differently. It appears he did not believe it a wife's duty to burn herself on her husband's funeral-pile, as did Christopher North ; and held the singular idea, that a wife had some rights as a human being as well as a husband.

Lady Byron's own statement appeared in

pamphlet form in 1830: at least, such is the date at the foot of the document. Thomas Campbell, in "The New Monthly Magazine," shortly after, printed a spirited, gentlemanly defence of Lady Byron, and administered a pointed rebuke to Moore for the rudeness and indelicacy he had shown in selecting from Byron's letters the coarsest against herself, her parents, and her old governess Mrs. Clermont, and by the indecent comparisons he had in stituted between Lady Byron and Lord Byron's last mistress.

It is refreshing to hear, at last, from somebody who is not altogether on his knees at the feet of the popular idol, and who has some chivalry for woman, and some idea of common humanity. He says, —

" I found my right to speak on this painful subject, on its now irrevocable publicity, brought up afresh as it has been by Mr. Moore, to be the theme of discourse to millions, and, if I err not much, the cause of misconception to innumerable minds. I claim to speak of Lady Byron in the right of a man, and of a friend to the rights of woman, and to liberty, and to natural

RESULTS AFTER LORD BYRONS DEATH.

religion. I claim a right, more especially, as one of the many friends of Lady Byron, who, one and all, feel aggrieved by this production. It has virtually dragged her forward from the shade of retirement, where she had hid her sorrows, and com pelled her to defend the heads of her friends and her parents from being crushed under the tombstone of Byron. Nay, in a general view, it has forced her to defend herself; though, with her true sense and her pure taste, she stands above all special pleading. To plenary explanation she ought not — she never shall be driven. Mr. Moore is too much a gentleman not to shudder at the thought of that; but if other Byronists, of a far different stamp, were to force the savage ordeal, it is her enemies, and not she, that would have to dread the burning ploughshares.

" We, her friends, have no wish to prolong the discussion : but a few words we must add, even to her admirable statement; for hers is a cause not only dear to her friends, but having become, from Mr. Moore and her misfortunes, a publicly-agitated cause, it concerns morality, and the most sacred rights of the sex, that she should (and that, too, without more special explanations) be acquitted out and out, and honorably ac quitted, in this business, of all share in the blame, which is one and indivisible. Mr. Moore, on further reflection, may see this ; and his return to candor will surprise us less than his momentary deviation from its path.

" For the tact of Mr. Moore's conduct in this affair, I have not to answer ; but, if indelicacy be charged upon me, I scorn

the charge. Neither will I submit to be called Lord Byron's accuser; because a word against him I wish not to say beyond what is painfully wrung from me by the necessity of owning or illustrating Lady Byron's unblamableness, and.of repelling certain misconceptions respecting her, which are now walking the fashionable world, and which have been fostered (though Heaven knows where they were born) most delicately and warily by the Christian godfathership of Mr. Moore.

" I write not at Lady Byron's bidding. I have never humiliated either her or myself by asking if I should write, or what I should write ; that is to say, I never applied to her for information against Lord Byron,,though I was justified, as one intending to criticise Mr. Moore, in inquiring into the truth of some of his statements. Neither will I suffer myself to be called her champion, if by that word be meant the advocate of her mere legal innocence; for that, I take it, nobody questions.

" Still less is it from the sorry impulse of pity that I speak of this noble woman ; for I look with wonder and even envy at the proud purity of her sense and conscience, that have car ried her exquisite sensibilities in triumph through such poign ant tribulations. But I am proud to be called her friend, the humble illustrator of her cause, and the advocate of those principles which make it to me more interesting than Lord Byron's. Lady Byron (if the subject must be discussed) belongs to sentiment and morality (at least as much as Lord Byron); nor is she to be suffered, when compelled to speak,

to raise her voice as in a desert, with no friendly voice to respond to her. Lady Byron could not have outlived her sufferings if she had not wound up her fortitude to the high point of trusting mainly for consolation, not to the opinion of the world, but to her own inward peace ; and, having said what ought to convince the world, I verily believe that she has less care about the fashionable opinion respecting her than any of her friends can have. But we, her friends, mix with the world ; and we hear offensive absurdities about her, which we have a right to put down.

" I proceed to deal more generally with Mr. Moore's book. You speak, Mr. Moore, against Lord Byron's censurers in a tone of indignation which is perfectly lawful towards calumnious traducers, but which will not terrify me, or any other man of courage who is no calumniator, from uttering his mind freely with regard to this part of your hero's conduct. I question your philosophy in assuming that all that is noble in Byron's poetry was inconsistent with the possibility of his being devoted to a pure and good woman; and I repudiate your morality for canting too complacently about ' the lava of his imagination,' and the unsettled fever of his passions, being any excuses for his planting the tic douloureux of domestic suffering in a meek woman's bosom.

" These are hard words, Mr. Moore ; but you have brought them on yourself by your voluntary ignorance of facts known to me: for you might and ought to have known both sides

of the question ; and, if the subject was too delicate for you to consult Lady Byron's confidential friends, you ought to have had nothing to do with the subject. But you cannot have sub mitted your book even to Lord Byron's sister, otherwise she would have set you right about the imaginary spy, Mrs. Clermont."

Campbell now goes on to print, at his own peril, he says, and without time to ask leave, the following note from Lady Byron in reply to an application he made to her, when he was about to review Moore's book, for an " estimate as to the correctness of Moore's statements."

The following is Lady Byron's reply : —

" DEAR MR. CAMPBELL, — In taking up my pen to point out for your private information * those passages in Mr. Moore's representation of my part of the story which were open to con tradiction, I find them of still greater extent than I had sup posed ; and to deny an assertion here and there would virtually admit the truth of the rest. If, on the contrary, I were to enter into a full exposure of the falsehood of the views taken by Mr. Moore, I must detail various matters, which, consistently with

" I [Campbell] had not time to ask Lady Byron's permission to print this private letter ; but it seemed to me important, and I have published it meo periculo."

my principles and feelings, I cannot under the existing circum stances disclose. I may, perhaps, convince you better of the difficulty of the case by an example : It is not true that pecu niary embarrassments were the cause of the disturbed state of Lord Byron's mind, or formed the chief reason for the arrange ments made by him at that time. But is it reasonable for me to expect that you or any one else should believe this, unless I show you what were the causes in question ? and this I cannot do. . " I am, &c.,

"A. I. NOEL BYRON."

Campbell then goes on to reprove Moore for his injustice to Mrs. Clermont, whom Lord Byron had denounced as a spy, but whose respecta bility and innocence were vouched for by Lord Byron's own family; and then he pointedly rebukes one false statement of great indelicacy and cruelty concerning Lady Byron's courtship, as follows : —

" It is a further mistake on Mr. Moore's part, and I can prove it to be so, if proof be necessary, to represent Lady Byron, in the course of their courtship, as one inviting her future husband to correspondence by letters after she had at first refused him. She never proposed a correspondence. On the contrary, he sent her a message after that first refusal, stating

that he meant to go abroad, and to travel for some years in the East; that he should depart with a heart aching, but not angry; and that he only begged a verbal assurance that she had still some interest in his happiness. Could Miss Milbanke, as a well-bred woman, refuse a courteous answer to such a message ? She sent him a verbal answer, which was merely kind and becoming, but which signified no encouragement that he should renew his offer of marriage.

" After that message, he wrote to her a most interesting letter about himself, — about his views, personal, moral, and reli gious, — to which it would have been uncharitable not to have replied. The result was an insensibly increasing corre spondence, which ended in her being devotedly attached to him. About that time, I occasionally saw Lord Byron; and though I knew less of him than Mr. Moore, yet I suspect I knew as much of him as Miss Milbanke then knew. At that time, he was so pleasing, that, if I had had a daughter with ample fortune and beauty, I should have trusted her in marriage with Lord Byron.

" Mr. Moore at that period evidently understood Lord Byron better than either his future bride or myself; but this speaks more for Moore's shrewdness than for Byron's ingenuousness of character.

" It is more for Lord Byron's sake than for his widow's that I resort not to a more special examination of Mr. Moore's mis conceptions. The subject would lead me insensibly into hateful disclosures against poor Lord Byron, who is more unfortunate

in his rash defenders than in his reluctant accusers. Happily, his own candor turns our hostility from himself against his de fenders. It was only in wayward and bitter remarks that he misrepresented Lady Byron. He would have defended himself irresistibly if Mr. Moore had left only his acknowledging pas sages. But Mr. Moore has produced a Life of him which reflects blame on Lady Byron so dexterously, that ' more is meant than meets the ear.' The almost universal impression produced by his book is, that Lady Byron must be a precise and a wan, unwarming spirit, a blue-stocking of chilblained learning, a piece of insensitive goodness.

" Who that knows Lady Byron will not pronounce her to be every thing the reverse ? Will it be believed that this person, so unsuitably matched to her moody lord, has written verses that would do no discredit to Byron himself; that her sensi tiveness is surpassed and bounded only by her good sense ; and that she is

' Blest with a temper, whose unclouded ray Can make to-morrow cheerful as to-day ' ?

" She brought to Lord Byron beauty, manners, fortune, meekness, romantic affection, and every thing that ought to have made her to the most transcendent man of genius— had he been what he should have been — his pride and his idol. I speak not of Lady Byron in the commonplace manner of attesting character : I appeal to the gifted Mrs. Siddons and Joanna Baillie, to Lady Charlemont, and to other ornaments of their

134 RESULTS AFTER LORD BYRON'S DEATH.

sex, whether I am exaggerating in the least when I say, that, in their whole lives, they have seen few beings so intellectual and well-tempered as Lady Byron.

" I wish to be as ingenuous as possible in speaking of her. Her manner, I have no hesitation to say, is cool at the first interview, but is modestly, and not insolently, cool : she con tracted it, I believe, from being exposed by her beauty and large fortune, in youth, to numbers of suitors, whom she could not have otherwise kept at a distance. But this manner could have had no influence with Lord Byron ; for it vanishes on nearer acquaintance, and has no origin in cold ness. All her friends like her frankness the better for being preceded by this reserve. This manner, however, though not the slightest apology for Lord Byron, has been inimical to Lady Byron in her misfortunes. It endears her to her friends; but it piques the indifferent. Most odiously unjust, therefore, is Mr. Moore's assertion, that she has had the advantage of Lord Byron in public opinion. She is, comparatively speaking, un known to the world ; for though she has many friends, that is, a friend in every one who knows her, yet her pride and purity and misfortunes naturally contract the circle of her acquaint ance.

" There is something exquisitely unjust in Mr. Moore com paring her chance of popularity with Lord Byron's, the poet who can command men of talents, — putting even Mr. Moore into the livery of his service, — and who has suborned the favor of almost all women by the beauty of his person and the volup-

RESULTS AFTER LORD BYRON S DEATH. 135

tuousness of his verses. Lady Byron has nothing to oppose to these fascinations but the truth and justice of her cause.

" You said, Mr. Moore, that Lady Byron was unsuitable to her lord : the word is cunningly insidious, and may mean as much or as little as may suit your convenience. But, if she was unsuitable, I remark that it tells all the worse against Lord Byron. I have not read it in your book (for I hate to wade through it); but they tell me that you have not only warily depreciated Lady Byron, but that you have described a lady that would have suited him. If this be true, 'it is the unkindest cut of all,' —to hold up a florid description of a woman suitable to Lord Byron, as if in mockery over the forlorn flower of vir tue that was drooping in the solitude of sorrow.

"But I trust there is no such passage in your book. Surely you must be conscious of your woman, with her ' -virtue loose about her, who would have suited Lord Byron? to be as imagi nary a being as the woman without a head. A woman to suit Lord Byron ! Poo, poo ! I could paint to you the woman that could have matched him, if I had not bargained to say as little as possible against him.

" If Lady Byron was not suitable to Lord Byron, so much the worse for his lordship ; for let me tell you, Mr. Moore, that neither your poetry, nor Lord Byron's, nor all our poetry put together, ever delineated a more interesting being than the woman whom you have so coldly treated. This was not kick ing the dead lion, but wounding the living lamb, who was already bleeding and shorn, even unto the quick. I know, that,

collectively speaking, the world is in Lady Byron's favor ; but it is coldly favorable, and you have not warmed its breath. Time, however, cures every thing ; and even your book, Mr. Moore, may be the means of Lady Byron's character being better appreciated. " THOMAS CAMPBELL."

Here is what seems to be a gentlemanly, high-spirited, chivalric man, throwing down his glove in the lists for a pure woman.

What was the consequence ? Campbell was crowded back, thrust down, overwhelmed, his eyes filled with dust, his mouth with ashes.

There was a general confusion and outcry, which re-acted both on him and on Lady Byron. Her friends were angry with him for having caused this re-action upon her ; and he found himself at once attacked by Lady Byron's ene mies, and deserted by her friends. All the lite rary authorities of his day took up against him with energy. Christopher North, professor of moral philosophy in the Edinburgh University, in a fatherly talk in " The Noctes," condemns Campbell, and justifies Moore, and heartily rec-

ommends his Biography, as containing nothing materially objectionable on the score either of manners or morals. Thus we have it in " The Noctes " of May, 1830 : -

" Mr. Moore's biographical book I admired; and I said so to my little world, in two somewhat lengthy articles, which many approved, and some, I am sorry to know, condemned."

On the point in question between Moore and Campbell, North goes on to justify Moore alto gether, only admitting that " it would have been better had he not printed any coarse expres sion of Byron's about the old people ;" and, finally, he closes by saying, —

"I do not think, that, under the circumstances, Mr. Camp bell himself, had he written Byron's Life, could have spoken, with the sentiments he then held, in a better., more manly, and more gentlemanly spirit, in so far as regards Lady Byron, than Mr. Moore did : and I am sorry he has been deterred from ' swim ming ' through Mr. Moore's work by the fear of ' wading ;' for the waters are clear and deep ; nor is there any mud, either at the bottom or round the margin."

Of the conduct of Lady Byron's so-called friends on this occasion it is more difficult to speak.

There has always been in England, as John Stuart Mill says, a class of women who glory in the utter self-abnegation of the wife to the hus band, as the special crown of womanhood. Their patron saint is the Griselda of Chaucer, who, when her husband humiliates her, and treats her as a brute, still accepts all with meek, unquestion ing, uncomplaining devotion. He tears her from her children ; he treats her with personal abuse ; he repudiates her, — sends her out to nakedness and poverty ; he installs another mistress in his house, and sends for the first to be her hand maid and his own : and all this the meek saint accepts in the words of Milton,—

" My guide and head, What thou hast said is just and right."

Accordingly, Miss Martineau tells us, that when Campbell's defence came out, coupled with a note from Lady Byron, —

" The first obvious remark was, that there was no real disclosure; and the whole affair had the appearance of a desire, on the part of Lady Byron, to exculpate herself, while yet no adequate information was given. Many, who had re garded her with favor till then, gave her up so far as to believe that feminine weakness had prevailed at last."

The saint had fallen from he'r pedestal! She had shown a human frailty ! Quite evidently she is not a Griselda, but possessed with a shocking desire to exculpate herself and her friends.

Is it, then, only to slandered men that the privilege belongs of desiring to exculpate them selves and their families and their friends from unjust censure ?

Lord Byron had made it a life-long object to vilify and defame his wife. He had used for that one particular purpose every talent that he possessed. He had left it as a last charge to Moore to pursue the warfare after death, which Moore had done to some purpose ; and Christo pher North had informed Lady Byron that her

private affairs were discussed, not only with the whiskey-toddy of the Noctes Club, but in every drawing-room in May Fair; and declared that the " Dear Duck " letter, and various other mat ters, must be explained, and urged somebody to speak; and then, when Campbell does speak with all the energy of a real gentleman, a general out cry and an indiscriminate melee is the result.

The world, with its usual injustice, insisted on attributing Campbell's defence to Lady Byron.

The reasons for this seemed to be, first, that Campbell states that he did not ask Lady By ron's leave, and that she did not authorize him to defend her ; and, second, that, having asked some explanations from her, he prints a note in which she declines to give any.

We know not how a lady could more gently yet firmly decline to make a gentleman her confidant than in this published note of Lady Byron ; and yet, to this day, Campbell is spoken of by the world as having been Lady Byron's confidant at this time. This simply shows how

very trustworthy are the general assertions about Lady Byron's confidants.

The final result of the matter, so far as Camp bell was concerned, is given in Miss Martineau's sketch, in the following paragraph : —

" The whole transaction was one of poor Campbell's freaks. He excused himself by saying it was a mistake of his ; that he did not know what he was about when he published the paper."

It is the saddest of all sad things to see a man, who has spoken from moral convictions, in advance of his day, and who has taken a stand for which he ought to honor himself, thus forced down and humiliated, made to doubt his own

better nature and his own honorable feelings,

f

by the voice of a wicked world.

Campbell had no steadiness to stand by the truth he saw. His whole story is told inci dentally in a note to " The Noctes," in which it is stated, that in an article in " Blackwood," January, 1825, on Scotch poets, the palm was given to Hogg over Campbell ; " one ground

being, that he could drink 'eight and twenty tumblers of punch, while Campbell is hazy upon seven.'"

There is evidence in " The Noctes," that in due time Campbell was reconciled to Moore, and was always suitably ashamed of having tried to be any more generous or just than the men of his generation.

And so it was settled as a law to Jacob, and an ordinance in Israel, that the Byron worship should proceed, and that all the earth should keep silence before him. " Don Juan," that, years before, had been printed by stealth, without Murray's name on the titlepage, that had been denounced as a book which no woman should read, and had been given up as a desperate enter prise, now came forth in triumph, with banners flying and drums beating. Every great periodi cal in England that had fired moral volleys of artillery against it in its early days, now humbly marched in the glorious procession of admirers to salute this edifying work of genius.

" Blackwood," which in the beginning had been the most indignantly virtuous of the whole, now grovelled and ate dust as the serpent in the very abjectness of submission. Odoherty (Maginn) declares that he would rather have written a page of " Don Juan " than a ton of " Childe Harold." * Timothy Tickler informs Christopher North that he means to tender Mur ray, as Emperor of the North, an interleaved copy f of " Don Juan," with illustrations, as the only work of Byron's he cares much about ; and Christopher North, professor of moral philoso phy in Edinburgh, smiles approval! We are not, after this, surprised to see the assertion, by a recent much-aggrieved writer in " The London Era," that " Lord Byron has been, more than any other man of the age, the teacher of the youth of England ; " and that he has " seen his works on the bookshelves of bishops palaces, no less than the tables of university under-gradu-ates."

* Noctes, July, 1822. t Noctes, September, 1832.

A note to "The Noctes " of July, 1822, in forms us of another instance of Lord Byron's triumph over English morals : —

"The mention of this" (Byron's going to Greece) "reminds me, by the by, of what the Guiccioli said in her visit to Lon don, where she was so lionized as having been the lady-love of Byron. She was rather fond of speaking on the subject, des ignating herself by some Venetian pet phrase, which she inter preted as meaning ' Love-Wife/ "

What was Lady Byron to do in such a world ? She retired to the deepest privacy, and devoted herself to works of charity, and the education of her only child, — that brilliant daughter, to whose eager, opening mind the whole course of current literature must bring so many trying questions in regard to the position of her father and mother, — questions that the mother might not answer. That the cruel inconsiderateness of the literary world added thorns to the intricacies of the path trodden by every mother who seeks to guide, restrain, and educate a strong, acute, and preco ciously intelligent child, must easily be seen.

What remains to be said of Lady Byron's life shall be said in the words of Miss Martineau, published in " The Atlantic Monthly : " —

" Her life, thenceforth, was one of unremitting bounty to society, administered with as much skill and prudence as be nevolence. She lived in retirement, changing her abode fre quently ; partly for the benefit of her child's education and the promotion of her benevolent schemes, and partly from a rest lessness which was one of the few signs of injury received from the spoiling of associations with home>

" She felt a satisfaction which her friends rejoiced in when, her daughter married Lord King, at present the Earl of Lovelace, in 1835 ; and when grief upon grief followed, in the appearance of mortal disease in her only child, her quiet patience stood her in good stead as before. She even found strength to ap propriate the blessings of the occasion, and took comfort, as did her dying daughter, in the intimate friendship, which grew closer as the time of parting drew nigh.

" Lady Lovelace died in 1852 ; and, for her few remaining years, Lady Byron was devoted to her grandchildren. But nearer calls never lessened her interest in remoter objects. Her mind was of the large and clear quality which could com prehend remote interests in their true proportions, and achieve each aim as perfectly as if it were the only one. Her agents used to say that it was impossible to mistake her directions;

and thus her business was usually well clone. There was no room, in her case, for the ordinary doubts, censures, and sneers about the misapplication of bounty.

" Her taste did not lie in the ' Charity-Ball' direction; her funds were not lavished in encouraging hypocrisy and improvidence among the idle and worthless ; and the quality of her charity was, in fact, as admirable as its quantity. Her chief aim was the extension and improvement of popular education ; but there was no kind of misery that she heard of that she did not palliate to the utmost, and no kind of solace that her quick imagination and sympathy could devise that she did not administer.

" In her methods, she united consideration and frankness with singular success. For one instance among a thousand : A lady with whom she had had friendly relations some time before, and who became impoverished in a quiet way by hope less sickness, preferred poverty with an easy conscience to a competency attended by some uncertainty about the perfect rectitude of the resource. Lady Byron wrote to an intermediate person exactly what she thought of the case. Whether the judgment of the sufferer was right or mistaken was nobody's business but her own : this was the first point. Next, a vol untary poverty could never be pitied by anybody : that was the second. But it was painful to others to think of the mortifica tion to benevolent feelings which attends poverty; and there could be no objection to arresting that pain. Therefore she, Lady Byron, had lodged in a neighboring bank the sum of

one hundred pounds, to be used for benevolent purposes ; and, in order to preclude all outside speculation, she had made the money payable to the order of the intermediate person, so that the sufferer's name need not appear at all.

" I^ive and thirty years of unremitting secret bounty like this must make up a great amount of human happiness ; but this was only one of a wide variety of methods of doing good. It \vas the unconcealable magnitude of her beneficence, and its wise quality, which made her a second time the theme of Eng lish conversation in all honest households within the four seas. Years ago, it was said far and wide that Lady Byron was doing more good than anybody else in England ; and it was difficult to imagine how anybody could do more.

" Lord Byron spent every shilling that the law allowed him out of her property while he lived, and left away from her every shilling that he could deprive her of by his will ; yet she had, eventually, a large income at her command. In the management of it, she showed the same wise consideration that marked all her practical decisions. She resolved to spend her whole income, seeing how much the world needed help at the moment. Her care was for the existing generation, rather than for a future one, which would have its own friends. She usually declined trammelling herself with annual subscrip tions to charities; preferring to keep her freedom from year to year, and to achieve definite objects by liberal bounty, rather than to extend partial help over a large surface which she could not herself superintend.

" It was her first industrial school that awakened the admira tion of the public, which had never ceased to take an interest in her, while sorely misjudging her character. We hear much now — and everybody hears it with pleasure —of the spread of education in ' common things ;' but long before Miss Coutts inherited her wealth, long before a name was found for such a method of training, Lady Byron had instituted the thing, and put it in the way of making its own name.

" She was living at Ealing, in Middlesex, in 1834 ; and there she opened one of the first industrial schools in England, if not the very first. She sent out a master to Switzerland, to be instructed in De Fellenburgh's method. She took, on lease, five acres of land, and spent several hundred pounds in render ing the buildings upon it fit for the purposes of the school. A liberal education was afforded to the children of artisans and laborers during the half of the day when they were not employed in the field or garden. The allotments were rented by the boys, who raised and sold produce, which afforded them a considerable yearly profit if they were good workmen. Those who worked in the field earned wages ; their labor being paid by the hour, according to the capability of the young laborer. They kept their accounts of expenditure and receipts, and acquired good habits of business while learning the occupation of their lives. Some mechanical trades were taught, as well as the arts of agriculture.

" Part of the wisdom of the management lay in making the pupils pay. Of one hundred pupils, half were boarders. They

paid little more than half the expenses of their maintenance, and the day-scholars paid threepence per week. Of course, a large part of the expense was borne by Lady Byron, besides the pay ments she made for children who could not otherwise have en tered the school. The establishment flourished steadily till 1852, when the owner of the land required it back for building-purposes. During the eighteen years that the Ealing schools were in action, they did a world of good in the way of incite ment and example. The poor-law commissioners pointed out their merits. Land-owners and other wealthy persons visited them, and went home and set up similar establishments. Dur ing those years, too, Lady Byron had herself been at work in various directions to the same purpose.

" A more extensive industrial scheme was instituted on her Leicestershire property, and not far off she opened a girls' school and an infant school; and when a season of distress came, as such seasons are apt to befall the poor Leicestershire stocking-weavers, Lady Byron fed the children for months to gether, till they could resume their payments. These school were opened in 1840. The next year, she built a schoolhouse on her Warwickshire property ; and, five years later, she set up an iron schoolhouse on another Leicestershire estate.

" By this time, her educational efforts were costing her several hundred pounds a year in the mere maintenance of existing establishments ; but this is the smallest consideration in the case. She has sent out tribes of boys and girls into life fit to do their part there with skill and credit and comfort. Perhaps it is a

still more important consideration, that scores of teachers and trainers have been led into their vocation, and duly prepared for it, by what they saw and learned in her schools. ' As for the best and the worst of the Ealing boys, the best have, in a few cases, been received into the Battersea Training School, whence they could enter on their career as teachers to the greatest ad vantage ; and the worst found their school a true reformatory, before reformatory schools were heard of. At Bristol, she bought a house for a reformatory for girls ; and there her friend, Miss Carpenter, faithfully and energetically carries out her own and Lady Byron's aims, which were one and the same.

" There would be no end if I were to catalogue the schemes of which these are a specimen. It is of more consequence to observe that her mind was never narrowed by her own acts, as the minds of benevolent people are so apt to be. To the last, her interest in great political movements, at home and abroad, was as vivid as ever. She watched every step won in philoso phy, every discovery in science, every token of social change and progress in every shape. Her mind was as liberal as her heart and hand. No diversity of opinion troubled her : she was respectful to every sort of individuality, and indulgent to all constitutional peculiarities. It must have puzzled those who kept up the notion of her being ' strait-laced ' to see how indul gent she was even to Epicurean tendencies, — the remotest of all from her own.

" But I must stop ; for I do not wish my honest memorial to degenerate into panegyric. Among her latest known acts were

her gifts to the Sicilian cause, and her manifestations on behalf of the antislavery cause in the United States. Her kindness to Williarft and Ellen Craft must be well known there ; and it is also related in the newspapers, that she bequeathed a legacy to a young American to assist him under any disadvantages he might suffer as an abolitionist.

" All these deeds were done under a heavy burden of ill health. Before she had passed middle life, her lungs were be lieved to be irreparably injured by partial ossification. She was subject to attacks so serious, that each one, for many years, was expected to be the last. She arranged her affairs in correspond ence with her liabilities : so that the same order would have been found, whether she died suddenly or after long warning.

" She was to receive one more accession of outward greatness before she departed. She became Baroness Wentworth in November, 1856. This is one of the facts of her history ; but it is the least interesting to us, as probably to her. We care more to know that her last days were bright in honor, and cheered by the attachment of old friends worthy to pay the duty she deserved. Above all, it is consoling to know that she who so long outlived her only child was blessed with the unre mitting and tender care of her grand-daughter. She died on the 16th of May, 1860.

" The portrait of Lady Byron as she was at the time of her marriage is probably remembered by some of my readers. It is very engaging. Her countenance afterwards became much worn ; but its expression of thoughtfulness and composure was

very interesting. Her handwriting accorded well with th* character of her mind. It was clear, elegant, and womanly. Her manners differed with circumstances. Her shrinking sen sitiveness might embarrass one visitor; while another would be charmed with her easy, significant, and vivacious conversation. It depended much on whom she talked with. The abiding cer tainty was, that she had strength for the hardest of human trials, and the composure which belongs to strength. For the rest, it is enough to point to her deeds, and to the mourning of her friends round the chasm which her departure has made in their life, and in the society in which it is spent. All that could be done in the way of personal love and honor was done while she lived : it only remains now to see that her name and fame are permitted to shine forth at last in their proper light."

We have simply to ask the reader whether a life like this was not the best, the noblest answer that a woman could make to a doubting world.

CHAPTER V.

THE ATTACK ON LADY BYRON'S GRAVE.

have now brought the review of the antagonism against Lady Byron down to the period of her death. During all this time, let the candid reader ask himself which of these two parties seems to be plotting against the other.

Which has been active, aggressive, unscrupu lous ? which has been silent, quiet, unoffending ? Which of the two has labored to make a party, and to make that party active, watchful, enthusi astic ?

Have we not proved that Lady Byron re mained perfectly silent during Lord Byron's life, patiently looking out from her retirement to see the waves of popular sympathy, that once bore her up, day by day retreating, while his ac-

cusations against her were resounding in his poems over the whole earth ? And after Lord Byron's death, when all the world with one con sent began to give their memorials of him, and made it appear, by their various " recollections of conversations," how incessantly he had ob truded his own version of the separation upon every listener, did she manifest any similar eager ness ?

Lady Byron had seen the " Blackwood" coming forward, on the first appearance of " Don Juan," to rebuke the cowardly lampoon in words eloquent with all the unperverted vigor of an honest Englishman. Under the power of the great conspirator, she had seen that " Black-wood " become the very eager recipient and chief reporter of .the stories against her, and the blind admirer of her adversary.

All this time, she lost sympathy daily by being silent. The world will embrace those who court it ; it will patronize those who seek its favor; it will make parties for those who

seek to make parties: but for the often ac cused who do not speak, who make no con fidants and no parties, the world soon loses sym pathy.

When at last she spoke, Christopher North says " she astonished tJie world!' Calm, clear, courageous, exact as to time, date, and circum stance, was that first testimony, backed by the equally clear testimony of Dr. Lushington.

It showed that her secret had been kept even from her parents. In words precise, firm, and fearless, she says, " If these statements on which Dr. Lushington and Sir Samuel Romilly formed their opinion were false, the responsi bility and the odium should rest with me only." Christopher North did not pretend to disbelieve this statement. He breathed not a doubt of Lady Byron's word. He spoke of the crime indicated, as one which might have been foul as the grave's corruption, unforgivable as the sin against the Holy Ghost. He rebuked the wife for bearing this testimony, even to save

the memory of her dead father and mother, and, in the same breath, declared that she ought now to go farther, and speak fully the one awful word, and then — " a mitigated sentence, or eternal silence!"

But Lady Byron took no counsel with the world, nor with the literary men of her age. One knight, with some small remnant of Eng land's old chivalry, set lance in rest for her: she saw him beaten back unhorsed, rolled in the dust, and ingloriously vanquished, and perceived that henceforth nothing but injury could come to any one who attempted to speak for her.

She turned from the judgments of man and the fond and natural hopes of human nature, to lose herself in sacred ministries to the down cast and suffering. What nobler record for woman could there be than that which Miss Martineau has given ?

Particularly to be noted in Lady Byron was her peculiar interest in reclaiming fallen women. Among her letters to Mrs. Prof. Pollen of

Cambridge was one addressed to a society of ladies who had undertaken this difficult work. It was full of heavenly wisdom and of a large and tolerant charity. Fenelon truly says, it is only perfection that can tolerate imperfection; and the very purity of Lady Byron's nature made her most forbearing and most tender towards the weak and the guilty. This letter, with all the rest of Lady Byron's, was returned to the hands of her executors after her death. Its publication would greatly assist the world in understanding the peculiarities of its writer's character.

Lady Byron passed to a higher life in 1860.* After her death, I looked for the publication of her Memoir and Letters as the event that should give her the same opportunity of be ing known and judged by her life and writ ings that had been so freely accorded to Lord Byron.

She was, in her husband's estimation, a woman

* Miss Martineau's Biographical Sketches.

of genius. She was the friend of many of the first men and women of her times, and corre sponded with them on topics of literature, morals, religion, and, above all, on the benevolent and philanthropic movements of the day, whose prin ciples she had studied with acute observation, and in connection with which she had acquired a large experience.

The knowledge of her, necessarily diffused by such a series of letters, would have created in America a comprehension of her character, of itself sufficient to wither a thousand slanders.

Such a Memoir was contemplated. Lady Byron's letters to Mrs. Pollen were asked for from Boston ; and I was applied to by a person in England, who I have recently learned is one of the existing trustees of Lady Byron's papers, to furnish copies of her letters to me for the purpose of a Memoir. Before I had time to have copies made, another letter came, stating that the trustees had concluded that it was not best to publish any Memoir of Lady Byron at all.

This left the character of Lady Byron in our American world precisely where the slanders of her husband, the literature of the Noctes Club, and the unanimous verdict of May Fair as recorded by " Blackwood," had placed it.

True, Lady Byron had nobly and quietly lived down these slanders in England by deeds that made her name revered as a saint among all those who valued saintliness.

But in France and Italy, and in these United States, I have had abundant oppor tunity to know that Lady Byron stood judged and condemned on the testimony of her brilliant husband, and that the feeling against her had a vivacity and intensity not to be overcome by mere allusions to a virtuous life in distant England.

This is strikingly shown by one fact. In the American edition of Moore's " Life of Byron," by Claxton, Remsen, and HafTelfinger, Philadel phia, 1869, which I have been consulting, Lady Byron's statement, which is found in the Appen-

dix of Murray's standard edition, is entirely omitted. Every other paper is carefully pre served. This one incident showed how the tide of sympathy was setting in this New World. Of course, there is no stronger power than a virtuous life ; but, for a virtuous life to bear testi mony to the world, its details must be told, so that the world may know them.

Suppose the memoirs of Clarkson and Wilber-force had been suppressed after their death, how soon might the coming tide have wiped out the record of their bravery and philanthropy ! Sup pose the lives of Francis Xavier and Henry •Martyn had never been written, and we had lost the remembrance of what holy men could do and dare in the divine enthusiasm of Christian faith! Suppose we had no Fenelon, no Book of Martyrs !

Would there not be an outcry through all the literary and artistic world if a perfect statue were allowed to remain buried forever because some painful individual history was connected

with its burial and its recovery ? But is not a noble life a greater treasure to mankind than any work of art ?

We have heard much mourning over the burned Autobiography of Lord Byron, and seen it treated of in a magazine as " the lost chapter in history." The lost chapter in history is Lady Byron's Auto biography in her life and letters ; and the sup pression of them is the root of this whole mischief.

We do not in this intend to censure the par ties who came to this decision.

The descendants of Lady Byron revere her memory, as they have every reason to do. That it was their desire to have a Memoir of her published, I have been informed by an indi vidual of the highest character in England, who obtained the information directly from Lady Byron's grandchildren.

But the trustees in whose care the papers were placed drew back on examination of them, and declared, that, as Lady Byron's papers could

not be fully published, they should regret any thing that should call public attention once more to the discussion of her history.

Reviewing this long history of the way in which the literary world had treated Lady Byron, we cannot wonder that her friends should have doubted whether there was left on earth any jus tice, or sense that any thing is due to woman as a human being with human rights. Evidently this lesson had taken from them all faith in the moral sense of the world. Rather than re-awaken the discussion, so unsparing, so painful, and so in delicate, which had been carried on so many years around that loved form, now sanctified by death, they sacrificed the dear pleasure of the memorials, and the interests of mankind, who have an indefeasible right to all the help that can be got from the truth of history as to the living power of virtue, and the reality of that great victory that overcometh the world.

There are thousands of poor victims suffering in sadness, discouragement, and poverty ; heart-

broken wives of brutal, drunken husbands ; women enduring nameless wrongs and horrors which the delicacy of their sex forbids them to utter, —to whom the lovely letters lying hidden away under those seals might bring courage and hope from springs not of this world.

But though the friends of Lady Byron, per haps from despair of their kind, from weariness of the utter injustice done her, wished to cherish her name in silence, and to confine the story of her virtues to that circle who knew her too well to ask a proof, or utter a doubt, the partisans of Lord Byron were embarrassed with no such scruple.

Lord Byron had artfully contrived during his life to place his wife in such an antagonistic position with regard to himself, that his inti mate friends were forced to believe that one of the two had deliberately and wantonly injured the other. The published statement of Lady Byron contradicted boldly and point-blank all the statement of her husband concerning the

separation : so that, unless she was convicted as a false witness, he certainly was.

The best evidence of this is Christopher North's own shocked, astonished statement, and the words of the Noctes Club.

The noble life that Lady Byron lived after this hushed every voice, and silenced even the most desperate calumny, while she was in the world. In the face of Lady Byron as the world saw her, of what use was the talk of Clytemnes-tra, and the assertion that she had been a mean, deceitful conspirator against her husband's honor in life, and stabbed his memory after death?

But when she was in her grave, when her voice and presence and good deeds no more spoke for her, and a new generation was grow ing up that knew her not, then was the time selected to revive the assault on her memory, and to say over her grave what none would ever have dared to say of her while living.

During these last two years, I have been grad ually awakening to the evidence of a new crusade

against the memory of Lady Byron, which re spected no sanctity, — not even that last and most awful one of death.

Nine years after her death, when it was fully understood that no story on her side or that of her friends was to be forthcoming, then her calumniators raked out from the ashes of her husband's sepulchre all his bitter charges, to state them over in even stronger and more indecent forms.

There seems to be reason to think that the materials supplied by Lord Byron for such a campaign yet exist in society.

To " The Noctes " of November, 1824, there is the following note apropos to a discussion of the Byron question : —

" Byron's Memoirs, given by him to Moore, were burned, as everybody knows. But, before this, Moore had lent them to several persons. Mrs. Home Purvis, afterwards Viscountess of Canterbury, is known to have sat up all one night, in which, aided by her daughter, she had a copy made. I have the strongest reason for believing that one other person made a

copy ; for the description of the first twenty-four hours after the marriage ceremonial has been in my hands. Not until after the death of Lady Byron, and Hobhouse, who was the poet's literary executor, can the poet's Autobiography see the light; but I am certain it will be published. "

Thus speaks Mackenzie in a note to a volume of "The Noctes," published in America in 1854. Lady Byron died in 1860.

Nine years after Lady Byron's death, when it was ascertained that her story was not to see the light, when there were no means of judging her character by her own writings, commenced a well-planned set of operations to turn the public attention once more to Lord Byron, and to represent him as an injured man, whose testimony had been unjustly suppressed.

It was quite possible, supposing copies of the Autobiography to exist, that this might occa sion a call from the generation of to-day, in answer to which the suppressed work might appear. This was a rather delicate operation to commence; but the instrument was not want-

ing. It was necessary that the subject should be first opened by some irresponsible party, whom more powerful parties might, as by accident, recognize and patronize, and on whose weakness they might build something stronger.

Just such an instrument was to be found in Paris. The mistress of Lord Byron could easily be stirred up and flattered to come before the world with a book which should re-open the whole controversy; and she proved a facile tool. At first, the work appeared prudently in French, and was called " Lord Byron juge par les Tc-moins de sa Vie," and was rather a failure. Then it was translated into English, and published by Bentley.

The book was inartistic, and helplessly, child ishly stupid as to any literary merits, — a mere mass of gossip and twaddle ; but after all, when one remembers the taste of the thousands of cir culating-library readers, it must not be consid ered the less likely to be widely read on that account. It is only once in a century that a writer of real genius has the art to tell his story so as to take both the cultivated few and the average many. De Foe and John Bunyan are almost the only examples. But there is a certain class of reading that sells and spreads, and exerts a vast influence, which the upper circles of literature despise too much ever to fairly esti mate its power.

However, the Guiccioli book did not want for patrons in the high places of literature. The " Blackwood " — the old classic magazine of England ; the defender of conservatism and aris tocracy ; the paper of Lockhart, Wilson, Hogg, Walter Scott, and a host of departed grandeurs — was deputed to usher into the world this book, and to recommend it and its author to the Christian public of the nineteenth century.

The following is the manner in which " Black-wood " calls attention to it : —

" ©ne of the most beautiful of the songs of Beranger is that addressed to his Lisette, in which he pictures her, in old age, narrating to a younger generation the loves of their youth ; deck-

ing his portrait with flowers at each returning spring, and reciting the verses that had been inspired by her vanished

charms : —

' When youthful eyes your wrinkles shall explore

To see what beauties once inspired my lays, Then will they say to thee, " Who was that friend So loved, so wept, so sung in ceaseless praise ? " Paint to their eyes, if possible, my love, Its ardors, its deliriums, e'en its fears ; And, good old friend, beside thy peaceful fire Repeat the love-songs of my early years.

" Ah ! " will they say, " was he so lovely, then ?"

•

And thou without a blush shalt say, " / loved." "Of wrong or evil was he guilty ever? " And thou with noble pride shalt answer, " Never ! " '

" This charming picture," " Blackwood " goes on to say, " has been realized in the case -of a poet greater than Beranger, and by a mistress more famous than Lisette. The Countess Guiccioli has at length given to the world her ' Recollections of Lord Byron.' The book first appeared in France under the title of ' Lord Byron juge par les Tcmoins de sa Vie,' without the name of the countess. A more unfortunate designation could hardly have been selected. The ' witnesses of his life ' told us nothing but what had been told before over and over again ; and the uniform and exaggerated tone of eulogy which per vaded the whole book was fatal to any claim on the part of the writer to be considered an impartial judge of the wonderfully mixed character of Byron.

" When, however, the book is regarded as the avowed pro-dttction of the Countess Guiccioli, it derives value and interest from its very faults* There is something inexpressibly touching in the picture of the old lady calling up the phan toms of half a century ago ; not faded and stricken by the hand of time, but brilliant and gorgeous as they were when Byron, in his manly prime of genius and beauty, first flashed upon her enraptured sight, and she gave her whole soul up to an absorb ing passion, the embers of which still glow in her heart.

" To her there has been no change, no decay. The god whom she worshipped with all the ardor of her Italian nature at seventeen is still the ' Pythian of the age ' to her at seventy. To try such a book by the ordinary canons of criticism would be as absurd as to arraign the authoress before a jury of British matrons, or to prefer a bill of indictment against the Sultan for bigamy to a Middlesex grand jury."

This, then, is the introduction which one of the oldest and most classical periodicals of Great Britain gives to a very stupid book, simply be cause it was written by Lord Byron's mistress. That fact, we are assured, lends grace even to its faults.

Having brought the authoress upon the stage,

* The Italics are mine. — H. B. S.

the review now goes on to define her position, and assure the Christian world that

" The Countess Guiccioli was the daughter of an impover ished noble. At the age of sixteen, she was taken from a con vent, and sold as third wife to the Count Guiccioli, who was old, rich, and profligate. A fouler prostitution never profaned the name of marriage. A short time afterwards, she accidentally met Lord Byron. Outraged and rebellious nature vindicated itself in the deep and devoted passion with which he inspired her. With the full assent of husband, father, and brother, and in compliance with the usages of Italian society, he was shortly afterwards installed in the office, and invested with all the privi leges, of her ' Cavalier Servente.' "

It has been asserted that the Marquis de Boissy, the late husband of this Guiccioli lady, was in the habit of introducing her in fashiona ble circles as "the Marquise de Boissy, my wife, formerly mistress to Lord Byron " ! We do not give the story as a verity ; yet, in the review of this whole history, we may be pardoned for thinking it quite possible.

The mistress, being thus vouched for and pre sented as worthy of sympathy and attention by

one of the oldest and most classic organs of English literature, may now proceed in her work of glorifying the popular idol, and casting abuse on the grave of the dead wife.

Her attacks on Lady Byron are, to be sure, less skilful and adroit than those of Lord Byron. They want his literary polish and tact ; but what of that ? " Blackwood " assures us that even the faults of manner derive a peculiar grace from the fact that the narrator is Lord Byron's mis tress ; and so we suppose the literary world must find grace in things like this : —

" She has been called, after his words, the moral Clytemnes-tra of her husband. Such a surname is severe : but the repug nance we feel to condemning a woman cannot prevent our lis tening to the voice of justice, which tells us that the comparison is still in favor of the guilty one of antiquity ; for she, driven to crime by fierce passion overpowering reason, at least only deprived her husband of physical life, and, in committing the deed, exposed herself to all its consequences ; while Lady Byron left her husband at the very moment that she saw him struggling amid a thousand shoals in the stormy sea of embarrassments created by his marriage, and precisely when he more than

ever required a friendly, tender, and indulgent hand to save him.

" Besides, she shut herself up in silence a thousand times more cruel than Clytemnestra's poniard : that only killed the body; whereas Lady Byron's silence was destined to kill the soul, — and such a soul! — leaving the door open to calumny, and making it to be supposed that her silence was magnanimity destined to cover over frightful wrongs, perhaps even depravity. In vain did he, feeling his conscience at ease, implore some inquiry and examination. She refused ; and the only favor she granted was to send him, one fine day, two persons to see whether he were not mad.

" And why, then, had she believed him mad ? Because she, a methodical, inflexible woman, with that unbendingness which a profound moralist calls the worship rendered to pride by a feelingless soul, — because she could not understand the possi bility of tastes and habits different to those of ordinary routine, or of her own starched life. Not to be hungry when she was ; not to sleep at night, but to write while she was sleeping, and to sleep when she was up ; in short, to gratify the require ments of material and intellectual life at hours different to hers, — all that was not merely annoying for her, but it must be mad ness ; or, if not, it betokened depravity that she could neither submit to nor tolerate without perilling her own morality.

" Such was the grand secret of the cruel silence which ex posed Lord Byron to the most malignant interpretations, to all the calumny and revenge of his enemies.

ATTACK ON LADY BYRON's GRAVE.

" She was, perhaps, the only woman in the world so strangely organized, — the only one, perhaps, capable of not feeling happy and proud at belonging to a man superior to the rest of humanity ; and fatally was it decreed that this woman alone of her species should be Lord Byron's wife ! "

In a note is added, —

" If an imaginary fear, and even an unreasonable jealousy, may be her excuse (just as one excuses a monomania), can one equally forgive her silence ? Such a silence is morally what are physically the poisons which kill at once, and defy all remedies ; thus insuring the culprit's safety. This silence it is which will ever be her crime ; for by it she poisoned the life of her hus band."

The book has several chapters devoted to Lord Byron's peculiar virtues ; and, under the one devoted to magnanimity and heroism, his forgiving disposition receives special attention. The climax of all is stated to be that he forgave Lady Byron. All the world knew that, since he had declared this fact in a very noisy and impas sioned manner in the fourth canto of "Childe Harold," together with a statement of the wrongs

which he forgave ; but the Guiccioli thinks his virtue, at this period, has not been enough appre ciated. In her view, it rose to the sublime. She says of Lady Byron, —

" An absolute moral monstrosity, an anomaly in the his tory of types of female hideousness, had succeeded in show ing itself in the light of magnanimity. But false as was this high quality in Lady Byron, so did it shine out in him true and admirable. The position in which Lady Byron had placed him, and where she continued to keep him by her harshness, silence, and strange refusals, was one of those which cause such suffer ing, that the highest degree of self-control seldom suffices to quiet the promptings of human weakness, and to cause persons of even slight sensibility to preserve moderation. Yet, with his sensibility and the knowledge of his worth, how did he act ? what did he say ? I will not speak of his ' Farewell;' of the care he took to shield her from blame by throwing it on others, by taking much too large a share to himself."

With like vivacity and earnestness does the narrator now proceed to make an incarnate angel of her subject by the simple process of denying every thing that he himself ever confessed,— every thing that has ever been confessed in regard

ATTACK ON LADY BYRONS GRAVE.

to him by his best friends. He has been in the world as an angel unawares from his cradle. His guardian did not properly appreciate him, and is consequently mentioned as that wicked Lord Car lisle. Thomas Moore is never to be sufficiently condemned for the facts told in his Biography. Byron's own frank and lawless admissions of evil are set down to a peculiar inability he had for speaking the truth about himself, — sometimes about his near relations ; all which does not in the least discourage the authoress from giving a separate chapter on " Lord Byron's Love of Truth."

In the matter of his relations with women, she complacently repeats (what sounds rather oddly as coming from her) Lord Byron's own assur ance, that he never seduced a woman ; and also the equally convincing statement, that he had told lier (the Guiccioli) that his married fidelity to his wife was perfect. She discusses Moore's account of the mistress in boy's clothes who used to share Byron's apartments in college, and ride

with him to races, and whom he presented to ladies as his brother.

She has her own view of this matter. The disguised boy was a lady of rank and fashion, who sought Lord Byron's chambers, as we are informed noble ladies everywhere, both in Italy and England, were constantly in the habit of doing ; throwing themselves at his feet, and im ploring permission to become his handmaids.

In the authoress's own words, " Feminine over tures still continued to be made to Lord Byron ; but the fumes of incense never hid from his sight his IDEAL." We are told, that, in case of these poor ladies, generally " disenchantment took place on his side without a corresponding result on the other: THENCE many heart-breakings." Nevertheless, we are informed that there fol lowed the indiscretions of these ladies " none of those proceedings that the world readily forgives, but which his feelings as a man of honor would have condemned."

As to drunkenness, and all that, we are in-

formed he was an anchorite. Pages are given to an account of the biscuits and soda-water that on this and that occasion were found to be the sole means of sustenance to this ethereal crea ture.

As to the story of using his wife's money, the lady gives, directly in the face of his own Letters and Journal, the same account given before by Medwin, and which caused such merriment when talked over in the Noctes Club, — that he had with her only a marriage-portion of ;£ 10,000 ; and that, on the separation, he not only paid it back, but doubled it.*

So on the authoress goes, sowing right and left the most transparent absurdities and mis- statements with what Carlyle well calls " a com-

* In the Noctes of November, 1824, Christopher North says, "I don't call Medwin a liar. . . . Whether Byron bammed him, or he, by virtue of his own stupidity, was the sole and sufficient bammifier of himself, I know not." A note says, that Murray had been much shocked by Byron's misstatements to Medwin as to money-matters with him. The note goes on to say, " Medwin could not have invented them, for they were mixed up with acknowledged facts; and the presumption is, tliat Byron mystified his gallant acquaintance. He was fond of such tricks."

posed stupidity, and a cheerful infinitude of ignorance." Who £&##///know, if not she, to be sure ? Had not Byron told her all about it ? and was not his family motto Crede Byron ?

The " Blackwood," having a dim suspicion that this confused style of attack and defence in reference to the two parties under consideration may not have great weight, itself proceeds to make the book an occasion for re-opening the controversy of Lord Byron with his wife.

The rest of the review is devoted to a power ful attack on Lady Byron's character, — the most fearful attack on the memory of a dead woman we have ever seen made by a living man. The author proceeds, like a lawyer, to gather up, arrange, and restate, in a most workmanlike manner, the confused accusations of the book.

Anticipating the objection, that such a re opening of the inquiry was a violation of the privacy due to womanhood and to the feelings of a surviving family, he says, that though mar riage usually is a private matter which the

world has no right to intermeddle with or dis cuss, yet —

" Lord Byron's was an exceptional case. It is not too much to say, that, had his marriage been a happy one, the course of events of the present century might have been materially changed; that the genius which poured itself forth in ' Don Juan ' and ' Cain' might have flowed in far different channels ; that the ardent love of freedom which sent him to perish at six and thirty at Missolonghi might have inspired a long career at home ; and that we might at this moment have been appealing to the counsels of his experience and wisdom at an age not exceeding that which was attained by Wellington, Lyndhurst, and Brougham.

" Whether the world would have been a gainer or a loser by the exchange is a question which every man must answer for himself, according to his own tastes and opinions ; but the possibility of such a change in the course of events warrants us in treating what would otherwise be a strictly private matter as one of public interest.

" More than half a century has elapsed, the actors have departed from the stage, the curtain has fallen ; and whether it will ever again be raised so as to reveal the real facts of the drama, may, as we have already observed, be well doubted. But the time has arrived when we may fairly gather up the fragments of evidence, clear them as far as possible from the incrustations of passion, prejudice, and malice, and place them

in such order, as, if possible, to enable us to arrive at some probable conjecture as to what the skeleton of the drama originally was."

Here the writer proceeds to put together all the facts of Lady Byron's case, just as an ad verse lawyer would put them as against her, and for her husband. The plea is made vigorously and ably, and with an air of indignant severity, as of an honest advocate who is thoroughly convinced that he is pleading the cause of a wronged man who has been ruined in name, shipwrecked in life, and driven to an early grave, by the arts of a bad woman, — a woman all the more horrible that her malice was disguised under the cloak of religion.

Having made an able statement of facts, adroitly leaving out ONE,* of which he could not have been ignorant had he studied the case care fully enough to know all the others, he proceeds to sum up against the criminal thus : —

* This one fact is, that Lord Byron might have had an open examination in court, if he had only persisted in refusing the deed of separation.

" We would deal tenderly with the memory of Lady Byron. Few women have been juster objects of compassion. It would seem as if Nature and Fortune had vied with each other which should be most lavish of her gifts, and yet that some malignant power had rendered all their bounty of no effect. Rank, beauty, wealth, and mental powers of no common order, were hers ; yet they were of no avail to secure her happiness. The spoilt child of seclusion, restraint, and parental idolatry, a fate (alike evil for both) cast her into the arms of the spoilt child of genius, passion, and the world. What real or fancied wrongs she suffered, we may never know; but those which she inflicted are sufficiently apparent.

" It is said that there are some poisons so subtle that they will destroy life, and yet leave no trace of their action. The murderer who uses them may escape the vengeance of the law ; but he is not the less guilty. So the slanderer who makes no charge ; who deals in hints and insinuations; who knows melancholy facts he would not willingly divulge,—things too painful to state ; who forbears, expresses pity, sometimes even affection, for his victim, shrugs his shoulders, looks with

' The significant eye, Which learns to lie with silence,' —

is far more guilty than he who tells the bold falsehood which may be met and answered, and who braves the punishment which must follow upon detection.

" Lady Byron has been called
' The moral Clytemnestra of her lord.'
The ' moral Brinvilliers ' would have been a truer designation.

"The conclusion at which we arrive is, that there is no proof whatever that Lord Byron was guilty of any act that need have caused a separation, or prevented a re-union, and that the imputations upon him rest on the vaguest conjecture ; that whatever real or fancied wrongs Lady Byron may have endured are shrouded in an impenetrable mist of her own creation, — a poisonous miasma in which she enveloped the character of her husband,—raised by her breath, and which her breath only could have dispersed.

' She dies, and makes no sign. O God ! forgive her.' "

As we have been obliged to review accusa tions on Lady Byron founded on old Greek tragedy, so now we are forced to abridge a passage from a modern conversations-lexicon, that we may understand what sort of compari sons are deemed in good taste in a conservative English review, when speaking of ladies of rank in their graves.

Under the article " Brinvilliers," we find as follows : —

"MARGUERITE D'AUBRAI, MARCHIONESS OF BRINVILLIERS.

— The singular atrocity of this woman gives her a sort of infamous claim to notice. She was born in Paris in 1651; being daughter of D'Aubrai, lieutenant-civil of Paris, who married her to the Marquis of Brinvilliers. Although possessed of attractions to captivate lovers, she was for some time much attached to her husband, but at length became madly in love with a Gascon officer. Her father imprisoned the officer in the Bastille ; and, while there, he learned the art of compounding subtle and most mortal poisons ; and, when he was released, he taught it to the lady, who exercised it with such success, that, in one year, her father, sister, and two brothers, became her victims. She professed the utmost tenderness for her victims, and nursed them assiduously. On her father she is said to have made eight attempts before she succeeded. She was very religious, and devoted to works of charity; and visited the hospitals a great deal, where it is said she tried her poisons on the sick."

People have made loud outcries lately, both in America and England, about violating the repose of the dead. We should like to know what they call this. Is this, then, what they mean by respecting the dead ?

Let any man imagine a leading review coming out with language equally brutal about his own mother, or any dear and revered friend.

Men of America, men of England, what do you think of this ?

When Lady Byron was publicly branded with the names of the foulest ancient and foulest modern assassins, and Lord Byron's mistress was publicly taken by the hand, and encouraged to go on and prosper in her slanders, by one of the oldest and most influential British reviews, what was said and what was done in England ?

That is a question we should be glad to have answered. Nothing was done that ever reached us.across the water.

And why was nothing done ? Is this language of a kind to be passed over in silence ?

Was it no offence to the .house of Wentworth to attack the pure character of its late venera ble head, and to brand her in her sacred grave with the name of one of the vilest of criminals ?

Might there not properly have been an indig nant protest of family solicitors against this in sult to the person and character of the Baroness Wentworth ?

If virtue went for nothing, benevolence for nothing, a long life of service to humanity for nothing, one would at least have thought, that, in aristocratic countries, rank might have had its rights to decent consideration, and its guar dians to rebuke the violation of those rights.

We Americans understand little of the advan tages of rank ; but we did understand that it secured certain decorums to people, both while living and when in their graves. From Lady Byron's whole history, in life and in death, it would appear that we were mistaken.

What a life was hers ! Was ever a woman more evidently desirous of the delicate and se cluded privileges of womanhood, of the sacred-ness of individual privacy ? Was ever a woman so rudely dragged forth, and exposed to the hardened, vulgar, and unfeeling gaze of mere curiosity? — her maiden secrets of love thrown open to be handled by roues; the sanctities of her marriage-chamber desecrated by leering satyrs ; her parents and best friends traduced

and slandered, till one indignant public protest was extorted from her, as by the rack, — a pro test which seems yet to quiver in every word with the indignation of outraged womanly deli cacy !

Then followed coarse blame and coarser com ment, — blame for speaking at all, and blame for not speaking more. One manly voice, raised for her in honorable protest, was silenced and overborne by the universal roar of ridicule and reprobation; and henceforth what refuge ? Only this remained : " Let them that suffer according to the will of God commit the keeping of their souls to him as to a faithful Creator."

Lady Byron turned to this refuge in silence, and filled up her life with a noble record of charities and humanities. So pure was she, so childlike, so artless, so loving, that those who knew her best, feel, to this day, that a memorial of her is like the relic of a saint. And could not all this preserve her grave from insult ? O England, England !

I speak in sorrow of heart to those who must have known, loved, and revered Lady Byron, and ask them, Of what were you thinking when you allowed a paper of so established literary rank as the " Blackwood " to present and earnestly recommend to our New World such a compendium of lies as the Guiccioli book ?

Is the great English-speaking community, whose waves toss from Maine to California, and whose literature is yet to come back in a thousand voices to you, a thing to be so despised ?

If, as the solicitors of the Wentworth family observe, you might be entitled to treat with si lent contempt the slanders of a mistress against a wife, was it safe to treat with equal contempt the indorsement and recommendation of those slanders by one of your oldest and most power ful literary authorities ?

No European magazine has ever had the weight and circulation in America that the " Blackwood" has held. In the days of my

youth, when New England was a comparatively secluded section of the earth, the wit and genius of the "Noctcs Ambrosianas " were in the mouths of men and maidens, even in our most quiet mountain-towns. There, years ago, we saw all Lady Byron's private affairs discussed, and felt the weight of Christopher North's decisions against her. Shelton Mackenzie, in his Ameri can edition, speaks of the American circulation of " Blackwood" being greater than that in England.* It was and is now reprinted monthly ; and, besides that, Littell's Magazine reproduces all its striking articles, and they come with the weight of long-established posi tion. From the very fact that it has long been considered the Tory organ, and the sup porter of aristocratic orders, all its admissions against the character of individuals in the privi leged classes have a double force.

When " Blackwood," therefore, boldly de nounces a lady of high rank as a modern Brin-villiers, and no sensation is produced, and no remonstrance follows, what can people in the New World suppose, but that Lady Byron's character was a point entirely given up ; that her depravity, was so well established and so fully conceded, that nothing was to be said, and that even the defenders of aristocracy were forced to admit it ?

I have been blamed for speaking on this sub ject without consulting Lady Byron's friends, trustees, and family. More than ten years had elapsed since I had had any intercourse with England, and I knew none of them. How was I to know that any of them were living ? It was perfectly fair for me to conclude that they were not; for, if they had been, they certainly must have taken some public steps to stop such a scandal. I was astonished to learn, for the

first time, by the solicitors' letters, that there were trustees, who held in their hands all Lady Byron's carefully-prepared proofs and documents, by which this falsehood might immediately have been refuted.

If they had spoken, they might have saved all this confusion. Even if bound by restric tions for a certain period of time, they still might have called on a Christian public to frown down such a cruel and indecent attack on the character of a noble lady who had been a benefactress to so many in England. They might have stated that the means of wholly refuting the slanders of the " Blackwood " were in their hands, and only delayed in coming forth from regard to the feelings of some in this gen eration. Then might they not have announced her Life and Letters, that the public might have the same opportunity as themselves for knowing and judging Lady Byron by her own writings ?

Had this been done, I had been most happy to have remained silent. I have been aston-

ished that any one should have supposed this speaking on my part to be any thing less than it is, — the severest act of self-sacrifice that one friend can perform for another, and the most solemn and difficult tribute to justice that a human being can be called upon to render.

I have been informed that the course I have taken would be contrary to the wishes of my friend. I think otherwise. I know her strong sense of justice, and her reverence for truth. Nothing ever moved her to speak to the public but an attack upon the honor of the dead. In her statement, she says of her parents, " There is no other near relative to vindicate their memory from insult: I am therefore compelled to break the silence I had hoped always to have observed."

If there was any near relative to vindicate Lady Byron's memory, I had no evidence of the fact; and I considered the utter silence to be strong evidence to the contrary. In all the storm of obloquy and rebuke that has raged in

consequence of my speaking, I have had two unspeakable sources of joy: first, that they could not touch her; and, second, that they could not blind the all-seeing God. It is worth being in darkness to see the stars.

It has been said that / have drawn on Lady Byron's name greater obloquy than ever before. I deny the charge. Nothing fouler has been asserted of her than the charges of the " Black-wood," because nothing fouler could be asserted. No satyr's hoof has ever crushed this pearl deeper in the mire than the hoof of the " Black-wood ; " but none of them have so defiled it or trodden it so deep that God cannot find it in the day "when he maketh up his jewels."

I have another word, as an American, to say about the contempt shown to our great people in thus suffering the materials of history to be falsified to subserve the temporary purposes of family feeling in England.

Lord Byron belongs not properly either to the Byrons or the Wentworths. He is not one

of their family jewels, to be locked up in their cases. He belongs to the world for which he wrote, to which he appealed, and before which he dragged his reluctant, delicate wife to a publicity equal with his own : the world has, therefore, a right to judge him.

We Americans have been made accessories, after the fact, to every insult and injury that Lord Byron and the literary men of his day have heaped upon Lady Byron. We have been betrayed into injustice, and a complicity with villany. After Lady Byron had nobly lived down slanders in England, and died full of years and honors, the " Blackwood" takes occasion to re-open the controversy by recommending a book full of slanders to a rising generation who knew nothing of the past. What was the con sequence in America ? My attention was first called to the result, not by reading the " Black-wood " article, but by finding in a popular monthly magazine two long articles, — the one an enthusiastic recommendation of the Guiccioli

book, and the other a lamentation over the burning of the Autobiography as a lost chapter in history.

Both articles represented Lady Byron as a cold, malignant, mean, persecuting woman, who had been her husband's ruin. They were so full of falsehoods and misstatements as to astonish me. Not long after, a literary friend wrote to me, " Will you, can you, reconcile it to your , conscience to sit still and allow that mistress so to slander that wife, — you, perhaps, the only one knowing the real facts, and able to set them forth ? "

Upon this, I immediately began collecting and reading the various articles and the book, and perceived that the public of this generation were in a way of having false history created, uncontradicted, under their own eyes.

I claim for my country men and women our right to true history. For years, the popular literature has held u.p publicly before our eyes the facts as to this man and this woman,

and called on us to praise or condemn. Let us have truth when we are called on to judge. It is our right.

There is no conceivable obligation on a human being greater than that of absolute justice. It is the deepest personal injury to an honorable mind to be made, through misrepre sentation, an accomplice in injustice. When a noble name is accused, any person who pos sesses truth which might clear it, and withholds that truth, is guilty of a sin against human nature and the inalienable claims of justice. I claim that I have not only a right, but an obliga tion, to bring in my solemn testimony upon this subject

For years and years, the silence-policy has been tried ; and what has it brought forth ? As neither word nor deed could be proved against Lady Byron, her silence has been spoken of as a monstrous, unnatural crime, "a poisonous mi asma," in which she enveloped the name of her husband.

Very well: since silence is the crime, I thought I would tell the world that Lady Byron had spoken.

Christopher North, years ago, when he con demned her for speaking, said that she should speak further, —

" She should speak, or some one for her. One word would suffice.' 5

That one word I have spoken.

PART II,

A

CHAPTER I.

LADY BYRON AS I KNEW HER.

N editorial in " The London Times" of Sept. 18 says, —

" The perplexing feature in this ' True Story' is, that it is impossible to distinguish what part in it is the editress's, and what Lady Byron's own. We are given the impression made on Mrs. Stowe's mind by Lady Byron's statements ; but it would have been more satisfactory if the statement itself had been reproduced as bare as possible, and been left to make its own impression on the public."

In reply to this, I will say, that in my article I gave a brief synopsis of the subject-matter of Lady Byron's communications; and I think it must be quite evident to the world that the main

fact on which the story turns was one which could not possibly be misunderstood, and the remembrance of which no lapse of time could ever weaken.

Lady Byron's communications were made to me in language clear, precise, terrible; and many of her phrases and sentences I could repeat at this day, word for word. But if I had reproduced them at first, as " The Times " suggests, word for word, the public horror and incredulity would have been doubled. ' It was necessary that the brutality of the story should, in some degree, be veiled and softened.

The publication, by Lord Lindsay, of Lady Anne Barnard's communication, makes it now possible to tell fully, and in Lady Byron's own words, certain incidents that yet remain untold. To me who know the whole history, the revela tions in Lady Anne's account, and the story re lated by Lady Byron, are like fragments of a dissected map : they fit together, piece by piece, and form one connected whole.

In confirmation of the general facts of this interview, I have the testimony of a sister who accompanied me on this visit, and to whom, im mediately after it, I recounted the story.

Her testimony on the subject is as follows : —

" MY DEAR SISTER, — I have a perfect recollection of going with you to visit Lady Byron at the time spoken of in your published article. We arrived at her house in the morning ; and, after lunch, Lady Byron and yourself spent the whole time till evening alone together.

" After we retired to our apartment that night, you related to me the story given in your published account, though with many more particulars than you have yet thought fit to give to the public.

" You stated to me that Lady Byron was strongly impressed with the idea that it might be her duty to publish a statement during her lifetime, and also the.reasons which induced her to think so. You appeared at that time quite disposed to think that justice required this step, and asked my opinion. We passed most of the night in conversation on the subject, — a conversation often resumed, from time to time, during several weeks in which you were considering what opinion to give.

" I was strongly of opinion that justice required the publica tion of the truth, but felt exceedingly averse to its being done by Lady Byron herself during her own lifetime, when she personally would be subject to the comments and misconcep tions of motives which would certainly follow such a communi cation. " Your sister,

" M. F. PERKINS."

I am now about to complete the account of my conversation with Lady Byron ; but as the credibility of a history depends greatly on the character of its narrator, and as especial pains have been taken to destroy the belief in this story by representing it to be the wanderings of a broken-down mind in a state of dotage and mental hallucination, I shall preface the narra tive with some account of Lady Byron as she was during the time of our mutual acquaintance and friendship.

This account may, perhaps, be deemed super fluous in England, where so many knew her ; but in America, where, from Maine to California, her character has been discussed and traduced, it is of importance to give interested thousands an opportunity of learning what kind of a wo man Lady Byron was.

Her character as given by Lord Byron in his Journal, after her first refusal of him, is this : —

" She is a very superior woman, and very little spoiled ; which is strange in an heiress, a girl of twenty, a peeress that is to be in her own right, an only child, and a savante, who has always had her'own way. She is a poetess, a mathemati cian, a metaphysician ; yet, withal, very kind, generous, and gentle, with very little pretension. Any other head would be turned with half her acquisitions and a tenth of her advan tages."

Such was Lady Byron at twenty. I formed her acquaintance in the year 1853, during my first visit in England. I met her at a lunch-party in the house of one of her friends.

The party had many notables ; but, among them all, my attention was fixed principally on Lady Byron. She was at this time sixty-one years of age, but still had, to a remarkable de gree, that personal attraction which is commonly considered to belong only to youth and beauty.

Her form was slight, giving an impression of

fragility ; her motions were both graceful and de cided ; her eyes bright, and full of interest and quick observation. Her silvery-white hair seemed to lend a grace to the transparent purity of her complexion, and her small hands had a pearly whiteness. I recollect she wore a plain widow's cap of a transparent material; arid was dressed in some delicate shade of lavender, which har monized well with her complexion.

When I was introduced to her, I felt in a mo ment the words of her husband : —

" There was awe in the homage that she drew; Her spirit seemed as seated on a throne."

Calm, self-poised, and thoughtful, she seemed to me rather to resemble an interested spectator of the world's affairs, than an actor involved in its trials ; yet the sweetness of her smile, and a certain very delicate sense of humor in her remarks, made the way of acquaintance easy.

Her first remarks were a little playful; but in a few moments we were speaking on what every

one in those days was talking to me about, — the slavery question in America.

It need not be remarked, that, when any one subject especially occupies the public mind, those known to be interested in it are compelled to listen to many weary platitudes. Lady Byron's remarks, however, caught rny ear and arrested my attention by their peculiar incisive quality, their originality, and the evidence they gave that she was as well informed on all our matters as the best American statesman could be. I had no wearisome course to go over with her as to the difference between the General Government and State Governments, nor explanations of the United-States Constitution; for she had the whole before her mind with a perfect clearness. Her morality upon the slavery question, too, im pressed me as something far higher and deeper than the common sentimentalism of the day. Many of her words surprised me greatly, and gave me new material for thought.

I found I was in company with a commanding mind, and hastened to gain instruction from her on another point where my interest had been aroused. I had recently been much excited by Kingsley's novels, "Alton Locke" and "Yeast," on the position of the religious thought in England. From these works I had gathered, that under the apparent placid uniformity of the Established Church of England, and of " good so ciety " as founded on it, there was moving a secret current of speculative inquiry, doubt, and dissent; but I had met, as yet, with no person among my. various acquaintances in England who seemed either aware of this fact, or able to guide my mind respecting it. The moment I mentioned the subject to Lady Byron, I received an answer which showed me that the whole ground was fa miliar to her, and that she was capable of giving me full information. She had studied with care ful thoughtfulness all the social and religious tendencies of England during her generation. One of her remarks has often since occurred to me. Speaking of the Oxford movement, she

said the time had come when the English Church could no longer remain as it was. It must either restore the past, or create a future. The Oxford movement attempted the former; and of the future she was beginning to speak, when our conversation was interrupted by the presenta tion of other parties.

Subsequently, in reply to a note from her on some benevolent business, I alluded to that con versation, and expressed a wish that she would finish giving me her views of the religious state of England. A portion of the letter that she wrote me in reply I insert, as being very charac teristic in many respects : —

" Various causes have been assigned for the decaying state of the English Church ; which seems the more strange, because the clergy have improved, morally and intellectually, in the last twenty years. Then why should their influence be diminished ? I think it is owing to the diffusion of a spirit of free inquiry.

" Doubts have arisen in the minds of many who are unhap pily bound by subscription not to doubt; and, in consequence, they are habitually pretending either to believe or to disbelieve. The state of Denmark cannot but be rotten, when to seem is the first object of the witnesses of truth.

" They may lead better lives, and bring forward abler argu ments ; but their efforts are paralyzed by that unsoundness. I see the High Churchman professing to believe in the existence of a church, when the most palpable facts must show him that no such church exists; the 'Low' Churchman professing to believe in exceptional interpositions which his philosophy secretly questions ; the ' Broad' Churchman professing as absolute an attachment to the Established Church as the nar rowest could feel, while he is preaching such principles as will at last pull it down.

" I ask you, my friend, whether there would not be more faith, as well as earnestness, if all would speak out. There would be more unanimity too, because they would all agree in a certain basis. Would not a wider love supersede the creed-bound charity of setts ?

" I am aware that I have touched on a point of difference between us, and I will not regret it; for I think the differences of mind are analogous to those differences of nature, which, in the most comprehensive survey, are the very elements of har mony.

" I am not at all prone to put forth my own opinions; but the tone in which you have written to me claims an unusual degree of openness on my part. I look upon creeds of all kinds as chains, — far worse chains than those you would break, — as the causes of much hypocrisy and infidelity. I hold it to be a sin to make a child say, 'I believe." 1 Lead it to utter that belief spontaneously. * I also consider the institution of an exclusive priesthood, though having been of service in some respects, as retarding the progress of Christianity at present. I desire to see a lay ministry.

" I will not give you more of my heterodoxy at present : perhaps I need your pardon, connected as you are with the Church, for having said so much.

" There are causes of decay known to be at work in my frame, which lead me to believe I may not have time to grow wiser ; and I must therefore leave it to others to correct the conclusions I have now formed from my life's experience. I should feel happy to discuss them personally with you; for it would be soul to soul. In that confidence I am yours most truly,

" A. I. NOEL BYRON."

%

It is not necessary to prove to the reader that this letter is not in the style of a broken-down old woman subject to mental hallucinations. It shows Lady Byron's habits of clear, searching analysis, her thoughtfulness, and, above all, that peculiar reverence for truth and sincerity which was a leading characteristic of her moral nature.* It also shows her views of the

* The reader is here referred to Lady Byron's other letters, printed in Part III.; which also show the peculiarly active and philosophical char acter of her mind, and the class of subjects on which it "habitually dwelt.

probable shortness of her stay on earth, derived from the opinion of physicians about her disease, which was a gradual ossification of the lungs. It has been asserted that pulmonary diseases, while they slowly and surely sap the physical life, often appear to give added vigor to the play of the moral and intellectual powers.

I parted from Lady Byron, feeling richer in that I had found one more pearl of great price on the shore of life.

Three years after this, I visited England to obtain a copyright for the issue of my novel of " Dred."

The hope of once more seeing Lady Byron was one of the brightest anticipations held out to me in this journey. I found London quite deserted; but, hearing that Lady Byron was still in town, I sent to her, saying in my note, that, in case she was not well enough to call, I would visit her. Her reply I give : —

" MY DEAR FRIEND, — I will be indebted to you for our meeting, as I am barely able to leave my room. It is not a time

for small personalities, if they could ever exist with you ; and, dressed or undressed, I shall hope to see you after two o'clock. " Yours very truly,

"A. I. NOEL BYRON."

I found Lady Byron in her sick-room, — that place which she made so different from the chamber of ordinary invalids. Her sick room seemed only a telegraphic station whence her vivid mind was flashing out all over the world.

By her bedside stood a table covered with books, pamphlets, and files of letters, all arranged with exquisite order, and each expressing some of her varied interests. From that sick-bed she still directed, with systematic care, her various works of benevolence, and watched with intelligent attention the course of science, literature, and religion ; and the versatility and activity of her mind, the flow of brilliant and penetrating thought on- all the topics of the day, gave to the conversations of her retired room a peculiar charm. You forgot that she was an invalid ; for

she rarely had a word of her own personalities, and the charm of her conversation . carried you invariably from herself to the subjects of which she was thinking. All the new books, the litera ture of the hour, were lighted up by her keen, searching, yet always kindly criticism ; and it was charming to get her fresh, genuine, clear-cut modes of expression, so different from the world-worn phrases of what is called good society. Her opinions were always perfectly clear and positive, and given with the freedom of one who has long stood in a position to judge the world and its ways from her own standpoint. But it was not merely in general literature and science that her heart lay : it was following always with eager interest the progress of humanity over the whole world.

This was the period of the great battle for liberty in Kansas. The English papers were daily filled with the thrilling particulars of that desperate struggle, and Lady Byron entered with heart and soul into it.

Her first letter to me, at this time, is on this subject. It was while " Dred " was going through the press.

"CAMBRIDGE TERRACE, Aug. 15.

"My DEAR MRS. STOWE, — Messrs. Chambers liked the proposal to publish the Kansas Letters. The more the public know of these matters, the better prepared they will be for your book. The moment for its publication seems well chosen. There is always in England a floating fund of sympathy for what is above the every-day sordid cares of life ; and these bet ter feelings, so nobly invested for the last two years in Florence Nightingale's career, are just set free. To what will they next be attached ? If you can lay hold of them, they may bring about a deeper abolition than any legislative one, — the abolition of the heart-heresy that man's worth comes, not from God, but from man.

"I have been obliged to give up exertion again, but hope soon to be able to call and make the acquaintance of your daughters. In case you wish to consult H. Martineau's pam phlets, I send more copies. Do not think of answering: I have occupied too much of your time in reading.

" Yours affectionately, " A. I. NOEL BYRON."

As soon as a copy of " Dred " was through the press, I sent it to her, saying that I had been
.**

reproved by some excellent people for repre senting too faithfully the profane language of some of the wicked characters. To this she sent the following reply : —

" Your book, dear Mrs. Stowe, is of the little leaven kind, and must prove a great moral force ; perhaps not manifestly so much as secretly. And yet I can hardly conceive so much power without immediate and sensible effects : only there will be a strong disposition to resist on the part of all hollow-hearted professors of religion, whose heathenisms you so unsparingly expose. They have a class feeling like others.

" To the young, and to those who do not reflect much on what is offered to their belief, you will do great good by showing how spiritual food is often adulterated. The bread from heaven is in the same case as baker's bread.

" If there is truth in what I heard Lord Byron say, that works of fiction live only by the amount of tmith which they contain, your story is sure of a long life. Of the few critiques I have seen, the best is in ' The Examiner/ I find an obtuseness as to the spirit and aim of the book, as if you had designed to make the best novel of the season, or to keep up the reputation of one. You are reproached, as Walter Scott was, with too much scrip tural quotation ; not, that I have heard, with phrases of an opposite character.

" The effects of such reading till a late hour one evening

appeared to influence me very singularly in a dream. The most horrible spectres presented themselves, and I woke in an agony of fear ; but a faith still stronger arose, and I became coura geous from trust in God, and felt calm. Did you do this ? It is very insignificant among the many things you certainly will do unknown to yourself. I know more than ever before how to value communion with you. I have sent Robertson's Sermons for you ; and, with kind regards to your family, am

"Yours affectionately, "A. I. NOEL BYRON."

I was struck in this note with the mention of Lord Byron, and, the next time I saw her, alluded to it, and remarked upon the pecu liar qualities of his mind as shown in some of his more serious conversations with Dr. Kennedy.

She seemed pleased to continue the subject, and went on to say many things of his singular character and genius, more penetrating and more appreciative than is often met with among critics.

I told her that I had been from childhood powerfully influenced by him ; and began to tell her how much, as a child, I, had been affected

f

by the news of his death, — giving up all my plays, and going off to a lonely hillside, where I spent the afternoon thinking of him. She interrupted me, before I had quite finished, with a quick, impulsive movement. " I know all that,"

she said : " I heard it all from Mrs. ; and it

was one of the things that made me wish to know you. I think you could understand him." We talked for some time of him then ; she, with her pale face slightly flushed, speaking, as any other great man's widow might, only of what was purest and best in his works, and what were his undeniable virtues and good traits, especially in early life. She told me many pleas ant little speeches made by him to herself; and, though there was running through all this a shade of melancholy, one could never have con jectured that there were under all any deeper recollections than the circumstances of an ordi nary separation might bring.

Not many days after, with the unselfishness which was so marked a trait with her, she chose

a day when she could be out of her room, and invited our family party, consisting of my hus band, sister, and children, to lunch with her.

What showed itself especially in this inter view was her tenderness for all young people. She had often inquired after mine ; asked about their characters, habits, and tastes ; and on this occasion she found an opportunity to talk with each one separately, and to make them all feel at ease, so that they were able to talk with her. She seemed interested to point out to them what they should see and study in London ; and the charm of her conversation left on their minds an impression that subsequent years have never effaced. I record this incident, because it shows how little Lady Byron assumed the privileges or had the character of an invalid absorbed in herself, and likely to brood over her own woes and wrongs.

Here was a family of strangers stranded in a dull season in London, and there was no manner of obligation upon her to exert herself to show

them attention. Her state of health would have been an all-sufficient reason why she should not do it; and her doing it was simply a specimen of that unselfish care for others, even down to the least detail, of which her life was full.

A little while after, at her request, I went, with my husband and son, to pass an evening at her house.

There were a few persons present whom she thought I should be interested to know, — a Miss Goldsmith, daughter of Baron Goldsmith, and Lord Ockham, her grandson, eldest son and heir of the Earl of Lovelace, to whom she in troduced my son.

I had heard much of the eccentricities of this young nobleman, and was exceedingly struck with his personal appearance. His bodily frame was of the order of the Farnese Hercules,

— a wonderful development of physical and muscu lar strength. His hands were those of a black smith. He was broadly and squarely made, with a finely-shaped head, and dark eyes of

surpassing brilliancy. I have seldom seen a more interesting combination than his whole appearance presented.

When all were engaged in talking, Lady Byron came and sat down by me, and glancing across to Lord Ockham and my son, who were talking together, she looked at me, and .smiled. I immediately expressed my admiration of his fine eyes and the intellectual expression of his coun tenance, and my wonder at the uncommon mus cular development of his frame.

She said that that of itself would account for many of Ockham's eccentricities. He had a body that required a more vigorous animal life than his station gave scope for, and this had often led him to seek it in what the world calls low society ; that he had been to sea as a sailor, and was now working as a mechanic on the iron work of " The Great Eastern." He had laid aside his title, and went in daily with the other workmen, requesting them to call him simply Ockham.

I said that there was something to my mind very fine about this, even though it might show some want of proper balance.

She said he had noble traits, and that she felt assured- he would yet accomplish something worthy of himself. " The great difficulty with our nobility is apt to be, that they do not understand the working-classes, so as to feel for them properly ; and Ockham is now going through an experience which may yet fit him to do great good when he comes to the peerage. I am trying to influence him to do good among the workmen, and to interest himself in schools for their children. I think," she added, " I have great influence over Ockham, — the greater, per haps, that I never make any claim to authority."

This conversation is very characteristic of Lady Byron, as showing her benevolent analysis of character, and the peculiar hopefulness she always had in regard to the future of every one brought in connection with her. Her moral hopefulness was something very singular ; and in

this respect she was so different from the rest of the world, that it would be difficult to make her understood. Her tolerance of wrong-doing would have seemed to many quite latitudinarian, and impressed them as if she had lost all just horror of what was morally wrong in transgres sion ; but it seemed her fixed habit to see faults only as diseases and immaturities, and to expect them to fall away with time.

She saw the germs of good in what others regarded as only evil. She expected valuable results to come from what the world looked on only as eccentricities ; * and she incessantly de voted herself to the task of guarding those whom the world condemned, and guiding them to those higher results of which she often thought that even their faults were prophetic.

Before I quit this sketch of Lady Byron as I knew her, I will give one more of her letters. My return from that visit in Europe was met by the sudden death of the son mentioned in the

* See her character of Dr. King, Part III., p. 469.

foregoing account. At the time of this sorrow, Lady Byron was too unwell to write to me. The letter given alludes to this event, and speaks also of two colored persons of remarka ble talent, in whose career in England she had taken a deep interest. One of them is the " friend " she speaks of.

"LONDON, Feb. 6, 1859.

"DEAR MRS. STOWE, — I seem to feel our friend as a bridge, over which our broken outward communication can be renewed without effort. Why broken ? The words I would have uttered at one time were like drops of blood from my heart. Now I sympathize with the calmness you have gained, and can speak of your loss as I do of my own. Loss and resto ration are more and more linked in my mind, but ' to the pres ent live.' As long as they are in God's world, they are in ours. I ask no other consolation.

" Mrs. W 's recovery has astonished me, and her hus band's prospects give me great satisfaction. They have achieved a benefit to their colored people. She had a mission which her burning soul has worked out, almost in defiance of death. But who is 'called' without being 'crucified,' man or woman ? I know of none.

"I fear that H. Martineau was too sanguine in her persuasion that the slave-power had received a serious check from the ruin

of so many of your Mammon-worshippers. With the return of commercial facilities, that article of commerce will again find purchasers enough to raise its value. Not that way is the iniquity to be overthrown. A deeper moral earthquake is needed.* We English had ours in India; and though the cases are far from being alike, yet a consciousness of what we ought to have been and ought to be toward the natives could not have been awakened by less than the reddened waters of the Ganges. So I fear you will have to look on a day of judg ment worse than has been painted.

" As to all the frauds and impositions which have been dis closed by the failures, what a want of the sense of personal responsibility they show. It seems to be thought that 'asso ciation ' will ' cover a multitude of sins ;' as if ' and Co.' could enter heaven. A firm may be described as a partnership for lowering the standard of morals. Even ecclesiastical bodies are not free from the 'and Co.;' very different from ' the goodly fellowship of the apostles.'

" The better class of young gentlemen in England are seized with a mediaeval mania, to which Ruskin has contributed much. The chief reason for regretting it is that taste is made to super sede benevolence. The money that would save thousands from perishing or suffering must be applied to raise the Gothic edifice where their last prayer may be uttered. Charity may be dead, while Art has glorified her. This is worse than Catholicism,

Alluding to the financial crisis in the United States in 1857.

which cultivates heart and eye together. The first cathedral was Truth, at the beginning of the fourth century, just as Christianity was exchanging a heavenly for an earthly crown. True religion may have to cast away the symbol for the spirit before ' the kingdom ' can come.

" While I am speculating to little purpose, perhaps you are doing —what? Might not a biography from your pen bring forth again some great, half-obscured soul to act on the world ? Even Sir Philip Sidney ought to be superseded by a still nobler type.

" This must go immediately, to be in time for the bearer, of whose meeting with you I shall think as the friend of both. May it be happy !

" Your affectionate " A. I. N. B."

One letter more from Lady Byron I give, — the last I received from her: —

" LONDON, May 3, 1859.

"DEAR FRIEND, — I have found, particularly as to your self, that, if I did not answer from the first impulse, all had evaporated. Your letter came by' The Niagara,' which brought Fanny Kemble to learn the loss of her best friend, the Miss F whom you saw at my house.

" Her death, after an illness in which she was to the last a minister of good to others, is a soul-loss to me also ; and your remarks are most appropriate to my feelings. I have been

taught, however, to accept survivorship ; even to feel it, in some cases, Heaven's best blessing.

" I have an intense interest in your new novel.* More power in these few numbers than in any of your former writ ings, relating, at least, to my own mind. It would amuse you to hear my grand-daughter and myself attempting to foresee the future of the love-story; being, for the moment, quite persuaded that James is at sea, and the minister about to ruin himself. We think that Mary will labor to be in love with the self-devot ed man, under her mother's influence, and from that hyper-conscientiousness so common with good girls ; but we don't wish her to succeed. Then what is to become of her older lover ? Time will show.

" The lady you desired to introduce to me will be welcomed as of you. She has been misled with respect to my having any house in Yorkshire (New Leeds). I am in London now

to be of a little use to A ; not ostensibly, for I can neither

go out, nor give parties : but I am the confidential friend to whom she likes to bring her social gatherings, as she can see something of the world with others. Age and infirmity seem to be overlooked in what she calls the harmony between us, — not perfect agreement of opinion (which I should regret, with almost fifty years of difference), but the spirit-union: can you say what it is ?

" I am interrupted by a note from Mrs. K . She says

* The Minister's Wooing, in the Atlantic Monthly.

that she cannot write of our lost friend yet, though she is less

sad than she will be. Mrs. F may like to hear of her

arrival, should you be in communication with our friend. She is the type of youth in age.

" I often converse with Miss S , a judicious friend of the

W s, about what is likely to await them. She would not

succeed here as well as where she was a novelty. The charac ter of our climate this year has been injurious to the respiratory organs ; but I hope still to serve them.

" I have just missed Dale Owen, with whom I wished to have conversed on spiritualism.* Harris is lecturing here on religion. I do not hear him praised.

" People are looking for helps to believe, everywhere but in life,—in music, in architecture, in antiquity, in ceremony; and upon all these is written, ' Thou shalt not believe.' At least, if this be faith, happier the unbeliever. I am willing to see through that materialism ; but, if I am to rest there, I would rend the veil.

"JUNE i.

" The day of the packet's sailing. I shall hope to be visited by you here. The best flowers sent me have been placed in your little vases, giving life to the remembrance of you, though not, like them, to pass away.

" Ever yours, " A. I. NOEL BYRON."

* See her letter on spiritualistic phenomena, Part III.

Shortly after, I was in England again, and had one more opportunity of resuming our personal intercourse. The first time that I called on Lady Byron, I saw her in one of those periods of utter physical exhaustion to which she was subject on account of the constant pressure of cares beyond her strength. All who knew her will testify, that, in a state of health which would lead most persons to become helpless absorbents of ser vice from others, she was assuming burdens, and making outlays of her vital powers in acts of love and service, with a generosity that often reduced her to utter exhaustion. But none who knew or loved her ever misinterpreted the cold ness of those seasons of exhaustion. We knew that it was not the spirit that was chilled, but only the frail mortal tabernacle. When I called on her at this time, she could not see me at first; and when, at last, she came, it was evident that she was in a state of utter prostration. Her hands were like ice ; her face was deadly pale; and she conversed with a

restraint and difficulty which showed what ex ertion it was for her to keep up at all. I left as soon as possible, with an appointment for another interview. That interview was my last on earth with her, and is still beautiful in memory. It was a long, still summer afternoon, spent alone with her in a garden, where we walked together. She was enjoying one of those bright intervals of freedom from pain and languor, in which her spirits always rose so buoyant and youthful; and her eye brightened, and her step became elastic.

One last little incident is cherished as most expressive of her. When it became time for me to leave, she took me in her carriage to the station. As we were almost there, I missed my gloves, and said, " I must have left them ; but there is not time to go back."

With one of those quick, impulsive motions which were so natural to her in doing a kind ness, she drew off her own, and said, " Take mine if they will serve you." -

I hesitated a moment; and then the thought, that I might never see her again, came over me, and I said, " Oh, yes! thanks." That was the last earthly word of love between us. But, thank God, those who love worthily never meet for the last time : there is always a future.

CHAPTER II.

T NOW come to.the particulars of that most painful interview which has been the cause of all this controversy. My sister and myself were going from London to Eversley to visit the Rev. C. Kingsley. On our way, we stopped, by Lady Byron's invitation, to lunch with her at her summer residence on Ham Common, near Richmond ; and it was then arranged, that on our return, we should make her a short visit, as she said she had a subject of importance on which she wished to converse with me alone.

On our return from Eversley, we arrived at her house in the morning.

It appeared to be one of Lady Byron's well

days. She was up and dressed, and moved 232

about her house with her usual air of quiet sim plicity ; as full of little acts of consideration for all about her as if they were the habitual inva lids, and she the well person.

There were with her two ladies of her most intimate friends, by whom she seemed to be re garded with a sort of worship. When she left the room for a moment, they looked after her with a singular expression of respect and affec tion, and expressed freely their admiration of her character, and their fears that her unselfishness might be leading her to over-exertion.

After lunch, I retired with Lady Byron ; and my sister remained with her friends. I should here remark, that the chief subject of the con versation which ensued was not entirely new to me. In the interval between my first and second visits to England, a lady who for many years had enjoyed Lady Byron's friendship and confidence, had, with her consent, stated the case generally to me, giving some of the incidents : so that I was in a manner prepared for what followed.

Those who accifse Lady Byron of being a per son fond of talking upon this subject, and apt to make unconsidered confidences, can have known very little of her, of her reserve, and of the apparent difficulty she had in speaking on sub jects nearest her heart.

Her habitual calmness and composure of man ner, her collected dignity on all occasions, are often mentioned by her husband, sometimes with bitterness, sometimes with admiration. He says, " Though I accuse Lady Byron of an excess of self-respect, I must in candor admit, that, if ever a person had excuse for an extraordinary portion of it, she has ; as, in all her thoughts, words, and deeds, she is the most decorous woman that ever existed, and must appear, what few I fancy could, a perfectly refined gentlewoman even to her femme de chambre^

This calmness and dignity were never more manifested than in this interview. In recalling the conversation at this distance of time, I can not remember all the language used. Some

particular words and forms of expression I do remember, and those I give ; and in other cases I give my t recollection of the substance of what was said.

There was something awful to me in the in tensity of repressed emotion which she showed as she proceeded. The great fact upon which all turned was stated in words that were unmis takable : —

" Mrs. Stowe, he was guilty of incest with his sister ! "

She here became so deathly pale, that I feared she would faint; and hastened to say, " My dear friend, I have heard that." She asked quickly, " From whom ? " and I answered, " From Mrs. ; " when she replied, " Oh, yes ! " as if recollecting herself.

I then asked her some questions ; in reply to which she said, " I will tell you."

She then spoke of her first acquaintance with Lord Byron ; from which I gathered that she, an only child, brought up in retirement, and living

much within herself, had been, as deep natures often were, intensely stirred by his poetry ; and had felt a deep interest in him personally, as one that had the germs of all that is glorious and noble.

When she was introduced to him, and per ceived his admiration of herself, and at last received his offer, although deeply moved, she doubted her own power to be to him all that a wife should be. She declined his offer, there fore, but desired to retain still his friendship. After this, as she said, a correspondence ensued, mostly on moral and literary subjects ; and, by this correspondence, her interest in him was constantly increased.

At last, she said, he sent her a very beautiful letter, offering himself again. " I thought," she added, "that it was sincere, and that I might now show him all I felt. I wrote just what was in my heart.

" Afterwards," she said, " I found in one of his journals this notice of my letter : ' A letter from Bell, — never rains but it pours.'"

There was through her habitual calm a shade • of womanly indignation as she spoke these words ; but it was gone in a moment. I said, " And did he not love you, then ? " She an swered, " No, my dear: he did not love me."

" Why, then, did he wish to marry you ? " She laid her hand on mine, and said in a low voice, " You will see."

She then told me, that, shortly after the de clared engagement, he came to her father's house to visit her as an accepted suitor. The visit was to her full of disappointment. His appearance was so strange, moody, and unac countable, and his treatment of her so peculiar, that she came to the conclusion that he did not love her, and sought an opportunity to converse with him alone.

She told him that she saw from his manner that their engagement did not give him pleasure; that she should never blame him if he wished to dissolve it; that his nature was exceptional; and if, on a nearer view of the situation, he shrank

from it, she would release him, and remain no less than ever his friend.

Upon this, she said, he fainted entirely away.

She stopped a moment, and then, as if speak ing with great effort, added, " Then I was sure he must love me."

"And did he not?" said I. "What other cause could have led to this emotion ?"

She looked at me very sadly, and said, " Fear of detection"

" What!" said I, " did that cause then exist ? "

" Yes," she said, "it did." And she explained that she now attributed Lord Byron's great agitation to fear, that, in some way, suspicion of the crime had been aroused in her mind, and that on this account she was seeking to break the engagement. She said, that, from that moment, her sympathies were aroused for him, to soothe the remorse and anguish which seemed preying on his mind, and which she then regarded as the sensibility of an unusually exacting moral nature, which judged itself by

higher standards, and condemned itself unspar ingly for what most young men of his times regarded as venial faults. She had every hope for his future, and all the enthusiasm of belief that so many men and women of those times and ours have had in his intrinsic nobleness. She said the gloom, however, seemed to be even deeper when he came to the marriage ; but she looked at it as the suffering of a peculiar being, to whom she was called to minister. I said to her, that, even in the days of my childhood, I had heard of something very painful that had passed as they were in the carriage, immediately after marriage. She then said that it was so; that almost his first words, when they were alone, were, that she might once have saved him ; that, if she had accepted him when he first offered, she might have made him any thing she pleased ; but that, as it was, she would find she had married a devil.

The conversation, as recorded in Lady Anne Barnard's Diary, seems only a continuation of

the foregoing, and just what might have followed upon it.

I then asked how she became certain of the true cause.

She said, that, from the outset of their married life, his conduct towards her was strange and unaccountable, even during the first weeks after the wedding, while they were visiting her friends, and outwardly on good terms. He seemed resolved to shake and combat both her religious principles and her views of the family state. He tried to undermine her faith in Christianity as a rule of life by argument and by ridicule. He set before her the Continental idea of the liberty of marriage ; it being a simple partnership of friendship and property, the parties to which were allowed by one another to pursue their own separate individual tastes. He told her, that, as he could not be expected to confine himself to her, neither should he expect or wish- that she should confine herself to him ; that she was young and pretty, and could have her lovers,

and he should never object; and that she must allow him the same freedom.

She said that she did not comprehend to what this was. tending till after they came to London, and his sister came to stay with them.

At what precise time the idea of an improper connection between her husband and his sister was first forced upon her, she did not say ; but she told me how it was done. She said that one night, in her presence, he treated his sister with a liberty which both shocked and astonished her. Seeing her amazement and alarm, he came up to her, and said, in a sneering tone, " I suppose you perceive you are not wanted here. Go to your own room, and leave us alone. We can amuse ourselves better without you."

She said, " I went to my room, trembling. I fell down on my knees, and prayed to my heav enly Father to have mercy on them. I thought, ' What shall I do ?' "

I remember, after this, a pause in the conver sation, during which she seemed struggling with

thoughts and emotions ; and, for my part, I was unable to utter a word, or ask a question.

She did not tell me what followed immediately upon this, nor how soon after she spoke on the subject with either of the parties. She first began to speak of conversations afterward held with Lord Byron, in which he boldly avow r ed the connection as having existed in time past, and as one that was to continue in time to come ; and implied that she must submit to it. She put it to his conscience as concerning his sister's soul, and he said that it was no sin ; that it was the way the world was first peopled : the Scrip tures taught that all the world descended from one pair ; and how could that be unless brothers married their sisters ? that, if not a sin then, it could not be a sin now.

I immediately said, " Why, Lady Byron, those are the very arguments given in the drama of ' Cain.' "

" The very same," was her reply. " He could reason very speciously on this subject." She went on to say, that, when she pressed him hard with the universal sentiment of mankind as to the horror and the crime, he took another turn, and said that the horror and crime were the very attraction ; that he had worn out all ordinary forms of sin, and that he " longed for the stimu lus of a new kind of vice" She set before him the dread of detection ; and then he became furious. She should never be the means of his detection, he said. She should leave him ; that he was resolved upon : but she should always bear all the blame of the separation. In the sneering tone which was common with him, he said, " The world will believe me, and it will not believe you. The world has made up its mind that ' By' is a glorious boy ; and the world will go for ' By,' right or wrong. Besides, I shall make it my life's object to discredit you : I shall use all my powers. Read ' Caleb Williams,' * and you will see that I shall do by you just as Falkland did by Caleb."

* This novel of Godwin's is a remarkably powerful story. It is related in the first person by the supposed hero, Caleb Williams. He represents

I said that all this seemed to me like insanity. She said that she was for a time led to think that it was insanity, and excused and pitied him ; that his treatment of her expressed such hatred and malignity, that she knew not what else to think of it; that he seemed resolved to drive her out of the house at all hazards, and

himself as private secretary to a gentleman of high family named Falkland. Caleb accidentally discovers that his patron has, in a moment of passion, committed a murder. Falkland confesses the crime to Caleb, and tells him that henceforth he shall always suspect him, and keep watch over him. Caleb finds this watchfulness insupportable, and tries to escape, but without success. He writes a touching letter to his patron, imploring him to let him go, and promising never to betray him. The scene where Falkland refuses this is the most highly wrought in the book. He says to him, " Do not im-gine that I am afraid of you ! I wear an armor against which all your weapons are impotent. I have dug a pit for you; and whichever way you move, backward or forward, to the right or the left, it is ready to swallow you. Be still! If once you Fall, call as loud as you will, no man on earth shall hear your cries : prepare a tale however plausible or however true, the whole world shall execrate you for an impostor. Your innocence shall be of no ser vice to you. I laugh at so feeble a defence. It is I that say it : you may believe what I tell you. Do you know, miserable wretch! " added he, stamping on the ground with fury, " that I have sworn to preserve my repu tation, whatever be the expense ; that I love it more than the whole world and its inhabitants taken together? and do you think that you shall wound it?" The rest of the book shows how this threat was executed.

threatened her, if she should remain, in a way to alarm the heart of any woman : yet, think ing him insane, she left him at last with the sorrow with which any one might leave a dear friend whose reason was wholly overthrown, and to whom in this desolation she was no longer permitted to minister.

i inquired in one of the pauses of the con versation whether Mrs. Leigh was a peculiarly beautiful or attractive woman.

" No, my dear: she was plain."

" Was she, then, distinguished for genius or talent of any kind ? "

" Oh, no ! Poor woman ! she was weak, rela tively, to him, and wholly under his control."

" And what became of her ?" I said.

" She afterwards repented, and became a truly good woman." I think it was here she men tioned that she had frequently seen and con versed with Mrs. Leigh in the latter part of her life ; and she seemed to derive comfort from the recollection.

246 LADY BYRON'S STORY AS TOLD ME.

I asked, " Was there a child ?" I had been

told by Mrs. that there was a daughter,

who had lived some years.

She said there was one, a daughter, who made her friends much trouble, being of a very difficult nature to manage. I had understood that at one time this daughter escaped from her friends to the Continent, and that Lady Byron assisted in efforts to recover her. Of Lady Byron's kindness both to Mrs. Leigh and the

child, I had before heard from Mrs. , who

gave me my first information.

It is also strongly impressed on my mind, that Lady Byron, in answer to some question of mine as to whether there was ever any meeting between Lord Byron and his sister after he left England, answered, that she had insisted upon it, or made it a condition, that Mrs. Leigh should not go abroad to him.

When the conversation as to events was over, as I stood musing, I said, " Have you no evi dence that he repented ?" and alluded to the

mystery of his death, and the message he en deavored to utter.

She answered quickly, and with great decision, that, whatever might have been his meaning at that hour, she felt sure he had finally repented ; and added with great earnestness, " I do not believe that any child of the heavenly Father is ever left to eternal sin."

I said that such a hope was most delightful to my feelings, but that I had always regarded the indulgence of it as a dangerous one.

Her look, voice, and manner, at that moment, are indelibly fixed in my mind. She looked at me so sadly, so firmly, and said, —

" Danger, Mrs. Stowe ! What danger can come from indulging that hope, like the danger that comes from not having it ?"

I said in my turn, " What danger comes from not having it ? "

" The danger of losing all faith in God," she said, " all hope for others, all strength to try and save them. I once knew a lady," she added,

248 LADY BYRON'S STORY AS TOLD ME.

"who was in a state of scepticism and despair from belief in that doctrine. I think I saved her by giving her my faith."

I was silent; and she continued : " Lord Byron believed in eternal punishment fully: for, though he reasoned against Christianity as it is com monly received, he could not reason himself out of it; and I think it made him desperate. He used to say, 'The worst of it is, I do believe/ Had he seen God as I see him, I am sure his heart would have relented."

She went on to say, that his sins, great as they were, admitted of much palliation and excuse ; that he was the child of singular and ill-matched parents ; that he had an organization originally fine, but one capable equally of great good or great evil; that in his childhood he had only the worst and most fatal influences ; that he grew up into manhood with no guide ; that there was every thing in the classical course of the schools to develop an unhealthy growth of passion, and no moral influence of any kind to restrain it;

that the manners of his day were corrupt ; that what were now considered vices in society were then spoken of as matters of course among young noblemen ; that drinking, gaming, and licentiousness everywhere abounded; and that, up to a certain time, he was no worse than mul titudes of other young men of his day, — only that the vices of his day were worse for him. The excesses of passion, the disregard of physical laws in eating, drinking, and living, wrought effects on him that they did not on less sensitively organized frames, and prepared him for the evil hour when he fell into the sin which shaded his whole life. All the rest was a strug gle with its consequences, — sinning more and more to conceal the sin of the past. But she be lieved he never outlived remorse; that he al ways suffered ; and that this showed that God had not utterly forsaken him. Remorse, she said, always showed moral sensibility; and, while that remained, there was always hope.

She now began to speak of her grounds for

thinking it might be- her duty fully to publish this story before she left the world.

First she said, that, through the whole course of her life, she had felt the eternal value of truth, and seen how dreadful a thing was falsehood, and how fearful it was to be an accomplice in it, even by silence. Lord Byron had demoralized the moral sense of England, and he had done it in a great degree by the sympathy excited by falsehood. This had been pleaded in extenua tion of all his crimes and vices, and led to a low ering of the standard of morals in the literary world. Now it was proposed to print cheap edi tions of his works, and sell them among the com mon people, and interest them in him by the circulation of this same story.

She then said to this effect, that she believed in retribution and suffering in the future life, and that the consequences of sins here follow us there; and it was strongly impressed upon her mind that Lord Byron must suffer in looking on the evil consequences of what he had done in this

life, and in seeing the further extension of that evil.

" It has sometimes strongly appeared to me," she said, " that he cannot be at peace until this injustice has been righted. Such is the strong feeling that I have when I think of going where he is."

These things, she said, had led her to inquire whether it might not be her duty to make a full and clear disclosure before she left the world.

Of course, I did not listen to this story as one who was investigating its worth. I received it as truth. And the purpose for which it was communicated was not to enable me to prove it to the world, but to ask my opinion whether she should show it to the world before leaving it. The whole consultation was upon the assumption that she had at her command such proofs as could not be questioned.

Concerning what they were I did not minutely inquire: only, in answer to a general question,

she said that she had letters and documents in proof of her story. Knowing Lady Byron's strength of mind, her clear-headedness, her ac curate habits, and her perfect knowledge of the matter, I considered her judgment on this point decisive.

I told her that I would take the subject into consideration, and give my opinion in a few days. That night, after my sister and myself had re tired to our own apartment, I related to her the whole history, and we spent the night in talking of it. I was powerfully impressed with the jus tice and propriety of an immediate disclosure; while she, on the contrary, represented the painful consequences that would probably come upon Lady Byron from taking such a step.

Before we parted the next day, I requested Lady Byron to give me some memoranda of such dates and outlines of the general story as would enable me better to keep it in its connection ; which she did.

On giving me the paper, Lady Byron requested

me to return it to her when it had ceased to be of use to me for the purpose indicated.

Accordingly, a day or two after, I enclosed it to her in a hasty note, as I was then leaving London for Paris, and had not yet had time fully to consider the subject.

On reviewing my note, I can recall that then the whole history appeared to me like one of those singular cases where unnatural impulses to vice are the result of a taint of constitutional in sanity. This has always seemed to me the only way of accounting for instances of utterly mo tiveless and abnormal wickedness and cruelty. These my first impressions were expressed in the hasty note written at the time: —

" LONDON, Nov. 5, 1856.

" DEAREST FRIEND, — I return these. They have held mine eyes waking! How strange ! how unaccountable ! Have you ever subjected the facts to the judgment of a medical man learned in nervous pathology ?

" Is it not insanity ?

' Great wits to madness nearly are allied, And thin partitions do their bounds divide.'

" But my purpose to-night is not to write you fully what I think of this matter. I am going to write to you from Paris more at leisure."

The rest of the letter was taken up in the final details of a charity in which Lady Byron had been engaged with me in assisting an un fortunate artist. It concludes thus : —

" I write now in all haste, en route for Paris. As to America, all is not lost yet.* Farewell ! I love you, my dear friend, as never before, with an intense feeling I cannot easily express. God bless you ! " H. B. S."

The next letter is as follows : —

" PARIS, Dec. 17, 1856.

" DEAR LADY BYRON, — The Kansas Committee have written

me a letter desiring me to express to Miss their gratitude

for the five pounds she sent them. I am not personally ac quainted with her, and must return these acknowledgments through you.

" I wrote you a day or two since, enclosing the reply of the Kansas Committee to you.

" On that subject on which you spoke to me the last time we were together, I have thought often and deeply.

* Alluding to Buchanan's election.

" I have changed my mind somewhat.

"Considering the peculiar circumstances of the case, I could wish that the sacred veil of silence, so bravely thrown over the past, should never be withdrawn during the time that you remain with us.

" I would say, then, Leave all with some discreet friends, who, after both have passed from earth, shall say what was due to justice.

" I am led to think this by seeing how low, how unjust, how unworthy, the judgments of this world are ; and I would not that what I so much respect, love, and revere, should be placed within reach of its harpy claw, which pollutes what it touches.

"The day will yet come which will bring to light every hidden thing. ' There is nothing covered that shall not be revealed, neither hid that shall not be known;' and so justice •will not fail.

" Such, my dear friend, are my thoughts ; different from what they were since first I heard that strange, sad history. Mean while, I love you ever, whether we meet again on earth or not.

" Affectionately yours, " H. B. S."

The following letter will here be inserted as confirming a part of Lady Byron's story : —

To THE EDITOR OF "MACMILLAN'S MAGAZINE." " SIR, — 1 trust that you will hold me excused from any desire to be troublesome, or to rush into print. Both these

things are far from my wish. But the publication of a book having for its object the vindication of Lord Byron's character, and the subsequent appearance in your magazine of Mrs. Stowe's article in defence of Lady Byron, having led to so much controversy in the various newspapers of the day, I feel con strained to put in a few words among the rest.

" My father was intimately acquainted with Lady Byron's family for many years, both before and after her marriage ; being, in fact, steward to Sir Ralph Milbanke at Seaham, where the marriage took place : and, from all my recollections of what he told me of the affair (and he used often to talk of it, up to the time of his death, eight years ago), I fully agree with Mrs. Stowe's view of the case, and desire to add my humble testi mony to the truth of what she has stated.

" Whilst Byron was staying at Seaham, previous to his mar riage, he spent most of his time pistol-shooting in the planta tions adjoining the hall, often making use of his glove as a mark; his servant being with him to load for him.

" When all was in readiness for the wedding-ceremony (which took place in the drawing-room of the hall), Byron had to be sought for in the grounds, where he was walking in his usual surly mood.

" After the marriage, they posted to Halnaby Lodge in York shire, a distance of about forty miles ; to which place my father accompanied them, and he always spoke strongly of Lady By ron's apparent distress during and at the end of the journey.

" The insulting words mentioned by Mrs. Stowe were spoken

by Byron before leaving the park at Seaham; after which he appeared to sit in moody silence, reading a book, for the rest of the journey. At Halnaby, a number of persons, tenants and others, were met to cheer them on their arrival. Of these he took not the slightest notice, but jumped out of the carriage, and walked away, leaving his bride to alight by herself. She shook hands with my father, and begged that he would see that some refreshment was supplied to those who had thus come to welcome them.

" I have in my possession several letters (which I should be glad to show to any one interested in the matter) both from Lady Byron, and her mother, Lady Milbanke, to my father, all showing the deep and kind interest which they took in the welfare of all connected with them, and directing the distribu tion of various charities, &c. Pensions were allowed both to the old servants of the Milbankes and to several poor persons in the village and neighborhood for the rest of their lives ; and Lady Byron never ceased to take a lively interest in all that concerned them.

" I desire to tender my humble thanks to Mrs. Stowe for having come forward in defence of one whose character has been much misrepresented; and to you, sir, for having published the same in your pages.

" I have the honor to be, sir, yours obediently,

" G. H. AIRD.

"DAOURTY, NORTHAMPTONSHIRE, Sept. 29, 1869."

17

CHAPTER III.

CHRONOLOGICAL SUMMARY OF EVENTS.

T HAVE now fulfilled as conscientiously as possible the requests of those who feel that they have a right to know exactly what was said in this interview. •

It has been my object, in doing this, to place myself "just where I should stand were I giving evidence under oath before a legal tribunal. In my first published account, there were given some smaller details of the story, of no particu lar value to the main purpose of it, which I received, not from Lady Byron, but from her confidential friend. One of these was the ac count of her seeing Lord Byron's favorite span iel lying at his door, and the other was the scene of the parting. 258

The first was communicated to me before I ever saw Lady Byron, and under these circum stances : I was invited to meet her, and had expressed my desire to do so, because Lord Byron had been all my life an object of great interest to me. I inquired what sort of a per son Lady Byron was. My friend spoke of her with enthusiasm. I then said, " But of course she never loved Lord Byron, or she would not have left him." The lady answered, " I can show you with what feelings she left him by relating this story;" and then followed the anecdote.

Subsequently, she also related to me the other story of the parting-scene between Lord and Lady Byron. In regard to these two incidents, my recollection is clear.

It will be observed by the reader that Lady Byron's conversation with me was simply for consultation on one point, and that point whether she herself should publish the story before her death. It was not, therefore, a complete history

of all events in their order, but specimens of a few incidents and facts. Her object was, not to prove her story to me, nor to put me in posses sion of it with a view to my proving it, but sim ply and briefly to show me what it was, that I might judge as to the probable results of its pub lication at that time.

It therefore comprised primarily these points : —

1. An exact statement, in so many words, of the crime.

2. A statement of the manner in which it was first forced on her attention by Lord Byron's words and actions, including his admissions and defences of it.

3. The admission of a period when she had ascribed his whole conduct to insanity.

4. A reference to later positive evidences of guilt, — the existence of a child, and Mrs. Leigh's subsequent repentance.

And here I have a word to say in reference to the alleged inaccuracies of my true story.

The dates that Lady Byron gave me on the memoranda did not relate either to the time of the first disclosure, or the period when her doubts became certainties ; nor did her conversa tion touch either of these points : and, on a care ful review of the latter, I see clearly that it omitted dwelling upon any thing which I might be supposed to have learned from her already published statement.

I re-enclosed that paper to her from London, and have never seen it since.

In writing my account, which I designed to do in the most general terms, I took for my guide Miss Martineau's published Memoir of Lady Byron, w r hich has long stood uncontra- dicted before the public, of which Macmillan's London edition is now before me. The reader is referred to page 316, which reads thus: —

" She was born 1792 ; married in January, 1814; returned to her father's house in 1816 ; died on May 16, 1860." This makes her mar ried life two years ; but we need not say that

the date is inaccurate, as Lady Byron was mar ried in 1815.

Supposing Lady Byron's married life to have covered two years, I could only reconcile its continuance for that length of time to her un certainty as to his sanity; to deceptions prac tised on her, making her doubt at one time, and believe at another; and his keeping her in a general state of turmoil and confusion, till at last he took the step of banishing her.

Various other points taken from Miss Marti-neau have also been attacked as inaccuracies ; for example, the number of executions in the house : but these points, though of no impor tance, are substantially borne out by Moore's statements.

This controversy, unfortunately, cannot be managed with the accuracy of a legal trial. Its course, hitherto, has rather resembled the course of a drawing-room scandal, where every one freely throws in an assertion, with or without proof. In making out my narrative, however, I

shall use only certain authentic sources, some of which have for a long time been before the public, and some of which have floated up from the waves of the recent controversy. I consider as authentic sources, —

Moore's Life of Byron ;

Lady Byron's own account of the separation, published in 1830 ;

Lady Byron's statements to me in 1856 ;

Lord Lindsay's communication, giving an extract from Lady Anne Barnard's diary, and a copy of a letter from Lady Byron dated 1818, about three years after her marriage ;

Mrs. Minn's testimony as given in a daily paper published at Newcastle, England ;

And Lady Byron's letters, as given recently in the late " London Quarterly."

All which documents appear to arrange them selves into a connected series.

From these, then, let us construct the story.

According to Mrs. Minn's account, which is likely to be accurate, the time spent by Lord

and Lady Byron in bridal-visiting was three weeks at Halnaby Hall, and six weeks at Seaham, when Mrs. Minn quitted their ser vice.

During this first period of three weeks, Lord Byron's treatment of his wife, as testified to by the servant, was such that she advised her young mistress to return to her parents; and, at one time, Lady Byron had almost resolved to do so.

What the particulars of his conduct were, the servant refuses to state; being bound by a prom ise of silence to her mistress. She, however, testifies to a warm friendship existing between Lady Byron and Mrs. Leigh, in a manner which would lead us to feel that Lady Byron received and was received by Lord Byron's sister with the greatest affection. Lady Byron herself says to Lady Anne Barnard, " I had heard that he was the best of brothers ;" and the infer ence is, that she, at an early period of her mar ried life, felt the .greatest confidence in his sister,

and wished to have her with them as much as possible. In Lady Anne's account, this wish to have the sister with her was increased by Lady Byron's distress at her husband's attempts to corrupt her principles with regard to religion and marriage.

In Moore's Life, vol. iii., letter 217, Lord By ron writes from Seaham to Moore, under date of March 8, sending a copy of his verses in Lady Byron's handwriting, and saying, " We shall leave this place to-morrow, and shall stop on our way to town, in the interval of taking a house there, at Col. Leigh's, near Newmarket, where any epistle of yours will find its welcome way. I have been very comfortable here, listen ing to that d d monologue which elderly gentlemen call conversation, in which my pious father-in-law repeats himself every evening, save one, when he played upon the fiddle. However, they have been vastly kind and hospitable, and I like them and the place vastly ; and I hope they will live many happy months. Bell is in

health and unvaried good-humor and behavior ; but we are in all the agonies of packing and parting."

Nine days after this, under date of March 17, Lord Byron says, " We mean to metropolize to-morrow, and you will address your next to Piccadilly." The inference is, that the days intermediate were spent at Col. Leigh's. The next letters, and all subsequent ones for six months, are dated from Piccadilly.

As we have shown, there is every reason to believe that a warm friendship had thus arisen between Mrs. Leigh and Lady Byron, and that, during all this time, Lady Byron desired as much of the society of her sister-in-law as pos sible. She was a married woman and a mother, her husband's nearest relative ; and Lady Byron could with more propriety ask, from her r counsel or aid in respect to his "peculiarities than she could from her own parents. If we consider the character of Lady Byron as given by Mrs. Minns, — that of a young person of warm but

repressed feeling, without sister or brother, long ing for human sympathy, and having so far found no relief but' in talking with a faithful depend ant, — we may easily see that the acquisition of a sister through Lord Byron might have been all in all to her, and that the feelings which he checked and rejected for himself might have flowed out towards his sister with enthusiasm. The date of Mrs. Leigh's visit does not appear.

The first domestic indication in Lord Byron's letters from London is the announcement of the death of Lady Byron's uncle, Lord Wentworth, from whom came large expectations of property. Lord Byron had. mentioned him before in his letters as so kind to Bell and himself, that he could not find it in his heart to wish him- in heaven if he preferred staying here. In his let ter of April 23, he mentions going to the play immediately after hearing this news, " although," as he says, " he ought to have staid at home in sackcloth for ' unc.' "

On June 12, he writes that Lady Byron is

more than three months advanced in her prog ress towards maternity; and that they have been out very little, as he wishes to keep her quiet. We are informed by Moore that Lord Byron was at this time a member of the Drury-Lane Theatre Committee ; and that, in this unlucky connection, one of the fatalities of the first year of trial as a husband lay. From the strain of Byron's letters, as given in Moore, it is appar ent, that, while he thinks it best for his wife to remain at home, he does not propose to share the retirement, but prefers running his own sep arate career with such persons as thronged the greenroom of the theatre in those days.

In commenting on Lord Byron's course, we must not by any means be supposed to indicate that he was doing any more or worse than most gay young men of his time. The license of the day as to getting drunk at dinner-parties, and leading, generally, what would, in these days, be called a disorderly life, was great. We should infer that none of the literary men of Byron's

time would have been ashamed of being drunk occasionally. The Noctes Ambrosianae Club of " Blackwood " is full of songs glorying, in the broadest terms, in out-and-out drunkenness, and inviting to it as the highest condition of a civil ized being.*

But drunkenness upon Lord Byron had a peculiar and specific effect, which he notices afterwards, in his Journal, at Venice : " The

*

effect of all wines and spirits upon me is, how ever, strange. It settles, but makes me gloomy, — gloomy at the very moment of their'effect: it composes, however, though sullenly" f And again, in another place, he says, " Wine and spirits make me sullen, and savage to ferocity."

* Shelton Mackenzie, in a note to the " Noctes " of July, 1822, gives the following saying of Maginn, one of the principal lights of the club: " No man, however much he might tend to civilization, was to be regarded as having absolutely reached its apex until he was drunk." He also records it as a further joke of the club, that a man's having reached this apex was to be tested by his inability to pronounce the -word " civilization," which, he says, after ten o'clock at night ought to be abridged to civilation, " by syn cope, or vigorously speaking by hic-cup."

t Vol. v. pp. 61, 75.

It is well known that the effects of alcoholic excitement are various as the natures of the subjects. But by far the worst effects, and the most destructive to domestic peace, are those that occur in cases where spirits, instead of act ing on the nerves of motion, and depriving the subject of power in that direction, stimulate the brain so as to produce there the ferocity, the steadiness, the utter deadness to compassion or conscience, which characterize a madman. How fearful to a sensitive young mother in the period of pregnancy might be the return of such a mad man to the domestic roof! Nor can we account for those scenes described in Lady Anne Bar nard's letters, where Lord Byron returned from his evening parties to try torturing experiments on his wife, otherwise than by his own state ment, that spirits, while they steadied "him, made him " gloomy, and savage to ferocity." Take for example this : —

" One night, coming home from one of his lawless parties, he saw me (Lady B.) so indignantly collected, and bearing all

with such a determined calmness, that a rush of remorse seemed to come over him. He called himself a monster, and, though his sister was present, threw himself in agony at my feet. ' I could not, no, I could not, forgiVe him such injuries ! He had lost me forever !' Astonished at this return to virtue, my tears, I believe, flowed over his face; and I said, ' Byron, all is forgotten : never, never shall you hear of it more.'

" He started up, and, folding his arms while he looked at me, burst out into laughter. 'What do you mean?' said I. < Only a philosophical experiment; that's all,' said he. ' I wished to ascertain the value of your resolutions.'"

To ascribe such deliberate cruelty as this to the effect of drink upon Lord Byron, is the most charitable construction that can be put upon his conduct.

Yet the manners of the period were such, that Lord Byron must have often come to this condition while only doing what many of his acquaintances did freely, and without fear of consequences.

Mr. Moore, with his usual artlessness, gives us an idea of a private supper between himself and Lord Byron. We give it, with our own Italics, as a specimen of many others : —

" Having taken upon me to order the repast, and knowing that Lord Byron for the last two days had done nothing towards sustenance beyond eating a few biscuits and (to appease appetite) chewing mastic, I desired that we should have a good supply of at least two kinds of fish. My com panion, however, confined himself to lobsters ; and of these finished two or three, to his own share, interposing, some times, a small liqueur-glass of strong white brandy, sometimes a tumbler of very hot water, and then pure brandy again, to the amount of near half a dozen small glasses of the latter, without which, alternately with the hot water, he appeared to think the lobster could not be digested. After this, we had claret, of which, having despatched two bottles between us, at about four o'clock in the morning we parted.

" As Pope has thought his ' delicious lobster-nights' worth commemorating, these particulars of one in which Lord Byron was concerned may also have some interest.

" Among other nights of the same description which I had the happiness of passing -with him, I remember once, in returning home from some assembly at rather a late hour, we saw lights in the windows of his old haunt, Stevens's in Bond Street, and agreed to stop there and sup. On entering, we found an old

friend of his, Sir G W , who joined our party; and, the

lobsters and brandy and water being put in requisition, it was (as usual on such occasions] broad daylight before we separated.' 1 " — Vol. iii. p. 83.

CHRONOLOGICAL SUMMARY OF EVENTS. 2/3

During the latter part of Lady Byron's preg nancy, it appears from Moore that Byron was, night after night, engaged out at dinner-parties, in which getting drunk was considered as of course \^Q finale, as appears from the following letters : —

[LETTER 228.] TO MR. MOORE.

"TERRACE, PICCADILLY, Oct. 31, 1815.

p

"I have not been able to ascertain precisely the time of duration of the stock-market; but I believe it is a good time for selling out, and I hope so. First, because I shall see you; and, next, because I shall receive certain moneys on behalf of Lady B., the which will materially conduce to my comfort; I wanting (as the duns say) ' to make up a sum.'

" Yesterday I dined out with a large-ish party, where were Sheridan and Colman, Harry Harris of C. G., and his brother, Sir Gilbert Heathcote, Ds. Kinnaird, and others of note and notoriety. Like other parties of the kind, it was Jirst silent, then talky, then argumentative, then disputatious % then imintelligible* then altogethery, then inarticulate, and then drunk. When we had reached the last step of this glorious ladder, it was difficult to get down again without stumbling; and, to crown all, Kin naird and I had to conduct Sheridan down a d d corkscrew

staircase, which had certainly been constructed before the dis-

* These Italics are ours. 18

2/4 CHRONOLOGICAL SUMMARY OF EVENTS.

covery of fermented liquors, and to which no legs, however crooked, could possibly accommodate themselves. We deposited him safe at home, where his man, evidently used to the business,* waited to receive him in the hall.

" Both he and Colman were, as usual, very good ; but I carried away much wine, and the wine had previously carried away my memory : so that all was hiccough and happiness for the last hour or so, and I am not impregnated with any of the con versation. Perhaps you heard of a late answer of Sheridan to the watchman who found him bereft of that 'divine particle of air' called reason. . . . He (the watchman) found Sherry in the street, fuddled and bewildered, and almost insensible. ' Who are you, sir ?' — No answer. ' What's your name ?' — A hiccough. ' What's your name ?' — Answer, in a slow, deliber ate, and impassive tone, ' Wilberforce !' Is not that Sherry all over ? — and, to my mind, excellent. Poor fellow ! his very dregs are better than the ' first sprightly runnings' of others.

" My paper is full, and I have a grievous headache.

" P.S. — Lady B. is in full progress. Next month will bring to light (with the aid of 'Juno Lucina, fer opem? or rather opes, for the last are most wanted) the tenth wonder of the world ; Gil Bias being the eighth, and he (my son's father) the ninth."

Here we have a picture of the whole story, — Lady Byron within a month of her confinement;

* These Italics are ours.

her money being used to settle debts ; her hus band out at a dinner-party, going through the iisual course of such parties, able to keep his legs and help Sheridan down stairs, and going home " gloomy, and savage to ferocity," to his wife.

Four days after this (letter 229), we find that this dinner-party is not an exceptional one, but one of a series : for he says, " To-day I dine with Kinnaird, — we are to have Sheridan and Colman again ; and to-morrow, once more, at Sir Gilbert Heathcote's."

Afterward, in Venice, he reviews the state of his health at this period in London ; and his account shows that his excesses in the vices of his times had wrought effects on his sensitive, nervous organization, very different from what they might on the more phlegmatic constitutions of ordinary Englishmen. In his journal, dated Venice, Feb. 2, 1821, he says,—

" I have been considering what can be the reason why I always wake at a certain hour in the morning, and always in

very bad spirits, — I may say, in actual despair and despond ency, in all respects, even of that which pleased me over night. In about an hour or two this goes off, and I compose either to sleep again, or at least to quiet. In England, five years ago, I had the same kind of hypochondria, but accompanied with so violent a thirst, that I have drunk as many as fifteen bottles of soda-water in one night, after going to bed, and been still thirsty, —calculating, however, some lost from the bursting-out and effervescence and overflowing of the soda-water in drawing the corks, or striking off the necks of the bottles from mere thirsty impatience. At present, I have not the thirst; but the depression of spirits is no less violent." — Vol. v. p. 96.

These extracts go to show what mtist have been the condition of the man whom Lady Byron was called to receive at the intervals when he came back from his various social excitements and pleasures. That his nerves were exacer bated by violent extremes of abstinence and reckless indulgence; that he was often day after day drunk, and that drunkenness made him savage and ferocious,—-such are the facts clearly shown by Mr. Moore's narrative. Of the natural peculiarities of Lord Byron's tern-

per, he thus speaks to the Countess of Blessing-ton : —

" I often think that I inherit my violence and bad temper from my poor mother, — not that my father, from all I could ever learn, had a much better : so that it is no wonder I have such a very bad one. As long as I can remember any thing, I recollect being subject to violent paroxysms of rage, so dispro-portioned to the cause as to surprise me when they were over; and this still continues. I eannot coolly view any thing which excites my feelings; and, once the lurking devil in me is roused, I lose all command of myself. I do not recover a good fit of rage for days after. Mind, I do not by this mean that the ill humor continues, as, on the contrary, that quickly subsides, ex hausted by its own violence ; but it shakes me terribly, and leaves me low and nervous after." — Lady Blessington's Conver sations, p. 142.

That during this time also his irritation and ill temper were increased by the mortification of duns, debts, and executions, is on the face of Moore's story. Moore himself relates one inci dent, which gives some idea of the many which may have occurred at these times, in a note on p. 215, vol. iv., where he speaks of Lord Byron's destroying a favorite old watch that had been his companion from boyhood, and gone with him to Greece. " In a fit of vexation and rage, brought upon him by some of these humiliating embarrassments, to which he was now almost daily a prey, he furiously dashed this watch on the hearth, and ground it to pieces with the poker among the ashes."

It is no wonder, that, with a man of this kind to manage, Lady Byron should have clung to the only female companionship she could dare to trust in the case, and earnestly desired" to retain with her the sister, who seemed, more than her self, to have influence over him.

The first letter given by " The Quarterly," from Lady Byron to Mrs. Leigh, without a date, evidently belongs to this period, when the sister's society presented itself as a refuge in her ap proaching confinement. Mrs. Leigh speaks of leaving. The young wife, conscious that the house presents no attractions, and that soon she herself shall be laid by, cannot urge Mrs. Leigh's stay as likely to give her any pleasure, but only as a comfort to herself.

" You will think me very foolish ; but I have tried two or three times, and cannot talk to you of your departure with a decent visage : so let me say one word in this way to spare my philosophy. With the expectations which I have, I never will nor can ask you to stay one moment longer than you are in clined to do. It would [be] the worst return for all I ever received from you. But in this at least I am ' truth itself,' when I say, that, whatever the situation may be, there is no one whose society is dearer to me, or can contribute more to my happiness. These feelings will not change under any cir cumstances, and I should be grieved if you did not understand them. Should you hereafter condemn me, I shall not love you less. I will say no more. Judge for yourself about going or staying. I wish you to consider yourself, if you could be wise enough to do that, for the first time in your life.

" Thine, " A. I. B."

Addressed on the cover, " To The Hon. Mrs. Leigh."

This letter not being dated, we have no clew but what we obtain from its own internal evi dence. It certainly is not written in Lady By ron's usual, clear, and elegant style ; and is, in this respect, in striking contrast to all her letters that I have ever seen.

But the notes written by a young woman under

such peculiar and distressing circumstances must not be judged by the standard of calmer'hours.

Subsequently to this letter, and during that stormy irrational period when Lord Byron's conduct became daily more and more unaccount able, may have come that startling scene in which Lord Byron took every pains to convince his wife of improper relations subsisting between himself and his sister.

What an utter desolation this must have been to the wife, tearing from her the last hold of friendship, and the last refuge to which she had clung in her sorrows, may easily be conceived.

In this crisis, it appears that the sister con vinced Lady Byron that the whole was to be attributed to insanity. It would be a convic tion gladly accepted, and bringing infinite relief, although still surrounding her path with fearful difficulties.

That such was the case, is plainly asserted by Lady Byron in her statement published in 1830. Speaking of her separation, Lady Byron says, —

" The facts are, I left London for Kirkby Mallory, the resi dence of my father and mother, on the I5th of January, 1816. Lord Byron had signified to me in writing, Jan. 6, his absolute desire that I should leave London on the earliest day that I could conveniently fix. It was not safe for me to encounter the fatigues of a journey sooner than the I5th. Previously to my departtire, it had been strongly impressed on my mind tJiat Lord Byron was under the influence of insanity.

" This opinion was in a great measure derived from the com munications made to me by his nearest relatives and personal attendant."

Now, there was no nearer relative than Mrs. Leigh; and the personal attendant was Fletcher. It was therefore presumably Mrs. Leigh who convinced Lady Byron of her husband's insan ity.

Lady Byron says, " It was even represented to me that he was in danger of destroying him self.

" With the concurrence of his family, I had consulted with Dr. Baillie, as a friend, on Jan. 8, as to his supposed malady." Now, Lord Byron's written order for her to leave came on Jan. 6.

It appears, then, that Lady Byron, acting in con currence with Mrs. Leigh and others of her hus band's family, consulted Dr. Baillie, on Jan. 8, as to what she should do ; the symptoms pre sented to Dr. Baillie being, evidently, insane hatred of his wife on the part of Lord Byron, and a determination to get her out of the house. Lady Byron goes on : —

" On acquainting him with the state of the case, and with Lord Byron's desire that I should leave London, Dr. Baillie thought my absence might be advisable as an experiment, assuming the fact of mental derangement; for Dr. Baillie, not having had access to Lord Byron, could not pronounce an opin ion on that point. He enjoined, that, in correspondence with Lord Byron, I should avoid all but light and soothing topics. Under these impressions, I left London, determined to follow the advice given me by Dr. Baillie. Whatever might have been the nature of Lord Byron's treatment of me from the time of my marriage, yet, supposing him to have been in a state of mental alienation, it was not for me, nor for any person of com mon humanity, to manifest at that moment a sense of injury."

It appears, then, that the domestic situation in Byron's house at the time of his wife's expulsion

was one so grave as to call for family counsel; for Lady Byron, generally accurate, speaks in the plural number. " His nearest relatives" certainly includes Mrs. Leigh. " His family" includes more. That some of Lord Byron's own relatives were cognizant of facts at this time, and that they took Lady Byron's side, is shown by one of his own *chance admissions. In vol. vi. p, 394, in a letter on Bowles, he says, speak ing of this time, " All my relations, save one, fell from me like leaves from a tree in autumn." And in Medwin's Conversations he says, " Even my cousin George Byron, who had been brought up with me, and whom I loved as a brother, took my wife's part." The conduct must have been marked in the extreme that led to this result.

We cannot help stopping here to say that Lady Byron's situation at. this time has been discussed in our days with a want of ordinary human feeling that is surprising. Let any father and mother, reading this, look on their own daughter, and try to make the case their own.

After a few short months of married life, — months full of patient endurance of the stran gest and most unaccountable treatment, — she comes to them, expelled from her husband's house, an object of hatred and aversion to him, and having to settle for herself the awful ques tion, whether he is a dangerous madman or a determined villain.

Such was this young wife's situation.

With a heart at times wrung with compassion for her husband as a helpless maniac, and fearful that all may end in suicide, yet compelled to leave him, she writes on the road the much-quoted letter, beginning " Dear Duck." This is an exaggerated and unnatural letter, it is true, but of precisely the character that might be ex pected from an inexperienced young wife when dealing with a husband supposed to be insane.

The next day,- she addressed to Augusta this letter : —

" MY DEAREST A., — It is my great comfort that you are still in Piccadilly."

And again, on the 23d : —

" DEAREST A., — I know you feel for me, as I do for you ; and perhaps I am better understood than I think. You have been, ever since I knew you, my best comforter; and will so re main, unless you grow tired of the office, — which may well be."

We can see here how self-denying and heroic appears to Lady Byron the conduct of the sister, who patiently remains to soothe and guide and restrain the moody madman, whose madness takes a form, at times, so repulsive to every wo manly feeling. She intimates that she should not wonder should Augusta grow weary of the office.

Lady Byron continues her statement thus : —

" When I arrived at Kirkby Mallory, my parents were unac quainted with the existence of any causes likely to destroy my prospects of happiness ; and, when I communicated to them the opinion that had been formed concerning Lord Byron's state of mind, they were most anxious to promote his restora tion by every means in their power. They assured those rela tions that were with him in London that ' they would devote their whole care and attention to the alleviation of his malady.' "

Here we have a quotation * from a letter written by Lady Milbanke to the anxious " rela tions " who are taking counsel about "Lord Byron in town. Lady Byron also adds, in justification of her mother from Lord Byron's slanders, " She had always treated him with an affectionate consideration and indulgence, which extended to every little peculiarity of his feelings. Never did an irritating word es cape her lips in her whole intercourse with him."

Now comes a remarkable part of Lady Byron's statement: —

" The accounts given me after I left Lord Byron, by those in constant intercourse with him,t added to those doubts

* This little incident shows the characteristic carefulness and accuracy of Lady Byron's habits. This statement was written fourteen years after the events spoken of; but Lady Byron carefully quotes a passage from her mother's letter written at that time. This shows that a copy of Lady Mil-banke's letter had been preserved, and makes it appear probable that copies of the whole correspondence of that period were also kept. Great light could be thrown on the whole transaction, could these documents be consulted.

t Here, again, Lady Byron's sealed papers might furnish light. The letters addressed to her at this time by those in constant intercourse with Lord Byron are doubtless preserved, and would show her ground of action.

which had before transiently occurred to my mind as to the reality of the alleged disease; and the reports of his medical attendants were far from establishing any thing like lunacy."

When these doubts arose in her mind, it is not natural to suppose, that they should, at first, involve Mrs. Leigh. She still appears to Lady Byron as the devoted, believing sister, fully con vinced of her brother's insanity, and endeavor ing to restrain and control him.

But if Lord Byron were sane, if the purposes he had avowed to his wife were real, he must have lied about his sister in the past, and per haps have the worst intentions for the future.

The horrors of that state of vacillation be tween the conviction of insanity and the com mencing conviction of something worse can scarcely be told.

At all events, the wife's doubts extend so far, that she speaks out to her parents. " UNDER THIS UNCERTAINTY," says the statement, " I deemed it right to communicate to my parents, that, if I were to consider Lord Byron's past

conduct as that of a person of sound mind, nothing could induce me to return to him. It therefore appeared expedient, both to them and to myself, to consult the ablest advisers. For that object, and also to obtain still further infor mation respecting appearances which indicated

mental derangement, my mother determined to

•* go to London. She was empowered by me to

take legal opinion on a written statement of mine; though I then had reasons for reserving a part of the case from the knowledge even of my father and mother!'

It is during this time of uncertainty that the next letter to Mrs. Leigh may be placed. It seems to be rather a fragment of a letter than a whole one: perhaps it is an extract; in which case it would be desirable, if possible, to view it in connection with the remaining text : —

"JAN. 25, 1816.

" MY DEAREST AUGUSTA, — Shall I still be your sister ? I must resign my rights to be so considered ; but I don't think that will make any difference in the kindness I have so uni formly experienced from you."

This fragment is not signed, nor finished in any way, but indicates that the writer is about to take a decisive step.

On the i/th, as we have seen, Lady Milbanke had written, inviting Lord Byron. Subsequently, she went to London to make more particular inquiries into his state. This fragment seems part of a letter from Lady Byron, called forth in view of some evidence resulting from her moth er's observations.*

Lady Byron now adds, —

" Being convinced by the result of these inquiries, and by the tenor of Lord Byron's proceedings, that the notion of in sanity was an illusion, I no longer hesitated to authorize such measures as were necessary in order to secure me from ever being again placed in his power.

" Conformably with this resolution, my father wrote to him, on the 2d of February, to request an amicable separation."

The following letter to Mrs. Leigh is dated the day after this application, and is in many respects a noticeable one : —

* Probably Lady Milbanke's letters are among the sealed papers, and would more fully explain the situation. 19

" KIRKBY MALLORY, Feb. 3, 1816.

" MY DEAREST. AUGUSTA, — You are desired by your broth er to ask if my father has acted with my concurrence in pro posing a separation. He has. It cannot be supposed, that, in my present distressing situation, I am capable of stating in a detailed manner the reasons which will not only justify this measure, but compel me to take it ; and it never can be my wish to remember Tinnecessarily \sic\ those injuries for which, however deep, I feel no resentment I will now only recall to Lord Byron's mind his avowed and insurmountable aversion to the married state, and the desire and determination he has expressed ever since its commencement to free himself from that bondage, as finding it quite insupportable, though can didly acknowledging that no effort of duty or affection has been wanting on my part. He has too painfully convinced me that all these attempts to contribute towards his happiness were wholly useless, and most unwelcome to him. I enclose this letter to my father, wishing it to receive his sanction. " Ever yours most affectionately,

" A. I. BYRON."

We observe in this letter that it is written to be shown to Lady Byron's father, and receive his sanction ; and, as that father was in ignorance of all the deeper causes of trouble in the case, it will be seen that the letter must necessarily be

a reserved one. This sufficiently accounts for the guarded character of the language when speaking of the causes of separation. One part of the letter incidentally overthrows Lord By ron's statement, which he always repeated dur ing his life, and which is repeated for him now ; namely, that his wife forsook him, instead of being, as she claims, expelled by him.

She recalls to Lord Byron's mind the " desire and determination he has expressed ever since his marriage to free himself from its bondage."

This is in perfect keeping with the " absolute desire," signified by writing, that she should leave his house on the earliest day possible ; and she places the cause of the separation on his having " too painfully " convinced her that he does not want her — as a wife.

It appears that Augusta hesitates to show this note to her brother. It is bringing on a crisis which she, above all others, would most wish to avoid.

In the mean time, Lady Byron receives a let-

ter from Lord Byron, which makes her feel it more than ever essential to make the decision final. I have reason to believe that this letter is preserved in Lady Byron's papers : —

" FEB. 4, 1816.

" I hope, my dear A., that you would on no account withhold from your brother the letter which I sent yesterday in answer to yours written by his desire, particularly as one which I have received from himself to-day renders it still more important that he should know the contents of that addressed to you. I am, in haste and not very well,

" Yours most affectionately,

"A. I. BYRON."

The last of this series of letters is less like the style, of Lady Byron than any of them. We cannot judge whether it is a whole consecutive letter, or fragments from a letter, selected and united. There is a great want of that clearness and precision which usually characterized Lady Byron's style. It shows, however, that the de cision is made, — a decision which she regrets on account of the sister who has tried so long to prevent it.

" KIRKBY MALLORY, Feb. 14, 1816.

"The present sufferings of all may yet be repaid in bless ings. Do not despair absolutely, dearest; and leave me but enough of your interest to afford you any consolation by par taking of that sorrow which I am most unhappy to cause thus unintentionally. You will be of my opinion hereafter ; and at present your bitterest reproach would be forgiven, though Heaven knows you have considered me more than a thousand would have done, —more than any thing but my affection for B., one most dear to you, could deserve. I must not remember these feelings. Farewell! God bless you from the bottom of my heart ! " A. I. B."

We are here to consider that Mrs. Leigh has stood to Lady Byron in all this long agony as her only confidante and friend ; that she has denied the charges her brother has made, and referred them to insanity, admitting insane at tempts upon herself which she has been obliged to watch over and control.

Lady Byron has come to the conclusion that Augusta is mistaken as to insanity; that there is a real wicked purpose and desire on the part of the brother, not as yet believed in by the sis-

ter. She regards the sister as one, who, though deceived and blinded, is still worthy of confi dence and consideration ; and so says to her, " You will be of my opinion hereafter"

She says, " You have considered me more than a thousand would have done." Mrs. Leigh is, in Lady Byron's eyes, a most abused and innocent woman, who, to spare her sister in her delicate situation, has taken on herself the whole charge of a maniacal brother, although suffering from him language and actions of the most inju rious kind. That Mrs. Leigh did not flee the house at once under such circumstances, and wholly decline the management of the case, seems to Lady Byron consideration and self-sacrifice greater than she can acknowledge.

The knowledge of the whole extent of the truth came to Lady Byron's mind at a later period.

We now take up the history from Lushing-ton's letter to Lady Byron, published at the close of her statement.

The application to Lord Byron for an act of separation was positively refused at first; it being an important part of his policy that all the responsibility and insistance should come from his wife, and that he should appear forced into it contrary to his will.

Dr. Lushington, however, says to Lady By ron,—

" I was originally consulted by Lady Noel on your behalf while you were in the country. The circumstances detailed by her were such as justified a separation ; but they were not of that aggravated description as to render such a measure indis pensable. On Lady Noel's representations, I deemed a reconciliation with Lord Byron practicable, and felt most sin cerely a wish to aid in effecting it. There was not, on Lady Noel's part, any exaggeration of the facts, nor, so far as I could perceive, any determination to prevent a return to Lord Byron : certainly none was expressed when I spoke of a recon ciliation."

In this crisis, with Lord Byron refusing the separation, with Lushington expressing a wish to aid in a reconciliation, and Lady Noel not ex pressing any aversion to it, the whole strain of

the dreadful responsibility comes upon the wife. She resolves to ask counsel of her lawyer, in view of a statement of the whole case.

Lady Byron is spoken of by Lord Byron (letter 233) as being in town with her father on the 29th of February ; viz., fifteen days after the date of the last letter to Mrs. Leigh. It must have been about this time, then, that she laid her whole case before Lushington ; and he gave it a thorough examination.

The result was, that Lushington expressed in the most decided terms his conviction that rec onciliation was impossible. The language he uses is very striking : —

" When you came to town in about a fortnight, or perhaps more, after my first interview with Lady Noel, I was, for the first time, informed by you of facts utterly unknown, as I have no doubt, to Sir Ralph and Lady Noel. On receiving this ad ditional information, my opinion was entirely changed. I con sidered a reconciliation impossible. I declared my opinion, and added, that, if such an idea should be entertained, I could not, either professionally or otherwise, take any part towards effecting it."

It does not appear in this note what effect the lawyer's examination of the case had on

Lady Byron's mind. By the expressions he uses, we should infer that she may still have been hesi tating as to whether a reconciliation might not be her duty.

This hesitancy he does away with most deci sively, saying, " A reconciliation is impossible ; " and, supposing Lady Byron or her friends desi rous of one, he declares positively that he can not, either professionally as a lawyer or privately as a friend, have any thing to do with effect ing it.

The lawyer, it appears, has drawn, from the facts of the case, inferences deeper and stronger than those which presented themselves to the mind of the young woman ; and he instructs her in the most absolute terms.

Fourteen years after, in 1830, for the first time the world was astonished by this declara tion from Dr. Lushington, in language so pro nounced and positive, that there could be no mistake.

298 CHRONOLOGICAL SUMMARY OF EVENTS.

Lady Byron had stood all these fourteen years slandered by her husband, and misunderstood by his friends, when, had she so chosen, this opinion of Dr. Lushington's could have been at once made public, which fully justified her con duct.

If, as the "Blackwood" of July insinuates, the story told to Lushington was a malignant slan der, meant to injure Lord Byron, why did she suppress the judgment of her counsel at a time when all the world was on her side, and this decision would have been the decisive blow against her husband ? Why, by sealing the lips of counsel, and of all whom she could influence, did she deprive herself finally of the very advan tage for which it has been assumed she fabri cated the story ?

CHAPTER IV.

THE CHARACTER OF THE TWO WITNESSES COMPARED.

T T will be observed, that, in this controversy, we are confronting two opposing stories, — one of Lord and the other of Lady Byron; and the statements from each are in point-blank con tradiction.

Lord Byron states that his wife deserted him. Lady Byron states that he expelled her, and re minds him, in her letter to Augusta Leigh, that the expulsion was a deliberate one, and that he had purposed it from the beginning of their marriage.

Lord Byron always stated that he was ignorant why his wife left him, and was desirous of her return. Lady Byron states that he told her that he would force her to leave him, and to leave him in such a way that the whole blame of the separation should always rest on her, and not on him.

To say nothing of any deeper or darker accu sations on either side, here, in the very outworks of the story, the two meet point-blank.

In considering two opposing stories, we al ways, as a matter of fact, take into account the character of the witnesses.

If a person be literal and exact in his usual modes of speech, reserved, careful, conscientious, and in the habit of observing minutely the minor details of time, place, and circumstances, we give weight to his testimony from these considera tions. But if a person be proved to have singular and exceptional principles with regard to truth ; if he be universally held by society to be so in the habit of mystification, that large allow ances must be made for his statements; if his assertions at one time contradict those made at another ; and if his statements, also, sometimes come in collision with those of his best friends, so that, when his language is re ported, difficulties follow, and explanations are made necessary, — all this certainly disqualifies him from being considered a trustworthy wit ness.

All these disqualifications belong in a remark able degree to Lord Byron, on the oft-repeated testimony of his best friends.

We shall first cite the following testimony, given in an article from " Under the Crown," which is written by an early friend and ardent admirer of Lord Byron : —

" Byron had one pre-eminent fault, —a fault which must be considered as deeply criminal by every one who does not, as I do, believe it to have resulted from monomania. He had a morbid love of a bad reputation. There was hardly an offence of which he would not, with perfect indifference, accuse himself. An old schoolfellow who met him on the Continent told me that he would continually write paragraphs against himself in the foreign journals, and delight in their republication by the English newspapers as in the success of a practical joke. Whenever anybody has related any thing discreditable of Byron, assuring me that it must be true, for he heard it from him-

self, I always felt that he could not have spoken upon worse authority ; and that, in all probability, the tale was a pure in vention. If I could remember, and were willing to repeat, the various misdoings which I have from time to time heard him attribute to himself, I could fill a volume. But I never believed them. I very soon became aware of this strange idiosyncrasy : it puzzled me to account for it ; but there it was, a sort of dis eased and distorted vanity. The same eccentric spirit would induce him to report things which were false with regard to his family, which anybody else would have concealed, though true. He told" me more than once that his father was insane, and killed himself. I shall never forget the manner in which he first told me this. While washing his hands, and singing a gay Neapolitan air, he stopped, looked round at me, and said, 'There always was madness in the family.' Then, after con tinuing his washing and his song, he added, as if speaking of a matter of the slightest indifference, ' My father cut his throat.' The contrast between the tenor of the subject and the levity of the expression was fearfully painful: it was like a stanza of ' Don Juan.' In this instance, I had no doubt that the fact was as he related it; but in speaking of it, only a few years since, to an old lady in whom I had perfect confidence, she assured me that it was not so. Mr Byron, who was her cousin, had been extremely wild, but was quite sane, and had died very quietly in his bed. What Byron's reason could have been for thus ca lumniating not only himself, but the blood which was flowing in his veins, who can divine ? But, for some reason or other, it

seemed to be his determined purpose to keep himself unknown to the great body of his fellow-creatures ; to present himself to their view in moral masquerade."

Certainly the character of Lord Byron here given by his friend is not the kind to make him a trustworthy witness in any case : on the con trary, it seems to show either a subtle delight in falsehood for falsehood's sake, or else the wary artifices of a man, who, having a deadly secret to conceal, employs many turnings and windings to throw the world off the scent. What in triguer, having a crime to cover, could devise a more artful course than to send half a dozen absurd stories to the press, which should, after a while, be traced back to himself, till the public should gradually look on all it heard from him as the result of this eccentric humor ?

The easy, trifling air with which Lord Byron made to this friend a false statement in regard to his father would lead naturally to the inquiry, on what other subjects, equally important to the good name of others, he might give false testi mony with equal indifference.

When Medwin's " Conversations with Lord Byron " were first published, they contained a number of declarations of the noble lord affect ing the honor and honesty of his friend and publisher Murray. These appear to have been made in the same way as those about his father, and with equal indifference. So serious were the charges, that Mr. Murray's friends felt that he ought, in justice to himself, to come for ward and confront them with the facts as stated in Byron's letters to himself; and in vol. x., p. 143, of Murray's standard edition, accord ingly, these false statements are confronted with the letters of Lord Byron. The statements, as reported, are of a most material and vital nature, relating to Murray's financial honor and honesty, and to his general truthfulness and sincerity. In reply, Murray opposes to them the accounts of sums paid for different works, and letters from Byron exactly contradicting his own state ments as to Murray's character.

The subject, as we have seen, was discussed

in " The Noctes." No doubt appears to be en tertained that Byron made the statements to Medwin ; and the theory of accounting for them is, that " Byron was ' bamming' him."

It seems never to have occurred to any of these credulous gentlemen, who laughed at oth ers for being "bammed," that Byron might be doing the very same thing by themselves. How many of his so-called packages sent to Lady Byron were real packages, and how many were mystifications ? We find, in two places at least in his Memoir, letters to Lady Byron, written and shown to others, which, he says, were never sent by him. He told Lady Blessington that he was in the habit of writing to her constantly, Was this " bamming " ? Was he " bamming," also, when he told the world that Lady Byron suddenly deserted him, quite to his surprise, and that he never, to his dying day, could find out why ?

Lady Blessington relates, that, in one of his conversations with her, he entertained her by repeating epigrams and lampoons, in which many of his friends were treated with severity. She inquired of him, in case he should die, and such proofs of his friendship come before the public, what would be the feelings of these friends, who had supposed themselves to stand so high in his good graces. She says, —

"'That,' said Byron, 'is precisely one of the ideas that most amuses me. I often fancy the rage and humiliation of my quondam friends in hearing the truth, at least from me, for the first time, and when I am beyond the reach of their malice. . . . What grief,' continued Byron, laughing, ' could resist the charges of ugliness, dulness, or any of the thousand name less defects, personal or mental, ' that flesh is heir to,' when reprisal or recantation was impossible ? . . . People are in such daily habits of commenting on the defects of friends, that they are unconscious of the unkindness of it. ... Now, I write down as well as speak my sentiments of those who think they have gulled me ; and I only wish, in case I die before them, that I might return to witness the effects my posthumous opinions of them are likely to produce in their minds. What good fun this would be ! ... You don't seem to value this as you ought,' said Byron with one of his sardonic smiles, see ing I looked, as I really felt, surprised at his avowed insincerity.

I feel the same pleasure in anticipating the rage and mor tification of my soi-disant friends at the discovery of my real sentiments of them that a miser may be supposed to feel while making a will that will disappoint all the expectants that have been toadying him for years. Then how amusing it will be to compare my posthumous with my previously given opinions, the one throwing ridicule on the other ! '"

It is asserted, in a note to " The Noctes," that Byron, besides his Autobiography, prepared a voluminous dictionary of all his friends and acquaintances, in which brief notes of their persons and character were given, with his opinion of them. It was not considered that the publication of this would add to the noble lord's popularity ; and it has never appeared.

In Hunt's Life of Byron, there is similar testimony. Speaking of Byron's carelessness in exposing his friends' secrets, and showing or giving away their letters, he says, -

" If his five hundred confidants, by a reticence as remarkable as his laxity, had not kept his secrets better than he did him self, the very devil might have been played with I don't know how many people. But there v/as always this saving reflection

to be made, that the man who could be guilty of such extrava gances for the sake of making an impression might be guilty of exaggeration, or inventing what astonished you ; and indeed, though he was a speaker of the truth on ordinary occasions, — that is to say, he did not tell you he had seen a dozen horses when he had seen only two, — yet, as he professed not to value the truth when in the way of his advantage (and there was nothing he thought more to his advantage than making you stare at him), the persons who were liable to suffer from his incontinence had all the right in the world to the benefit of this consideration." *

With a person of such mental and moral habits as to truth, the inquiry always must be, Where does mystification end, and truth begin ?

If a man is careless about his father's reputa tion for sanity, and reports him a crazy suicide ; if he gayly accuses his publisher and good friend of double-dealing, shuffling, and dishonesty ; if he tells stories about Mrs. Clermont,f to which

* Hunt's Byron, p. 77. Philadelphia, 1828.

t From the Temple-Bar article, October, 1860. " Mrs. Leigh, Lord Byron's sister, had other thoughts of Mrs Clermont, and wrote to her, offer ing public testimony to her tenderness and forbearance under circumstances which must have been trying to any friend of Lady Byron." — Campbell, in the New Monthly Magazine, 1830, p. 380.

his sister offers a public refutation, — is it to be supposed that he will always tell the truth about his wife, when the world is pressing him hard, and every instinct of self-defence is on the alert ?

And then the ingenuity that could write and publish false documents about himself, that they might re-appear in London papers, — to what other accounts might it not be turned ? Might it not create documents, invent statements, about his wife as well as himself?

The document so ostentatiously given to M. G. Lewis "for circulation among friends in Eng land " was a specimen of what the Noctes Club would call " bamming."

If Byron wanted a legal investigation, why did he not take it in the first place, instead of signing the separation ? If he wanted to cancel it, as he said in this document, why did he not go to London, and enter a suit for the restitution of conjugal rights, or a suit in chancery to get possession of his daughter ? That this was in his mind, passages in Medwin's Conversations

show. He told Lady Blessington also that he might claim his daughter in chancery at any time.

Why did he not do it ? Either of these two steps would have brought on that public inves tigation he so longed for. Can it be possible that all the friends who passed this private docu ment from hand to hand never suspected that they were being "bammed " by it?

But it has been universally assumed, that though Byron was thus remarkably given to mystification, yet all his statements in regard to this story are to be accepted, simply because he makes them. Why must we accept them, any more than his statements as to Murray or his own father ?

So we constantly find Lord Byron's incidental statements coming in collision with those of oth ers : for example, in his account of his marriage, he tells Medwin that Lady Byron's maid was put between his bride and himself, on the same seat, in the wedding-journey. The lady's maid her self, Mrs. Minns, says she was sent before them

to Halnaby, and was there to receive them when they alighted.

He said of Lady Byron's mother, " She al ways detested me, and had not the decency to conceal it in her own house. Dining with her one clay, I broke a tooth, and was in great pain; which I could not help showing. ' It will do you good/ said Lady Noel. ' I am glad of it!"

Lady Byron says, speaking of her mother, " She always treated him with an affectionate consideration and indulgence, which extended to every little peculiarity of his feelings. Never did an irritating word escape her."

Lord Byron states that the correspondence between him and Lady Byron, after his refusal, was first opened by her. Lady Byron's friends deny the statement, and assert that the direct contrary is the fact.

Thus we see that Lord Byron's statements are directly opposed to those of his family in relation to his father ; directly against Murray's accounts, and his own admission to Murray ;

directly against the statement of the lady's maid as to her position in the journey; directly against Mrs. Leigh's as to Mrs. Clermont, and against Lady Byron as to her mother.

We can see, also, that these misstatements were so fully perceived by the men of his times, that Medwin's Conversations were simply laughed at as an amusing instance of how far a man might be made the victim of a mystification. Christopher North thus sentences the book : —

" I don't mean to call Medwin a liar. . . . The captain lies, sir; but it is under a thousand mistakes. Whether Byron bammed him, or he, by virtue of his own egregious stupidity, was the sole and sufficient bammifier of himself, I know not; neither greatly do I care. This much is certain, . . . that the book throughout is full of things that were not, and most re-splendently deficient quoad the things that were."

Yet it is on Medwin's Conversations alone that many of the magazine assertions in regard to Lady Byron are founded.

It is on that authority that Lady Byron is accused of breaking open her husband's writing-desk in his absence, and sending the letters she found there to the husband of a lady compro mised by them ; and likewise that Lord Byron is declared to have paid back his wife's ten-thousand-pound wedding-portion, and doubled it. Moore makes no such statements ; and his remarks about Lord Byron's use of his wife's money are unmistakable evidence to the con trary. Moore, although Byron's ardent partisan, was too well informed to make assertions with regard to him, which, at that time, it would have been perfectly easy to refute.

All these facts go to show that Lord Byron's character for accuracy or veracity was not such as to entitle him to ordinary confidence as a witness, especially in a case where he had the strongest motives for misstatement.

And if we consider that the celebrated Auto biography was the finished, careful work of such a practised " mystifier," who can wonder that it presented a web of such intermingled truth and lies, that there was no such thing as disen-

tangling it, and pointing out where falsehood ended, and truth began ?

But, in regard to Lady Byron, what has been the universal impression of the world ? It has been alleged against her that she was a precise, straightforward woman, so accustomed to plain, literal dealings, that she could not understand the various mystifications of her husband ; and that from that cause arose her unhappiness. Byron speaks, in " The Sketch," of her peculiar truthfulness ; and even in the " Clytemnestra " poem, when accusing her of lying, he speaks of her as departing from

" The early truth that was her proper praise."

Lady Byron's careful accuracy as to dates, to time, place, and circumstances, will probably be vouched for by all the very large number of persons whom the management of her extended property and her works of benevolence brought to act as co-operators or agents with her. She was not a person in the habit of making exag-

gerated or ill-considered statements. Her pub lished statement of 1830 is clear, exact, accurate, and perfectly intelligible. The dates are careful ly ascertained and stated, the expressions are moderate, and all the assertions firm and perfect ly definite.

It therefore seems remarkable that the whole reasoning on this Byron matter has generally been conducted by assuming all Lord Byron's statements to be true, and requiring all Lady Byron's statements to be sustained by other evidence.

If Lord Byron asserts that his wife deserted him, the assertion is accepted without proof; but, if Lady Byron asserts that he ordered her to leave, that requires proof. Lady Byron asserts that she took counsel, on this order of Lord Byron, with his family friends and physician, under the idea that it originated in insanity. The " Blackwood " asks, " What family friends ? " says it doesn't know of any ; and asks proof.

If Lord Byron asserts that he always longed

for a public investigation of the charges against him, the " Quarterly " and " Blackwood " quote the saying with ingenuous confidence. They are obliged to admit that he refused to stand that public test ; that he signed the deed of separation rather than meet it. They know, also, that he could have at any time instituted suits against Lady Byron that would have brought the whole matter into court, and that he did not. Why did he not? The "Quarterly" simply intimates that such suits would have been unpleasant. Why ? On account of per sonal^ delicacy ? The man that wrote " Don Juan," and furnished the details of his wedding-night, held back from clearing his name by delicacy ! It is astonishing to what extent this controversy has consisted in simply repeating Lord Byron's assertions over and over again, and calling the result proof.

Now, we propose a different course. As Lady Byron is not stated by her warm admirers to have had any monomania for speaking un-

truths on any subject, we rank her value as a witness at a higher rate than Lord Byron's. She never accused her parents of madness or suicide, merely to make a sensation ; never " bammed " an acquaintance by false statements concerning the commercial honor of any one with whom she was in business relations ; never wrote and sent to the press as a clever jest false statements about herself; and never, in any other .ingenious way, tampered with truth. We therefore hold it to be a mere dictate of reason and common sense, that, in all cases where her statements conflict with her husband's, hers are to be taken as the more trustworthy.

" The London Quarterly," in a late article, distinctly repudiates Lady Byron's statements as sources of evidence, and throughout quotes statements of Lord Byron as if they had the force of self-evident propositions. We con sider such a course contrary to common sense as well as common good manners.

The state of the case is just this : If Lord

.Byron did not make false statements on this subject, it was certainly an exception to his usual course. He certainly did make such on a great variety of other subjects. By his own showing, he had a peculiar pleasure in falsify ing language, and in misleading and betraying even his friends.

But, if Lady Byron gave false witness upon this subject, it was an exception to the whole course of her life.

The habits of her mind, the government of her conduct, her life-long reputation, all were those of a literal, exact truthfulness.

The accusation of her being untruthful was first brought forward by her husband in the " Clytemnestra" poem, in the autumn of 1816; but it never was publicly circulated till after his death, and it was first formally made the basis of a published attack on Lady Byron in the July " Blackwood" of 1869. Up to that time, we look in vain through current literature for any indications that the world regarded Lady Byron

otherwise than as a cold, careful, prudent wo man, who made no assertions, and had no confi dants. When she spoke in 1830, it is perfectly evident that Christopher North and his circle believed what she said, though reproving her for saying it at all.

The " Quarterly " goes on to heap up a num ber of vague assertions, — that Lady Byron, about the time of her separation, made a confidant of a young officer ; that she told the clergyman of Ham of some trials with Lord Ockham; and that she told stories of different things at differ ent times.

All this is not proof: it is mere assertion, and assertion made to produce prejudice. It is like raising a whirlwind of sand to blind the eyes that are looking for landmarks. It is quite probable Lady Byron told different stories about Lord Byron at various times. No woman could have a greater variety of stories to tell ; and no woman ever was so persecuted and pursued and harassed, both by public literature and pri-

vate friendship, to say something. She had plenty of causes for a separation, without the fatal and final one. In her conversations with Lady Anne Barnard, for example, she gives reasons enough for a separation, though none of them are the chief one. It is not different stories, but contradictory stories, that must be relied on to disprove the credibility of a witness. The " Quarterly " has certainly told a great number of different stories, — stories which may prove as irreconcilable with each other as any attributed to Lady Byron ; but its denial of all weight to her testimony is simply begging the whole ques tion under consideration.

A man gives testimony about the causes of a railroad accident, being the only eye-witness.

The opposing counsel begs, whatever else you do, you will not admit that man's testimony. You ask, " Why ? Has he ever been accused of want of veracity on other subjects ? " — " No : he has stood high as a man of probity and honor for years." — " Why, then, throw out his testi mony ?"

" Because he lies in this instance," says the adversary : " his testimony does not agree with this and that." — " Pardon me, that is the very point in question," say you : " we expect to prove that it does agree with this and that,"

Because certain letters of Lady Byron's do not agree with the " Quarterly's" theory of the facts of the separation, it at once assumes that she is an untruthful witness, and proposes to throw out her evidence altogether.

We propose, on the contrary, to regard Lady Byron's evidence with all the attention due to the statement of a high-minded, conscientious person, never in any other case accused of vio lation of truth ; we also propose to show it to be in strict agreement with all well-authenti cated facts and documents ; and we propose to treat Lord Byron's evidence as that of a man of great subtlety, versed in mystification and de lighting in it, and who, on many other subjects, not only deceived, but gloried in deception ; and then we propose to show that it contra-

diets well-established facts and received docu ments.

One thing more we have to say concerning the laws of evidence in regard to documents presented in this investigation.

This is not a London West-End affair, but a grave historical inquiry, in which the whole English-speaking world are interested to know the truth.

As it is now too late to have the securities of a legal trial, certainly the rules of historical evidence should be strictly observed. All im portant documents should be presented in an entire state, with a plain and open account of their history, — who had them, where they were found, and how preserved.

There have been most excellent, credible, and authentic documents produced in this case ; and, as a specimen of them, we shall mention Lord Lindsay's letter, and the journal and letter it authenticates. Lord Lindsay at once comes forward, gives his name boldly, gives the history of the papers he produces, shows how they came to be in his hands, why never produced before, and why now. We feel confidence at once.

But, in regard to the important series of letters presented as Lady Byron's, this obviously proper course has not been pursued. Though assumed to be of the most critical importance, no such distinct history of them was given in the first instance. The want of such evidence being noticed by other papers, the " Quarterly" ap pears hurt that the high character of the maga zine has not been a sufficient guaranty; and still deals in vague statements that the letters have been freely circulated, and that two noble men of the highest character would vouch for them if necessary.

In our view, it is necessary. These noblemen should imitate Lord Lindsay's example, — give a fair account of these letters, under their own names ; and then, we would add, it is needful for complete satisfaction to have the letters entire, and not in fragments.

The " Quarterly " gave these letters with the evident implication that they are entirely de structive to Lady Byron's character as a wit ness. Now, has that magazine much reason to be hurt at even an insinuation on its own character when making such deadly assaults on that of another ? The individuals who bring forth documents that they suppose to be deadly to the character of a noble person, always in her generation held to be eminent for virtue, cer tainly should not murmur at being called upon to substantiate these documents in the manner usually expected in historical investigations.

We have shown that these letters do not con tradict, but that they perfectly confirm the facts, and agree with the dates in Lady Byron's pub lished statements of 1830; and this is our reason for deeming them authentic.

These considerations with regard to the man ner of conducting the inquiry seem so obviously proper, that we cannot but believe that they will command a serious attention.

CHAPTER V.

THE DIRECT ARGUMENT TO PROVE THE CRIME.

\T ^E shall now proceed to state the argu ment against Lord Byron.

ist, There is direct evidence that Lord Byron was guilty of some unusual immorality.

The evidence is .not, as the " Blackwood" says, that Lushington yielded assent to the ex parte statement of a client; nor, as the " Quar terly" intimates, that he was affected by the charms of an attractive young woman.

The first evidence of it is the fact that Lushington and Romilly offered to take the case into court, and make there a public exhibi tion of the proofs on which their convictions were founded.

2d, It is very strong evidence of this fact,

that Lord Byron, while loudly declaring that he wished to know with what he was charged, de clined this open investigation, and, rather than meet it, signed a paper which he had before refused to sign.

3d, It is also strong evidence of this fact, that although secretly declaring to all his intimate friends that he still wished open investigation in a court of justice, and affirming his belief that his character was being ruined for want of it, he never afterwards took the means to get it. In stead of writing a private handbill, he might have come to England and entered a suit; and he did not do it.

That Lord Byron was conscious of a great crime is further made probable by the peculiar malice he seemed to bear to his wife's legal counsel.

If there had been nothing to fear in that legal investigation wherewith they threatened him, why did he not only flee from it, but regard with a peculiar bitterness those who advised and pro-

TO PROVE THE CRIME.

posed it ? To an innocent man falsely accused, the certainties of law are a blessing and a ref uge. Female charms cannot mislead in a court of justice ; and the atrocities of rumor are there sifted, and deprived of power. A trial is not a threat to an innocent man : it is an invitation, an opportunity. Why, then, did he hate Sir Samuel Romilly, so that he exulted like a fiend over his tragical death ? The letter in which he pours forth this malignity was so brutal, that Moore was obliged, by the general outcry of society, to suppress it. Is this the lan guage of an innocent man who has been offered a fair trial under his country's laws ? or of a guil ty man, to whom the very idea of public trial means public exposure ?

4th, It is probable that the crime was the one now alleged, because that was the most impor tant crime charged against him by rumor at the period. This appears by the following ex tract of a letter from Shelley, furnished by the "Quarterly," dated Bath, Sept. 29, 1816: —

" I saw Kinnaird, and had a long talk with him. He informed me that Lady Byron was now in perfect health ; that she was living with your sister. I felt much pleasure from this intelli gence. I consider the latter part of it as affording a decisive contradiction to the only important calumny that ever was ad vanced against you. On this ground, at least, it will become the world hereafter to be silent."

It appears evident here that the charge of improper intimacy with his sister was, in the mind of Shelley, the only important one that had yet been made against Lord Byron.

It is fairly inferable, from Lord Byron's own statements, that his family friends believed this charge. Lady Byron speaks, in her statement, of " nearest relatives" and family friends who were cognizant of Lord Byron's strange conduct at the time of the separation ; and Lord Byron, in the letter to Bowles, before quoted, says that every one of his relations, except his sister, fell from him in this crisis like leaves from a tree in autumn. There was, therefore, not only this report, but such appearances in support of it as

convinced those nearest to the scene, and best apprised of the facts ; so that they fell from him entirely, notwithstanding the strong influence of family feeling. The Guiccioli book also men tions this same allegation as having arisen from peculiarities in Lord Byron's manner of treating his sister: —

" This deep, fraternal affection assumed at times, under the influence of his powerful genius, and under exceptional circum stances, an almost too passionate expression, which opened a fresh field to his enemies." *

It appears, then, that there was nothing in the character of Lord Byron and of his sister, as they appeared before their generation, that pre vented such a report from arising : on the con trary, there was something in their relations that made it seem probable. And it appears that his own family friends were so affected by it, that they, with one accord, deserted him. The " Quarterly " presents the fact, that Lady Byron went to visit Mrs. Leigh at this time, as triumph-

* My Recollections, p. 238.

ant proof that she did not then believe it. Can the "Quarterly" show just what Lady Byron's state of mind was, or what her motives were, in making that visit ?

The " Quarterly" seems to assume, that no woman, without gross hypocrisy, can stand by a sister proven to have been guilty. We can appeal on this subject to all women. We fear lessly ask any wife, " Supposing your husband and sister were involved together in an infamous crime, and that you were the mother of a young daughter whose life would be tainted by a knowl edge of that .crime, what would be your wish ? Would you wish to proclaim it forthwith ? or would you wish quietly to separate from your husband, and to cover the crime from the eye of man ?"

It has been proved that Lady Byron did not reveal this even to her nearest relatives. It is proved that she sealed the mouths of her coun sel, and even of servants, so effectually, that they remain sealed even to this day. This is evidence

that she did not wish the thing known. It is proved also, that, in spite of her secrecy with her parents and friends, the rumor got out, and was spoken of by Shelley as the only important one.

Now, let us see how this note, cited by the " Quarterly," confirms one of Lady Byron's own statements. She says to Lady Anne Barnard, —

" I trust you understand my wishes, which never were to injure Lord Byron in any way : for, though he would not suffer me to remain his wife, he cannot prevent me from continuing his friend; and it was from considering myself as such that I silenced tJie accusations by which my own conduct might have been more fully justified"

How did Lady Byron silence accusations f First, by keeping silence to her nearest relatives ; second, by shutting the mouths of servants ; third, by imposing silence on her friends,—as Lady Anne Barnard ; fourth, by silencing her legal counsel ; fifth, and most entirely, by treating Mrs. Leigh, before the world, with un altered kindness. In the midst of the rumors,

Lady Byron went to visit her ; and Shelley says that the movement was effectual. Can the " Quarterly" prove, that, at this time, Mrs. Leigh had not confessed all, and thrown herself on Lady Byron's mercy ?

It is not necessary to suppose great horror and indignation on the part of Lady Byron. She may have regarded her sister as the victim of a most singularly powerful tempter. Lord Byron, as she knew, had tried to corrupt her own morals and faith. He had obtained a power over some women, even in the highest circles in Eng land, which had led them to forego the usual decorums of their sex, and had given rise to great scandals. He was a being of wonderful personal attractions. He had not only strong poetical, but also strong logical power. He was daring in speculation, and vigorous in sophistical argument ; beautiful, dazzling, and possessed of magnetic power of fascination. His sister had been kind and considerate to Lady Byron when Lord Byron was brutal and cruel. She had been

overcome by him, as a weaker nature sometimes sinks under the force of a stronger one ; and Lady Byron may really have considered her to be more sinned against than sinning.

Lord Byron, if we look at it rightly, did not corrupt Mrs. Leigh any more than he did the whole British public. They rebelled at the im morality of his conduct and the obscenity of his writings; and he resolved that they should ac cept both. And he made them do it. At first, they execrated " Don Juan." Murray was afraid to publish it. Women were determined not to read it. In'1819, Dr. William Maginn of the Noctes wrote a song against it in the following virtuous strain : —

•" Be ' Juan,' then, unseen, unknown ;
It must, or we shall rue it. We may have virtue of our own :
Ah ! why should we undo it ? The treasured faith of days long past
We still would prize o'er any, And grieve to hear the ribald jeer
Of scamps like Don Giovanni."

Lord Byron determined to conquer the virtu ous scruples of the Noctes Club ; and so we find this same Dr. William Maginn, who in 1819 wrote so valiantly, in 1822 declaring that he would rather have written a page of " Don Juan " than a ton of " Childe Harold." All English morals were, in like manner, formally surrendered f to Lord Byron. Moore details his adulteries in Venice with unabashed particularity: artists send for pictures of his principal mistresses ; the literary world call for biographical sketches of their points ; Moore compares his wife and his last mistress in a neatly-turned sentence ; and yet the professor of morals in Edinburgh Uni versity recommends the biography as pure, and having no mud in it. The mistress is lion ized in London, and in 1869 i s introduced to the world of letters by " Blackwood," and bid, " without a blush, to say she loved " —

This much being done to all England, it is quite possible that a woman like Lady Byron, standing silently aside and surveying the course

of things, may have thought that Mrs. Leigh was no more seduced than all the rest of the world, and have said, as we feel disposed to say of that generation, and of a good many in this, " Let him that is without sin among you cast the first stone."

The peculiar bitterness of remorse expressed in his works by Lord Byron is a further evi dence that he had committed an unusual crime. We are aware that evidence cannot be drawn in this manner from an author's works merely, if unsupported by any external probability. For example, the subject most frequently and power fully treated by Hawthorne is the influence of a secret, unconfessed crime on the soul: neverthe less, as Hawthorne is well known to have al ways lived a pure and regular life, nobody has ever suspected him of any greater sin than a vigorous imagination. But here is a man believed guilty of an uncommon immorality by the two best lawyers in England, and threatened with an open exposure, which he does not dare to meet.

The crime is named in society; his own relations fall away from him on account of it; it is only set at rest by the heroic conduct of his wife. Now, this man is stated by many of his friends to have had all the appearance of a man se cretly laboring under the consciousness of crime. Moore speaks of this propensity in the following language:—

" I have known him more than once, as we sat together after dinner, and he was a little under the influence of wine, to fall seriously into this dark, self-accusing mood, and throw out hints of his past life with an air of gloom and mystery designed evidently to awaken curiosity and interest."

Moore says that it was his own custom to dis pel these appearances by ridicule, to which his friend was keenly alive. And he goes on to

say,—

" It has sometimes occurred to me, that the occult causes of his lady's separation from him, round which herself and her legal adviser have thrown such formidable mystery, may have been nothing more than some imposture of this kind, some dimly-hinted confession of undefined horror, which, though in-

tended by the relater to mystify and surprise, the hearer so little understood as to take in sober seriousness." *

All we have to say is, that Lord Byron's con duct in this respect is exactly what might have been expected if he had a crime on his con science.

The energy of remorse and despair expressed in " Manfred " were so appalling and so vividly personal, that the belief was universal on the Continent that the experience was wrought out of some actual crime. Goethe expressed this idea, and had heard a murder imputed to Byron as the cause.

The allusion to the crime and consequences^ of incest is so plain in " Manfred," that it isJ astonishing that any one can pretend, as Gait does, that it had any other application.

The hero speaks of the love between himself and the imaginary being whose spirit haunts him as having been the deadliest sin, and one

* Vol. vi. p. 242.

that has, perhaps, caused her eternal destruc tion : —

" What is she now ? A sufferer for my sins ; A thing I dare not think upon."

He speaks of her blood as haunting him, and as being

" My blood, — the pure, warm stream That ran in the veins of my fathers, and in ours When we were in our youth, and had one heart, And loved each other as we should not love."

This work was conceived in the commotion of mind immediately following his separation. The scenery of it was sketched in a journal sent to his sister at the time.

In letter 377, defending the originality of the conception, and showing that it did not arise from reading " Faust," he says, -

" It was the Steinbach and the Jungfrau, and something else, more than Faustus, that made me write ' Manfred.' "

In letter 288, speaking of the various accounts given by critics of the origin of the story, he says, —

" The conjecturer is out, and knows nothing of the matter. I had a better origin than he could devise or divine for the soul of him."

In letter 299, he says, —

" As to the germs of ' Manfred,' they may be found in the journal I sent to Mrs. Leigh, part of which you saw."

It may be said, plausibly, tkat Lord Byron, if conscious of this crime, would not have expressed it in his poetry. But his nature was such, that he could not help it. Whatever he wrote that had any real power was generally wrought out of self; and, when in a tumult of emotion, he could not help giving glimpses of the cause. It appears that he did know that he had been ac cused of incest, and that Shelley thought that accusation the only really important one; and yet, sensitive as he was to blame and reproba tion, he ran upon this very subject most likely to re-awaken scandal.

But Lord Byron's strategy was always of the bold kind. It was the plan of the fugitive, who, instead of running away, stations himself so near

to danger, that nobody would ever think of look ing for him there. Pie published passionate verses to his sister, on this principle. He imi tated the security of an innocent man in every thing but the unconscious energy of the agony which seized him when he gave vent to his nature in poetry. The boldness of his strategy is evident through all his life. He began by charging his wife with the very cruelty and deception which he was himself practising. He had spread a net for her feet, and he accused her of spreading a net for his. He had placed her in a position where she could not speak, and then leisurely shot arrows at her; and he represented her as having done the same by him. When he at tacked her in " Don Juan," and strove to take from her the very protection* of womanly sacred-ness by putting her name into the mouth of every ribald, he did a bold thing, and he knew it. He meant to do a bold thing. There was a general

* The reader is here referred to the remarks of " Blackwood " on " Don Juan "in Part III.

outcry against it; and he fought it down, and gained his point. By sheer boldness and perse verance, he turned the public from his wife, and to himself, in the face of their very groans and protests. His "Manfred" and his "Cain" were parts of the same game. But the involuntary cry of remorse and despair pierced even through his own artifices, in a manner that produced a con viction of reality.

His evident fear and hatred of his wife were other symptoms of crime. There was no ap parent occasion for him to hate her. He ad mitted that she had been bright, amiable, good, agreeable ; that her marriage had been a very un comfortable one ; and he said to Madame de Stael, that he did not doubt she thought him deranged. Why, then, did he hate her for wanting to live peaceably by herself? Why did he so fear her, that not one year of his life passed without his concocting and circulating some public or private accusation against her ? She, by his own showing, published none against him. It

is remarkable, that, in all his zeal to represent himself injured, he nowhere quotes a -single re mark from Lady Byron, nor a story coming either directly or indirectly from her or her family. He is in a fever in Venice, not from what she has spoken, but because she has sealed the lips of her counsel, and because she and her family do not speak : so that he professes himself utterly ignorant what form her allegations against him may take. He had heard from Shelley that his wife silenced the most important calumny by going to make Mrs. Leigh a visit ; and yet he is afraid of her, — so afraid/that he tells Moore he expects she will attack him after death, and charges him to defend his grave.

Now, if Lord Byron knew that his wife had a deadly secret that she could tell, all this conduct is explicable: it is in the ordinary course of human nature. Men always distrust those who hold facts by which they can be ruined. They fear them ; they are antagonistic to them ; they cannot trust them. The feeling of Falk-

land to Caleb Williams, as portrayed in God win's masterly sketch, is perfectly natural; and it is exactly illustrative of what Byron felt for his wife. He hated her for having his secret ; and, so far as a human being could do it, he tried to destroy her character before the world, that she might not have the power to testify against him. If we admit this solution, Byron's conduct is at least that of a man who is acting as men ordi narily would act under such circumstances : if we do not, he is acting like a fiend. Let us look at admitted facts. He married his wife without love, in a gloomy, melancholy, mo rose state of mind. The servants testify to strange, unaccountable treatment of her imme diately after marriage ; such that her confidential maid advises her return to her parents. In Lady Byron's letter to Mrs. Leigh, she reminds Lord Byron that he always expressed a desire and determination to free himself from the marriage. Lord Byron himself admits to Madame de Stael that his behavior was such, that his wife must

have thought him insane. Now, we are asked to believe, that simply because, under these circum stances, Lady Byron wished to live separate from her husband, he hated and feared her so that he could never let her alone afterward ; that he charged her with malice, slander, deceit, and deadly intentions against himself, merely out of spite, because she preferred not to live with him. This last view of the case certainly makes Lord Byron more unaccountably wicked than the other.

The first supposition shows him to us as a man in an agony of self-preservation ; the sec ond as a fiend, delighting in gratuitous deceit and cruelty.

Again : the evidence of this crime appears in Lord Byron's admission, in a letter to Moore, that he had an illegitimate child born before he left England, and still living at the time.

In letter 307, to Mr. Moore, under date Ven ice, Feb. 2, 1818, Byron says, speaking of Moore's loss of a child, —

" I know how to feel with you, because I am quite wrapped up in my own children. Besides my little legitimate, I have made unto myself an illegitimate since [since Ada's birth], to say nothing of one before; and I look forward to one of these as the pillar of my old age, supposing that I ever reach, as I hope I never shall, that desolating period."

The illegitimate child that he had made to himself since Ada's birth was Allegra, born about nine or ten months after the separation. The other illegitimate alluded to was born be fore, and, as the reader sees, was spoken of as still living.

Moore appears to be puzzled to know who this child can be, and conjectures that it may possibly be the child referred to in an early poem, written, while a schoolboy of nineteen, at Harrow.

On turning back to the note referred to, we find two things : first, that the child there men tioned was not claimed by Lord Byron as his own, but that he asked his mother to care for it as belonging to a schoolmate now dead ; sec-

ond, that the infant died shortly after, and, con sequently, could not be the child mentioned in this letter.

Now, beside this fact, that Lord Byron admit ted a living illegitimate child born before Ada, we place this other fact, that there was a child in England which was believed to be his by those who had every opportunity of knowing.

On this subject we shall cite a passage from a letter recently received .by us from England, and written by a person who appears well in formed on the subject of his letter: —

" The fact is, the incest was first committed, and the child of it born before^ shortly before, the Byron marriage. The child (a daughter) must not be confounded with the natural daughter of Lord Byron, born about a year after his separation.

" The history, more or less, of that child of incest, is known to many; for in Lady Byron's attempts to watch over .her, and rescue her from ruin, she was compelled to employ various agents at different times."

This letter contains a full recognition, by an intelligent person in England, of a child corre-

spending well with Lord Byron's declaration of an illegitimate, born before he left England.

Up to this point, we have, then, the circum stantial evidence against Lord Byron as fol lows : —

A good and amiable woman, who had married him from love, determined to separate from him.

Two of the greatest lawyers of England con firmed her in this decision, and threatened Lord Byron, that, unless he consented to this, they would expose the evidence against him in a •suit for divorce. He fled from this exposure, and never afterwards sought public investiga tion.

He was angry with and malicious toward the counsel who supported his wife ; he was angry at and afraid of a wife who did nothing to injure him, and he made it a special object to defame and de grade her. He gave such evidence of remorse and fear in his writings as to lead eminent literary men to believe he had committed a great crime. The public rumor of his day specified

what the crime was. His relations, by his own showing, joined against him. The report was silenced by his wife's efforts only. Lord Byron subsequently declares the existence of an illegiti mate child, born before he left England. Cor responding to this, there is the history, known in England, of a child believed to be his, in whom his wife took an interest.

All these presumptions exist independently of any direct testimony from Lady Byron. They are to be admitted as true, whether she says a word one way or the other.

From this background of proof, I come for ward, and testify to an interview with Lady By ron, in which she gave me specific information of the facts in the case. That I report the facts just as I received them from her, not altered or misremembered, is shown by the testimony of my sister, to whom I related them at the time. It cannot, then, be denied that I had this interview, and that this communication was made. I therefore testify that Lady Byron,

for a proper purpose, and at a proper time, stated to me the following things : —

i; That the crime which separated her from Lord Byron was incest. 2. That she first dis covered it by improper actions towards his sister, which, he meant to make her understand, indicated the guilty relation. 3. That he ad mitted it, reasoned on it, defended it, tried to make her an accomplice, and, failing in that, hated her and expelled her. 4. That he threat ened her that he would make it his life's object to destroy her character. 5. That for a period she was led to regard this conduct as insanity, and to consider him only as a diseased person. 6. That she had subsequent proof that the facts were really as she suspected ; that there had been a child born of the crime, whose history she knew ; that Mrs. Leigh had repented.

The purpose for which this was stated to me was to ask, Was it her duty to make the truth fully known during her lifetime ?

Here, then, is a man believed guilty of an

unusual crime by two lawyers, the best in Eng land, who have seen the evidence, —a man who dares not meet legal investigation. The crime is named in society, and deemed so far probable to the men of his generation as to be spoken of by Shelley as the only important allegation against him. He acts through life exactly like a man struggling with remorse, and afraid of'de tection ; he has all the restlessness and hatred and fear that a man has who feels that there is evidence which might destroy him. He admits an illegitimate child besides Allegra. A child believed to have been his is known to many in England. Added to all this, his widow, now advanced in years, and standing on the borders of eternity, being, as appears by her writings and conversation, of perfectly sound mind at the time, testifies to me the facts before named, which exactly correspond to probabilities.

I publish the statement; and the solicitors who hold Lady Byron's private papers do not deny the truth of the story. They try to cast

discredit on me for speaking; but they do not say that I have spoken falsely, or that the story is not true. The lawyer who knew Lady Byron's story in 1816 does not now deny that this is the true one. Several persons in England testify, that at various times, and for various purposes, the same story has been told to them. Moreover, it appears from my last letter addressed to Lady Byron on this subject that I recommended her to leave all necessary papers in the hands of some discreet persons, who, after both had passed away, should see that justice was done. The solicitors admit that Lady Byron has left sealed papers of great importance in the hands of trus tees, with discretionary power. I have been informed very directly that the nature of these documents was such as to lead to the suppres sion of Lady Byron's life and writings. This is all exactly as it would be, if the story related by Lady Byron were the true one.

The evidence under this point of view is so strong, that a great effort has been made to throw out Lady Byron's testimony.

This attempt has been made on two grounds, ist, That she was under a mental hallucination. This theory has been most ably refuted by the very first authority in England upon the sub ject. He says, —

" No person practically acquainted with the true characteris tics of insanity would affirm, that, had this idea of' incest' been an insane hallucination, Lady Byron could, from the lengthened period which intervened between her unhappy marriage and death, have refrained from exhibiting it, not only to legal ad visers and trustees (assuming that she revealed to them the fact), but to others, exacting no pledge of secrecy from them as to her mental impressions. Lunatics do for a time, and for some special purpose, most cunningly conceal their delusions ; but they have not the capacity to struggle for thirty-six years, as Lady Byron must have done, with so frightful an hallucination, without the insane state of mind becoming obvious to those with whom they are daily associating. Neither is it consistent with experience to suppose, that, if Lady Byron had been a monomaniac, her state of disordered understanding would have been restricted to one hallucination. Her diseased brain, af fecting the normal action of thought, would, in all probability, have manifested other symptoms besides those referred to of aberration of intellect.

" During the last thirty years, I have not met with a case of

insanity (assuming the hypothesis of hallucination) at all par allel with that of Lady

Byron. In my experience, it is unique. I never saw a patient with such a delusion."

We refer our readers to a careful study of Dr. Forbes Winslow's consideration of this subject given on p. 458 of our Part III. Any one who has been familiar with the delicacy and acuteness of Dr. Winslow, as shown in his work on obscure diseases of the brain and nerves, must feel that his positive assertion on this ground is the best possible evidence. We here gratefully acknowledge our obligations to Dr. Winslow for the corrected proof of his valuable letter, which he has done us the honor to send for this work. We shall consider that his argument, in connection with what the reader may observe of Lady Byron's own writ ings, closes that issue of the case completely.

The other alternative is, that Lady Byron deliberately committed false witness. This was the ground assumed by the " Blackwood," when in July, 1869, it took upon itself the responsi-

23

bility of re-opening the Byron controversy. It is also the ground assumed by " The London Quarterly" of to-day.

Both say, in so many words, that no crime was imputed to Lord Byron; that the representa tions made to Lushington in the beginning were false ones ; and that the story told to Lady Byron's confidential friends in later days was also false.

Let us examine this theory. In the first place, it requires us to believe in the existence of a moral monster, of whom Madame Brinvilliers is cited as the type. The " Blackwood," let it be remembered, opens the controversy with the statement that Lady Byron was a Madame Brinvilliers. The " Quarterly " does not shrink from the same assumption.

Let us consider the probability of this ques tion.

If Lady Byron were such a woman, and wished to ruin her husband's reputation in order to save her own, and, being perfectly unscrupu- lous, had circulated against him a story of un natural crime which had no proofs, how came two of the first lawyers of England to assume the responsibility of offering to present her case in open court ? How came her husband, if he knew himself guiltless, to shrink from that pub lic investigation which must have demonstrated his innocence ? Most astonishing of all, when he fled from trial, and the report got abroad against him in England,.and was believed even by his own relations, w r hy did not his wife avail herself of the moment to complete her vic tory ? If at that moment she had publicly broken with Mrs. Leigh, she might have con firmed every rumor. Did she do it ? and why not ? According to the " Blackwood," we have here a woman who has made up a frightful story to ruin her husband's reputation, yet who takes every pains afterward to prevent its being ruined. She fails to do the very thing she undertakes ; and for years after, rather than injure him, she loses public sympathy, and, by sealing the lips of her legal counsel, deprives herself of the ad vantage of their testimony.

Moreover, if a desire for revenge could have been excited in her, it would have been provoked by the first publication of the fourth canto of "Childe Harold," when she felt that Byron was attacking her before the world. Yet we have Lady Anne Barnard's testimony, that, at this time, she was so far from wishing to injure him, that all her commu nications were guarded, by cautious secrecy. At this time, also, she had a strong party in England, to whom she could have appealed. Again: when " Don Juan " was first printed, it excited a vio lent re-action against Lord Byron. Had his wife chosen then to accuse him, and display the evi dence she had shown to her counsel, there is little doubt that all the world would have stood with her ; but she did not. After his death, when she spoke at last, there seems little doubt, from the strength of Dr. Lushington's language, that Lady Byron had a very strong case, and that, had she been willing, her counsel could have

told much more than he did. She might then have told her whole story, and been believed. Her word was believed by Christopher North, and accepted as proof that Byron had been a great criminal. Had revenge been her motive, she could have spoken the ONE WORD more that North called for.

The " Quarterly" asks why she waited till everybody concerned was dead. There is an obvious answer. Because, while there was any body living to whom the testimony would have been utterly destructive, there were the best reasons for withholding it. When all were gone from earth, and she herself was in constant expec tation of passing away, there was a reason, and a proper one, why she should speak. By nature and principle truthful, she had had the oppor tunity of silently watching the operation of a permitted lie upon a whole generation. She had been placed in a position in which it was neces sary, by silence, to allow the spread and propaga tion through society of a radical falsehood. Lord

Byron's life, fame, and genius had all struck their roots into this lie, been nourished by it, and had derived thence a poisonous power.

In reading this history, it will be remarked that he pleaded his personal misfortunes in his marriage as excuses for every offence against morality, and that the literary world of England accepted the plea, and tolerated and justified the crimes. Never before, in England, had adultery been spoken of in so respectful a manner, and an adulteress openly praised and feted, and ob scene language and licentious images publicly tolerated ; and all on the plea of a man's private misfortunes.

There was, therefore, great force in the sug gestion made to Lady Byron, that she owed a testimony in this case to truth and justice, irre spective of any personal considerations. There is no more real reason for allowing the spread of a hurtful falsehood that affects ourselves than for allowing one that affects our neighbor. This falsehood had corrupted the literature and

morals of both England and America, and led to the public toleration, by respectable authorities, of forms of vice at first indignantly rejected. The question was, Was this falsehood to go on corrupting literature as long as history lasted ? Had the world no right to true history ? Had she who possessed the truth no responsibility to the world ? Was not a final silence a con firmation of a lie with all its consequences ?

This testimony of Lady Byron, so far from being thrown out altogether, as the " Quarterly" proposes, has a peculiar and specific value from the great forbearance and reticence which char acterized the greater part of her life.

The testimony of a person who has shown in every action perfect friendliness to another comes with the more weight on that account. Testimony extorted by conscience from a parent against a child, or a wife against a husband, where all the other actions of the life prove the existence of kind feeling, is held to be the strongest form of evidence.

The fact that Lady Byron, under the severest temptations and the bitterest insults and inju ries, withheld every word by which Lord Byron could be criminated, so long as he and his sister were living, is strong evidence, that, when she did speak, it was not under the influence of ill-will, but of pure conscientious convictions; and the fullest weight ought, therefore, to be given to her testimony.

We are asked now why she ever spoke at all. The fact that her story is known to several per sons in England is brought up as if it were a crime. To this we answer, Lady Byron had an undoubted moral right to have exposed the whole story in a public court in 1816, and thus cut herself loose from her husband by a divorce. For the sake of saving her husband and sister from destruction, she waived this right to self-justification, and stood for years a silent sufferer under calumny and misrepresentation. She de sired nothing but to retire from the whole sub ject ; to be permitted to enjoy with her child the

peace and seclusion that belong to her sex. Her husband made her, through his life and after his death, a subject of such constant discussion, that she must either abandon the current literature of her day, or .run the risk of reading more or less about herself in almost every magazine of her time. Conversations with Lord Byron, notes of interviews with Lord Byron, journals of time spent with Lord Byron, were constantly spread before the public. Leigh Hunt, Gait, Medwin, Trelawney, Lady Blessington, Dr. Kennedy, and Thomas Moore, all poured forth their •memo rials ; and in all she figured prominently. All these had their tribes of reviewers and critics, who also discussed her. The profound mystery of her silence seemed constantly to provoke in quiry. People could not forgive her for not speaking. Her privacy, retirement, and silence were set down as coldness, haughtiness, and contempt of human sympathy. She was con stantly challenged to say something : as, for ex ample, in the " Noctes " of November, 1825, six

months after Byron's death, Christopher North says, speaking of the burning of the Autobiog raphy,—

" I think, since the Memoir was burned by these people, these people are bound to put us in possession of the best evi dence they still have the power of producing, in order that we may come to a just conclusion as to a subject upon which, by their act, at least, as much as by any other people's act, we are compelled to consider it our duty to make up our deliberate opinion, — deliberate and decisive. Woe be to those who pro voke this curiosity, and will not allay it! Woe be to them ! say I. Woe to them ! says the world."

When Lady Byron published her statement, which certainly seemed called for by this lan guage, Christopher North blamed her for doing it, and then again said that she ought to go on and tell the whole story. If she was thus ad jured to speak, blamed for speaking, and adjured to speak further, ail in one breath, by public prints, there is reason to think that there could not have come less solicitation from private sources, — from friends who had access to her

at all hours, whom she loved, by whom she was beloved, and to whom her refusal to explain might seem a breach of friendship. Yet there is no evidence on record, that we have seen, that she ever had other confidant than her legal counsel, till after all the actors in the events were in their graves, and the daughter, for whose sake largely the secret was guarded, had fol lowed them.

Now, does any one claim, that because a woman has sacrificed for twenty years all cravings for human sympathy, and all possibility of perfectly free *and unconstrained intercourse with her friends, that she is obliged to go on bearing this same lonely burden to the end of her days ?'

Let any one imagine the frightful constraint and solitude implied in this sentence. Let any one, too, think of its painful complications in life. The roots of a falsehood are far-reaching. Conduct that can only be explained by criminat ing another must often seem unreasonable and unaccountable ; and the most truthful person,

who feels bound to keep silence regarding a radical lie of another, must often be placed in positions most trying to conscientiousness. The great merit of " Caleb Williams " as a nqyel con sists in its philosophical analysis of the utter helplessness of an innocent person who agrees to keep the secret of a guilty one. One sees there how that necessity of silence produces all the effect of falsehood on his part, and deprives him of the confidence and sympathy of those with whom he would take refuge.

For years, this unnatural life was forced on Lady Byron, involving her as in a network,^

even in her dearest family relations.

That, when all the parties were dead, Lady Byron should allow herself the sympathy of a circle of intimate friends, is something so per fectly proper and natural, that we cannot but wonder that her conduct in this respect has ever been called in question. If it was her right to have had a public expose in 1816, it was certainly her right to show to her own intimate

circle the secret of her life when all the principal actors were passed from earth.

The " Quarterly " speaks as if, by thus waiting, she deprived Lord Byron of the testimony of living witnesses. But there were as many wit nesses and partisans dead on her side as on his. Lady Milbanke and Sir Ralph, Sir Samuel Rom-illy and Lady Anne Barnard, were as much dead as Hobhouse, Moore, and others of Byron's par tisans.

The " Quarterly" speaks of Lady Byron as " running round, and repeating her story to peo ple mostly below her own rank in life."

To those who know the personal dignity of Lady Byron's manners, represented and dwelt on by her husband in his conversations with Lady Blessington, this coarse and vulgar attack • only proves the poverty of a cause which can defend itself by no.better weapons.

Lord Byron speaks of his wife as " highly cul tivated ;" as having " a degree of self-control I never saw equalled."

" I am certain," he says, " that Lady Byron's first idea is what is due to herself: I mean that it is the undeviating rule of her conduct. . . . Now, my besetting sin is a want of that self-respect which she has in excess. . . . But, though I accuse Lady Byron of an excess of self-respect, I must, in candor, admit, that, if any person ever had excuse for an ex traordinary portion of it, she has ; as, in all her thoughts, words, and actions, she is the most decorous woman that ever existed."

This is the kind of woman who has lately been accused in the public prints as a babbler of secrets and a gossip in regard to her private difficulties with children, grandchildren, and ser vants. It is a fair specimen of the justice that has generally been meted out to Lady Byron.

In 1836, she was accused of having made a confidant of Campbell, on the strength of having written him a note declining to give him any information, or answer any questions. In July, 1869, she was denounced by " Blackwood " as a Madame Brinvilliers for keeping such perfect silence on the matter of her husband's character ; and, in the last " Quarterly," she is

spoken of as a gossip "running round, and repeating her story to people below her in - rank."

While we are upon this subject, we have a suggestion to make. John Stuart Mill says that utter self-abnegation has been preached to women as a peculiarly feminine virtue. It is true ; but there is a moral limit to the value of self-abnegation.

It is a fair question for the moralist, whether it is right and proper wholly to ignore one's personal claims to justice. The teachings of the Saviour give us warrant for submitting to personal injuries; but both the Saviour and St. Paul manifested bravery in denying false accusations, and asserting innocence.

Lady Byron was falsely accused of having ruined the man of his generation, and caused all his vices.and crimes, and all their evil effects on society. She submitted to the accusation for a certain number of years for reasons which commended themselves to her conscience; but

when all the personal considerations were re moved, and she was about passing from life, it was right, it was just, it was strictly in accord ance with the philosophical and ethical character of her mind, and with her habit of considering all things in their widest relations to the good of mankind, that she should give serious attention and consideration to the last duty which she might owe to abstract truth and justice in her generation.

In her letter on the religious state of Eng land, we find her advocating an absolute frank ness in all religious parties. She would have all openly confess those doubts, which, from the best of motives, are usually suppressed ; and believed, that, as a result of such perfect truthfulness, a wider love would prevail among Christians. This shows the strength of her conviction of the power and the importance of absolute truth; and shows, therefore, that her doubts and con scientious inquiries respecting her duty on this subject are exactly what might have been ex-

pected from a person of her character and prin ciples.

Having thus shown that Lady Byron's testi mony is the testimony of a woman of strong and sound mind, that it was not given from malice nor ill-will, that it was given at a proper time and in a proper manner, and for a purpose in accordance with the most elevated moral views, and that it is co-incident with all the established facts of this history, and furnishes a perfect solution of every mystery of the case, we think we shall carry the reader with us in say ing that it is to be received as absolute truth.

This conviction we arrive at while as yet we are deprived of the statement prepared by Lady Byron, and the proof by which she expected to sustain it; both which, as we understand, are now in the hands of her trustees.

CHAPTER VI.

PHYSIOLOGICAL ARGUMENT.

HE credibility of the accusation of the unnatural crime charged to Lord Byron is greater than if charged to most men. He was born of parents both of whom were remark able for perfectly ungoverned passions. There appears to be historical evidence that he was speaking literal truth when he says to Medwin of his father,—

" He would have made a bad hero for Hannah More. He ran out three fortunes, and married or ran away with three women. . . . He seemed born for his own ruin and that of the other sex. He began by seducing Lady Carmarthen, and spent her four thousand pounds; and, not content with one adventure of this kind, afterwards eloped with Miss Gordon." — Medwin 'j Conversations, p. 31. • 370

Lady Carmarthen here spoken of was the mother of Mrs. Leigh. Miss Gordon became Lord Byron's mother.

By his own account, and that of Moore, she was a passionate, ungoverned, though affection ate woman. Lord Byron says to Medwin, —

" I lost my father when I was only six years of age. My mother, when she was in a passion with me (and I gave her cause enough), used to say, " O you little dog ! you are a Byron all over ! you are as bad as your father ! " — Ibid., p. 31.

By all the accounts of his childhood and early youth, it is made apparent that ancestral causes had sent him into the world with a most peril ous and exceptional sensitiveness of brain and nervous system, which it would have required the most judicious course of education to direct safely and happily.

Lord Byron often speaks as if he deemed himself subject to tendencies which might ter minate in insanity. The idea is so often men tioned and dwelt upon in his letters, journals,

and conversations, that we cannot but ascribe it to some very peculiar experience, and not to mere affectation.

But, in the history of his early childhood and youth, we see no evidence of any original male-formation of nature. We see only evidence of one of those organizations, full of hope and full of peril, which adverse influences might easily drive to insanity, but wise physiological training and judicious moral culture might have guided to the most splendid results. But of these he had neither. He was alternately the pet and victim of his mother's tumultuous na ture, and equally injured both by her love and her anger. A Scotch maid of religious charac ter gave him early serious impressions of reli gion, and thus added the element of an awakened conscience to the conflicting ones of his char acter.

Education, in the proper sense of the word, did not exist in England in those days. Physiologi cal considerations of the influence of the body

on the soul, of the power of brain and nerve over moral development, had then not even entered the general thought of society. The school and college education literally taught him nothing but the ancient classics, of whose power in exciting and developing the animal passions Byron often speaks.

The morality of the times is strikingly exem plified even in its literary criticism.

For example : One of Byron's poems, written while a schoolboy at Harrow, is addressed to " My Son." Mr. Moore, and the annotator of the standard edition of Byron's poems, gravely give the public their speculations on the point, whether Lord Byron first became a father while a schoolboy in Harrow ; and go into par ticulars in relation to a certain infant, the claim to which lay between Lord Byron and another schoolfellow. It is not the nature - of the event itself, so much as the cool, unembarrassed man ner in which it is discussed, that gives the im pression of the state of public morals. There

is no intimation of any thing unusual, or discred itable to the school, in the event, and no appar ent suspicion that it will be regarded as a serious imputation on Lord Byron's character.

Modern physiological developments would lead any person versed in the study of the recip rocal influence of physical and moral laws to anticipate the most serious danger to such an organization as Lord Byron's, from a precocious development of the passions. Alcoholic and narcotic stimulants, in the case of such a person, would be regarded as little less than suicidal, and an early course of combined drinking and licentiousness as tending directly to estab lish those unsound conditions which lead towards moral insanity. Yet not only Lord Byron's tes timony, but every probability from the license of society, goes to show that this was exactly what did take place.

Neither restrained by education, nor warned by any correct physiological knowledge, nor held in check by any public sentiment, he drifted directly upon the fatal rock.

Here we give Mr. Moore full credit for all his abatements in regard to Lord Byron's excesses in his early days. Moore makes the point very strongly, that he was not, de facto, even so bad as many of his associates ; and we agree with him. Byron's physical organization was originally as fine and as sensitive as that of the most delicate woman. He possessed the faculty of moral ideali ty in a high degree ; and he had not, in the earlier part of his life, an attraction towards mere brutal vice. His physical sensitiveness was so remark able, that he says of himself, " A dose of salts has the effect of a temporary inebriation, like light champagne, upon me." Yet this excep tionally delicately-organized boy and youth was in a circle where not to conform to the coarse drinking-customs of his day was to incur cen sure and ridicule. That he early acquired the power of bearing large quantities of liquor is manifested by the record in his Journal, that, on the day when he read the severe " Edinburgh " article upon his schoolboy poems, he drank three bottles of claret at a sitting.

Yet Byron was so far" superior to his times, that some vague impulses to physiological pru dence seem to have suggested themselves to him, and been acted upon with great vigor. He never could have lived so long as he did, under the exhaustive process of every kind of excess, if he had not re-enforced his physical nature by an assiduous care of his muscular system. He took boxing-lessons, and distinguished himself in all athletic exercises.

He also had periods in which he seemed to try vaguely to retrieve himself from dissipation, and to acquire self-mastery by what he called temperance.

But, ignorant and excessive in all his move ments, his very efforts at temperance were in temperate. From violent excesses in eating and drinking, he would pass to no less unnatural periods of utter abstinence. Thus the very conservative power which Nature has of adapt ing herself to any settled course was lost. The extreme sensitiveness produced by long periods

of utter abstinence made the succeeding debauch more maddening and fatal. He was like a fine musical instrument, whose strings were every day alternating between extreme tension and perfect laxity. We have in his Journal many passages, .'of which the following is a speci men : —

" I have dined regularly to-day, for the first time since Sun day last; this being sabbath too, — all the rest, tea and dry biscuits, six per diem. I wish to God I had not dined, now 1 It kills me with heaviness, stupor, and horrible dreams; and yet it was but a pint of bucellas, and fish. Meat I never touch, nor much vegetable diet. I wish I were* in the country, to take exercise, instead of being obliged to cool by abstinence, in lieu of it. I should not so much mind a little accession of flesh: my bones can well bear it. But the worst -is, the Devil always came with it, till I starved him out; and I will not be the slave of any appetite. If I do err, it shall be my heart, at least, that heralds the way. O my head ! how it aches ! The horrors of digestion! I wonder how Bonaparte's dinner agrees with him." Moore's Life> vol. ii. p. 264.From all the contemporary history and litera ture of the times, therefore, we have reason to believe that Lord Byron spoke the exact truth when he said to Medwin,

" My own master at an age when I most required a guide, left to the dominion of my passions when they were the strong est, with a fortune anticipated before I came into possession of it, and a constitution impaired by early excesses, I commenced my travels, in 1809, with a joyless indifference^to the world and all that was before me." — Medwin^s Conversations, p. 42.

Utter prostration of the whole physical man from intemperate excess, the deadness to temp tation which comes from utter exhaustion, was his condition, according to himself and Moore, when he first left England, at twenty-one years of age.

In considering his subsequent history, 'we are to take into account that it was upon the brain and nerve-power, thus exhausted by early excess, that the draughts of sudden and rapid literary composition began to be made. There was something unnatural and unhealthy in the ra pidity, clearness, and vigor with which his va rious works followed each other. Subsequently

to the first two cantos of "Childe Harold," "The Bride of Abydos," "The Corsair," "The Giaour," " Lara," " Parisina," and " The Siege of Corinth," all followed close upon each other, in a space of less than three years, and those the three most critical years of his life. " The Bride of Abydos" came out in the autumn of 1813, and was written in a week ; and " The Corsair " was composed in thirteen days. A few months more than a year before his marriage, and the brief space of his married life, was the period in which all this literary labor was performed, while yet he was running the wild career of intrigue and fashionable folly. He speaks of " Lara " as being tossed off in the intervals between mas querades and balls, &c. It is with the physical results of such unnatural efforts that we have now chiefly to do. Every physiologist would say that the demands of such poems on a healthy brain, in that given space, must have been ex hausting ; but when we consider that they were checks drawn on a bank broken by early extrav-

agance, and that the subject was prodigally spending vital forces in every other direction at the same time, one can scarcely estimate the physiological madness of such a course as Lord Byron's.

It is evident from his Journal, and Moore's account, that any amount of physical force which was for the time restored by his first for eign travel was recklessly spent in this period, when he threw himself with a mad recklessness into London society in the time just preceding his marriage. The revelations made in Moore's Memoir of this period are sad enough : those to

Medwin are so appalling as to the state of contemporary society in England, as to require, at least, the benefit of the doubt for which Lord Byron's habitual carelessness of truth gave scope. His adventures with ladies of the high est rank in England are there paraded with a freedom of detail that respect for womanhood must lead every woman to question. The only thing that is unquestionable is, that Lord Byron

made these assertions to Medwin, not as re morseful confessions, but as relations of his bonnes fortunes, and that Medwin published them in the very face of the society to which they related.

When Lord Byron says, " I have seen a great deal of Italian society, and swum in a gondola ; but nothing could equal the profligacy of high life in England . . . when I knew it," he makes certainly strong assertions, if we remem ber what Mr. Moore reveals of the harem kept in Venice.

But when Lord Byron intimates that three married women in his own rank in life, who had once held illicit relations with him, made wedding-visits to his wife at one time, we must hope that he drew on his active imagination, as he often did, in his statements in regard to women.

When he relates at large his amour with Lord Melbourne's wife, and represents her as pursu ing him with an insane passion, to which- he

with difficulty responded ; and when he says that she tracked a rival lady to his lodgings, and came into them herself, disguised as a carman, — one hopes that he exaggerates. And what are we to make of passages like this ? —

" There was a lady at that time, double my own age, the mother of several children who were perfect angels, with whom I formed a liaison that continued without interruption for eight months. She told me she was never in love till she was thirty, and I thought myself so with her when she was forty. I never felt a stronger passion, which she returned with equal ardor. .. .

" Strange as it may seem, she gained, as all women do, an influence over me so strong, that I had great difficulty in break ing with her."

Unfortunately, these statements, though prob ably exaggerated, are, for substance, borne out in the history of the times. With every possible abatement for exaggeration in these statements, there remains still undoubted evidence from other sources that Lord Byron exercised a most peculiar and fatal power over the moral sense of the women with whom he was brought in re-

lation ; and -that love for him, in many women, became a sort of insanity, depriving them of the just use of their faculties. All this makes his fatal history both possible and probable.

Even the article in " Blackwood," written in 1825 for the express purpose of vindicating his character, admits that his name had been coupled with those of three, four, or more women of rank, whom it speaks of as " licen tious, unprincipled, characterless women."

That such a course, in connection with alter nate extremes of excess and abstinence in eating and drinking, and the immense draughts on the brain-power of rapid and brilliant composition, should have ended in that abnormal state in which cravings for unnatural vice give indica tions of approaching brain-disease, seems only too probable.

This symptom of exhausted vitality becomes often a frequent type in periods of very corrupt society. The dregs of the old Greek and Ro man civilization were foul with it ; and the

apostle speaks of the turning of the use of the natural into that which is against nature, as the last step in abandonment.

The very literature of such periods marks their want of physical and moral soundness. Having lost all sense of what is simple and nat ural and pure, the mind delights to dwell on horrible ideas, which give a shuddering sense of guilt and crime. All the writings of this fatal period of Lord Byron's life are more or less in tense histories of unrepentant guilt and remorse or of unnatural crime. A recent writer in " Temple Bar" brings to light the fact, that " The Bride of Abydos," the first of the brilliant and rapid series of poems which began in the period immediately preceding his marriage, was, in its first composition, an intense story of love between a brother and sister in a Turkish ha rem ; that Lord Byron declared, in a letter to Gait, that it was drawn from real life; that, in compliance with the prejudices of the age, he altered the relationship to that of cousins before publication.

This same writer goes on to show, by a series of extracts from Lord Byron's published letters and journals, that his mind about this time was in a fearfully unnatural state, and suffering sin gular and inexplicable agonies of remorse ; that, though he was accustomed fearlessly to confide to his friends immoralities which would be looked upon as damning, there was now a secret to which he could not help alluding in his let ters, but which he told Moore he could not tell now, but "some day or other when we are veterans" He speaks of his heart as eating itself out; of a mysterious person, whom he says, " God knows I love too well, and the Devil prob ably too. He wrote a song, and sent it to Moore, addressed to a partner in some awful guilt, whose very name he dares not mention, because

" There is grief in the sound, there is guilt in the fame."

He speaks of struggles of remorse, of efforts at repentance, and returns to guilt, with a sort of horror very different from the well-pleased

air with which he relates to Medwin his com mon intrigues and adulteries. He speaks of himself generally as oppressed by a frightful, un natural gloom and horror, and, when occasionally happy, " not in a way that can or ought to last."

" The Giaour," " The Corsair," " Lara," " Pari-sina," " The Siege of Corinth," and " Man fred," all written or conceived about this period of his life, give one picture of a desperate, despairing, unrepentant soul, whom suffering maddens, but cannot reclaim.

In all these he paints only the one woman, of concentrated, unconsidering passion, ready to sacrifice heaven and defy hell for a guilty man, beloved in spite of religion or reason. In this unnatural literature, the stimulus of crime is represented as intensifying love. Medora, Gul-nare, the Page in " Lara," Parisina, and the lost sister of Manfred, love the more intensely because the object of the love is a criminal, out lawed by God and man. The next step beyond this is — madness.

The work of Dr. Forbes Winslow on " Ob scure Diseases of the Brain and Nerves " * con tains a passage so very descriptive of the case of Lord Byron, that it might seem to have been written for it. The sixth chapter of his work, on " Anomalous and Masked Affections of the Mind," contains, in our view, the only clew that can unravel the sad tragedy of Byron's life. He says, p. 87, -

" These forms of unrecognized mental disorder are not always accompanied by any well-marked disturbance of the bodily health requiring medical attention, or any obvious de parture from a normal state of thought and conduct such as to justify legal interference; neither do these affections always incapacitate the party from engaging in the ordinary business of life. . . . The change may have progressed insidiously and stealthily, having slowly and almost imperceptibly induced important molecular modifications in the delicate vesicular neurine of the brain, ultimately resulting in some aberration of the ideas, alteration of the affections, or perversion of the pro pensities or instincts. . . .

" Mental disorder of a dangerous character has been known

* The article in question is worth a careful reading. Its industry and accuracy in amassing evidence are worthy attention.

for years to be stealthily advancing, without exciting the slightest notion of its presence, until some sad and terrible catastrophe, homicide, or suicide, has painfully awakened attention to its existence. Persons suffering from latent insanity often affect singularity of dress, gait, conversation, and phraseology. The most trifling circumstances stimulate their excitability. They are martyrs to ungovernable paroxysms of passion, are inflamed to a state of demoniacal fury by the most insignificant of causes, and occasionally lose all sense of delicacy of feeling, sentiment, refinement of manners and con versation. Such manifestations of undetected mental disorder may be seen associated with intellectual and moral qualities of the highest order."

In another place, Dr. Winslow again adverts to this latter symptom, which was strikingly marked in the case of Lord Byron : —

" All delicacy and decency of thought are occasionally banished from the mind, so effectually does the principle of thought in these attacks succumb to the animal instincts and passions. . . .

" Such cases will commonly be found associated with organic predisposition to insanity or cerebral disease. . . . Modifica tions of the malady are seen allied with genius. The biogra phies of Cowper, Burns, Byron, Johnson, Pope, and Haydon,

establish that the most exalted intellectual conditions do not escape unscathed.

" In early childhood, this form of mental disturbance may, in many cases,'be detected. To its existence is often to be traced the motiveless crimes of the young."

No one can compare this passage of Dr. Forbes Winslow with the incidents we have already cited as occurring in that fatal period before the separation of Lord and Lady Byron, and not feel that the hapless young wife was in deed struggling with those inflexible natural

laws, which, at some stages of retribution, in-

p volve in their awful sweep the guilty with the

innocent. She longed to save; but he was gone past redemption. Alcoholic stimulants and licentious excesses, without doubt, had produced those unseen changes in the brain, of which Dr.

Forbes Winslow speaks ; and the re sults were terrible in proportion to the peculiar fineness and - delicacy of the organism deranged. Alas ! the history of Lady Byron is the his tory of too many women in every rank of life

who are called in agonies of perplexity and fear to watch that gradual process by which physical excesses change the organism of the brain, till slow, creeping, moral insanity comes on. The woman who is the helpless victim of cruelties which only unnatural states of the brain could invent; who is heart-sick to-day, and dreads to morrow, — looks in hopeless horror on the fatal process by which a lover and a protector changes under her eyes, from day to day, to a brute and a fiend.

Lady Byron's married life — alas ! it is lived over in many a cottage and tenement-house, with no understanding on either side of the woful misery.

Dr. Winslow truly says, " The science of these brain-affections is yet in its infancy in England." At that time, it had not even begun 'to be. Mad ness was a fixed point; and the inquiries into it had no nicety. Its treatment, if established, had no redeeming power. Insanity simply locked a man up as a dangerous being ; and the very

suggestion of it, therefore, was resented as an injury.

A most peculiar and affecting feature of that form of brain-disease which hurries its victim, as by an overpowering mania, into crime, is, that

often the moral faculties and the affections re-

• main to a degree unimpaired, and protest with all

their strength against the outrage. Hence come conflicts and agonies of remorse proportioned to the strength of the moral nature. Byron, more than any other one writer, may be called the poet of remorse. His passionate pictures of this feeling seem to give new power to the English language: —

" There is a war, a chaos of the mind, When all its elements convulsed—combined, Lie dark and jarring with perturbed force, And gnashing with impenitent remorse That juggling fiend, who never spake before, But cries, ' I -warned thee !' when the deed is o'er."

It was this remorse that formed the only re deeming feature of the case. Its eloquence, its

agonies, won from all hearts the interest that we give to a powerful nature in a state of danger and ruin ; and it may be hoped that this feel ing, which tempers the stern justice of human judgments, may prove only a faint image of the wider charity of Him whose thoughts are as far above ours as the heaven is above the earth.

CHAPTER VII.

HOW COULD SHE LOVE HIM f

T T has seemed, to some, wholly inconsistent, that Lady Byron, if this story were true, could retain any kindly feeling for Lord Byron, or any tenderness for his memory; that the pro fession implied a certain hypocrisy : but, in this sad review, we may see how the woman who once had loved him, might, in spite of every wrong he had heaped upon her, still have looked on this awful wreck and ruin chiefly with pity. While she stood afar, and refused to justify or join in the polluted idolatry which defended his vices, there is evidence in her writings that her mind often went back mournfully, as a mother's would, to the early days when he might have been saved.

394 HOW COULD SHE LOVE HIM ? •

One of her letters in Robinson's Memoirs, in regard to his religious opinions, shows with what intense earnestness she dwelt upon the unhappy influences of his childhood and youth, and those early theologies which led him to re gard himself as one of the reprobate. She says, —

" Not merely from casual expressions, but from the whole tenor of Lord Byron's feelings,

I could not but conclude that he was a believer in the inspiration of the Bible, and had the gloomiest Calvinistic tenets. To that unhappy view of the relation of the creature to the Creator I haVe always ascribed the misery of his life.

" It is enough for me to know that he who thinks his trans gression beyond forgiveness . . . has righteousness beyond that of the self-satisfied sinner. It is impossible for me to doubt, that, could he once have been assured of pardon, his living faith in moral duty, and love of virtue (' I love the virtues that I can not claim'), would have conquered every temptation. Judge, then, how I must hate the creed that'made him see God as an Avenger, and not as a Father ! My own impressions were just the reverse, but could have but little weight; and it was in vain to seek to turn his thoughts from that fixed idea with which he connected his personal peculiarity as a stamp. Instead of being made happier by any apparent good, he felt convinced that

every blessing would be turned into a curse to him. . . . ' The worst of it is, I do believe,' he said. 7, like all connected with him, was broken against the rock of predestination. I may be pardoned for my frequent reference to the sentiment (expressed by him), that I was only sent to show him the happiness he was forbidden to enjoy."

In this letter we have the heart, not of the wife, but of the mother, — the love that searches everywhere for extenuations of the guilt it is forced to confess.

That Lady Byron was not alone in ascribing such results to the doctrines of Calvinism, in certain cases, appears from the language of the Thirty-nine Articles, w,hich says, —

" As the godly consideration of predestination, and our elec tion in Christ, is full of sweet, pleasant, and unspeakable com fort to godly persons, and such as feel in themselves the workings of the spirit of Christ; ... so, for curious and carnal persons, lacking the spirit of Christ, to have continually before their eyes the sentence of God's predestination, is a most dangerous downfall, whereby the Devil doth thrust them either into des peration, or into wretchedness of most unclean living, —no less perilous than desperation."

Lord Byron's life is an exact commentary on these words, which passed under the revision of Calvin himself.

The whole tone of this letter shows not only that Lady Byron never lost her deep interest in her husband, but that it was by this experience that all her religious ideas were modified. There is another of these letters in which she thus speaks of her husband's writings and charac ter: —

" The author of the article on " Goethe " appears to me to have the mind which could dispel the illusions about another poet, without depreciating his claims ... to the truest inspira tion.

" Who has sought to distinguish between the holy and the unholy in that spirit ? to prove, by the very degradation of the one, how high the other was ? A character is never done jus tice to by extenuating its faults : so I do not agree to nisi bonum. It is kinder to read the blotted page."

These letters show that Lady Byron's idea was, that, even were the whole mournful truth about Lord Byron fully told, there was still a foundation left for pity and mercy. She seems

to have remembered, that if his sins were pecu liar, so also were his temptations ; and to have schooled herself for years to gather up, and set in order in her memory, all that yet remained precious in this great ruin. Probably no Eng lish writer that ever has made the attempt could have done this more perfectly. Though Lady Byron was not a poet par excellence, yet she belonged to an order of souls fully equal to Lord Byron. Hers was more the analytical mind of the philosopher than the creative mind of the poet; and it was, for that reason, the one mind in our day capable of estimating him fully both with justice and mercy. No person in England had a more intense sensibility to genius, in its loftier acceptation, than Lady Byron ; and none more completely sympathized with what was pure and exalted in her husband's writings.

There is this peculiarity in Lord Byron, that the pure and the impure in his poetry often run side by side without mixing, — as one may see at Geneva the muddy stream of the Arve

and the blue waters of the Rhone flowing together unmingled. What, for example, can be nobler, and in a higher and tenderer moral strain, than his lines on the dying gladiator, in " Childe Harold " ? What is more like the vigor of the old Hebrew Scriptures than his thunder storm in the Alps ? What can more perfectly express moral ideality of the highest kind than the exquisite descriptions of Aurora Raby,— pure and high in thought and language, occur ring, as they do, in a work full of the most utter vileness ?

Lady Byron's hopes for her husband fastened themselves on all the noble fragments yet re maining in that shattered temple of his mind which lay blackened and thunder-riven ; and she looked forward to a sphere beyond this earth, where infinite mercy should bring all again to symmetry and order. If the strict theologian -must regret this as an undue latitude of charity, let it at least be remembered that it was a char ity which sprang from a Christian virtue, and

which she extended to every human being, how ever lost, however low. In her view, the mercy which took him was mercy that could restore all.

In my recollections of the interview with Lady Byron, when this whole history was presented, I can remember that it was with a softened and saddened feeling that I contemplated the story, as one looks on some awful, inexplicable ruin.

The last letter which I addressed to Lady Byron upon this subject will show that such was the impression of the whole interview. It was in reply to the one written on the death of my son : —

"JAN. 30, 1858.

" MY DEAR FRIEND, — I did long to hear from you at a time when few knew how to speak, because I knew that ^<?« had known every thing that sorrow can teach, — you, whose whole life has been a crucifixion, a long ordeal.

" But I believe that the Lamb, who stands forever • in the midst of the throne, as it had been slain,' has everywhere his followers, — those who seem sent into the world, as he was, to suffer for the redemption of others ; and, like him, they must look to the joy set before them, — of redeeming others.

" I often think that God called you to this beautiful and terrible ministry when he suffered you to link your destiny with one so strangely gifted and so fearfully tempted. Perhaps the reward that is to meet you when you enter within the veil where you must so soon pass will be to see that spirit, once chained and defiled, set free and purified; and to know that to you it has been given, by your life of love and faith, to accom plish this glorious change.

" I think increasingly on the subject on which you conversed with me once, — the future state of retribution. It is evident to me that the spirit of Christianity has produced in the human spirit a tenderness of love which wholly revolts from the old doctrine on this subject; and I observe, that, the more Christ-like any one becomes, the more difficult it seems for them to accept it as hitherto presented. And yet, on the contrary, it was Christ who said, ' Fear Him that is able to destroy soul and body in hell;' and the most appalling language is that of Christ himself.

" Certain ideas, once prevalent, certainly must be thrown off. An endless infliction for past sins was once the doctrine : that we now generally reject. The doctrine now generally taught is, that an eternal persistence in evil necessitates ever lasting "suffering, since evil induces misery by an eternal nature of things; and this, I fear, is inferrible from the analogies of Nature, and confirmed by the whole implication of the Bible.

" What attention have you given to this subject ? and is there

any fair way of disposing of the current of assertion, and the still deeper under-current of implication, on this subject, without admitting one which loosens all faith in revelation, and throws us on pure naturalism ? But of one thing I always feel sure : probation does not end with this present life ; and the number of the saved may therefore be infinitely greater than the world's history leads us to suppose.

" I think the Bible implies a great crisis, a struggle, an agony, in which God and Christ and all the good are engaged in redeeming from sin; and we are not to suppose that the little portion that is done for souls as they pass between the two doors of birth and death is all.

" The Bible is certainly silent there. The primitive Church believed in the mercies of an intermediate state ; and it was only the abuse of it by Romanism that drove the Church into its present position, which, I think, is wholly indefensible, and wholly irreconcilable with the spirit of Christ. For if it were the case, that probation in all cases begins and ends here, God's ex ample would surely be one that could not be followed, and he would seem to be far less persevering* than even human beings in efforts to save.

" Nothing is plainer than that it would' be wrong to give up any mind to eternal sin till every possible thing had been done for its recovery ; and that is so clearly not the case here, that I can see, that, with thoughtful minds, this belief would cut the very roots of religious faith in God : for there is a difference between facts that we do not understand, and facts which we do 26

understand, and perceive to be wholly irreconcilable with a cer tain character professed by God.

" If God says he is love, and certain ways of explaining Scripture make him less loving and patient than man, then we make Scripture contradict itself. Now, as no passage of Scripture limits probation to this life, and as one passage in Peter certainly unequivocally asserts that Christ preached to the spirits in prison while his body lay in the grave, I am clear upon this point.

" But it is also clear, that if there be those who persist in refusing God's love, who choose to dash themselves forever against the inflexible laws of the universe, such souls must forever suffer.

" There may be souls who hate purity because it reveals their vileness ; who refuse God's love, and prefer eternal conflict with it. For such there can be no peace. Even in this life, we see those whom the purest self-devoting love only inflames to madness; and we have only to suppose an eternal persistence in this to suppose eternal misery.

" But on this subject we can only leave all reverently in the hands of that Being whose almighty power is ' declared chiefly in showing mercy.'"

CHAPTER VIII.

CONCLUSION.

T N leaving this subject, I have one appeal to make to the men, and more especially to the women, who have been my readers.

In justice to Lady Byron, it must be remem bered that this publication of her story is not her act, but mine. I trust you have already con ceded, that, in so severe and peculiar a trial, she had a right to be understood fully by her imme diate circle of friends, and to seek of them coun sel in view of the moral questions to which such very exceptional circumstances must have given rise. Her communication to me was not an address to the public: it was a statement of the case for advice. True, by leaving the whole,

unguarded by pledge or promise, it left discre tionary power with me to use if needful.

You, my sisters, are to judge whether the accusation laid against Lady Byron by the "

Blackwood," in 1869, was not of so barbarous a nature as to justify my producing the truth I held in my hands in reply.

The " Blackwood " claimed a right to re-open the subject because it was not a private but a public matter. It claimed that Lord Byron's unfortunate marriage might have changed not only his own destiny, but that of all England. It suggested, that but for this, instead of wear ing out his life in vice, and corrupting society by impure poetry, he might, at this day, have been leading the counsels of the State, and helping the onward movements of the world. Then directly it charged Lady Byron with meanly for saking her husband in a time of worldly mis fortune ; with fabricating a destructive accusa tion of crime against him, and confirming this accusation by years of persistent silence more guilty than open assertion.

It has been alleged, that, even admitting that Lady Byron's story were true, it never ought to have been told.

Is it true, then, that a woman has not the same right to individual justice that a man has ? If the cases were reversed, would it have been thought just that Lord Byron should go down in history loaded with accusations of crime because he could be only vindicated by exposing the crime of his wife ?

It has been said that the crime charged on Lady Byron was comparatively unimportant, and the one against Lord Byron was deadly.

But the " Blackwood," in opening the contro versy, called Lady Byron by the name of an unnatural female criminal, whose singular atroci ties alone entitle her to infamous notoriety ; and the crime charged upon her was sufficient to warrant the comparison:

Both crimes are foul, unnatural, horrible ; and there is no middle ground between the admission of the one or the other.

You must either conclude that a woman, all whose other works, words, and deeds were gen erous, just, and gentle, committed this one mon strous exceptional crime, without a motive, and against all the analogies of her character and all the analogies of her treatment of others ; or you must suppose that a man known by all tes timony to have been boundlessly licentious, who took the very course, which, by every physiologi cal law, would have led to unnatural results, did, at last, commit an unnatural crime.

The question, whether I did right, when Lady Byron was thus held up as an abandoned crimi nal by the " Blackwood," to interpose my knowl edge of the real truth in her defence, is a serious one ; but it is one for which I must account to God alone, and in which, without any contempt of the opinions of my fellow-creatures, I must say, that it is a small thing to be judged of man's judgment.

I had in the case a responsibility very dif ferent from that of many others. I had been consulted in relation to the publication of this story by Lady Byron, a-t a time when she had it in her power to have exhibited it with all its proofs, and commanded an instant conviction. I have reason to think that my advice had some weight in suppressing that disclosure. I gave that advice under the impression that the Byron controversy was a thing forever passed, and never likely to return.

It had never occurred to me, that, nine years after Lady Byron's death, a standard English periodical would declare itself free to re-open this controversy, when all the generation who were her witnesses had passed from earth ; and that it would re-open it in the most savage form of accusation, and with the indorsement and commendation of a book of the vilest slanders, edited by Lord Byron's mistress.

Let the reader mark the retributions of justice. The accusations of the " Blackwood," in 1869, were simply an intensified form of those first concocted by Lord Byron in his "

Clytemnestra "

poem of 1816. He forged that weapon, and be queathed it to his party. The " Blackwood " took it up, gave it a sharper edge, and drove it to the heart of Lady Byron's fame. The result has been the disclosure of this history. It is, then, Lord Byron himself, who, by his network of wiles, his ceaseless persecutions of his wife, his efforts to extend his partisanship beyond the grave, has brought on this tumultuous exposure. He, and he alone, is the cause of this revela tion.

And now I have one word to say to those in England, who, with all the facts and documents in their hands which could at once have cleared Lady Byron's fame, allowed the barbarous assault of the " Blackwood" to go over the civilized world without a reply. I speak to those, who, knowing that I am speaking the truth, stand silent ; to those who have now the ability to produce the facts and documents by which this cause might be instantly settled, and who do not produce them.

I do not judge them ; but I remind them that a day is coming when they and I must stand side by side at the great judgment-seat, — I to give an account for my speaking, they for their silence.

In that day, all earthly considerations will have vanished like morning mists, and truth or falsehood, justice or injustice, will be the only realities.

In that day, God, who will judge the secrets of all men, will judge between this man and this woman. Then, if never before, the full truth shall be told both of the depraved and dissolute man who made it his life's object to defame the innocent, the silent, the self-denying woman who made it her life's object to give space for repent ance to the guilty.

PART III.

CONTAINING MISCELLANEOUS DOCUMENTS REFERRED TO IN THE FOREGOING CHAPTERS.

PART III.

MISCELLANEOUS DOCUMENTS.

THE TRUE STORY OF LADY BYRON'S LIFE,

AS ORIGINALLY PUBLISHED IN "THE ATLANTIC MONTHLY."

THE reading world of America has lately been presented with a book which is said to sell rapidly, and which appears to meet with universal favor;

The subject of the book may be thus briefly stated : The mis tress of Lord Byron comes before the world for the sake of vindicating his fame from slanders and aspersions cast on him by his wife. The story of the mistress versus wife may be summed up as follows : —

Lord Byron, the hero of the story, is represented as a human being endowed with every natural charm, gift, and grace, who, by the one false step of an unsuitable marriage, wrecked his whole life. A narrow-minded, cold-hearted precisian, without sufficient intellect to comprehend his genius, or heart to feel for his temptations, formed with him one of those mere worldly marriages common in high life ; and, finding that she could not reduce him to the mathematical proprieties and conventional rules of her own mode of life, suddenly, and without warning, abandoned him in the most cruel and inexplicable manner.

It is alleged that she parted from him in apparent affection and good-humor, wrote him a playful, confiding letter upon the

414 • MISCELLANEOUS DOCUMENTS.

way, but, after reaching her father's house, suddenly, and with out explanation, announced to him that she would never see him again ; that this sudden abandonment drew down upon him a perfect storm of scandalous stories, which his wife never contradicted ; that she never in any way or shape stated what the exact reasons for her departure had been, and thus silently gave scope to all the maliqe of thousands of enemies. The sensitive victim was actually driven from England, his home broken up, and he doomed to be a lonely wanderer on foreign shores.

In Italy, under bluer skies, and among a gentler people, with more tolerant modes of judgment, the authoress intimates that he found peace and consolation. A lovely young Italian count ess falls in love with him, and, breaking her family ties for his sake, devotes herself to him; and, in blissful retirement with her, he finds at last that domestic life for which he was so fitted.

Soothed, calmed, and refreshed, he writes " Don Juan," which the world is at this late hour informed was a poem with a high moral purpose, designed to be a practical illustration of the doctrine of total depravity among young gentlemen in high life.

Under the elevating influence of love, he rises at last to higher realms of moral excellence, and resolves to devote the rest of his life to some noble and heroic purpose ; becomes the savior of Greece; and dies untimely, leaving a nation to mourn his loss.

The authoress dwells with a peculiar bitterness on Lady Byron's entire silence during all these years, as the most aggra vated form of persecution and injury. She informs the world that Lord Byron wrote his Autobiography with the purpose of giving a fair statement of the exact truth in the whole matter; and that Lady Byron bought up the manuscript of the publisher, and insisted on its being destroyed, unread; thus inflexibly depriving her husband of his last chance of a hearing before the tribunal of the public.

As a result of this silent, persistent cruelty on the part of a cold, correct, narrow-minded woman, the character of Lord Byron has been misunderstood, and his name transmitted to after-ages clouded with aspersions and accusations which it is the object of this book to remove.

Such is the story of Lord Byron's mistress, — a story which is going the length of this American continent, and rousing up new sympathy with the poet, and doing its best to bring the youth of America once more under the power of that brilliant, seductive genius, from which it was hoped they had escaped. Already we are seeing it revamped in magazine-articles, which take up the slanders of the paramour and enlarge on them, and wax eloquent in denunciation of the marble-hearted, insensible wife.

All this while, it does not appear to occur to the thousands of unreflecting readers that they are listening merely to the story of Lord Byron's mistress and of Lord Byron ; and that, even by their own showing, their heaviest accusation against Lady Byron is that she has not spoken at all. Her story has never been told.

For many years after the rupture between Lord Byron and his wife, that poet's personality, fate, and happiness had an interest for the whole civilized world, which, we will venture to say, was unparalleled. It is within the writer's recollection, how, in the obscure mountain-town where she spent her early days, Lord Byron's separation from his wife was, for a season, the all-engrossing topic.

She remembers hearing her father recount at the breakfast-table the facts as they were given in the public papers, together with his own suppositions and theories of the causes.

Lord Byron's " Fare thee well," addressed to Lady Byron, was set to music, and sung with tears by young school-girls, even in this distant America.

Madame de Stael said of this appeal, that she was sure it would have drawn her at once to his heart and his arms ; she could have forgiven every thing : and so said all the young ladies all over the world, not only in England, but in France and Germany, wherever Byron's poetry appeared in transla tion.

Lady Byron's obdurate cold-heartedness in refusing even to listen to his .prayers, or to have any intercourse with him whi^ch might lead to reconciliation, was the one point conceded on all sides.

The stricter moralists defended her ; but gentler hearts throughout all the world regarded her as a marble-hearted monster of correctness and morality, a personification of the law unmitigated by the gospel.

Literature in its highest walks busied itself with Lady Byron. Hogg, in the character of the Ettrick Shepherd, devotes sev eral eloquent passages to expatiating on the conjugal fidelity of a poor Highland shepherd's wife, who, by patience and prayer and forgiveness, succeeds in reclaiming her drunken husband, and making a good man of him ; and then points his moral by contrasting with this touching picture the cold-heart ed, pharisaical correctness of Lady Byron.

Moore, in his " Life of Lord Byron," when beginning the recital of the series of disgraceful amours which formed the staple of his life in Venice, has this passage : —

" Highly censurable in point of morality and decorum as
was his course of life while under the roof of Madame ,
it was (with pain I am forced to confess) venial in comparison with the strange, headlong career of license to which, when weaned from that connection, he so unrestrainedly, and, it may be added, defyingly abandoned himself. Of the state of his mind on leaving England, I have already endeavored to convey some idea ; and among the feelings that went to make up that self-centred spirit of resistance which he then opposed to his fate was an indignant scorn for his own countrymen for the wrongs lie thought they had done him. For a time, the kindly sentijnents which he still harbored toward Lady Byron, and a sort of vague hope, perhaps, that all would yet come right again, kept his mind in a mood somewhat more softened and docile, as well as sufficiently under the influence of English opinions to pre vent his breaking out into open rebellion against it, as he un luckily did afterward.

" By the failure of the attempted mediation with Lady Byron, his last link with home was severed : while, notwithstanding the quiet and unobtrusive life which he led at Geneva, there was as

MISCELLANEOUS DOCUMENTS.

yet, he found, no cessation of the slanderous warfare against his character ; the same busy and misrepresenting spirit which had tracked his every step at home, having, with no less malicious watchfulness, dogged him into exile."

We should like to know what the misrepresentations and slanders must have been, when this sort of thing is admitted in Mr. Moore's justification. It seems to us rather wonderful how anybody, unless it were a person like the Countess Guiccioli, could misrepresent a life such as even Byron's friend admits he was leading.

During all these years, when he was setting at defiance every principle of morality and decorum, the interest of the female mind all over Europe in the conversion of this brilliant prodigal son was unceasing, and reflects the greatest credit upon the faith of the sex.

Madame de Stae'l commenced the first effort at evangelization immediately after he left England, and found her catechumen in a most edifying state of humility. He was, metaphorically, on his knees in penitence, and confessed himself a miserable sin ner in the loveliest manner possible. Such sweetness and hu mility took all hearts. His conversations with Madame de Stael were printed, and circulated all over the world ; making it to appear that only the inflexibility of Lady Byron stood in the way of his entire conversion.

Lady Blessington, among many others, took him in hand five or six years afterward, and was greatly delighted with his docil ity, and edified by his frank and free confessions of his miserable offences. Nothing now seemed wanting to bring the wanderer home to the fold but a kind word from Lady Byron. But, when the fair countess offered to mediate, the poet only shook his head in tragic despair ; " he had so many times tried in vain ; Lady Byron's course had been from the first that of obdurate silence."

Any one who would wish to see a specimen of the skill of the honorable poet in mystification will do well to read a letter to Lady Byron, which Lord Byron, on parting from Lady Bles sington, enclosed for her to read just before he went to Greece. He says, —

" The letter which I enclose I was prevented from sending by my despair of its doing any good. I was perfectly sincere when I wrote it, and am so still. But it is difficult for me to with stand the thousand provocations on that subject which both friends and foes have for seven years been throwing in the way • of a man whose feelings were once quick, and whose temper was never patient."

" TO LADY BYRON, CARE OF THE HON. MRS. LEIGH, LONDON.

" PISA, Nov. 17, 1821.

" I have to acknowledge the receipt of ' Ada's hair,' which is very soft and pretty, and nearly as dark already as mine was at twelve years old, if I may judge from what I recollect of some in Augusta's possession, taken at that age. But it don't curl, —perhaps from its being let grow.

" I also thank you for the inscription of the date and name ; and I will tell you why : I believe that they are the only two or three words of your handwriting in my possession. For your letters I returned ; and except the two words, or rather the one word, ' Household,' written twice in an old account-book, I have no other. I burnt your last note, for two reasons : firstly, it was written in a style not very agreeable ; and, sec ondly, I wished to take your word without documents, which are the worldly resources of suspicious people.

" I suppose that this note will reach you somewhere about kAda's birthday, — the loth of December, I believe. She will then be six: so that, in about twelve more, I shall have some chance of meeting her ; perhaps sooner, if I am obliged to go to England by business or otherwise. Recollect, however, one thing, either in distance or nearness, —every day which keeps us asunder should, after so long a period, rather soften our mutual feelings; which must always have one rallying-point a* long as our child exists, which, I presume, we both hope will be long after either of her parents.

" The time which has elapsed since the separation has been considerably more than the whole brief period of our union, and the not much longer one of our prior acquaintance. We both made a bitter mistake ; but now it is over, and irrevocably so. For at thirty-three on my part, and a few years less on yours, though it is no very extended period of life, still it is one when the habits and thought are generally so formed as to admit of no modification ; and, as we could not agree when younger, we should with difficulty do so now.

" I say all this, because I own to you, that, notwithstanding every thing, I considered our re-union as not impossible for more than a year after the separation ; but then I gave up the hope entirely and forever. But this very impossibility of re union seems to me at least a reason why, on all the few points of discussion which can arise between us, we should preserve the courtesies of life, and as much of its kindness as people who are never to meet may preserve, — perhaps more easily than nearer connections. For my own part, I am violent, but not malignant; for only fresh provocations can awaken my resent ments. To you, who are colder and more concentrated, I would just hint, that you may sometimes mistake the depth of a cold anger for dignity, and a worse feeling for duty. I assure you that I bear you now (whatever I may have done) no resentment whatever. Remember, that, if you have injured me in aught, this forgiveness is something ; and that, if I have injured yoii, it is something more still, if it be true, as the moralists say, that the most offending are the least forgiving.

" Whether the offence has been solely on my side, or recip rocal, or on yours chiefly, I have ceased to reflect upon any but two things ; viz., that you are the mother of my child, and that we shall never meet again. I think, if you also consider the two corresponding points with reference to myself, it will be better for all three.

" Yours ever, " NOEL BYRON."

The artless Thomas Moore introduces this letter in the " Life " with the remark, —

" There are few, I should think, of my readers, who will not agree with me in pronouncing, that, if the author of the follow ing letter had not right on his side, he had at least most of those good feelings which are found in general to accompany it."

The reader is requested to take notice of the important ad mission, that the letter was never sent to Lady Byron at all. It was, in fact, never intended for her, but was a nice little dra matic performance, composed simply with the view of acting on the sympathies of Lady Blessington and Byron's numerous female admirers ; and the reader will agree with its, we think, that, in this point of view, it was very neatly done, and deserves immortality as a work of high art. For six years, he had been plunging into every kind of vice and excess, pleading his shat tered domestic joys, and his wife's obdurate heart; as the apol ogy and the impelling cause ; filling the air with his shrieks and complaints concerning the slander which pursued him, while he filled letters to his confidential correspondents with records of new mistresses. During all these years, the silence of Lady Byron was unbroken ; though Lord Byron not only drew in private on the sympathies of his female admirers, but employed his talents and position as an author in holding her up to contempt and ridicule before thousands of readers. We shall quote at length his side of the story, which he published in the first canto of " Don Juan," that the reader may see how much reason he had for assuming the injured tone which he did in the letter to Lady Byron quoted above. That letter never was sent to her; and the unmanly and indecent caricature of her, and the indelicate exposure of the whole story on his own side, which we are about to quote, were the only communications that could have reached her solitude.

In the following verses, Lady Byron is represented as Donna Inez, and Lord Byron as Don Jose ; but the incidents and allusions were so very pointed, that nobody for a moment doubted whose history the poet was narrating.

" His mother was a learned lady, famed
For every branch of every science known In every Christian language ever named,
With virtues equalled by her wit alone ; She made the cleverest people quite ashamed ;
And even the good with inward envy groaned, Finding themselves so very much exceeded In their own way by all the things that she did.
Her favorite science was the mathematical;
Her noblest virtue was her magnanimity ; Her wit (she sometimes tried at wit) was Attic all;
Her serious sayings darkened to sublimity : In short, in all things she was fairly what I call
A prodigy. Her morning-dress was dimity ; Her evening, silk ; or, in the summer, muslin, And other stuffs witl*which I won't stay puzzling.
Some women use their tongues : she looked a lecture, Each eye a sermon, and her brow a homily,
An all-in-all sufficient self-director,
Like the lamented late Sir Samuel Romilly.
In short, she was a walking calculation, — Miss Edgeworth's novels stepping from their covers,
Or Mrs. Trimmer's books on education, Or Cceleb's wife set out in quest of lovers,

Morality's prim personification,

In which not envy's self a flaw discovers.

To others' share 'let female errors fall;'

For she had not even one, —the worst of all.

Oh 1 she was perfect, past all parallel Of any modern female saint's comparison ;

So far above the cunning powers of hell, Her guardian angel had given up his garrison :

Even her minutest motions went as well As those of the best timepiece made by Harrison

;

In virtues, nothing earthly could surpass her

Save thine ' incomparable oil,' Macassar.

Perfect she was ; but as perfection is Insipid in this naughty world of ours,

Don Jose, like a lineal son of Eve,

Went plucking various fruits without her leave.

He was a mortal of the careless kind,

With no great love for learning or the learned,

Who chose to go where'er he had a mind, And never dreamed his lady was concerned.

The world, as usual, wickedly inclined To see a kingdom or a house o'erturned,

Whispered he had a mistress ; some said two: But, for domestic quarrels, one will do.

Now, Donna Inez had, with all her merit, A great opinion of her own good qualities:

Neglect, indeed, requires a saint to bear it; And such indeed she was in her moralities:

But then she had a devil of a spirit, And sometimes mixed up fancies with realities,

And let few opportunities escape

Of getting her liege lord into a scrape.

This was an easy matter with a man

Oft in the wrong, and never on his guard :

And even the wisest, do the best they can,

Have moments, hours, and days so unprepared,

That you might' brain them with their lady's fan ;' And sometimes ladies hit exceeding

hard,

And fans turn into falchions in fair hands,

And why and wherefore no one understands.

'Tis a pity learned virgins ever wed With persons of no sort of education ;

Or gentlemen, who, though well born and bred, Grow tired of scientific conversation.

I don't choose to say much upon this head ; I'm a plain man, and in a single station :

But, O ye lords of ladies intellectual!

Inform us truly, have they not henpecked you all ?

Don Jose and the Donna Inez led For some time an unhappy sort of life,

Wishing each other not divorced, but dead : They lived respectably as man and wife ;

Their conduct was exceedingly well bred, And gave no outward sign of inward strife ;

Until at length the smothered fire broke out,

And put the business past all kind of doubt.

For Inez called some druggists and physicians, And tried to prove her loving lord was

mad ;

But, as he had some lucid intermissions, She next decided he was only bad.

Yet, when they asked her for her depositions, No sort of explanation could be had,

Save that her duty both to man and God * Required this conduct ; which seemed very

odd.

She kept a journal where his faults were noted, And opened certain trunks of books and letters,

(All which might, if occasion served, be quoted ;) And then she had all Seville for abettors,

Besides her good old grandmother (who doted) : The hearers of her case became repeaters,

Then advocates, inquisitors, and judges,—
Some for amusement, others for old grudges.
And then this best and meekest woman bore With such serenity her husband's woes !
Just as the Spartan ladies did of yore,
Who saw their spouses killed, and nobly chose
Never to say a word about them more. Calmly she heard each calumny that rose,
And saw his agonies with such sublimity,
That all the world exclaimed, ' What magnanimity !'

This is the longest and most elaborate version of his own story that Byron ever published; but he busied himself with many others, projecting at one time a Spanish romance, in which the same story is related in the same transparent man ner : but this he was dissuaded from printing. The book-sell ers, however, made a good speculation in publishing what they called his domestic poems ; that is, poems bearing more or less relation to this subject.

Every person with whom he became acquainted with any degree of intimacy was made familiar with his side of the story. Moore's Biography is from first to last, in its representations, founded upon Byron's communicativeness, and Lady Byron's silence ; and the world at last settled down to believing that the account so often repeated, and never contradicted, must be sub stantially a true one.

The true history of Lord and Lady Byron has long been per fectly understood in many circles in England ; but the facts were of a nature that could not be made public. While there was a young daughter living whose future might be prejudiced by its

recital, and while there were other persons on whom* the dis closure of the real truth would have been crushing as an ava lanche, Lady Byron's only course was the perfect silence in which she took refuge, and those sublime works of charity and mercy to which she consecrated her blighted earthly life.

But the time is now come when the truth may be told. All the actors in the scene have disappeared from the stage of mortal existence, and passed, let us have faith to hope, into a world where they would desire to expiate their faults by a late publica tion of the truth.

No person in England, we think, would as yet take the responsibility of relating the true history which is to clear Lady Byron's memory ; but, by a singular concurrence of circum stances, all the facts of the case, in the most undeniable and authentic form, were at one time placed in the hands of the writer of this sketch, with authority to make such use of them as she should judge best. Had this melancholy history been allowed to sleep, no public use would have been made of them ; but the appearance of a popular attack on the character of Lady Byron calls for a vindication, and the true story of her married life will therefore now be related.

Lord Byron has described in one of his letters the impres sion left upon his mind by a young person whom' he met one evening in society, and who attracted his attention by the sim plicity of her dress, and a certain air of singular purity and calmness with which she surveyed the scene around her.

On inquiry, he was told that this young person was Miss Milbanke, an only child, and one of the largest heiresses in England.

Lord Byron was fond of idealizing his experiences in poetry; and the friends of Lady Byron had no difficulty in recognizing the portrait of Lady Byron, as she appeared at this time of her life, in his exquisite description of Aurora Raby : —

" There was Indeed a certain fair and fairy one,
Of the best class, and better than her class, — Aurora Raby, a young star who shone
O'er life, too sweet an image for such glass ;
A lovely being scarcely formed or moulded ; A rose with all its sweetest leaves yet folded.

Early in years, and yet more infantine In figure, she had something of sublime
In eyes which sadly shone as seraphs' shine ; All youth, but with an aspect beyond time ;
Radiant and grave, as pitying man's decline ; Mournful, but mournful of another's crime,
She looked as if she sat by Eden's door,
And grieved for those who could return no more.
She gazed upon a world she scarcely knew,
As seeking not to know it; silent, lone, As grows a flower, thus quietly she grew,
And kept her heart serene within its zone. There was awe in the homage which she drew ;
Her spirit seemed as seated on a throne, Apart from the surrounding world, and strong In its own strength, — most strange in one so young ! "

Some idea of the course which their acquaintance took, and of the manner in which he was piqued into thinking of her, is given in a stanza-or two : —

" The dashing and proud air of Adeline
Imposed not upon her : she saw her blaze Much as she would have seen a glow-worm shine ;
Then turned unto the stars for loftier rays. Juan was something she could not divine,
Being no sibyl in the new world's ways; Yet she was nothing dazzled by the meteor, Because she did not pin her faith on feature.
His fame too (for he had that kind of fame Which sometimes plays the deuse with womankind, —
A heterogeneous mass of glorious blame,
Half virtues and whole vices being combined ;
Faults which attract because they are not tame ; Follies tricked out so brightly that they blind), —
These seals upon her vrax made no impression,
Such was her coldness or her self-possession.
Aurora sat with that indifference
Which piques a preux chevalier, — as it ought. Of all offences, that's the worst offence
Which seems to hint you are not worth a thought.
To his gay nothings, nothing was replied, Or something which was nothing, as urbanity
Required. Aurora scarcely looked aside, Nor even smiled enough for any vanity.
The Devil was in the girl! Could it be pride, Or modesty, or absence, or inanity ?
Juan was drawn thus into some attentions, Slight but select, and just enough to express,
To females of perspicuous comprehensions,
That he would rather make them more than less.
Aurora at the last (so history mentions, Though probably much less a fact than guess)
So far relaxed her thoughts from their sweet prison
As once or twice to smile, if not to listen.
But Juan had a sort of winning way,

A proud humility, if such there be, Which showed such deference to what females say,

As if each charming word were a decree. His tact, too, tempered him from grave to gay,

And taught him when to be reserved or free. He had the art of drawing people out,
Without their seeing what he was about.

Aurora, who, in her indifference, Confounded him in common with the crowd

Of flatterers, though she deemed he had more sense Than whispering foplings or than witlings loud,

Commenced (from such slight things will great commence) To feel that flattery which attracts the proud,

Rather by deference than compliment,

And wins even by a delicate dissent.

And then he had good looks ; that point was carried Nem. con. amongst the women.

Now, though we know of old that looks deceive, And always have done, somehow these good looks Make more impression than the best of books.

Aurora, who looked more on books than faces,

Was very young, although so very sage ; Admiring more Minerva than the Graces,

Especially upon a printed page. But Virtue's self, with all her tightest laces,

Has not the natural stays of strict old age ; And Socrates, that model of all duty, Owned to a penchant, though discreet, for beauty."

The presence of this high-minded, thoughtful, unworldly woman is described through two cantos of the wild, rattling " Don Juan," in a manner that shows how deeply the poet was capable of being affected by such an appeal to his higher nature.

For instance, when Don Juan sits silent and thoughtful amid a circle of persons who are talking scandal, the poet says, —

" 'Tis true, he saw Aurora look as though

She approved his silence : she perhaps mistook Its motive for that charity we owe, But seldom pay, the absent.

He gained esteem where it was worth the most;

And certainly Aurora had renewed In him some feelings he had lately lost

Or hardened, — feelings which, perhaps ideal, Are so divine that I must deem them real:
—

The love of higher things and better days;

The unbounded hope and heavenly ignorance Of what is called the world and the world's ways ;

The moments when we gather from a glance More joy than from all future pride or praise,

Which kindled manhood, but can ne'er entrance The heart in an existence of its own Of which another's bosom is the zone.

And, full of sentiments sublime as billows „ Heaving between this world and worlds beyond,

Don Juan, when the midnight hour of pillows Arrived, retired to his." . . .

In all these descriptions of a spiritual, unworldly nature acting on the spiritual and unworldly part of his own nature,

every one who ever knew Lady Byron intimately must have recognized the model from which he drew, and the experience from which he spoke, even though nothing was further from his mind than to pay this tribute to the woman he had injured, and though before these lines, which showed how truly he knew her real character, had come one stanza of ribald, vulgar caricature, designed as a slight to her : —

" There was Miss Millpond, smooth as summer's sea,

That usual paragon, an only daughter, Who seemed the cream of equanimity

'Till skimmed ; and then there was some milk and water ; With a slight shade of blue, too, it might be,

Beneath the surface : but what did it matter? Love's riotous ; but marriage should have quiet, And, being consumptive, live on a milk diet."

The result of Byron's intimacy with Miss Milbanke and the enkindling of his nobler feelings was an offer of marriage, which she, though at the time deeply interested in him, declined with many expressions of friendship and interest. In fact, she already loved him, but had that doubt of her power to be to him all that a wife should be which would be likely to arise in a mind so sensitively constituted and so unworldly. They, how ever, continued a correspondence as friends : on her part, the interest continually increased ; on his, the transient rise of bet ter feelings was choked and overgrown by the thorns of base, unworthy passions.

From the height at which he might have been happy as the husband of a noble woman, he fell into the depths of a secret adultercfus intrigue with a blood relation, so near in consanguin ity, that discovery must have been utter ruin, and expulsion from civilized society.

From henceforth, this damning guilty secret became the rul ing force' in his life ; holding him with a morbid fascination, yet filling him with remorse and anguish, and insane dread of detec tion. Two years after his refusal by Miss Milbanke, his various friends, seeing that for some cause he was wretched, pressed marriage upon him.

Marriage has often been represented as the proper goal and terminus of a wild and dissipated career; and it has been sup posed to be the appointed mission of good women to receive wandering prodigals, with all the rags and disgraces of their old life upon them, and put rings on their hands, and shoes on their feet, and introduce them, clothed and in their right minds, to an honorable career in society.

Marriage was, therefore, universally recommended to Lord Byron by his numerous friends and well-wishers ; and so he determined to marry, and, in an hour of reckless desperation, sat down and wrote proposals to two ladies. One was declined : the other, which was accepted, was to Miss Milbanke. The world knows well that he had the gift of expression, and will not be surprised that he wrote a very beautiful letter, and that the woman who had already learned to love him fell at once into the snare.

Her answer was a frank, outspoken avowal of her love for him, giving herself to him heart and hand. The good in Lord Byron was not so utterly obliterated that he could receive such a letter without emotion, or practise such unfairness on a loving, trusting heart without pangs of remorse. He had sent the letter in mere recklessness ; he had not seriously expected to be accepted ; and the discovery of the treasure of affection which he had secured was like a vision of lost heaven to a soul in hell.

But, nevertheless, in his letters written about the engage ment, there are sufficient evidences that his self-love was flat tered at the preference accorded him by so superior a woman, and one who had been so much sought. He mentions with an air of complacency that she has employed the last two years in refusing five or six of his acquaintance ; that he had no idea she loved him, admitting that it was an old attachment on his part. He dwells on her virtues with a sort of pride of owner ship. There is a sort of childish levity about the frankness of these letters, very characteristic of the man who skimmed over the deepest abysses v with the lightest jests. Before the world, and to his intimates, he was acting the part of the suc cessful fiance, conscious all the while of the deadly secret that lay cold at the bottom of his heart.

When he went to visit Miss Milbanke's parents as her ac cepted lover, she was struck with his manner and appearance : she saw him moody and gloomy, evidently wrestling with dark and desperate thoughts, aad any thing but what a happy and accepted lover should be. She sought an interview with him alone, and told him that she had observed that he was not happy in the engagement; and magnanimously added, that if, on review, he found he had been mistaken in the nature of his feelings, she would immediately release him, and they should remain only friends.

Overcome with the conflict of his feelings, Lord Byron fainted away. Miss Milbanke was convinced that his heart must really be deeply involved in an attachment with reference to which he showed such strength of emotion, and she spoke no more of a dissolution of the engagement.

There is no reason to doubt that Byron was, as he relates in his " Dream," profoundly agonized and agitated when he stood before God's altar with the trusting young creature whom he was leading to a fate so awfully tragic ; yet it was not the mem ory of Mary Chaworth, but another guiltier and more damning memory, that overshadowed that hour.

The moment the carriage-doors were shut upon the bride groom and the bride, the paroxysm of remorse and despair — unrepentant remorse and angry despair — broke forth upon her gentle head : —

" You might have saved me from this, madam ! You had all in your own power when I offered myself to you first. Then you might have made me what you pleased ; but now you will find that you have married a devil! "

In Miss Martineau's Sketches, recently published, is an account of the termination of this wedding-journey, which brought them to one of Lady Byron's ancestral country-seats, where they were to spend the honeymoon.

Miss Martineau says, —

" At the altar she did not know that she was a sacrifice ; but before sunset of that winter day she knew it, if a judgment may be formed from her face, and attitude of -despair, when she alighted from the carriage on the afternoon of her marriage-

day. It was not the traces of tears which won the sympathy of the old butler who stood at the open door. The bride groom jumped out of the carriage, and walked away. The bride alighted, and came up the steps alone, with a countenance and frame agonized and listless with evident horror and despair. The old servant longed to offer his arm to the young, lonely creature, as an assurance of sympathy and protection. From this shock she certainly rallied, and soon. The pecuniary diffi culties of her new home were exactly what a devoted spirit like hers was fitted to encounter. Her husband bore testimony, after the catastrophe, that a brighter being, a more sympathiz ing and agreeable companion, never blessed any man's home. When he afterward called her cold and mathematical, and over-pious, and so forth, it was when public opinion had gone against him, and when he had discovered that her fidelity and mercy, her silence and magnanimity, might be relied on, so that he was at full liberty to make his part good, as far as she was concerned.

" Silent she was even to her own parents, whose feelings she magnanimously spared. She did not act rashly in leaving him, though she had been most rash in marrying him."

Not all at once did the full knowledge of the dreadful reality into which she had entered come upon the young wife. She knew faguely, from the wild avowals of the first hours of their marriage, that there was a dreadful secret of guilt; that Byron's soul was torn with agonies of remorse, and that he had no love to give to her in return for a love which was ready to do and dare all for him. Yet bravely she addressed herself to the task of soothing and pleasing and calming the man whom she had taken " for better or for worse."

Young and gifted; with a peculiar air of refined and spiritual beauty ; graceful in every movement; possessed of exquisite taste; a perfect companion to his mind in all the higher walks of literary culture; and with that infinite pliability to all his varying, capricious moods which true love alone can give ; bearing in her hand a princely fortune, which, with a woman's uncalculating generosity, was thrown at his feet, — there is no wonder that she might feel for a while as if she could enter

the lists with the very Devil himself, and fight with a woman's weapons for the heart of her husband.

There are indications scattered through the letters of Lord Byron, which, though brief indeed,'showed that his young wife was making every effort to accommodate herself to him, and to give him a cheerful home. One of the poems that he sends to his publisher about this time, he speaks of as being copied by her. He had always the highest regard for her literary judg ments and opinions ; and this little incident shows that she was already associating herself in a wifely fashion with his aims as an author.

The poem copied by her, however, has a sad meaning, which she afterwards learned to understand only too well : —

" There's not a joy the world can give like that it takes away When the glow of early thought declines in feeling's dull decay : 'Tis not on youth's smooth cheek the blush alone that fades so fast; But the tender bloom of heart is gone e'er youth itself be past.

Then the few whose spirits float above the wreck of happiness Are driven o'er the shoals of guilt, or ocean of excess : The magnet of their course is gone, or only points in vain The shore to which-their shivered sail shall never stretch again."

Only a few days before she left him forever, LorB Byron sent Murray manuscripts, in Lady Byron's handwriting, of the " Siege of Corinth," and ' Parisina," and wrote, —

" I am very glad that the handwriting was a favorable omen of the morale of the piece : but you must not trust to that; for my copyist would write out any thing I desired, in all the igno rance of innocence."

There were lucid intervals in which Lord Byron felt the charm of his wife's mind, and the strength of her powers. " Bell, you could be a poet too, if you only thought so," he would say. There were summer-hours in her stormy life, the memory of which never left her, when Byron was as gentle and tender as he was beautiful; when he seemed to be possessed by a good angel: and then for a little time all the ideal possibil ities of his nature stood revealed.

The most dreadful men to live with are those who thus alternate between angel and devil. The buds of hope and love called out by a day or- two of sunshine are frozen again and again, till the tree is killed.

But there came an hour of revelation, — an hour when, in a manner which left no kind of room for doubt, Lady Byron saw the full depth of the abyss of infamy which her marriage was expected to cover, and understood that she was expected to be the cloak and the accomplice of this infamy.

Many women would have been utterly crushed by such a disclosure ; some would have fled from him immediately, and exposed and denounced the crime. Lady Byron did neither. When all the hope of womanhood, died out of her heart, there arose within her, stronger, purer, and brighter, that immortal kind of love such as God feels for the sinner, — the love of which Jesus spoke, and which holds the one wanderer of more account than the ninety and nine that went not astray. She would neither leave her husband nor betray him, nor yet would she for one moment justify his sin ; and hence came two years of convulsive struggle, in which sometimes, for a while, the good angel seemed to gain ground, and then the evil one returned with sevenfold vehemence,

Lord Byron argued his case with himself and with her with all the sophistries of his powerful mind. He repudiated Christianity as authority; asserted the right of every human being to follow out what he called " the impulses of nature." Subsequently he introduced into one of his dramas the reason ing by which he justified himself in incest.

In the drama of " Cain," Adah, the sister and the wife of Cain, thus addresses him : —

" Cain, walk not with this spirit. Bear with what we have borne, and love me : I Love thee.

Lucifer. More than thy mother and thy sire ?

Adah. I do. Is that a sin too?

Lucifer. No, not yet :

It one day will be in your children.

Adah. What!

Must not my daughter love her brother Enoch? 28

Lucifer. Not as thou lovest Cain.

Adah. O my God I

Shall they not love, and bring forth things that love Out of their loVe ? Have they not drawn their milk Out of this bosom ? Was not he, their father, Born of the same sole womb, in the same hour With me ? Did we not love each other, and, In multiplying our being, multiply Things which will love each other as we love Them ? And as I love thee, my Cain, go not Forth with this spirit: he is not of ours.

Lucifer. The sin I speak of is not of my making ; And cannot be a sin in you, whate'er It seems in those who will replace ye in Mortality.

Adah. What is the sin which is not Sin in itself? Can circumstance make sin Of virtue ? If it doth, we are the slaves Of" —

Lady Byron, though slight and almost infantine in her bodily presence, had the soul, not only of an angelic woman, but of a strong, reasoning man. It was the writer's lot to know her at a period when she formed the personal acquaint ance of many of the very first minds of England; but, among all with whom this experience brought her in connection, there was none who impressed her so strongly as Lady Byron. There was an almost supernatural power of moral divination, a grasp of the very highest and most comprehensive things, that made her lightest opinions singularly impressive. No doubt, this result was wrought out in a great degree from the anguish and conflict of these two years, when, with no one to help or counsel her but Almighty God, she wrestled and struggled with fiends of darkness for the redemption of her husband's soul.

She followed him through all his sophistical reasonings with a keener reason. She besought and implored, in the name of his better nature, and by all the glorious things that he was capable of being and doing ; and she had just power enough to convulse and shake and agonize, but not power enough to subdue.

One of the first of living writers, in the novel of " Romola," has given, in her masterly sketch of the character of Tito, the whole history of the conflict of a woman like Lady Byron with a nature like that of her husband. She has described a being full of fascinations and sweetnesses, full of generosities and of good-natured impulses ; a nature that could not bear to give pain, or to see it in others, but entirely destitute of any firm moral principle : she shows how such a being, merely by yielding step by step to the impulses of passjon, and disregard ing the claims of truth and right, becomes involved in a fatality of evil, in which deceit, crime, and cruelty are a necessity, forcing him to persist in the basest ingratitude to the father who has done all for him, and hard-hearted treachery to the high-minded wife who has given herself to him wholly.

There are few scenes in literature more fearfully tragic than the one between Romola and Tito, when he finally discovers that she knows him fully, and can be deceived by him no more.

Some such hour always must come for strong, decided natures irrevocably pledged, — one to the service of good, and the other to the slavery of evil. The demoniac cried out, " What have I to do with thee, Jesus of Nazareth ? Art thou come to tor ment me before the time ? " The presence of all-pitying purity and love was a torture to the soul possessed by the demon of evil.

These two years in which Lady Byron was with all her soul struggling to bring her husband back to his better self were a series of passionate convulsions.

During this time, such was the disordered and desperate state of his worldly affairs, that there were ten executions for debt levied on their family establishment; and it was Lady Byron's fortune each time which settled the account.

Toward the last, she and her husband saw less and less of each other ; and he came more and more decidedly under evil influences, and seemed to acquire a sort of hatred of her.

Lady Byron once said significantly to a friend who spoke of some* causeless dislike in another, " My dear, I have known people to be-hated for no other reason than because they im personated conscience."

The biographers of Lord Byron, and all his apologists, are careful to narrate how sweet and amiable and obliging he was to everybody who approached him ; and the saying of Fletcher, his man-servant, that " anybody could do any thing with my Lord, except my Lady," has often been quoted.

The reason of all this will now be evident. " My Lady" was the only one, fully understanding the deep and dreadful secrets of his life, who had the courage resolutely and persist ently and inflexibly to plant herself in his way, and insist upon it, that, if he went to destruction, it should be in spite of her best efforts.

He had tried his strength with her fully. The first attempt had been to make her an accomplice by sophistry ; by destroy ing her fait'h in Christianity, and confusing her sense of right and wrong, to bring her into the ranks of those convenient women who regard the marriage-tie only as a friendly alliance to cover license on both sides.

When her husband described to her the Continental latitude (the good-humored marriage, in which complaisant couples mutually agreed to form the cloak for each other's infidelities), and gave her to understand that in this way alone she could have a peaceful and friendly life with him, she answered him simply, " I am too truly your friend to do this."

When Lord Byron found that he had to do with one who would not yield, who knew him fully, who could not be blinded and could not be deceived, he determined to rid himself of her altogether.

It was when the state of affairs between herself and her husband seemed darkest and most hopeless, that the only child of this union was born. Lord Byron's treatment of his wife during the sensitive period that preceded the birth of this child, and during her confinement, was marked by paroxysms of un manly brutality, for which the only possible charity on her part was the supposition of insanity. Moore sheds a significant light on this period, by telling us, that, about this time, Byron was often drunk, day after day, with Sheridan. There had been insanity in the family ; and this was the plea which Lady Byron's love put in for him. She regarded him as, if not insane, at

least so nearly approaching the boundaries of insanity as to be a subject of forbearance and tender pity ; and ~she loved him with that love resembling a mother's, which good wives often feel when thev have lost all faith in their husbands' principles, and all hopes of their affections. Still, she was in heart and soul his best friend; true to him with a truth which he himself could not shake.

In the verses addressed to his daughter, Lord Byron speaks of her as
" The child of iove, though born in bitterness, And nurtured in convulsion."

A day or two after the birth of this child, Lord Byron came suddenly into Lady Byron's room, and told her that her mother was dead. It was an utter falsehood; but it was only one of the many nameless injuries and cruelties by which he expressed his hatred of her. A short time after her confinement, she was informed by him, in a note, that, as soon as she was able to travel, she must go ; that he could not and would not longer have her about him; and, when her child was only five weeks old, he carried this threat of expulsion into effect.

Here we will insert briefly Lady Byron's own account (the only one she ever gave to the public) of this separation. The circumstances under which this brief story was written are affecting.

Lord Byron was dead. The whole account between him and her was closed forever in this world. Moore's Life had been prepared, containing simply and solely Lord Byron's own version of their story. Moore sent this version to Lady Byron, and requested to know if she had any remarks to make upon it. In reply, she sent a brief statement to him, —the first and only one that had come from her during all. the years of the separation, and which appears to have mainly for its object the exculpation of her father and mother from the charge, made by the poet, of being the instigators of the separation.

In this letter, she says, with regard to their separation, —

" The facts are, I left London for Kirkby Mallory, the resi dence of my father and mother, on the I5th of January, 1816.

LORD BYRON HAD SIGNIFIED TO ME IN WRITING, JAN. 6, HIS ABSOLUTE DESIRE THAT I SHOULD LEAVE LONDON ON

THE EARLIEST DAY THAT I COULD CONVENIENTLY FIX.

It was not safe for me to undertake the fatigue of a journey sooner than the I5th. Previously to my departure, it had been strongly impressed upon my mind that Lord Byron was under the influence of insanity. This opinion was derived, in a great measure, from the communications made me by his nearest rela tives and personal attendant, who had more opportunity than myself for observing him during the latter part of my stay in town. It was even represented to me that he was in danger of destroying himself.

" With the concurrence ' of his family, I had consulted Dr. Baillie as a friend (Jan. 8) respecting the supposed malady. On acquainting him with the state of the case, and with Lord Byron's desire that I should leave London, Dr. Baillie thought that my absence might be advisable as an experiment, assuming the fact of mental derangement; for Dr. Baillie, not having had access to Lord Byron, could not pronounce a positive opinion on that point. He enjoined, that, in correspondence with Lord Byron, I should avoid all but light and soothing topics. Under these impressions, I left London, determined to follow the advice given by Dr. Baillie. Whatever might have been the conduct of Lord Byron toward me from the time of my marriage, yet, supposing him to be hi a state of mental aliena tion, it was not for me, nor for any person of common humanity, to manifest at that moment a sense of injury."

Nothing more than this letter from Lady Byron is necessary to substantiate the fact, that she did not leave her husband, but was driven from him, — driven from him that he might give himself up to the guilty infatuation that was consuming him, without being tortured by her imploring face, and by the silent power of her presence and her prayers.

For a long time before this, she had seen little of him. On the day of her departure,.she passed by the door of his room, and stopped to caress his favorite spaniel, which was lying there;

and she confessed to a friend the weakness of feeling a willingness even to be something as humble as that poor little

creature, might she only be allowed to remain and watch over him. She went into the room where he and the partner of his sins were sitting together, and said, " Byron, I come to say good-by ; " offering, at the same time, her hand.

Lord Byron put his hands behind him, retreated to the mantle-piece, and, looking round on the two that stood there, with a sarcastic smile said, " When shall we three meet again ? " Lady Byron answered, '* In heaven, I trust." And those were her last words to him on earth.

Now, if the reader wishes to understand the real talents of Lord Byron for deception and dissimulation, let him read, with this story in his mind, the " Fare thee well," which he addressed to Lady Byron through the printer : —

" Fare thee well ; and if forever,

Still forever fare thee well! Even though unforgiving, never 'Gainst thee shall my heart rebel.

Would that breast were bared before thee
Where thy head so oft hath lain, While that placid sleep came o'er thee
Thou canst never know again !
Though my many faults defaced me,
Could no other arm be found
* Than the one which once embraced me
To inflict a careless wound ? "

The re-action of society against him at the time of the sepa ration from his wife was something which he had not expected, and for which, it appears, he was entirely unprepared. It broke up the guilty intrigue, and ,drove him from England. He had not courage to meet or endure it. The world, to be sure, was very far from suspecting what the truth was : but the tide was setting against him with such vehemence as to make him trem ble every hour lest the whole should be known ; and henceforth it became a warfare of desperation to make his story good, no matter at whose expense.

He had tact enough to perceive at first that the assumption of the pathetic and the magnanimous, and general confessions of faults, accompanied with admissions of his wife's goodness,

would be the best policy in his case. In this mood, he thus writes to Moore : —

"The fault was not in my choice (unless in choosing at all) ; for I do not believe (and I must say it in the very dregs of all this bitter business) that there ever was a better, or 'even a brighter, a kinder, or a more amiable, agreeable being than Lady Byron. I never had, nor can have, any reproach to make her while with me. Where there is blame, it belongs to myself."

As there must be somewhere a scapegoat to bear the sin of the affair, Lord Byron wrote a poem called " A Sketch," in which he lays the blame of stirring up strife on a friend and former governess of Lady Byron's ; but in this sketch he intro duces the following just eulogy on Lady Byron : —

" Foiled was perversion by that youthful mind Which flattery fooled not, baseness could not blind, Deceit infect not, near contagion soil, Indulgence weaken, nor example spoil, Nor mastered science tempt her to look down On humbler talents with a pitying frown, Nor genius swell, nor beauty render vain, Nor envy ruffle to retaliate pain, Nor fortune change, pride raise, nor passion bow, Nor virtue teach austerity, — till now ; Serenely purest of her sex that live, But wanting one sweet weakness, —to forgive ; Too shocked at faults her soul can never know, She deemed that all could be like her below : Foe to all vice, yet hardly Virtue's friend ; For Virtue pardons those she would amend."

In leaving England, Lord Byron 'first went to Switzerland, where he conceived and in part wrote out the tragedy of " Man fred." Moore speaks of his domestic misfortunes, and the sufferings which he underwent at this time, as having an influence in stimulating his genius, so that he was enabled to write with a greater power.

Anybody who reads the tragedy of " Manfred " with this story in his mind will see that it is true.

The hero is represented as a gloomy misanthrope, dwelling with impenitent remorse on the memory of an incestuous pas-

sion which has been the destruction of his sister for this life and the life to come, but which, to the very last gasp, he despairingly refuses to repent of, even while he sees the fiends of darkness rising to take possession of his departing soul. That Byron knew his own guilt well, and judged himself severely, may be gathered from passages in this poem, which are as powerful as human language can be made ; for instance, this part of the " incantation," which Moore says was written at this time : —

" Though thy slumber may be deep,
Yet thy spirit shall not sleep :
There are shades which will not vanish ;
There are thoughts thou canst not banish.
By a power to thee unknown,
Thou canst never be alone :
Thou art wrapt as with a shroud ;
Thou art gathered in a cloud ;
And forever shalt thou dwell
In the spirit of this spell.

From thy false tears I did distil An essence which had strength to kill ; From thy own heart I then did wring The black blood in its blackest spring ; From thy own smile I snatched the snake, For there it coiled as in a brake ; From thy own lips I drew the charm Which gave all these their chiefest harm : In proving every poison known,

I found the strongest was thine own.
By thy cold breast and serpent smile,
By thy unfathomed gulfs of guile,
By that most seeming virtuous eye,
By thy shut soul's hypocrisy,
By the perfection of thine art
Which passed for human thine own heart,
By thy delight in others' pain,
And by thy brotherhood of Cain,
I call upon thee, and compel
Thyself to be thy proper hell 1"

Again : he represents Manfred as saying to the old abbot, who seeks to bring him to repentance, —

" Old man, there is no power in holy men, Nor charm in prayer, nor purifying form Of penitence, nor outward look, nor fast, Nor agony, nor, greater than all these, The innate tortures of that deep despair, Which is remorse without the fear of hell, But, all in all sufficient to itself,

Would make a hell of heaven, can exorcise From out the unbounded spirit the quick sense Of its own sins, wrongs, sufferance, and revenge Upon itself: there is no future pang Can deal that justice on the self-condemned He deals on his own soul."

And when the abbot tells him,

" All this is well;

For this will pass away, and be succeeded By an auspicious hope, which shall look up With calm assurance to that blessed place Which all who seek may win, whatever be Their earthly errors,"

He answers,

Then the old abbot soliloquizes : —

" This should have been a noble creature : he Hath all the energy which would have made A goodly frame of glorious elements, Had they been wisely mingled ; as it is, It is an awful chaos, —light and darkness, And mind and dust, and passions and pure thoughts, Mixed, and contending without end or order."

The world can easily see, in Moore's Biography, what, after this, was the course of Lord Byron's life ; how he went from shame to shame, and dishonor to dishonor, and used the fortune which his wife brought him in the manner described in those private letters which his biographer was left to print. Moore, indeed, says Byron had made the resolution not to touch his lady's fortune; but adds, that it re'quired more self-command than he possessed to carry out so honorable a purpose.

Lady Byron made but one condition with him. She had him in her power ; and she exacted that the unhappy partner of his sins should not follow him out of England, and^that the ruinous intrigue should be given up. Her inflexibility on this point kept up that enmity which was constantly expressing itself in some publication or other, and which drew her and her private relations with him before the public.

The story of what Lady Byron did with the portion of her fortune .which was reserved to her is a record of noble and skilfully administered charities. Pitiful and wise and strong, there was no form of human suffering or sorrow that did not find with her refuge and help. She gave not only systemati cally, but also impulsively.-

Miss Martineau claims for her the honor of having first invented practical schools, in which the children of the poor were turned into agriculturists, artisans, seamstresses, and good wives for poor men. While she managed with admirable skill and economy permanent institutions of this sort, she was always ready to relieve suffering in any form. The fugitive slaves William and Ellen Crafts, escaping to England, were fostered by her protecting care.

In many cases where there was distress or anxiety from poverty among those too self-respecting to make their sufferings known, the delicate hand of Lady Byron ministered to the want with a consideration which spared the most refined feel ings.

As a mother, her course was embarrassed by peculiar trials. The daughter inherited from the father not only brilliant talents, but a restlessness and morbid sensibility which might be too surely traced to the storms and agitations of the period in which she was born. It was necessary to bring her up in ignorance of the true history of her mother's life ; and the consequence was, that she could not fully understand that mother.

During her early girlhood, her career was a source of more anxiety than of comfort. She married a man of fashion, ran a brilliant course as a gay woman of fashion, and died early of a lingering and painful disease.

In the silence and shaded retirement of the sick-room, the

444 MISCELLANEOUS DOCUMENTS.

daughter came wholly back to her mother's arms and heart; and it was on that mother's bosom that she leaned as she went down into the dark valley. It was that mother who placed her weak and dying hand ih that of her Almighty Saviour.

To the children left by her daughter, she ministered with the faithfulness of a guardian angel ; and it is owing to her influ ence that those who yet remain are among the best and noblest of mankind.

The person whose relations with Byron had been so disas trous, also, in the latter years of her life, felt Lady Byron's loving and ennobling influences, and, in her last sickness and dying hours, looked to her for consolation and help.

There was an unfortunate child of sin, born with the curse upon her, over whose wayward nature Lady Byron watched with a mother's tenderness. She was the one who could have patience when the patience of every one else failed ; and though her task was a difficult one, from the strange, abnormal propen sities to evil in the object of her cares, yet Lady Byron never faltered, and never gave over, till death took the responsibility from her hands.

During all this trial, strange to say, her belief that the good in Lord Byron would finally conquer was unshaken.

To a friend who said to her, " Oh ! how could you love him ? " she answered briefly, " My dear, there was the angel in him." It is in us all.

It was in this angel that she had faith. It was for the deliv erance of this angel from degradation and shame and sin that she unceasingly prayed. She read every work that Byron wrote, —read it with a deeper knowledge than any human being but herself could possess. The ribaldry and the obscenity and the insults with which he strove to make her ridiculous in the world fell at her pitying feet unheeded.

When he broke away from all this unworthy life to devote himself to a manly enterprise for the redemption of Greece, she thought that she saw the beginning of an answer to her prayers. Even although one of his latest acts concerning her was to repeat to Lady Blessington the false accusation which made Lady Byron, the author of all his errors, she still had hopes from the one step taken in the right direction.

        «

In the midst of these hopes came the news of his sudden death. On his death-bed, it is well known that he called his confidential English servant to him, and said to him, " Go to my sister; tell her— Go to Lady Byron, — you will see her,— and say " —

Here followed twenty minutes of indistinct mutterings, in which the names of his wife, daughter, and sister, frequently occurred. He then said, " Now I have told you all."

" My lord," replied Fletcher, " I have not understood a word your lordship has been saying."

" Not understand me ! " exclaimed Lord Byron with a look of the utmost distress : " what a pity ! Then it is j;oo late, — all is over ! " He afterwards, says Moore, tried to utter a few words, of which none were intelligible except " My sister — my child."

When Fletcher returned to London, Lady Byron sent for him, and walked the room in convulsive struggles to repress her tears and sobs, while she over and over again strove to elicit something from him which should enlighten her upon what that last message had been ; but in vain : the gates of eternity were shut in her face, and not-a word had passed to tell her if he had repented.

For all that, Lady Byron never doubted his salvation. Ever before her, during the few remaining years of her widowhood, was the image of her husband, purified and ennobled, with the shadows of earth forever dissipated, the stains of sin forever removed ; " the angel in him," as she expressed it, " made per fect, according to its divine ideal."

Never has more divine strength of faith and love existed in woman. Out of the depths of her own loving and merciful nature, she gained such views of the divine love and mercy as made all hopes possible. There was no soul of whose future Lady Byron despaired, — such was her boundless faith in the redeeming power of love.

After Byron's death, the life of this delicate creature — so frail in body that she seemed always hovering on the brink of the eternal world, yet so strong in spirit, and so unceasing in her various ministries of mercy — was a miracle of mingled weakness and strength.

To talk with her seemed to the writer of this sketch the nearest possible approach to talking with one of the spirits of the just made perfect.

She was gentle, artless ; approachable as a little child; with ready, outflowing sympathy for the cares and sorrows and interests of all who approached her ; with a naive and gentle playfulness, that adorned, without hiding, the breadth and strength of her mind ; and, above all, with a clear, divining, moral discrimination; never mistaking wrong for right in the slightest shade, yet with a mercifulness that made allowance for every weakness, and pitied every sin.

There was^so much of Christ in her, that to have seen her seemed to be to have drawrt near to heaven. She was one of those few whom absence cannot estrange from friends ; whose mere presence in this world seems always a help to every gener ous thought, a strength to every good purpose, a comfort in every sorrow.

Living so near the confines of the spiritual world, she seemed already to see into it : hence the words of comfort which she addressed to a friend who had lost a son : —

" Dear friend, remember, as long as our loved ones are in God's world, they are in ours"

It has been thought by some friends who have read the proof-sheets of the foregoing that the author should state more specifically her authority for these statements.

The circumstances which led the writer to England at a certain time originated a friendship and correspondence with Lady Byron, which was always regarded as one of the greatest acquisitions of that visit.

On the occasion of a second visit to England, in 1856, the writer received a note from Lady Byron, indicating that she wished to have some private, confidential conversation upon important subjects, and inviting her, for that purpose, to spend a day with her at her country-seat near London.

The writer went and spent a day with Lady Byron alone ;

and the object of the invitation was explained to her. Lady Byron was in such a state of health, that her physicians had warned her that she had very little time to live. She was engaged in those duties and retrospections which every thoughtful person" finds necessary, when coming deliberately, and with open eyes, to the boundaries of this mortal life*

At that time, there was a cheap edition of Byron's works in contemplation, intended to bring his writings into circulation among the masses ; and the pathos arising from the story of his domestic misfortunes was one great means relied on for giving it currency.

Under these circumstances, some of Lady Byron's friends had proposed the question to her, whether she had not a respon sibility to society for the truth; whether she did right to allow thgse writings to gain influence over the popular mind by giving a silent consent to what she knew to be utter falsehoods.

Lady Byron's whole, life had been passed in the most heroic self-abnegation and self-sacrifice : and she had now to consider whether one more act of self-denial was not required of her before leaving this world; namely, to declare the absolute truth, no matter at what expense to her own feelings.

For this reason, it was her desire to recount the whole history to a person of another country, and entirely out of the sphere of personal and local feelings which might be supposed to influence those in the country and station in life where the events really happened, in order that she might be helped by such a person's views in making up an opinion as to her own duty.

The interview had almost the solemnity of a death-bed avowal. Lady Byron stated the facts which have been em bodied in this article, and gave to the writer a paper containing a brief memorandum of the whole, with the dates affixed.

We have already spoken of that singular sense of the reality of the spiritual world which seemed to encompass Lady Byron during the last part of her life, and which made her words and actions seem more like those of a blessed being detached from earth than of an ordinary mortal. All her modes of looking at things, all her motives of action, all her involuntary exhi-bitions of emotion, were so high above any common level, and so entirely regulated by the most unworldly causes, that it would seem difficult to make the ordinary world understand exactly how the thing seemed to lie before her mind. Wnat impressed the writer more strongly than any thing else was Lady Byron's perfect convictionathat her husband was now a redeemed spirit; that he looked back with pain and shame and regret on all that was unworthy in . his past life ; and that, if he could speak or could act in the case, he would desire to prevent the further circulation of base falsehoods, and of seductive poetry, which had been made the vehicle of morbid and unworthy passions.

Lady Byron's experience*had led her to apply the powers of her strong philosophical mind to the study of mental pathology : and she had become satisfied that the solution of the painfinl problem which first occurred to her as a young wife, was, after all, the true one ; namely, that Lord Byfon had been one of those unfortunately constituted persons in whom the balance of nature is so critically hung, that it is always in danger of dipping towards insanity; and that, in certain periods of his life, he was so far under the influence of mental disorder as not to be fully responsible for his actions.

She went over with a brief and clear analysis the history of his whole life as she had thought it out during the lonely musings of her widowhood. She dwelt on the ancestral causes that gave him a nature of exceptional and dangerous suscepti bility. She went through the mismanagements of his child hood, the history of his school-days, the influence of the ordinary school-course of classical reading on such a mind as his. She sketched boldly and clearly the internal life of the young men of the time, as she, with her purer eyes, had looked through it; and showed how habits, which, with less susceptible fibre and coarser strength of nature, were tolerable for his com panions, were deadly to him, unhinging his nervous system, and intensifying the dangers of ancestral proclivities. Lady Byron expressed the feeling too, that the Calvinistic theology, as heard in Scotland, had proved in his case, as it often does in certain minds, a subtle poison. He never could either dis-believe or become reconciled to it ; and the sore problems it proposes imbittered his spirit against Christianity.

"The worst of it is, I do believe" he would often say with violence, when he had been employing all his powers of reason, wit, and ridicule upon these subjects.

Through all this sorrowful history was to be seen, not the care of a slandered woman to make her story good, but the pathetic anxiety of a mother, who treasures every particle of hope, every intimation of good, in the son whom she cannot cease to love. With indescribable resignation, she dwelt on those last hours, those words addressed to her, never to be understood till repeated in eternity.

But all this she looked upon as fSrever past; believing, that, with the dropping of the earthly life, these morbid impulses aad influences ceased, and that higher nature which he often so beautifully expressed in his poems became the triumphant one.

While speaking on this subject, her pale, ethereal face became luminous with a heavenly radiance : there was some thing so sublime in her belief in the victory of love over evil, that faith with her seemed to have become sight. She seemed so clearly to perceive the divine ideal of the man she had loved, and for whose salvation she had been called to suffer and labor and pray, that all memories of his past unworthiness fell away, and were lost.

Her love was never the doting fondness of weak women ; it was the appreciative and discriminating love by which a higher nature recognized godlike capabilities under all the dust and defilement of misuse and passion : and she never doubted that the love which in her was so strong, that no injury or insult could shake it, was yet stronger in the God who made her capable of such a devotion, and that in him it was accompanied by power to subdue all things to itself.

The writer was so impressed and excited by the whole scene and recital, that she begged for two or three days to deliberate before forming any opinion. She took the memorandum with her, returned to London, and gave a day or two to the con sideration of the subject. The decision which she made was

chiefly influenced by her reverence and affection for Lady Byron. She seemed so frail, she had suffered so much, she stood at such a height above the comprehension of the coarse and common world, that the author had a feeling that it would almost be like violating a shrine to ask her to come forth from the sanctuary of a silence where she had so long abode, and plead her cause. She wrote to Lady Byron, that while this act of justice did seem to be called for, and to be in some respects most desirable, yet, as it would involve so much that was painful to her, the writer considered that Lady Byron would be entirely justifiable in leaving the truth to be disclosed after her death; and recommended that all the facts necessary should be put in the hands of some person, to be so published.

Years passed on. Lady Byron lingered four years after this interview, to the wonder of her physicians and all her friends.

After Lady Byron's death, the writer looked anxiously, hoping to see a Memoir of the person whom she considered the most remarkable woman that England has produced in the century. No such Memoir has appeared on the part of her friends ; and the mistress of Lord Byron has the ear of the public, and is sowing far and wide unworthy slanders, which are eagerly gathered up and read by an undiscriminating com munity.

There may be family reasons in England which prevent Lady Byron's friends from speaking. But Lady Byron has an American name and an American existence ; and reverence for pure womanhood is, we think, a national characteristic of the American; and, so far as this country is concerned, we feel that the public should have this refutation of the slanders of the Countess Guiccioli's book.

LORD LINDSAY'S LETTER TO "THE LONDON TIMES."

TO THE EDITOR OF " THE TIMES."

SIR, — I have waited in expectation of a categorical denial of the horrible charge brought by Mrs. Beecher Stowe against Lord Byron and his sister on the alleged authority of the la^s Lady Byron. Such denial has been only indirectly given by the letter of Messrs. Wharton and Fords in your impression of yesterday. That letter is sufficient to prove that Lady Byron never contemplated the use made of her name, and that her descendants and representatives disclaim any countenance of Mrs. B. Stowe's article ; but it does not specifically meet Mrs. Stowe's allegation, that Lady Byron, in conversing with her thirteen years ago, affirmed the charge now before -us. It re mains open, therefore, to a scandal-loving world, to credit the calumny through the advantage of this flaw, involuntary, I believe, in the answer produced against it. My object in addressing you is to supply that deficiency by proving that what is now stated on Lady Byron's supposed authority is at variance, in all respects, with what she stated immediately after the separation, when every thing was fresh in her memory in relation to the time 'during which, according to Mrs. B. Stowe, she believed that Byron and his sister were living together in guilt. I publish this evidence*with reluctance, but in obedience to that higher obligation of justice to the voiceless and defence less dead which bids me break through a reserve that other wise I should have held sacred. The Lady Byron of 1818 would, I am certain, have sanctioned my doing so, had she fore seen the present unparalleled occasion, and the bar that the conditions of her will present (as I infer from Messrs. Wharton and Fords' letter) against any fuller communication. Calumnies such as the present sink deep and with^sapidity into the public mind, and are not easily eradicated. The fame of one of our greatest poets, and that of the kindest and truest and most constant friend that Byron ever had, is at stake ; and it'will not do to wait for revelations from the fountain-head, which are not promised, and possibly may never reach us.

The late Lady Anne Barnard, who died in 1825, a contem porary and friend of Burke, Windham, Dundas, and a host of the wise and good of that generation, and remembered in letters as the authoress of " Auld Robin Gray," had known the late Lady Byron from infancy, and took a warm interest in her; holding Lord Byron in corresponding repugnance, not to say jirejudice, in consequence of what she believed to be his harsh and cruel treatment of her young friend. I transcribe the fol lowing passages, and a letter from Lady Byron herself (written in 1818) from ricordi, or private family memoirs, in Lady Anne's autograph, now before me. I include the letter, because, although treating only in general terms of the matter and causes of the separation, it affords collateral evidence bearing strictly upon the point of the credibility of the charge now in question : —

" The separation of Lord and Lady Byron astonished the world, which believed him a reformed man as to his habits, and a becalmed man as to his remorses. He had written nothing that appeared after his marriage till the famous ' Fare thee well,' which had the power of compelling those to pity the writer who were not well aware that he. was not the unhappy person he affected to be. Lady Byron's misery was whispered soon after her marriage and his ill usage ; but no word transpired, no sign escaped, from her. She gave birth, shortly, to a daughter; and when she went, as soon as she was recovered, on a visit to her father's, taking her little Ada with her, no one knew that it was to return to her lord no more. At that period, a severe fit of illness had confined me to bed for two months. I heard of Lady Byron's distress ; of the pains he took to give a harsh impression of her character to the world. I wrote to her, and entreated her to come and let me see and hear her, if she conceived my symnfithy or counsel could be any comfort to her. She came ; but what a tale was unfolded by this interest ing young creature, who had so fondly hoped to have made a young man of genius and romance (as she supposed) happy ! They had not beeft an hour in the carriage which conveyed them from the church, when, breaking into a malignant sneer,

' Oh ! what a dupe you have been to your imagination ! How is it possible a woman of your sense could form the wild hope of reforming me ? Many are the tears you will have to shed ere that plan is accomplished. It is enough for me that you are my wife for me to hate you. If you were the wife of any other man, I own you might have charms,' &c. I who listened was astonished. ' How could you go on after this,' said I, ' rfly dear ? Why did you not return to your father's ?' — ' Because I had not a conception he was in earnest ; because I reckoned it a bad jest, and told him so,—that my. opinions of him were very different from his of himself, otherwise he would not find me by his side. He laughed it over when he saw me appear hurt; and I forgot what had passed, till forced to remember it. I believe he was pleased with me, too, for a little while. I sup pose it had escaped his memory that I was his wife.' But she described the happiness they enjoyed to have been unequal and perturbed. Her situation, in- a short time, might have entitled her to some tenderness; but she made no claim on him for any. He sometimes reproached her for the motives that had induced her to marry him : all was ' vanity, the vanity of Miss Milbanke carrying the point of reforming Lord Byron ! He always knew her inducements ; her pride shut her eyes to his: he wished to build up his character and his fortunes ; both were somewhat deranged : she had a high name, and would have a fortune worth his attention,—let her look to'that for his motives!' — 'O Byron, Byron!' she said, ' how you desolate me!' He would then accuse himself of being mad,'and throw himself on the ground in a frenzy, which she believed was affected to conceal the coldness and malignity of his heart, — an affectation which at that time never failed to meet with the tenderest commiseration. I could find by some impli-catio'ns, not followed up by me, lest she might have condemned herself afterwards for her involuntary disclosures, that he soon attempted to corrupt her principles, both with respect to her own conduct and her latitude for his. She saw the precipice on which she stood, and kept his sister with her as much as possible. He returned in the evenings from the haunts of vice, where he made her understand he had been, with manners so

profligate ! ' O the wretch !' said I. ' And had he no moments of remorse ?' — ' Sometimes he appeared to have them. One night, coming home from one of his lawless parties, he saw me so indignantly collected, and bearing all with such a determined calmness, that a rush of remorse seemed to come over him. He called himself a monster, though his sister was present, and threw himself in agony at my feet. "I could not — no — I could not forgive him such injuries. He had lost me forever ! " Astonished at the return of virtue, my tears, I believe, flowed over his face, and I said, " Byron, all is forgotten : never, never, shall you hear of it more ! " He started up, and, folding his arms while he looked at me, burst into laughter. " What do you mean ?" said I. " Only a philosophical experiment; that's all," said he. " I wished to ascertain the value of your resolutions." ' I need not say more of this prince of duplicity, except that varied were his methods of rendering her wretched, even to the last. When her lovely little child was born, and it was laid beside its mother on the bed, and he was informed he might see his daughter, after gazing at it with an exulting smile, this was the ejaculation that broke from him : ' Oh, what an implement of torture have I acquired in you !' Such he rendered it by his eyes and manner, keeping her in a perpetual alarm for its safety when in his presence. All this 'reads madder than I believe he was : but she had not then made up her mind to disbelieve his pretended insanity, and conceived it best to intrust her secret with the excellent Dr. Baillie ; telling him* all that seemed to regard the state of her husband's mind, and letting his advice regulate her conduct. Baillie doubted of his derangement; but, as he did not reckon his own opinion infallible, he wished her to take precautions as if her husband was so. He recommended her going to the country, but to give him no suspicion of her intentions of remaining there, and, for a short time, to show no coldness in her letters, till she could better ascertain his state. She went, regretting, as she told me, to wear any semblance but the truth. A short time disclosed the story to the world. He acted the part of a man driven to despair by her inflexible resentment and by the arts of a governess (once a servant in the family) who hated him.

I will give you," proceeds Lady Anne, " a few paragraphs transcribed from one of Lady Byron's own letters to me. It is sorrowful to think, that, in a very little time, this young and amiable creature, wise, patient, and feeling, will have her character mistaken by every one who reads Byron's works. To rescue her from this, I preserved her letters; and, when she a/terwards expressed a fear that any thing of her writings should ever fall into hands to injure him (I suppose she meant by publication), I safely assured her that it never should. But here this letter shall be placed, a sacred record in her favor, unknown to herself: —

" ' I am a very incompetent judge of the impression which the last canto of " Childe Harold " may produce on the minds of indifferent readers. It contains the usual trace of a con science restlessly awake ; though his object has been too long to aggravate its burden, as if it could thus be oppressed into eternal stupor. I will hope, as you clo, that it survives for his ultimate good. It was the acuteness of his remorse, impenitent in its character, which so long seemed to demand from my compassion to spare every semblance of reproach, every look of grief, which might have said to his conscience, " You have made me wretched." I am decidedly of opinion that he is responsible. He has wished to be thought partially deranged, or on the brink of it, to perplex observers, and prevent them from tracing effects to their real causes through all the intrica cies of his conduct. I was, as I told you, at one time the dupe of his acted insanity, and clung to the former delusions in regard to the motives that concerned me personally, till the whole system was laid bare. He is the absolute monarch of words, and uses them, as Bonaparte did lives, for conquest, without more regard to their intrinsic value ; considering them only as ciphers, which must derive all their import from the situation in which he places them, and the ends to which he adapts them with such consummate skill. Why, then, you will say, does he not employ them to give a better color to his own character ? Because he is too good an actor to over-act, or to assume a moral garb which it would be easy to strip off. In

MISCELLANEOUS DOCUMENTS.

regard to his poetry, egotism is the vital principle of his imagi nation, which it is difficult for him to kindle on any subject with which his own character and interests are not identified : but by the introduction of fictitious incidents, by change of scene or time, he has enveloped his poetical disclosures in a system impenetrable except to a very few ; and his constant desire of creating a sensation makes him not averse to be tie object of wonder and curiosity, even though accompanied by some dark and vague suspicions. Nothing has contributed more to the misunderstanding of his real character than the lonely grandeur in which he shrouds it, and his affectation of being above mankind, when he exists almost in their voice. The romance of -his sentiments is another feature of this mask of state. I know no one more habitually destitute of that enthusiasm he so beautifully expresses, and to which he can work up his fancy chiefly by contagion. I had heard he was the best of brothers, the most generous of friends; and I thought such feelings only required to be warmed and cherished into more diffusive beVievolence. Though these opinions are eradicated, and could never return but with the decay of my memory, you will not wonder if there are still moments when the association of feelings which arose from them soften and sadden my thoughts. But I have not thanked you, dearest Lady Anne, for your kindness in regard to a principal object, — that of rectifying false impressions. I trust you understand my wishes, which never were to injure Lord Byron in any way : for, though he would not suffer me to remain his wife, he cannot prevent me from continuing his friend ; and it was from con sidering myself as such that I silenced the accusations by which my own conduct might have been more fully justified. It is not necessary to speak ill of his heart in general : it is sufficient that to me it was hard and impenetrable ; that my own must have been broken before his could have been touched. I would rather represent this as my misfortune than as his guilt ; but surely that misfortune is not to be made .my crime ! Such are my feelings : you will judge how to act. His allusions to me in "Childe Harold " are cruel and cold, but with such a semblance as to make me appear so, and to attract

all sympathy to himself. It is said in this poem that hatred of him will be taught as a lesson to his child. I might appeal to ail who have ever heard me speak of him, and still more to my own heart, to witness that there has been no moment when I have remembered injury otherwise than affectionately and sorrowfully. It is not my duty to give way to hopeless and wholly unrequited affection ; but, so long as I live, my chief struggle will probably be not to remember him too kindly. I do not seek the sympathy of the world ; but I wish to be known by those whose opinion is valuable, and whose kindness is dear to me. Among such, my dear Lady Anne, you will ever be remembered by your truly affectionate,

"'A. BYRON.'"

It is the province of your readers, and of the world at large, to judge between the two testimonies now before them, — Lady Byron's in 1816 and 1818, and that put forward in 1869 by Mrs. B. Stowe, as communicated by Lady Byron thirteen years ago. In the face of the evidence now given, positive, negative, and circumstantial, there can be but two alternatives in the case: either Mrs. B. Stowe must have entirely misunderstood Lady Byron, and been thus led into error and misstatement; or we must conclude, that, under the pressure of a lifelong and secret sorrow, Lady Byron's mind had become clouded with an hallu cination in respect of the particular point in question.

The reader will admire the noble but severe character dis played in Lady Byron's letter; but those who keep in view what her first impressions were, as above recorded, may probably place a more lenient interpretation than hers upon some of the incidents alleged to Byron's discredit. I shall conclude with some remarks upon his character, written shortly after his death by a wise, virtuous, and charitable judge, the ki':e Sir Walter Scott, likewise in a letter to. Lady Anne Bar nard : —

" Fletcher's account of poor Byron is extremely interesting. I had always a strong attachment to that unfortunate though most richly-gifted man, because I thought I saw that his virtues

(and tie had many) were his own; and his eccentricities the result of an irritable temperament, which sometimes approached nearly to mental disease. Those who are gifted with strong nerves, a regular temper, and habitual self-command, are not, perhaps, aware how much of what they may think virtue they owe to constitution ; and such are but too severe judges of men like Byron, whose mind, like a day of alternate storm and sunshine, is all dark shades and stray gleams of light, instead of the twilight gray which illuminates happier though less distinguished mortals. I always thought, that, when a moral proposition was placed plainly before Lord Byron, his mind yielded a pleased and willing assent to it; but, if there was any side-view given in the way of raillery or otherwise, he was willing enough to evade conviction. ... It augurs ill for the cause of Greece that this master-spirit should have been with drawn from their assistance just as he was obtaining a complete ascendency over their counsels. I have seen several letters from the Ionian Islands, all of which unite in speaking in the highest praise of the wisdom and temperance of his counsels, and the ascendency he was obtaining over the turbulent and ferocious chiefs of the insurgents. I have some verses written by him on his last birthday : they breathe a spirit of affection towards his wife, and a desire of dying in battle, which seems like an anticipation of his approaching fate."

I remain, sir, your obedient servant,
LINDSAY.
DUNECHT, Sept. 3.
DR. FORBES WINSLOW'S LETTER TO "THE LONDON TIMES."
TO THE EDITOR.
SIR, — Your paper of the 4th of September, containing an able and deeply interesting " Vindication of Lord Byron," has followed me to this place. With the general details of the " True

Story " (as it is termed) of Lady Byron's separation from

her husband, as recorded in " Macmillan's Magazine," I have no desire or intention to grapple. It is only with the hypothesis of insanity, as suggested by the clever writer of the " Vindica tion " to account for Lady Byron's sad revelations to Mrs. Beecher Stowe, with which I propose to deal. I do not be lieve that the mooted theory of mental aberration can, in this case, be for a moment maintained. If Lady Byron's statement of facts to Mrs. B. Stowe is to be viewed as the creation of a distempered fancy, a delusion or hallucination of an insane mind, at what part of the narrative are we to draw the bounda ry-line between fact and delusion, sanity and insanity ? Where are we to fix the point cTappui of the lunacy ? Again : is the alleged " hallucination " to be considered as strictly confined to the idea that Lord Byron had committed the frightful sin of in cest ? or is the whole of the " True Story " of her married life, as reproduced with such terrible minuteness by Mrs. Beecher Stowe, to be viewed as the delusion of a disordered fancy ? If Lady Byron was the subject of an " hallucination " with regard to her husband, I think it not unreasonable to conclude that the mental alienation existed on the day of her marriage. If this proposition be accepted, the natural inference will be, that the details of the conversation which Lady Byron represents to have occurred between herself and Lord Byron as soon as they entered the carriage never took place. Lord Byron is said to have remarked to Lady Byron, " You might have prevented this (or words to this effect): you will now find that you have married a devil." Is this alleged conversation to be viewed as facf, or fiction ? evidence of sanity, or insanity ? Is the revelation which Lord Byron is said to have made to his wife of his "in cestuous passion " another delusion, having no foundation ex cept in his wife's disordered imagination ? Are his alleged attempts to justify to Lady Byron's mind the morale of the plea of "Continental latitude, — the good-humored marriage, in which complaisant couples mutually agree to form the cloak for each other's infidelities," — another morbid perversion of her imagination ? Did this conversation ever take place ? It will be difficult to separate one part of the "True Story " from another, and maintain that this portion indicates insanity, and that por-

tion represents sanity. If we accept the hypothesis of hallu cination, we are bound to view the whole of Lady Byrou's conversations with Mrs. B. Stowe, and the written statement laid before her, as the wild and incoherent representations of a lunatic. On the day when Lady Byron parted from her hus band, did she enter his private room, and find him with the " object of his guilty passion " ? and did he say, as they parted, " When shall we three meet again ? " Is this to be considered as an actual occurrence, or as another form of hallucination ? It is quite inconsistent with the theory of Lady Byron's insanity to imagine that her delusion was restricted to the idea of his having committed " incest." In common fairness, we are bound to view the aggregate mental phenomena which she exhibited from the day of the marriage to their final separation and her death. No person practically acquainted with the true charac teristics of insanity would affirm, that, had this idea of " incest" been an insane hallucination, Lady Byron could, from the lengthened period which intervened between her unhappy mar riage and death, have refrained from exhibiting her mental alien ation, not only to her legal advisers and trustees, but to others, exacting no pledge of secrecy from them as to her disordered impressions. Lunatics do for a time, and for some special pur pose, most cunningly conceal their delusions; but they have not the capacity to struggle for thirty-six years with a frightful hal lucination, similar to the one Lady Byron is alleged to have had, without the insane state of mind becoming obvious to those with whom they are daily associating. Neither is it consistent with experience to suppose, that, if Lady Byron had been a monomaniac, her state of disordered understanding would have been restricted to one hallucination. Her diseased brain, affect ing the normal action of thought, would, in all probability, have manifested other symptoms besides those referred to of aberra tion of intellect.

During the last thirty years, I have not met with a case of insanity (assuming the hypothesis of hallucination) at all paral lel with that of Lady Byron's. In my experience, it is unique. I never saw a patient with such a delusion. If it should be es tablished, by the statements of those who are the depositors of

the secret (and they are now bound, in vindication of Lord By ron's memory, to deny, if they have the power of doing so, this most frightful accusation), that the idea of incest did unhappily cross Lady Byron's mind prior to her finally leaving him, it no doubt arose from a most inaccurate knowledge of facts and per fectly unjustifiable data, and was not, in the right psychological acceptation of the phrase, an insane hallucination.

Sir, I remain your obedient servant,

FORBES WINSLOW, M.D. ZARINGERHOF, FREBURG-EN-BREISGAU, Sept. 8, 1869.

EXTRACT FROM LORD BYRON'S EXPUNGED LETTER.

TO MR. MURRAY.

" BOLOGNA, June 7, 1819.

..." Before I left Venice, I had returned to you your late, and Mr. Hobhouse's sheets of 'Juan.' Don't wait for further answers from me, but address yours to Venice as usual. I know nothing of my own movements. I may return there in a few days, or not for some time : all this depends on circumstances. I left Mr. Hoppner very well. My daughter Allegra is well too, and is growing pretty : her hair is growing darker, and her eyes are blue. Her temper and her ways, Mr. Hoppner says, are like mine, as well as her features : she will make, in that case, a manageable young lady.

" I have never seen any thing of Ada, the little Electra 'of my Mycenae. . . . But there will come a day of reckoning, even if

I should not live to see it. I have at least seen shivered,

who was one of my assassins. When that man was doing his worst to uproot my whole family, — tree, branch, and blossoms ; when, after taking my retainer, he went over to them ; when he was bringing desolation on my hearth, and destruction on my household gods, — did he think, that, in less than three years, a natural event, a severe domestic, but an expected and com mon calamity, would lay his carcass in a cross-road, or stamp

462 MISCELLANEOUS DOCUMENTS.

his name in a verdict of lunacy ? Did he (who in his sexage nary . . .) reflect or consider what my feelings must have been when wife and child and sister, and name and fame and country, were to be my sacrifice on his legal altar ? — and this at a moment when my health was declining, my fortune embarrassed, and my mind had been shaken by many kinds of disappointment ? while I was yet young, and might have reformed what might be wrong in my conduct, and retrieved what was perplexing in my affairs ? But he is in his grave, and —" What a long letter I have scrib bled ! " .

IN order that the reader may measure the change of moral tone with regard to Lord Byron, wrought by the constant efforts of himself and his party, we give the two following extracts from " Blackwood."

The first is " Blackwood " in 1819, just after the publication of " Don Juan : " the second is " Blackwood " in 1825.

" In the composition of this work, there is, unquestionably, a more thorough and intense infusion of genius and vice, power and profligacy, than in any poem which had ever before been written in the English, or, indeed, in any other modern language. Had the wickedness been less inextricably mingled with the beauty and the grace and the strength of a most inimitable and incomprehensible Muse, our task would have been easy. ' Don Juan' is by far the most admirable specimen of the mixture of ease, strength, gayety, and seriousness, extant in the whole body of English poetry : the author has devoted his powers to ihe worst of purposes and passions ; and it increases his guilt and our sorrow that he has devoted them entire.

" The moral strain of the whole poem is pitched in the lowest key. Love, honor, patriotism, religion, are mentioned only to be scoffed at, as if their sole resting-place were, or ought to be, in the bosoms of fools. It appears, in short, as if this misera ble man, having exhausted every species of sensual gratification, having drained the cup of sin even to its bitterest dregs, were resolved to show us that he is no longer a' human being, even

in his frailties, but a cool, unconcerned fiend, laughing with a detestable glee over the whole of the better and worse elements of which human life is composed; treating well-nigh with equal derision the most pure of virtues, and the most odious of vices; dead alike to the beauty of the one, and the deformity of the other ; a mere heartless despiser of that frail but noble human ity, whose type was never exhibited in a shape of more deplora ble degradation than in his own contemptuously distinct deline ation of himself. To confess to his Maker, and weep over in secret agonies the wildest and most fantastic transgressions of heart and mind, is the part of a conscious sinner, in whom sin has not become the sole principle of life and action ; but to lay bare to the eye of man and of woman all the hidden con vulsions of a wicked spirit, and to do all this without one symp tom of contrition, remorse, or hesitation, with a calm, careless ferociousness of contented and satisfied depravity, — this was an insult which no man of genius had ever before dared to put upon his Creator or his species. Impiously railing against his God, madly and meanly disloyal to his sovereign and his coun try, and brutally outraging all the best feelings of female honor, affection, and confidence, how small a part of chivalry is that which remains to the descendant of the Byrons ! — a gloomy visor and a deadly weapon!

" Those who are acquainted (as who is not ?) with the main incidents in the private life of Lord Byron, and who have not seen this production, will scarcely believe that malignity should have carried him so far as to make him commence a filthy and impious poem with an elaborate satire on the character and manners of his wife, from whom, even by his own confession, he has been separated only in consequence of his own cruel and heartless misconduct. It is in vain for Lord Byron to attempt in any way to justify his own behavior in that affair ; and, now that he has so openly and audaciously invited inquiry and reproach, we do not see any good reason why he should not be plainly told so by the general voice of his countrymen. It would not be an easy matter to persuade any man who has any knowledge of the nature of woman, that a female such as Lord Byron has himself described his wife to be would rashly or

464 MISCELLANEOUS DOCUMENTS.

hastily or lightly separate herself from the love with which she had once been inspired for such a man as he is or was. Had he not heaped insult upon insult, and scorn upon scorn, had he not forced the iron of his contempt into her very soul, there is no woman of delicacy and virtue, as he admitted Lady Byron to be, who would not have hoped all things, and suffered all things, from one, her love of whom must have been inwoven with so many exalting elements of delicious pride, and more delicious humility. To offend the love of such a woman -was wrong, but it might be forgiven ; to desert her was unmanly, but he might have returned, and wiped forever from her eyes the tears of her desertion: but to injure and to desert, and then to turn back and wound her widowed privacy with unhallowed strains of cold-blooded mockery, was brutally, fiendishly, inex-piably mean. For impurities there might be some possibility of pardon, were they supposed to spring only from the reckless buoyancy of young blood and fiery passions ; for impiety there might at least be pity, were it visible that the misery of the impious soul equalled its darkness : but for offences such as this, which cannot proceed either from the madness of sudden impulse or the bewildered agonies of doubt, but which speak the wilful and determined spite of an unrepenting, unsoftened, smiling, sarcastic, joyous sinner, there can be neither pity nor pardon. Our knowledge that it is committed by one of the most powerful intellects our island ever has produced lends intensity a thousand-fold to the bitterness of our indignation. Every high thought that was ever kindled in our breasts by the Muse of Byron, every pure and lofty feeling that ever responded from within us to the sweep of his majestic inspirations, every re membered moment of admiration and enthusiasm, is up in arms against him. We look back with a mixture of wrath and scorn to the delight with which we suffered ourselves to be filled by one, who, all the while he was furnishing us with delight, must, we cannot doubt it, have been mocking us with a cruel mock ery ; less cruel only, because less peculiar, than that with which he has now turned him from the lurking-place of his selfish and polluted exile to pour the pitiful chalice of his contumely on the surrendered devotion of a virgin bosom, and the holy hopes

of the mother of his child. It is indeed a sad and a humiliating thing to know, that, in the same year, there proceeded from the same pen two productions in all things so different as the fourth canto of ' Childe Harold ' and this loathsome ' Don Juan.'

" We have mentioned one, and, all will admit, the worst in stance of the private malignity which has been embodied in so many passages of ' Don Juan ;' and we are quite sure the lofty-minded and virtuous men whom Lord Byron has debased himself by insulting will close the volume which contains their own injuries, with no feelings save those of pity for him that has inflicted them, and for her who partakes so largely in the same injuries." — August, 1819.

" BLACKWOOD," — itcrum.

" WE shall/like all others who say any thing about Lord By ron, begin, sans apologie, with his personal character. This is the great object of attack, the constant theme of open vituperation to one set, and the established mark for all the petty but deadly artillery of sneers, shrugs, groans, to another. Two widely different matters, however, are generally, we might say univer sally, mixed up here, — the personal character of the man, as proved by his course of life ; and his personal character, as revealed in or guessed from his books. Nothing can be more unfair than the style in which this mixture is made use of. Is there a noble sentiment, a lofty thought, a sublime conception, in the book ? ' Ah, yes !' is the answer. ' But what of that ? It is only the roue Byron that speaks !' Is a kind, a generous action of the man mentioned ? ' Yes, yes !' comments the sage; ' but only remember the atrocities of " Don Juan : " depend on it, this, if it be true, must have been a mere freak of caprice, or perhaps a bit of vile hypocrisy.' Salvation is thus shut out at either entrance : the poet damns the man, and the man the poet.

" Nobody will suspect us of being so absurd as to suppose that it is possible for people to draw no inferences as to the 3°

character of an author from his book, or to shut entirely out of view, in judging of a book, that which they may happen to know about the man who writes it. The cant of the day sup poses such things to be practicable ; but they are not. But what we complain of and scorn is the extent to which they are carried in the case of this particular individual, as compared with others ; the impudence with which things are at once assumed to be facts in regard to his private, history; and the absolute unfairness of never arguing from his writings to him, but for evil.

" Take the man, in the first place, as unconnected, in so far as we can thus consider him, with his works ; and ask, What, after all, are the bad things we know of him ? Was he dis honest or dishonorable ? had he ever done any thing to forfeit, or even endanger, his rank as a gentleman ? Most assuredly, no such accusations have ever been maintained against Lord Byron the private nobleman, although something of the sort may have been insinuated against the author/ ' But he was such a profligate in his morals, that his name- cannot be men tioned with any thing like tolerance.' Was he so x indeed? We should like extremely to have the catechising of the in dividual man who says so. That he indulged in sensual vices, to some extent, is certain, and to be regretted and condemned. But was he worse, as to such matters, than the enormous majority of those who join in'the cry of horror upon this occa sion ? We most assuredly believe exactly the reverse ; and we rest our belief upon very plain and intelligible grounds. First, we hold it impossible that the majority of mankind, or that any thing beyond a very small minority, are or can be entitled to talk of sensual profligacy as having formed a part of the life and character of the man, who, dying at -six and thirty, bequeathed a collection of works such as Byron's to the world. Secondly, we hold it impossible, that laying the. extent of his intellectual labors out of the question, and looking only to the nature of the intellect which generated, and delighted in gene rating, such beautiful and noble conceptions as are to be found in almost all Lord Byron's works, — we hold it impossible that very many men can be at once capable of comprehending these

conceptions, and entitled to consider sensual profligacy as having formed the principal, or even a principal, trait in Lord Byron's character. Thirdly, and lastly, we have never been able to hear any one fact established which could prove Lord Byron to deserve any thing like the degree or even kind of odium which has, in regard to matters of this class, been heaped upon his name. We have no story of base unmanly seduction, or false -and villanous intrigue, against him, — none whatever. It seems to us quite clear, that, if he had been at all what is called in society an unprincipled sensualist, there must have been many such stories, authentic and authenticated. But there are none such, — absolutely none. His name has been coupled with the names of three, four, or more women of some rank : but what kind of women ? Every one of them, in the first place, about as old as himself in years, and therefore" a great deal older in character ; every one of them utterly battered in reputation long before he came into contact with them, — licentious, unprincipled, characterless women. What father has ever reproached him with the ruin of his daughter ? What husband has denounced him as the destroyer of his peace ?

"Let us not be mistaken. We are not defending the offences of which Lord Byron unquestionably was guilty; neither are we finding fault with those, who, after looking honestly within and around themselves, condemn those offences, no matter how severely : but we are speaking of society in general as it now exists ; and we say that there is vile hypocrisy in the tone in which Lord Byron is talked of there. We say, that, although all offences against purity of life are miserable things, and condemnable things, the degrees of guilt attached to different offences of this class are as widely different as are the degrees of guilt between an assault and a murder ; and we con fess our belief, that no man of Byron's station and age could have run much risk in gaining a very bad name in society, had a course of life similar (in so far as we know any thing of that) to Lord Byron's been the only thing chargeable against him.

" The last poem he wrote was produced upon his birthday, not many weeks before he died. We consider it as one of the

finest and most touching effusions of his noble genius. We think he who reads it, and can ever after bring himself to regard even the worst transgressions that have been charged against Lord Byron with any feelings but those of humble sor row and manly pity, is not deserving of the name of man. The deep and passionate struggles with the inferior elements of his nature (and ours) which it records ; the lofty thirsting after purity ; the heroic devotion of a soul half weary of life, because unable to believe in its own powers to live up to what it so intensely felt to be, and so reverentially honored as, the right; the whole picture of this mighty spirit, often darkened, but never sunk, — often erring, but never ceasing to see and to worship the beauty of virtue ; the repentance of it; the anguish ; the aspira tion, almost stifled in despair, the whole of this is such a whole, that we are sure no man can read these solemn verses too often ; and we recommend them for repetition, as the best and most conclusive of all possible answers whenever the name of Byron is insulted by those who permit themselves to forget nothing, either in his life or in his writings, but the good." [1825.]

THE following letters of Lady Byron's are reprinted from the Memoirs of H. C. Robinson. They are given that the reader may form some judgment of the strength and activity of her mind, and the elevated class of subjects upon which it habitually dwelt.

LADY BYRON TO H. C. R.

"DEC. 31, 1853.

"DEAR MR. CRABB ROBINSON, — I have an inclination, if I were not afraid of trespassing on your time (but you can put my letter by for any leisure moment), to enter upon the history of a character which I think less appreciated than it ought to be. Men, I observe, do not understand men in certain points, with out a woman's interpretation. Those points, of course, relate to feelings.

" Here is a man taken by most of those who come in his way either for Dry-as-dust, Matter-of-fact, or for a ' vain visionary.' There are, doubtless, some defective or excessive characteristics which give rise to those impressions.

" My acquaintance was made, oddly enough, with him twenty-seven years ago. A pauper said to me of him, * He's the poor man's doctor.' Such a recommendation seemed to me a good one : and I also knew that his organizing head had formed the first district society in England (for Mrs. Fry told me she could not have effected it without his aid); yet he has always ignored his own share of it. I felt in him at once the curious combina tion of the Christian and the cynic, —of reverence for man, and contempt of. men. It was then an internal war, but one in which it was evident to me that the holier cause would be vic torious, because there was deep belief, and, as far as I could learn, a blameless and benevolent life. He appeared only to want sunshine. It was a plant which could not be brought to perfection in darkness. He had begun life by the most painful conflict between filial duty and conscience, — a large provision in the church secured for him by his father ; but he could not sign. There was discredit, as you know, attached to such Scru ples.

" He was also, when I first knew him, under other circum stances of a nature to depress him, and to make him feel that he was unjustly treated. The gradual removal of these called forth his better nature in thankfulness to God. Still the old misanthropic modes of expressing himself obtruded themselves at times. This passed in '48 between him and Robertson. Robertson said to me, ' I want to know something about ragged schools.' I replied, ' You had better ask Dr.- King: he knows more about them.' — 'I?' said Dr. King. 'I take care to know nothing of ragged schools, lest they should make me ragged.' Robertson did not see through it. Perhaps I had been taught to understand such suicidal speeches by my cousin, Lord Melbourne.

" The example of Christ, imperfectly as it may be understood by him, has been ever before his eyes : he woke to the thought of following it, and he went to rest consoled or rebuked by it

After nearly thirty years of intimacy, I may, without presump tion, form that opinion. There is something pathetic to me in seeing any one so unknown. Even the other medical friends of Robertson, when I knew that Dr. King felt a woman's tenderness, said on one occasion to him, ' But we know that you, Dr. King, are above all feeling."

" If I have made the character more consistent to you by putting in these bits of mosaic, my pen will not have been ill employed, nor unpleasingly to you.

" Yours truly,

"A. NOEL BYRON."

LADY'BYRON TO H. C. R.

"BRIGHTON, Nov. 15, 1854.

" The thoughts of all this public and private suffering have taken the life out of my pen when I tried to write on matters which would otherwise have been most interesting to me : these seemed the shadows, that the stern reality. It is good, how ever, to be drawn out of scenes in which one is absorbed most unprofitably, and to have one's natural interests revived by such a letter as I have to thank you for, as well as its predecessor. You touch upon the very points which do interest me the most, habitually. The change of form, and enlargement of design, in ' The Prospective' had led me to express to one of the promoters of that object my desire to contribute. The religious crisis is instant; but the man for it ? The next best thing, if, as I believe, he is not to be found in England, is an association of such men as are to edit the new periodical. An address delivered by Freeman Clarke at Boston, last May, makes me think him bet ter fitted for a leader than any other of the religious ' Free thinkers.' I wish I could send you my one copy; but you do not need it, and others do. His object is the same as that of the ' Alliance Universelle :' only he is still more free from ' partialism ' (his own word) in his aspirations and practical suggestions with respect to an ultimate ' Christian synthesis.' He so far adopts Comte's theory as to speak of religion it self under three successive aspects, historically,— i. Thesis;

MISCELLANEOUS DOCUMENTS. 4/1

2. Antithesis; 3. Synthesis. I made his acquaintance in Eng land ; and he inspired confidence at once by his brave inde pendence (incomptis capillis] and seif-zmconsciousness. J. J. Tayler's address of last month follows in the same path, —all in favor of the ' irenics,' instead of polemics.

" The answer which you gave me so fully and distinctly to the questions I proposed for your consideration was of value in turning to my view certain aspects of the case which I had not before observed. I had begun a second attack on your patience, when all was forgotten in the news of the day."

LADY BYRON TO H. C. R.

" BRIGHTON, Dec. 25, 1854.

" With J. J. Tayler, though almost a stranger to him, I have a peculiar reason for sympathizing. A book of his was a treas ure to my daughter on her death-bed.*

" I must confess to intolerance of opinion as, to these two points,— eternal evil in any form, and (involved in it) eternal suffering. To believe in these would take away my God, who is all-loving. With a God with whom omnipotence and omni science were all, evil might be eternal; but why do I say to you what has been better said elsewhere ? "

LADY BYRON TO H. C. R.

" BRIGHTON, Jan. 31, 1855.

. . . " The great difficulty in respect to ' The Review' t seems to be to settle a basis, inclusive and exclusive; in short, a boundary question. From what you said, I think you agreed with me, that a latitudinarian Christianity ought to be the character of the periodical; but the depth of the roots should correspond with the width of the branches of that tree of knowledge. Of some of those minds one might say, ' They

* Probably " The Christian Aspects of Faith and Duty." Mr. Tayler has also written " A Retrospect of the Religious Life of England." i "The National Review."

have no root;' and then, the richer the foliage, the more danger that the trunk will fall. ' Grounded in Christ' has to me a most practical significance and value. I, too, have anxiety about a friend (Miss Carpenter) whose life is of public im portance : she, more than any of the English reformers, un less Nash and Wright, has found the art of drawing out the good of human nature, and proving its existence. She makes these discoveries by the light of love. I hope she may re cover, from to-day's report. The object of a Reformatory in Leicester has just been secured at a county meeting. . . . Now the desideratum is well-qualified masters and mistresses. If you hear of such by chance, pray let me know. The regular schoolmaster is an extinguisher. Heart, and familiarity .with the class to be educated, are all important. At home and abroad, the evidence is conclusive on that point; for I have for many years attended to such experiments in various parts of Europe. ' The Irish Quarterly' has taken up the subject with rather more zeal than judgment. I had hoped that a sound and temperate exposition of the facts might form an article in the ' Might-have-been Review.' "

LADY BYRON TO H. C. R.
" BRIGHTON, Feb. 12, 1855.

" I have at last earned the pleasure of writing to you by having settled troublesome matters of little moment, except locally ; and I gladly take a wider range by sympathizing in your interests. There is, besides, no responsibility — for me at least—in canvassing the merits of Russell or Palmerston, but much in deciding whether the ' village politician ' Jack son or Thompson shall be leader in the school and public-house.

" Has not the nation been brought to a conviction that the system should be broken up ? and is Lord Palmerston, who has used it so long and so cleverly, likely to promote that object ?

" But, whatever obstacles there may be in state affairs, that general persuasion must modify other departments of action and knowledge. * Unroasted coffee ' will no longer be acceptec

under the official seal,—another reason for a new literary combination for distinct special objects, a review in which every separate article should be convergent. If, instead of the problem to make a circle pass through three given points, it were required to find the centre from which to describe a circle through any three articles in the ' Edinburgh' or ' Westminster Review,' who would accomplish it ? Much force is lost for want of this one-mindedness amongst the contributors. It would not exclude variety or freedom in the unlimited discussion of means towards the ends unequivocally recognized. If St. Paul had edited a review, he might have admitted Peter as well as Luke or Barnabas. . . .

" Ross gave us an excellent sermon, yesterday, on ' Hallow ing Hie Name.' Though far from commonplace, it might have been delivered in any church.

" We have had Fanny Kemble here last week. I only heard her ' Romeo and Juliet," — not less instructive, as her readings always are, than exciting; for in her glass Shakspeare is a philosopher. I know her, and honor her for her truthfulness amidst all trials."

LADY BYRON TO H. C. R.
" BRIGHTON, March 5, 1855.

" I recollect only those passages of Dr. Kennedy's book wh ; " u bear upon the opinions of Lord Byron. Strange as it may seem, Dr. Kennedy is most faithful where you doubt his being so. Not merely from casual expressions, but from the wa' 1 : tenor of Lord Byron's feelings, I could not but conclude he was a believer in the inspiration of the Bible, and had the gloomiest Calvinistic tenets. To that unhappy view of the re lation of the creature to the Creator, I have always ascribed the misery of his life. ... It is enough for me to remember, that he who thinks his transgressions beyond forgiveness (and such w«s nis own deepest feeling) has righteousness beyond that of the self-satisfied sinner, or, perhaps, of the half-awakened. It was impossible for me to doubt, that, could he have been at once asoured of pardon, his living faith in a moral duty, and love of

virtue ('I love the virtues which I cannot claim'), would have conquered every temptation. Judge, then, how I must hate the creed which made him see God as an Avenger, not a Father ! My own impressions were just the reverse, but could have little weight; and it was in vain to seek to turn his thoughts for long from that idee fixe with which he connected his physical peculiarity as a stamp. Instead of being made happier by any apparent good, he felt convinced that every blessing would be ' turned into a curse ' to him. Who, pos sessed by such ideas, could lead a life of love and service to God or man ? They must, in a measure, realize themselves. 'The worst of it is, I do believe,' he said. I, like all con nected with him, was broken against the rock of predestina tion. I may be pardoned for referring to his frequent expres sion of the sentiment that I was only sent to show him the happiness he was forbidden to enjoy. You will now better understand why ' The Deformed Transformed' is too painful to me for discussion. Since writing the above, I have read Dr. Granville's letter on the Emperor of Russia, some passages of which seem applicable to the prepossession I have described. I will not mix up less serious matters with these, which forty years have not made less than present still to me."

LADY BYRON TO H. C. R.

- •-• " BRIGHTON, April 8, 1855.

..." The book which has interested me most, lately, is that on ' Mosarsm,' translated by Miss Goldsmid, and which I read, as you will believe, without any Christian (unchristian?) prejudice. The missionaries of the Unity were always, from my childhood, regarded by me as in that sense the people ; and I believe they were true to that mission, though blind, intel lectually, in demanding the crucifixion. The present aspect of Jewish opinions, as shown in that book, is all but Christian. The author is under the error of taking, as the representatives of Christianity, the Mystics, Ascetics, and Quietists; and therefore he does not know how near he is to the true spirit of the gospel. If you should happen to see Miss Goldsmid, pray

tell her what a great service I think she has rendered to us soi-disants Christians in translating a book which must make us sensible of the little we have done, and the much we have to do, to justify our preference of the later to the earlier dispen sation." ...

LADY BYRON TO H. C. R.

"BRIGHTON, April u, 1855.

" You appear to have more definite information respecting ' The Review ' than I have obtained. ... It was also said that ' The Review ' would, in fact, be ' The Prospective' amplified, — not satisfactory to me, because I have always thought that periodical too Unitarian, in the sense of separating itself from other Christian churches, if not by a high wall, at least by a wire-gauze fence. Now, separation is to me the aipeoie. The revelation through Nature never separates : it is the revelation through the Book which separates. Whewell and Brewster would have been one, had they not, I think, equally dimmed their lamps of science when reading their Bibles. As long as we think a truth better for being shut up in a text, we are not of the wide-world religion, which is to include all in one fold : for that text will not be accepted by the followers of other books, or students of the same ; and separation will ensue. The Christian Scripture should be dear to us, not as the charter of a few, but of mankind; and to fashion it into cages is to deny its ultimate objects. These thoughts hot, like the roll at break fast, where your letter was so welcome an addition."

THREE DOMESTIC POEMS BY LORD BYRON.

FARE THEE WELL.

FARE thee well! and if forever,
Still forever fare thee well! Even though unforgiving, never
'Gainst thee shall my heart rebel.
Would that breast were bared before thee Where thy head so oft hath lain,
While that placid sleep came o'er thee Which thou ne'er canst know again !
Would that breast, by thee glanced over, Every inmost thought could show 1
Then thou wouldst at last discover * 'Twas not well to spurn it so.
Though the world for this commend thee, Though it smile upon the blow,
Even its praises must offend thee, Founded on another's woe.
Though my many faults defaced me, Could no other arm be found,
Than the one which once embraced me, To inflict a cureless wound ?
Yet, oh ! yet, thyself deceive not: Love may sink by slow decay;
But, by sudden wrench, believe not Hearts can thus be torn away :
Still thine own its life retaineth ;
Still must mine, though bleeding, beat; And the undying thought which paineth
Is — that we no more may meet.
These are words of deeper sorrow Than the wail above the dead:
Both shall live, but every morrow Wake us from a widowed bed.
And when thou wouldst solace gather, When our child's first accents flow,
Wilt thou teach her to say " Father," Though his care she must forego ?
When her little hand shall press thee,
When her lip to thine is pressed, Think of him whose prayer shall bless thee ;
Think of him thy love had blessed.
Should her lineaments resemble
Those thou never more mayst see, Then thy heart will softly tremble
With a pulse yet true to me.
All my faults, perchance, thou knowest;
All my madness none can know : All my hopes, where'er thou goest,
Wither; yet with thee they go.
Every feeling hath been shaken :
Pride, which not a world could bow, Bows to thee, by thee forsaken;
Even my soul forsakes me now.
But 'tis done : all words are idle;
Words from me are vainer still; But the thoughts we cannot bridle
Force their way without the will.
Fare thee well! — thus disunited,
Torn from every nearer tie, Seared in heart, and lone and blighted,
More than this I scarce can die.

A SKETCH.

BORN in the garret, in the kitchen bred ; Promoted thence to deck her mistress' head ;
Next — for some gracious service unexpressed, And from its wages only to be guessed — Raised

from the toilette to the table, where Her wondering betters wait behind her chair.

> With eye unmoved, and forehead unabashed, She dines from off the plate she lately washed. Quick with the tale, and ready with the lie, The genial confidante and general spy, Who could, ye gods ! her next employment guess ? -An only infant's earliest governess ! She taught the child to read, and taught so well, That she herself, by teaching, learned to spell. An adept next in penmanship she grows, As many a nameless slander deftly shows : What she had made the pupil of her art, None know ; but that high soul secured the heart, And panted for the truth it could not hear, With longing breast and undeluded ear. Foiled was perversion by that youthful mind Which flattery fooled not, baseness could not blind, Deceit infect not, near contagion soil, Indulgence weaken, nor example spoil, Nor mastered science tempt her to look down On humbler talents with a pitying frown, Nor genius swell, nor beauty render vain, Nor envy ruffle to retaliate pain, Nor fortune change, pride raise, nor passion bow, Nor virtue teach austerity, till now. Serenely purest of her sex that live; But wanting one sweet weakness, —to forgive; Too shocked at faults her soul can never know, She deems that all could be like her below : Foe to all vice, yet hardly Virtue's friend; For Virtue pardons those she would amend.

But to the theme, now laid aside too long, — The baleful burthen of this honest song. Though all her former functions are no more, She rules the circle which she served before. If mothers —none know why — before her quake ; If daughters dread her for the mothers' sake; If early habits — those false links, which bind At times the loftiest to the meanest mind —

Have given her power too deeply to instil
The angry essence of her deadly will;
If like a snake she steal within your walls
Till the black slime betray her as she crawls;
If like a viper to the heart she wind,
And leave the venom there she did not find, —
What marvel that this hag of hatred works
Eternal evil latent as she lurks,
To make a Pandemonium where she dwells,
And reign the Hecate of domestic hells ?
Skilled by a touch to deepen scandal's tints
With all the kind mendacity of hints,
While mingling truth with falsehood, sneers with smiles,
A thread of candor with a web of wiles ;
A plain blunt show of briefly-spoken seeming,
To hide her bloodless heart's soul-hardened scheming;
A lip of lies; a face formed to conceal,
And, without feeling, mock at all who feel;
With a vile mask the Gorgon would disown ;
A cheek of parchment, and an eye of stone.
Mark how the channels of her yellow blood
Ooze to her skin, and stagnate there to mud !
Cased like the centipede in saffron mail,
Or darker greenness of the scorpion's scale,
(For drawn from reptiles only may we trace
Congenial colors in that soul or face,) —
Look on her features ! and behold her mind
As in a mirror of itself defined.

Look on the picture ! deem it not o'ercharged ;
There is no trait which might not be enlarged :
Yet true to " Nature's journeymen," who made
This monster when their mistress left off trade,
This female dog-star of her little sky,
Where all beneath her influence droop or die.
O wretch without a tear, without a thought, Save joy above the ruin thou hast wrought 1
The time shall come, nor long remote, when thou
Shalt feel far more than thou inflictest now, —
Feel for thy vile self-loving self in vain,
And turn thee howling in unpitied pain.
May the strong curse of crushed affections light
Back on thy bosom with reflected blight,
And make thee, in thy leprosy of mind,
As loathsome to thyself as to mankind,
Till all thy self-thoughts curdle into hate
Black as thy will for others would create ;
Till thy hard heart be calcined into dust,
And thy soul welter in its hideous crust!
Oh, may thy grave be sleepless as the bed,
The widowed couch of fire, that thou hast spread !
Then, when thou fain wouldst weary Heaven with prayer,
Look on thine earthly victims, and despair !
Down to the dust ! and, as thou rott'st away,
Even worms shall perish on thy poisonous clay.
But for the love I bore, and still must bear,
To her thy malice from all ties would tear,
Thy name, thy human name, to every eye
The climax of all scorn, should hang on high,
Exalted o'er thy less abhorred compeers,
And festering in the infamy of years.

LINES

ON HEARING THAT LADY BYRON WAS ILL.

AND thou wert sad, yet I was not with thee !
And thou wert sick, and yet I was not near ! Methought that joy and health alone could be
Where I was not, and pain and sorrow here. And is it thus ? It is as I foretold,
And shall be more so ; for the mind recoils Upon itself, and the wrecked heart lies cold,
While heaviness collects the shattered spoils.
It is not in the storm nor in the strife
We feel benumbed, and wish to be no more, But in the after-silence on the shore, When all is lost except a little life. I am too well avenged ! But 'twas my right:
Whate'er my sins might be, thou wert not sent To be the Nemesis who should requite ;
Nor did Heaven choose so near an instrument Mercy is for the merciful! — if thou Hast been of such, 'twill be accorded now. Thy nights are banished from the realms of sleep!
Yes ! they may flatter thee; but thou shalt feel
A hollow agony which will not heal; For thou art pillowed on a curse too deep : Thou hast sown in my sorrow, and must reap

The bitter harvest in a woe as real! I have had many foes, but none like thee;
For 'gainst the rest myself I could defend,
And be avenged, or turn them into friend: But thou in safe implacability
Hadst nought to dread, in thy own weakness shielded; And in my love, which hath but too much yielded,
And spared, for thy sake, some I should not spare. And thus upon the world, — trust in thy truth, And the wild fame of my ungoverned youth,
On things that were not and on things that are, — Even upon such a basis hast thou built A monument, whose cement hath'been guilt! The moral Clytemnestra of thy lord, And hewed down, with an unsuspected sword, Fame, peace, and hope, and all the better life,
Which, but for this cold treason of thy heart, Might still have risen from out the grave of strife,
And found a nobler duty than to part. But of thy virtues didst thou make a vice,
Trafficking with them in a purpose cold,
For present anger and for future gold, And buying others' grief at any price.
And thus, once entered into crooked ways, The early truth, which was thy proper praise, Did not still walk beside thee, but at times, And with a breast unknowing its own crimes, Deceit, averments incompatible, Equivocations, and the thoughts which dwell
In Janus-spirits; the significant eye Which learns to lie with silence; the pretext Of prudence, with advantages annexed; The acquiescence in all things which tend, No matter how, to the desired end, —
All found a place in thy philosophy. The means were worthy, and the end is won : I would not do by thee as thou hast done !

THE END

Made in the USA
Coppell, TX
10 December 2019